W9-BEB-275

RAVES FOR
THE BLACK DAHLIA

"High-intensity prose. Reading it aloud could shatter your wineglasses."
—ELMORE LEONARD

"An absolute masterpiece and Ellroy's finest work to date . . . played out against a beautifully dark, moody, '40s L.A. jazz score. The ultimate novel noir."
—JONATHAN KELLERMAN

"If you don't read James Ellroy's THE BLACK DAHLIA, you will have only yourself to blame, my friend."
—LARRY KING

"The toughest tough-guy book you'll ever read! Big, ambitious, with passionate characters, grand obsessions, a fine sense of period and ambiance . . . Much more than a mystery, this is a real novel."
—WILLIAM BAYER

more . . .

more . . .

"A dark, compelling work of fiction . . . This is a tough book. It's a good one, too."
—*San Jose Mercury News*

"Ellroy's seventh mystery and his best . . . The texture of his writing—dark, moody, tense—gains originality with each novel. If you want to go to hell and back, this book is for you."
—*Los Angeles Daily Breeze/News Pilot*

"The novelistic equivalent of film noir."
—*Christian Science Monitor*

"Ellroy's apocalyptic visions are keenly realized, and his strong moral convictions are conveyed to the reader. This powerful and unforgettable novel should *not* be missed."
—*Rave Reviews*

"Haunting . . . A book of deep friendships, conflicted love, and the brooding and merciless obsession of the characters with the Black Dahlia."
—*Los Angeles* magazine

"Ellroy's best yet . . . Ellroy is here to stay. Our great-grandchildren will be reading this book."
—RICHARD LAYMAN

"A fast-moving, brutal, and enjoyable police novel . . . This is red-hot writing."
—*Milwaukee Journal*

"Masterful . . . A shocker that other writers would kill to have written. This one is not to be missed; it'll hang you out to dry."
—HARLAN ELLISON

"Building like a symphony . . . a wonderful, complicated but accessible tale of ambition, insanity, passion, and deceit, with the perfect setting of booming, postwar Los Angeles."
—*Publishers Weekly*

Also by James Ellroy

Destination: Morgue!

The Cold Six Thousand

Crime Wave

My Dark Places

American Tabloid

Hollywood Nocturnes

White Jazz

L.A. Confidential

The Big Nowhere

Suicide Hill

Killer on the Road

Because the Night

Blood on the Moon

Clandestine

Brown's Requiem

THE BLACK DAHLIA

JAMES ELLROY

NEW YORK   BOSTON

The author gratefully acknowledges Houghton Mifflin to quote *All My Pretty Ones*, copyright © 1962 by Anne Sexton

Mysterious Press
Hachette Book Group USA
1271 Avenue of the Americas, New York, NY 10020

Mysterious Press is an imprint of Warner Books, Inc.
The Mysterious Press name and logo are trademarks of Warner Books, Inc.

Cover artwork licensed by Universal Studios Licensing LLLP

Printed in the United States of America

ISBN-13: 978-0-7394-7360-3

Prologue

I never knew her in life. She exists for me through others, in evidence of the ways her death drove them. Working backward, seeking only facts, I reconstructed her as a sad little girl and a whore, at best a could-have-been—a tag that might equally apply to me. I wish I could have granted her an anonymous end, relegated her to a few terse words on a homicide dick's summary report, carbon to the coroner's office, more paperwork to take her to potter's field. The only thing wrong with the wish is that she wouldn't have wanted it that way. As brutal as the facts were, she would have wanted all of them known. And since I owe her a great deal and am the only one who does know the entire story, I have undertaken the writing of this memoir.

But before the Dahlia there was the partnership, and before that there was the war and military regulations and manuevers at Central Division, reminding us that cops were also soldiers, even though we were a whole lot less popular than the ones battling the Germans and Japs. After duty every day, patrolmen were subjected to participation in air raid drills, blackout drills and fire evacuation drills that had us standing at attention on Los Angeles Street, hoping for a Messerschmitt attack to make us feel less like fools. Daywatch roll call featured alphabetical formations, and shortly after graduating the Academy in August of '42, that was where I met Lee.

I already knew him by reputation, and had our respective records down pat: Lee Blanchard, 43-4-2 as a heavyweight, formerly a regular attraction at the Hollywood Legion Stadium; and me: Bucky Bleichert, light-heavy, 36-0-0, once ranked tenth by *Ring* magazine, probably because Nat Fleisher was amused by the way I taunted opponents with my big buck teeth. The statistics didn't tell the whole story, though. Blanchard hit hard, taking six to give one, a classic headhunter; I danced and counterpunched and hooked to the liver, always keeping my guard up, afraid that catching too many head shots would ruin my looks worse than my teeth already had. Stylewise, Lee and I were like oil and water, and every time our shoulders brushed at roll call, I would wonder: who would win?

For close to a year we measured each other. We never talked boxing or police work, limiting our conversation to a few words about the weather. Physically, we looked as antithetical as two big men could: Blanchard was blond and ruddy, six feet tall and huge in the chest and shoulders, with stunted bowlegs and the beginning of a hard, distended gut; I was pale and dark-haired, all lanky muscularity at 6 foot 3. Who would win?

I finally quit trying to predict a winner. But other cops had taken up the question, and during that first year at Central I heard dozens of opinions: Blanchard by early KO; Bleichert by decision; Blanchard stopped/stopping on cuts—everything but Bleichert by knockout.

When I was out of eye shot, I heard whispers of our non–ring stories: Lee coming on the LAPD, assured of rapid promotion for fighting private smokers attended by the high brass and their political buddies, cracking the Boulevard-Citizens bank heist back in '39 and falling in love with one of the heisters' girlfriends, blowing a certain transfer to the Detective Bureau when the skirt moved in with him—in violation of departmental regs on shack jobs—and begged him to quit boxing. The Blanchard rumors hit me like little feint-jabs, and I wondered how true they were. The bits of my own story felt like body blows, because they were 100 percent straight dope: Dwight Bleichert joining the Department in flight from tougher main events, threatened with expulsion from the Academy when his father's German-American Bund membership came to light, pressured into snitching the Japanese guys he grew up with to the Alien Squad in order to secure his LAPD appointment. Not asked to fight smokers, because he wasn't a knockout puncher.

4

Blanchard and Bleichert: a hero and a snitch.

Remembering Sam Murakami and Hideo Ashida manacled en route to Manzanar made it easy to simplify the two of us—at first. Then we went into action side by side, and my early notions about Lee—and myself—went blooey.

It was early June of '43. The week before, sailors had brawled with zoot suit wearing Mexicans at the Lick Pier in Venice. Rumor had it that one of the gobs lost an eye. Skirmishing broke out inland: navy personnel from the Chavez Ravine naval base versus pachucos in Alpine and Palo Verde. Word hit the papers that the zooters were packing Nazi regalia along with their switchblades, and hundreds of in-uniform soldiers, sailors and marines descended on downtown LA, armed with two-by-fours and baseball bats. An equal number of pachucos were supposed to be forming by the Brew 102 Brewery in Boyle Heights, supplied with similar weaponry. Every Central Division patrolman was called in to duty, then issued a World War I tin hat and an oversize billy club known as a nigger knocker.

At dusk, we were driven to the battleground in personnel carriers borrowed from the army, and given one order: restore order. Our service revolvers had been taken from us at the station; the brass did not want .38's falling into the hands of reet pleat, stuff cuff, drape shape, Argentine ducktail Mexican gangsters. When I jumped out of the carrier at Evergreen and Wabash holding only a three-pound stick with a friction-taped handle, I got ten times as frightened as I had ever been in the ring, and not because chaos was coming down from all sides.

I was terrified because the good guys were really the bad guys.

Sailors were kicking in windows all along Evergreen; marines in dress blues were systematically smashing streetlights, giving themselves more and more darkness to work in. Eschewing inter-service rivalry, soldiers and jarheads overturned cars parked in front of a bodega while navy youths in skivvies and white bell-bottoms truncheoned the shit out of an outnumbered bunch of zooters on the sidewalk next door. At the periphery of the action I could see knots of my fellow officers hobnobbing with Shore Patrol goons and MPs.

I don't know how long I stood there, numbed, wondering what to do. Finally I looked down Wabash toward 1st Street, saw small houses, trees and no pachucos, cops or blood-hungry GIs. Before I knew what I was doing, I ran there full speed. I would have kept running until I dropped, but a high-pitched laugh issuing from a front porch stopped me dead.

I walked toward the sound. A high-pitched voice called out,

"You're the second young copper to take a powder from the commotion. I don't blame you. Kinda hard to tell who to put the cuffs on, ain't it?"

I stood on the porch and looked at the old man. He said, "Radio says cabdrivers been makin' runs to the USO up in Hollywood, then bringin' the sailor boys down here. KFI called it a naval assault, been playin' 'Anchors Aweigh' every hour on the half hour. I saw some gyrenes down the street. You think this is what you call an amphibious attack?"

"I don't know what it is, but I'm going back."

"You ain't the only one turned tail, you know. 'Nuther big fella came runnin' this way pronto."

Pops was starting to look like a wily version of my father. "There's some pachucos who need their order restored."

"Think it's that simple, laddy?"

"I'll make it that simple."

The old man cackled with delight. I stepped off the porch and headed back to duty, tapping the knocker against my leg. The streetlights were now all dead; it was almost impossible to distinguish zooters from GIs. Knowing that gave me an easy way out of my dilemma, and I got ready to charge. Then I heard *"Bleichert!"* behind me, and knew who the other runner had been.

I ran back. There was Lee Blanchard, "The Southland's good but not great white hope," facing down three marines in dress blues and a pachuco in a full-drape zoot suit. He had them cornered in the center walkway of a ratty bungalow court and was holding them off with parries from his nigger knocker. The jarheads were taking roundhouse swipes at him with their two-by-fours, missing as Blanchard moved sideways and back and forth on the balls of his feet. The pachuco fondled the religious medals around his neck, looking bewildered.

"Bleichert code three!"

I waded in, jabbing with my stick, the weapon hitting shiny brass buttons and campaign ribbons. I caught clumsy truncheon blows on my arms and shoulders and pressed forward so the marines would be denied swinging room. It was like being in a clinch with an octopus, and no referee or three-minute bell, and on instinct I dropped my baton, lowered my head and started winging body punches, making contact with soft gabardine midsections. Then I heard, "Bleichert step back!"

I did, and there was Lee Blanchard, the nigger knocker held high above his head. The marines, dazed, froze; the club descended: once, twice, three times, clean shots to the shoulders. When the trio was reduced to a dress blue rubble heap,

6

Blanchard said, "To the halls of Tripoli, shitbirds," and turned to the pachuco. "Hola, Tomas."

I shook my head and stretched. My arms and back ached; my right knuckles throbbed: Blanchard was cuffing the zooter, and all I could think to say was, "What was that all about?"

Blanchard smiled. "Forgive my bad manners. Officer Bucky Bleichert, may I present Señor Tomas Dos Santos, the subject of an all-points fugitive warrant for manslaughter committed during the commission of a Class B Felony. Tomas snatched a purse off a hairbag on 6th and Alvarado, she keeled of a heart attack and croaked, Tomas dropped the purse, ran like hell. Left a big fat juicy set of prints on the purse, eyeball witnesses to boot." Blanchard nudged the man. "Habla Ingles, Tomas?"

Dos Santos shook his head no; Blanchard shook his head sadly. "He's dead meat. Manslaughter Two's a gas chamber jolt for spics. Hepcat here's about six weeks away from the Big Adios."

I heard shots coming from the direction of Evergreen and Wabash. Standing on my toes, I saw flames shooting out of a row of broken windows, crackling into blue and white flak when they hit streetcar wires and phone lines. I looked down at the marines, and one of them gave me the finger. I said, "I hope those guys didn't get your badge number."

"Fuck them sideways if they did."

I pointed to a clump of palm trees igniting into fireballs. "We'll never be able to get him booked tonight. You ran down here to roust them? You thought—"

Blanchard silenced me with a playful jab that stopped just short of my badge. "I ran down here because I knew there wasn't a goddamn thing I could do about restoring order, and if I just stood around I might have gotten killed. Sound familiar?"

I laughed. "Yeah. Then you—"

"Then I saw the shitbirds chasing hepcat, who looked suspiciously like the subject of felony warrant number four eleven dash forty-three. They cornered me here, and I saw you walking back looking to get hurt, so I thought I'd let you get hurt for a reason. Sound reasonable?"

"It worked."

Two of the marines had managed to get to their feet, and were helping the other one up. When they started for the sidewalk three abreast, Tomas Dos Santos sent a hard right foot at the biggest of the three asses. The fat PFC it belonged to turned to face his attacker; I stepped forward. Surrendering their East LA campaign, the three hobbled out to the street, gunshots and flaming palm trees. Blanchard ruffled Dos Santos' hair. "You cute little shit, you're a dead man. Come on, Bleichert, let's find a place to sit this thing out."

* * *

We found a house with a stack of daily papers on the porch a few blocks away and broke in. There were two fifths of Cutty Sark in the kitchen cupboard, and Blanchard switched the cuffs from Dos Santos' wrists to his ankles so he could have his hands free to booze. By the time I made ham sandwiches and highballs, the pachuco had killed half the jug and was belting "Cielito Lindo" and a Mex rendition of "Chattanooga Choo Choo." An hour later the bottle was dead and Tomas was passed out. I lifted him onto the couch and threw a quilt over him, and Blanchard said, "He's my ninth hard felon for 1943. He'll be sucking gas inside of six weeks, and I'll be working Northeast or Central Warrants inside of three years."

His certainty rankled me. "Ixnay. You're too young, you haven't made sergeant, you're shacking with a woman, you lost your high brass buddies when you quit fighting smokers and you haven't done a plainsclothes tour. You—"

I stopped when Blanchard grinned, then walked to the living room window and looked out. "Fires over on Michigan and Soto. Pretty."

"Pretty?"

"Yeah, pretty. You know a lot about me, Bleichert."

"People talk about you."

"They talk about you, too."

"What do they say?"

"That your old man's some sort of Nazi drool case. That you ratted off your best friend to the feds to get on the Department. That you padded your record fighting built-up middle-weights."

The words hung in the air like a three-count indictment. "Is that it?"

Blanchard turned to face me. "No. They say you never chase cooze and they say you think you can take me."

I took the challenge. "All those things are true."

"Yeah? So was what you heard about me. Except I'm on the Sergeants List, I'm transferring to Highland Park Vice in August and there's a Jewboy deputy DA who wets his pants for boxers. He's promised me the next Warrants spot he can wangle."

"I'm impressed."

"Yeah? You want to hear something even more impressive?"

8

"Hit me."

"My first twenty knockouts were stumblebums handpicked by my manager. My girlfriend saw you fight at the Olympic and said you'd be handsome if you got your teeth fixed, and maybe you *could* take me."

I couldn't tell if the man was looking for a brawl then and there or a friend; if he was testing me or taunting me or pumping me for information. I pointed to Tomas Dos Santos, twitching in his booze sleep. "What about the Mex?"

"We'll take him in tomorrow morning."

"You'll take him in."

"The collar's half yours."

"Thanks, but no thanks."

"Okay, partner."

"I'm not your partner."

"Maybe someday."

"Maybe never, Blanchard. Maybe you work Warrants and pull in repos and serve papers for the shysters downtown, maybe I put in my twenty, take my pension and get a soft job somewhere."

"You could go on the feds. I know you've got pals on the Alien Squad."

"Don't push me on that."

Blanchard looked out the window again. "Pretty. Make a good picture postcard. 'Dear Mom, wish you were here at the colorful East LA race riot.'"

Tomas Dos Santos stirred, mumbling, "Inez? Inez? Qué? Inez?" Blanchard walked to a hall closet and found an old wool overcoat and tossed it on top of him. The added warmth seemed to calm him down; the mumbles died off. Blanchard said, "Cherchez la femme. Huh, Bucky?"

"What?"

"Look for the woman. Even with a snootful of juice, old Tomas can't let Inez go. I'll lay you ten to one that when he hits the gas chamber she'll be right there with him."

"Maybe he'll cop a plea. Fifteen to life, out in twenty."

"No. He's a dead man. Cherchez la femme, Bucky. Remember that."

I walked through the house looking for a place to sleep, finally settling on a downstairs bedroom with a lumpy bed way too short for my legs. Lying down, I listening to sirens and gunshots in the distance. Gradually I dozed off, and dreamed of my own few and far between women.

●   ●   ●

By the morning the riot had cooled off, leaving the sky hung with soot and the streets littered with broken liquor bottles and discarded two-by-fours and baseball bats. Blanchard called Hollenbeck Station for a black-and-white to transport his ninth hard felon of 1943 to the Hall of Justice jail, and Tomas Dos Santos wept when the patrolmen took him away from us. Blanchard and I shook hands on the sidewalk and walked separate routes downtown, him to the DA's office to write up his report on the capture of the purse snatcher, me to Central Station and another tour of duty.

The LA City Council outlawed the wearing of the zoot suit, and Blanchard and I went back to polite conversation at roll call. And everything he stated with such rankling certainty that night in the empty house came true.

Blanchard was promoted to Sergeant and transferred to Highland Park Vice early in August, and Tomas Dos Santos went to the gas chamber a week later. Three years passed, and I continued to work a radio car beat in Central Division. Then one morning I looked at the transfer and promotion board and saw at the top of the list: Blanchard, Leland C., Sergeant; Highland Park Vice to Central Warrants, effective 9/15/46.

And, of course, we became partners. Looking back, I know that the man possessed no gift of prophecy; he simply worked to assure his own future, while I skated uncertainly toward mine. It was his flat-voiced "Cherchez la femme" that still haunts me. Because our partnership was nothing but a bungling road to the Dahlia. And in the end, she was to own the two of us completely.

1

Fire and Ice

CHAPTER ONE

The road to the partnership began without my knowing it, and it was a revival of the Blanchard-Bleichert fight brouhaha that brought me the word.

I was coming off a long tour of duty spent in a speed trap on Bunker Hill, preying on traffic violators. My ticket book was full and my brain was numb from eight hours of following my eyes across the intersection of 2nd and Beaudry. Walking through the Central muster room and a crowd of blues waiting to hear the P.M. crime sheet, I almost missed Johnny Vogel's, "They ain't fought in years, and Horrall outlawed smokers, so I don't think that's it. My dad's thick with the Jewboy, and he says he'd try for Joe Louis if he was white."

Then Tom Joslin elbowed me. "They're talking about you, Bleichert."

I looked over at Vogel, standing a few yards away, talking to another cop. "Hit me, Tommy."

Joslin smiled. "You know Lee Blanchard?"

"The Pope know Jesus?"

"Ha! He's working Central Warrants."

"Tell me something I don't know."

"How's this? Blanchard's partner's topping out his twenty. Nobody thought he'd pull the pin, but he's gonna. The

Warrants boss is this felony court DA, Ellis Loew. He got Blanchard his appointment, now he's looking for a bright boy to take over the partner's spot. Word is he creams for fighters and wants you. Vogel's old man's in the Detective Bureau. He's simpatico with Loew and pushing for his kid to get the job. Frankly, I don't think either of you got the qualifications. Me, on the other hand . . ."

I tingled, but still managed to come up with a crack to show Joslin I didn't care. "Your teeth are too small. No good for biting in the clinches. Lots of clinches working Warrants."

• • •

But I did care.

That night I sat on the steps outside my apartment and looked at the garage that held my heavy bag and speed bag, my scrapbook of press clippings, fight programs and publicity stills. I thought about being good but not really good, about keeping my weight down when I could have put on an extra ten pounds and fought heavyweight, about fighting tortilla-stuffed Mexican middleweights at the Eagle Rock Legion Hall where my old man went to his Bund meetings. Light heavyweight was a no-man's-land division, and early on I pegged it as being tailor-made for me. I could dance on my toes all night at 175 pounds, I could hook accurately to the body from way outside and only a bulldozer could work in off my left jab.

But there were no light heavyweight bulldozers, because any hungry fighter pushing 175 slopped up spuds until he made heavyweight, even if he sacrificed half his speed and most of his punch. Light heavyweight was safe. Light heavyweight was guaranteed fifty-dollar purses without getting hurt. Light heavyweight was plugs in the *Times* from Braven Dyer, adulation from the old man and his Jew-baiting cronies and being a big cheese as long as I didn't leave Glassell Park and Lincoln Heights. It was going as far as I could as a natural—without having to test my guts.

Then Ronnie Cordero came along.

He was a Mex middleweight out of El Monte, fast, with knockout power in both hands and a crablike defense, guard high, elbows pressed to his sides to deflect body blows. Only nineteen, he had huge bones for his weight, with the growth potential to jump him up two divisions to heavyweight and the big money. He racked up a string of fourteen straight early-round KOs at the Olympic, blitzing all the top LA middles. Still growing and anxious to jack up the quality of his opponents, Cordero issued me a challenge through the *Herald* sports page.

I knew that he would eat me alive. I knew that losing to a taco bender would ruin my local celebrity. I knew that running from the fight would hurt me, but fighting it would kill me. I started looking for a place to run to. The army, navy and marines looked good, then Pearl Harbor got bombed and made them look great. Then the old man had a stroke, lost his job and pension and started sucking baby food through a straw. I got a hardship deferment and joined the Los Angeles Police Department.

I saw where my thoughts were going. FBI goons were asking me if I considered myself a German or an American, and would I be willing to prove my patriotism by helping them out. I fought what was next by concentrating on my landlady's cat stalking a bluejay across the garage roof. When he pounced, I admitted to myself how bad I wanted Johnny Vogel's rumor to be true.

Warrants was local celebrity as a cop. Warrants was plainclothes without a coat and tie, romance and a mileage per diem on your civilian car. Warrants was going after the real bad guys and not rousting winos and wienie waggers in front of the Midnight Mission. Warrants was working in the DA's office with one foot in the Detective Bureau, and late dinners with Mayor Bowron when he was waxing effusive and wanted to hear war stories.

Thinking about it started to hurt. I went down to the garage and hit the speed bag until my arms cramped.

•　•　•

Over the next few weeks I worked a radio car beat near the northern border of the division. I was breaking in a fat-mouthed rookie named Sidwell, a kid just off a three-year MP stint in the Canal Zone. He hung on my every word with the slavish tenacity of a lapdog, and was so enamored of civilian police work that he took to sticking around the station after our end of tour, bullshitting with the jailers, snapping towels at the wanted posters in the locker room, generally creating a nuisance until someone told him to go home.

He had no sense of decorum, and would talk to anybody about anything. I was one of his favorite subjects, and he passed station house scuttlebutt straight back to me.

I discounted most of the rumors: Chief Horrall was going to start up an interdivisional boxing team, and was shooting me Warrants to assure that I signed on along with Blanchard; Ellis Loew, the felony court comer, was supposed to have won a bundle betting on me before the war and was now handing me a belated reward; Horrall had rescinded his order banning smokers, and some high brass string puller wanted me happy so he could line his pockets betting on me. Those tales sounded too farfetched, although I knew boxing was somehow behind my front-runner status. What I credited was that the Warrants opening was narrowing down to either Johnny Vogel or me.

Vogel had a father working Central dicks; I was a padded 36-0-0 in the no-man's-land division five years before. Knowing the only way to compete with nepotism was to make the weight, I punched bags, skipped meals and skipped rope until I was a nice, safe light heavyweight again. Then I waited.

CHAPTER TWO

I was a week at the 175-pound limit, tired of training and dreaming every night of steaks, chili burgers and coconut cream pies. My hopes for the Warrants job had waned to the point where I would have sold them down the river for pork chops at the Pacific Dining Car, and the neighbor who looked after the old man for a double sawbuck a month had called me to say that he was acting up again, taking BB potshots at the neighborhood dogs and blowing his Social Security check on girlie magazines and model airplanes. It was reaching the point where I would have to *do* something about him, and every toothless geezer I saw on the beat hit my eyes as a gargoyle version of Crazy Dolph Bleichert. I was watching one stagger across 3rd and Hill when I got the radio call that changed my life forever.

"11-A-23, call the station. Repeat: 11-A-23, call the station."

Sidwell nudged me. "We got a call, Bucky."

"Roger it."

"The dispatcher said to call the station."

I hung a left and parked, then pointed to the call box on the corner. "Use the gamewell. The little key next to your handcuffs."

Sidwell obeyed, trotting back to the cruiser moments later,

looking grave. "You're supposed to report to the Chief of
Detectives immediately," he said.

My first thoughts were of the old man. I leadfooted the six
blocks to City Hall and turned the black-and-white over to
Sidwell, then took the elevator up to Chief Thad Green's fourth-
floor offices. A secretary admitted me to the Chief's inner
sanctum, and sitting in matched leather chairs were Lee
Blanchard, more high brass than I had ever seen in one place
and a spider-thin man in a three-piece tweed suit.

The secretary said, "Officer Bleichert," and left me standing
there, aware that my uniform hung on my depleted body like a
tent. Then Blanchard, wearing cord slacks and a maroon
letterman's jacket, got to his feet and played MC.

"Gentlemen, Bucky Bleichert. Bucky, left to right in uniform,
we have Inspector Malloy, Inspector Stensland and Chief
Green. The gentleman in mufti is Deputy DA Ellis Loew."

I nodded, and Thad Green pointed me to an empty chair
facing the assembly. I settled into it; Stensland handed me a
sheaf of papers. "Read this, Officer. It's Braven Dyer's editorial
for this coming Saturday's *Times*."

The top page was dated 10/14/46, with a block printed title—
"Fire and Ice Among LA's Finest"—directly below it. Below
that, the typed text began:

Before the war, the City of the Angels was graced
with two local fighters, born and raised a scant five
miles apart, pugilists with styles as different as fire
and ice. Lee Blanchard was a bowlegged windmill of a
leather slinger, and sparks covered the ringside seats
when he threw punches. Bucky Bleichert entered the
ring so cool and collected that it was easy to believe he
was immune to sweat. He could dance on his toes
better than Bojangles Robinson, and his rapier jabs
peppered his opponents' faces until they looked like
the steak tartare at Mike Lyman's Grill. Both men
were poets: Blanchard the poet of brute strength,
Bleichert the counter poet of speed and guile. Collec-
tively they won 79 bouts and lost only four. In the ring
as in the table of elements, fire and ice are tough to
beat.

Mr. Fire and Mr. Ice never fought each other.
Divisional boundaries kept them apart. But a sense of
duty brought them together in spirit, and both men
joined the Los Angeles Police Department and continued fighting out of the ring—this time in the war

against crime. Blanchard cracked the baffling Boulevard-Citizens bank robbery case in 1939, and captured thrill-killer Tomas Dos Santos; Bleichert served with distinction during the '43 Zoot Suit Wars. And now they are both officers in Central Division: Mr. Fire, 32, a sergeant in the prestigious Warrants Squad; Mr. Ice, 29, a patrolman working a dangerous beat in downtown LA. I recently asked both Fire and Ice why they gave up their best ring years to become cops. Their responses are indicative of the fine men they are:

Sergeant Blanchard: "A fighter's career doesn't last forever, but the satisfaction of serving your community does."

Officer Bleichert: "I wanted to fight more dangerous opponents, namely criminals and Communists."

Lee Blanchard and Bucky Bleichert made great sacrifices to serve their city, and on Election Day, November 5, Los Angeles voters are going to be asked to do the same thing—vote in a five-million-dollar bond proposal to upgrade the LAPD's equipment and provide for an 8 percent pay raise for all personnel. Keep in mind the examples of Mr. Fire and Mr. Ice. Vote "Yes" on Proposition B on Election Day.

Finishing, I handed the pages back to Inspector Stensland. He started to speak, but Thad Green shushed him with a hand on his shoulder. "Tell us what you thought of it, Officer. Be candid."

I swallowed to keep my voice steady. "It's subtle."

Stensland flushed, Green and Malloy grinned, Blanchard hooted outright. Ellis Loew said, "Proposition B is going to lose hands down, but there's a chance to reintroduce it in the off-year election next spring. What we had in—"

Green said, "Ellis, please," and turned his attention to me. "One of the reasons the bond is going to fail is that the public is less than pleased with the service we've been giving them. We were shorthanded during the war, and some of the men we hired to remedy that turned out to be rotten apples and made us look bad. Also, we're top-heavy with rookies since the war ended, and a lot of good men have retired. Two station houses need to be rebuilt and we need to offer higher starting salaries to attract better men. All this takes money, and the voters aren't going to give it to us in November."

I was beginning to get the picture. Malloy said, "It was your idea, counselor. You tell him."

Loew said, "I'm laying dollars to doughnuts we can pass the proposal in the '47 Special. But we need to drum up enthusiasm for the Department to do it. We need to build up morale within the Department, and we need to impress the voters with the quality of our men. Wholesome white boxers are a big draw, Bleichert. You know that."

I looked at Blanchard. "You and me, huh?"

Blanchard winked. "Fire and Ice. Tell him the rest of it, Ellis."

Loew winced at his first name, then continued. "A ten-round bout three weeks from now at the Academy gym. Braven Dyer is a close personal friend of mine, and he'll be building it up in his column. Tickets will go for two dollars apiece, with half allotted for policemen and their families, half for civilians. The gate goes to the police charity program. From there we build up an interdivisional boxing team. All good wholesome white boys. The team members get one duty day off a week to teach underprivileged kids the art of self-defense. Publicity all the way, straight to the '47 Special Election."

All eyes were on me now. I held my breath, waiting for the offer of the Warrants spot. When no one said a word, I glanced sidelong at Blanchard. His upper body looked brutally powerful, but his stomach had gone to flab and I was younger, taller and probably a whole lot faster. Before I could give myself reasons to back down, I said, "I'm in."

The brass gave my decision a round of applause; Ellis Loew smiled, exposing teeth that looked like they belonged on a baby shark. "The date is October 29, a week before the election," he said. "And both of you will have unlimited use of the Academy gym for training. Ten rounds is a lot to ask of men as inactive as you two have been, but anything else would look sissy. Don't you agree?"

Blanchard snorted, "Or communistic"; Loew shot him a shark-tooth grimace. I said, "Yes, sir," and Inspector Malloy raised a camera, chirping, "Watch the birdy, son."

I stood up and smiled without parting my lips; a flashbulb popped. I saw stars and got a back pounding, and when the camaraderie stopped and my vision cleared, Ellis Loew was standing in front of me, saying, "I'm betting on great things from you. And if I don't miss my bet, I expect we'll be colleagues soon."

I thought, You're a subtle bastard, but said, "Yes, sir." Loew gave me a limp handshake and walked away. I rubbed the last of the stars out of my eyes and saw that the room was empty.

I took the elevator down to street level, thinking of tasty

ways to regain the weight I had lost. Blanchard probably weighed 200, and if I came in at my safe old 175 against him he would wear me down every time he managed to get inside. I was trying to decide between the Pantry and Little Joe's when I hit the parking lot and saw my adversary in the flesh—talking to a woman blowing smoke rings up at a picture postcard sky.

I went over. Blanchard was leaning against an unmarked cruiser, gesturing at the woman, still intent on her rings, putting them out three and four at a time. She was in profile as I approached, head tilted up, back arched, one hand on the cruiser's door for support. Auburn hair in a pageboy cut brushed her shoulders and long, thin neck; the fit of her Eisenhower jacket and wool skirt told me she was thin all over.

Blanchard caught sight of me and nudged her. Letting out a lungful of smoke, she turned. Up close, I saw a strong-pretty face, all mismatched parts: high forehead that made her hairdo look incongruous, crooked nose, full lips and big black-brown eyes.

Blanchard made the introductions. "Kay, this is Bucky Bleichert. Bucky, Kay Lake."

The woman ground out her cigarette. I said, "Hello," wondering if this was the girlfriend that Blanchard met at the Boulevard-Citizens robbery trial. She didn't play as a heister's quail, even if she had been shacking with a cop for years.

Her voice had a slight prairie twang. "I saw you box several times. You won."

"I always won. Are you a fight fan?"

Kay Lake shook her head. "Lee used to drag me. I was taking art classes back before the war, so I brought my sketch pad and drew the boxers."

Blanchard put an arm around her shoulders. "Made me quit fighting smokers. Said she didn't want me doing the vegetable shuffle." He went into an imitation of a punch-drunk fighter sparring, and Kay Lake flinched away from him. Blanchard shot a quick look at her, then fired off some left jabs and right crosses at the air. The punches were telegraphed, and in my mind I countered a one-two at his jaw and midsection.

I said, "I'll try not to hurt you."

Kay smoldered at the remark; Blanchard grinned. "It took weeks to talk her into letting me do it. I promised her a new car if she didn't pout too much."

"Don't make any bets you can't cover."

Blanchard laughed, then moved into a side-by-side drape with Kay. I said, "Who thought this thing up?"

"Ellis Loew. He got me Warrants, then my partner put in his

papers and Loew started thinking about you to replace him. He got Braven Dyer to write that Fire and Ice horseshit, then he took the whole pie to Horrall. He never would have gone for it, but all the polls said the bond issue was heading for the deep six, so he said okay."

"And he's got money on me? And if I win I get Warrants?"

"Something like that. The DA himself don't like the idea, thinks the two of us wouldn't work as partners. But he's going along—Horrall and Thad Green convinced him. Personally, I almost hope you do win. If you don't, I get Johnny Vogel. He's fat, he farts, his breath stinks and his daddy's the biggest nosebleed in Central dicks, always running errands for the Jewboy. Besides—"

I tapped Blanchard's chest with a soft forefinger. "What's in it for you?"

"Betting works both ways. My girl's got a taste for nice things, and I can't afford to let her down. Right, babe?"

Kay said, "Keep talking about me in the third person. It sends me."

Blanchard put up his hands in mock surrender; Kay's dark eyes burned. Curious about the woman, I said, "What do you think about the whole thing, Miss Lake?"

Now her eyes danced. "For aesthetic reasons, I hope you both look good with your shirts off. For moral reasons, I hope the Los Angeles Police Department gets ridiculed for perpetrating this farce. For financial reasons, I hope Lee wins."

Blanchard laughed and slapped the hood of the cruiser; I forgot vanity and smiled with my mouth open. Kay Lake stared me straight in the eye, and for the first time—strangely but surely—I sensed that Mr. Fire and I were becoming friends. Sticking out my hand, I said, "Luck short of winning"; Lee grabbed it and said, "The same."

Kay took in the two of us with a look that said we were idiot children. I tipped my hat to her, then started to walk away. Kay called out "Dwight," and I wondered how she knew my real name. When I turned around, she said, "You'd be very handsome if you got your teeth fixed."

CHAPTER THREE

The fight became the rage of the Department, then LA, and the Academy gym was sold out within twenty-four hours of Braven Dyer's announcement of it in the *Times* sports page. The 77th Street lieutenant tapped as official LAPD oddsmaker installed Blanchard as an early 3 to 1 favorite, while the real bookie line had Mr. Fire favored by knockout at 2½ to 1 and decision by 5 to 3. Interdepartmental betting was rampant, and wager pools were set up at all station houses. Dyer and Morrie Ryskind of the *Mirror* fed the craze in their columns, and a KMPC disc jockey composed a ditty called the "Fire and Ice Tango." Backed by a jazz combo, a sultry soprano warbled, "Fire and Ice ain't sugar and spice; four hundred pounds tradin' leather, that sure ain't nice. But Mr. Fire light my torch and Mr. Ice cool my brow, to me that's all-night service with a capital wow!"

I was a local celebrity again.

At roll call I watched betting markers change hands and got attaboys from cops I had never met before; Fat Johnny Vogel gave me the evil eye every time he passed me in the locker room. Sidwell, ever the rumor monger, said that two night-watch blues had bet their cars, and the station commander, Captain Harwell, was holding the pink slips until after the fight. The dicks in Administrative Vice had suspended their bookie shakedowns because Mickey Cohen was taking in ten grand a day in markers and was kicking back 5 percent to the advertising agency employed by the city in its effort to pass the bond issue. Harry Cohn, Mr. Big at Columbia Pictures, had put down a bundle on me to win by decision, and if I delivered I got a hot weekend with Rita Hayworth.

None of it made sense, but all of it felt good, and I kept myself from going crazy by training harder than I ever had before.

At end of watch each day I headed straight for the gym and *worked*. Ignoring Blanchard and his brownnosing entourage and the off-duty cops who hovered around me, I hit the heavy bag, left jab—right cross—left hook, five minutes at a crack, on my toes the whole time; I sparred with my old pal Pete Lukins and rolled sets at the speed bag until sweat blinded me and my arms turned to rubber. I skipped rope and ran through the Elysian Park hills with two-pound weights strapped to my ankles, jabbing at tree limbs and bushes, outracing the trash can dogs who prowled there. At home, I gorged myself on liver, porterhouse steak and spinach and fell asleep before I could get out of my clothes.

Then, with the fight nine days away, I saw the old man and decided to take a dive for the money.

The occasion was my once-a-month visit, and I drove out to Lincoln Heights feeling guilty that I hadn't shown up since I got the word that he was acting crazy again. I brought gifts to assuage that guilt: canned goodies scrounged from the markets on my beat and confiscated girlie mags. Pulling up in front of the house, I saw that they wouldn't be enough.

The old man was sitting on the porch, swigging from a bottle of cough syrup. He had his BB pistol in one hand, absently taking shots at a formation of balsa wood airplanes lined up on the lawn. I parked, then walked over to him. His clothes were flecked with vomit and his bones protruded underneath them, poking out like they were joined to him at all the wrong angles. His breath stank, his eyes were yellow and filmy and the skin I could see underneath his crusty white beard was flush with broken veins. I reached down to help him to his feet; he swatted my hands, jabbering, "Scheisskopf! Kleine Scheisskopf!"

I pulled the old man up into a standing position. He dropped the BB pistol and Expectolar pint and said, "Guten Tag, Dwight," like he had just seen me the day before.

I brushed tears from my eyes. "Speak English, Papa."

24

The old man grabbed the crook of his right elbow and shook his fist at me in a slapdash fungoo. "Englisch Scheisser! Churchill Scheisser! Amerikanisch Juden Scheisser!"

I left him on the porch and checked out the house. The living room was littered with model airplane parts and open cans of beans with flies buzzing around them; the bedroom was wallpapered with cheesecake pics, most of them upside down. The bathroom stank of stale urine and the kitchen featured three cats snouting around in half-empty tunafish cans. They hissed at me as I approached; I threw a chair at them and went back to my father.

He was leaning on the porch rail, fingering his beard. Afraid he would topple over, I held his arm; afraid I would start to cry for real, I said, "Say something, Papa. Make me mad. Tell me how you managed to fuck up the house so bad in a month."

My father tried to pull free. I held on tighter, then loosened my grip, afraid of snapping the bone like a twig. He said, "Du, Dwight? Du?" and I knew he'd had another stroke and lost his memory of English again. I searched my own memory for phrases in German and came up empty. As a boy I'd hated the man so much that I made myself forget the language he'd taught me.

"Wo ist Greta? Wo, mutti?"

I put my arms around the old man. "Mama's dead. You were too cheap to buy her bootleg, so she got some raisinjack from the niggers in the Flats. It was rubbing alcohol, Papa. She went blind. You put her in the hospital, and she jumped off the roof."

"Greta!"

I held him harder. "Ssssh. It was fourteen years ago, Papa. A long time."

The old man tried to push me away; I shoved him into the porch stanchion and pinned him there. His lips curled to shout invective, then his face went blank, and I knew he couldn't come up with the words. I shut my eyes and found words for him: "Do you know what you cost me, you fuck? I could have gone to the cops clean, but they found out my father was a fucking subversive. They made me snitch off Sammy and Ashidas, and Sammy died at Manzanar. I know you only joined the Bund to bullshit and chase snatch, but you should have known better, because I didn't."

I opened my eyes and found them dry; my father's eyes were expressionless. I eased off his shoulders and said, "You couldn't have known better, and the snitch jacket's all on me. But you were a cheap stingy fuck. You killed Mama, and that's yours."

I got an idea how to end the whole mess. "You go rest now, Papa. I'll take care of you."

• • •

That afternoon I watched Lee Blanchard train. His regimen was four-minute rounds with lanky light heavys borrowed from the Main Street Gym, and his style was total assault. He crouched when he moved forward, always feinting with his upper body; his jab was surprisingly good. He wasn't the headhunter or sitting duck I expected, and when he hooked to the breadbasket I could feel the punches twenty yards away. For the money he was no sure thing, and money was the fight now.

So money made it a tank job.

I drove home and called up the retired postman who kept an eye on my father, offering him a C-note if he cleaned up the house and stuck to the old man like glue until after the fight. He agreed, and I called an old Academy classmate working Hollywood Vice and asked him for the names of some bookies. Thinking I wanted to bet on myself, he gave me the numbers of two independents, one with Mickey Cohen and one with the Jack Dragna mob. The indies and the Cohen book had Blanchard a straight two to one favorite, but the Dragna line was even money, Bleichert or Blanchard, the new odds coming from scouting reports that said I looked fast and strong. I could double every dollar I put in.

In the morning I called in sick, and the daywatch boss bought it because I was a local celebrity and Captain Harwell wouldn't want him rattling my cage. With work out of the way, I liquidated my savings account, cashed in my Treasury bonds and took out a bank loan for two grand, using my almost new '46 Chevy ragtop as collateral. From the bank, it was just a short ride out to Lincoln Heights and a talk with Pete Lukins. He agreed to do what I wanted, and two hours later he called me with the results.

The Dragna bookie I had sent him to had taken his money on Blanchard by late-round knockout, offering him two to one odds against. If I took my dive in rounds eight through ten, my net would be $8,640—enough to maintain the old man in a class rest home for at least two or three years. I had traded Warrants for a close-out on bad old debts, with the late-round stipulation just enough of a risk to keep me from feeling too much like a coward. It was a tradeoff that someone was going to help me pay for, and that someone was Lee Blanchard.

With seven days left before the fight, I ate myself up to 192, increased the distance on my roadwork and upped my heavy bag stints to six minutes. Duane Fisk, the officer assigned as my trainer and second, warned me about overtraining, but I ignored him and kept pushing up until forty-eight hours before the bout. Then I decelerated to light calisthenics and studied my opponent.

From the back of the gym I watched Blanchard spar in the center ring. I looked for flaws in his basic attack and gauged his reactions when his sparring partners got cute. I saw that in clinches his elbows were tucked in to deflect body shots, leaving him open for jarring little uppercuts that would bring up his guard and set him up for counter hooks to the ribs. I saw that his best punch, the right cross, was always telegraphed with two half steps to the left and a head feint. I saw that on the ropes he was deadly, that he could keep lighter opponents pinned there with elbow steers alternated with short body blows. Moving closer, I saw eyebrow scar tissue that I would have to avoid in order to prevent a stoppage on cuts. That rankled, but a long scar running down the left side of his ribcage looked like a juicy place to throw him a lot of hurt.

"At least he looks good with his shirt off."

I turned to face the words. Kay Lake was staring at me; out of the corner of my eye I saw Blanchard, resting on his stool, staring at us. "Where's your sketch pad?" I asked.

Kay waved at Blanchard; he blew her a kiss with two gloved hands. The bell rang, and he and his partner moved toward each other popping jabs. "I gave that up," Kay said. "I wasn't very good, so I changed my major."

"To what?"

"To pre-med, then psychology, then English lit, then history."

"I like a woman who knows what she wants."

Kay smiled. "So do I, but I don't know any. What do *you* want?"

I eyeballed the gym. Thirty or forty spectators were seated in folding chairs around the center ring, most of them off-duty cops and reporters, most of them smoking. A dissipating haze hung over the ring, and the spotlight shining down from the ceiling gave it a sulfurous glow. All eyes were on Blanchard and his punchy, and all the shouts and catcalls were for him—but without me getting ready to avenge old business none of it meant a thing. "I'm part of this. That's what I want."

Kay shook her head. "You quit boxing five years ago. It's not your life anymore."

The woman's aggressiveness was making me itchy. I blurted,

27

"And your boyfriend's a never-was just like me, and you were some sort of gang skirt before he picked you up. You—"

Kay Lake stopped me by laughing. "Have you been reading my press clippings?"

"No. You been reading mine?"

"Yes."

I didn't have a retort for *that*. "Why'd Lee quit fighting? Why'd he join the Department?"

"Catching criminals gives him a sense of order. Do you have a girlfriend?"

"I'm saving myself for Rita Hayworth. Do you flirt with a lot of cops, or am I a special case?"

Shouts rose from the crowd. I glanced over and saw Blanchard's sparring partner hit the canvas. Johnny Vogel climbed into the ring and popped out his mouthpiece; the punchy expelled a long jet of blood. When I turned to Kay she was pale, hunching into her Ike jacket. I said, "Tomorrow night'll be worse. You should stay home."

Kay shuddered. "No. It's a big moment for Lee."

"He told you to come?"

"No. He would never do that."

"The sensitive type, huh?"

Kay dug in her pockets for cigarettes and matches, then lit up. "Yes. Like you, but without the chip on the shoulder."

I felt myself go red. "You're always there for each other? thick and thin and all that?"

"We try."

"Then why aren't you married? Shacking's against the regs, and if the brass decided to get snotty they could nail Lee for it."

Kay blew rings at the floor, then looked up at me. "We can't."

"Why not? You've been shacked for years. He quit fighting smokers for you. He lets you flirt with other men. Sounds like an ace deal to me."

More shouts echoed. Glancing sidelong, I saw Blanchard pounding a new punchy. I countered the shots, duking the stale gym air. After a few seconds I saw what I was doing and stopped. Kay flipped her cigarette in the direction of the ring and said, "I have to go now. Good luck, Dwight."

Only the old man called me that. "You didn't answer my question."

Kay said, "Lee and I don't sleep together," then walked away before I could do anything but stare.

• • •

I hung around the gym for another hour or so. Toward dusk, reporters and cameramen started arriving, making straight for center ring, Blanchard and his boring knockdowns of glass-chinned pugs. Kay Lake's exit line stayed with me, along with flashes of her laughing and smiling and turning sad at the drop of a hat. When I heard a newshound yell, "Hey! There's Bleichert!" I exited, running out to the parking lot and my twice-mortgaged Chevy. Pulling away, I realized I had no place to go and nothing I wanted to do except satisfy my curiosity about a woman who was coming on like gangbusters and a big load of grief.

So I drove downtown to read her press clippings.

The clerk at the *Herald* morgue, impressed with my badge, led me to a reading table. I told him I was interested in the Boulevard-Citizens bank robbery and the trial of the captured robber, and that I thought the date was sometime early in '39 for the heist, maybe fall of the same year for the legal proceedings. He left me sitting there and returned ten minutes later with two large, leather-bound scrapbooks. Newspaper pages were glued to heavy black cardboard sheets, arranged chronologically, and I flipped from February 1 to February 12 before I found what I wanted.

On February 11, 1939, a four-man gang hijacked an armored car on a quiet Hollywood side street. Using a downed motor-cycle as a diversion, the robbers overpowered the guard who left the car to investigate the accident. Putting a knife to his throat, they forced the other two guards still inside the car to let them in. Once inside, they chloroformed and trussed all three men and substituted six bags filled with phone book scraps and slugs for six bags filled with cash.

One robber drove the armored car to downtown Hollywood; the other three changed into uniforms identical to the ones the guards wore. The three in uniform walked in the door of Boulevard-Citizens Savings & Loan on Yucca and Ivar, carry-ing the sacks of paper and slugs, and the manager opened the vault for them. One of the robbers sapped the manager; the other two grabbed sacks of real money and headed for the door. By this time, the driver had entered the bank, and had rounded up the tellers. He herded them into the vault and sapped them, then shut the door and locked it. All four robbers were back on the sidewalk when a Hollywood Division patrol car, alerted by a bank-to-station alarm, arrived. The officers ordered the heisters to halt; they opened fire; the cops fired back. Two robbers were killed and two escaped—with four bags filled with unmarked fifties and C-notes.

When I saw no mention of Blanchard or Kay Lake, I

skimmed a week of page one and two accounts of the LAPD investigation.

The dead heisters were identified as Chick Geyer and Max Ottens, San Francisco muscle with no known LA associates. Eyeball witnesses at the bank could not identify the two escapers from mug shots or provide adequate descriptions of them—their guard hats were pulled low and both wore lacquered sunglasses. There were no witnesses at the hijack scene, and the chloroformed guards had been overpowered before they got good looks at their attackers.

The heist went from page two and three to the scandal columns. Bevo Means featured it for three days running, milking the angle that the Bugsy Siegel mob was chasing the escaped heisters because one of the armored car's stops was the Bug Man's haberdashery front. Siegel had sworn to find them, even though it was the bank's money that the two got away with—not his.

Means' columns got further and further afield, and I turned pages until I hit the February 28 headline: "Tip From Ex-Boxer Cop Cracks Bloody Bank Robbery."

The account was loaded with praise for Mr. Fire, but was short on facts. Officer Leland C. Blanchard, 25, a Los Angeles policeman attached to Central Division and a former "popular fixture" at the Hollywood Legion Stadium, questioned his "fight game acquaintances" and "informants" and got tips that Robert "Bobby" De Witt was the brains behind the Boulevard-Citizens job. Blanchard relayed the tip to Hollywood Division detectives, and they raided De Witt's Venice Beach house. They found stashes of marijuana, guard uniforms and money bags from Boulevard-Citizens Savings & Loan. De Witt protested his innocence, and was arrested and charged with two counts of Armed Robbery One, five counts of Aggravated Assault, one count of Grand Theft Auto, and one count of Harboring Felonious Drugs. He was held without bail—and there was still no mention of Kay Lake.

Tiring of cops and robbers, I kept flipping pages. De Witt, a San Berdoo native with three pimping priors, kept yelping that the Siegel mob or the police had framed him: the mob because he sometimes ran cooze in Siegel territory, the cops because they needed a patsy for the Boulevard-Citizen job. He had no alibi for the day of the heist, and said he didn't know Chick Geyer, Max Ottens or the still-at-large fourth man. He went to trial, and the jury didn't believe him. He was convicted on all counts, and drew a ten-to-life jolt at San Quentin.

Kay finally appeared in a June 21 human interest piece titled

"Gang Girl Falls In Love—With Cop! Going Straight? To Altar?" Beside the story there were photographs of her and Lee Blanchard, along with a mug shot of Bobby De Witt, a hatchet-faced guy sporting a greasy pompadour. The piece started with a recounting of the Boulevard-Citizens job and Blanchard's part in solving it, then segued to sugar:

> . . . and at the time of the robbery, De Witt was providing shelter for an impressionable young girl. Katherine Lake, 19, came west from Sioux Falls, South Dakota, in 1936, not seeking Hollywood stardom, but seeking a college education. What she got was a degree in the college of criminal hard knocks.
>
> "I fell in with Bobby because I had no place to go," "Kay" Lake told *Herald Express* reporter Aggie Underwood. "It was still the Depression, and jobs were scarce. I used to take walks near this awful boarding-house where I had a cot, and that was how I met Bobby. He gave me my own room at his house, and he said he'd enroll me at Valley J.C. if I kept the house clean. He didn't do that, and I got more than I bargained for."
>
> Kay thought Bobby De Witt was a musician, but he was really a dope peddler and procuror. "At first he was nice to me," Kay said. "Then he made me drink laudanum and stay home all day to answer the telephone. After that it got worse."
>
> Kay Lake declined to state how it "got worse," and she was not surprised when police arrested De Witt for his part in the bloody February 11 robbery. She found lodging at a career girl's residence in Culver City, and when called by the prosecution to testify at De Witt's trial, she did—even though she was terrified of her former "benefactor."
>
> "It was my duty," she said. "And of course at the trial I met Lee."
>
> Lee Blanchard and Kay Lake fell in love. "As soon as I saw her I knew she was the girl for me," Officer Blanchard told crime scribe Bevo Means. "She has that waiflike beauty I'm a sucker for. She's had a rough life, but now I'm going to set it straight."
>
> Lee Blanchard is no stranger to tragedy himself. When he was 14, his 9-year-old sister disappeared, never to be seen again. "I think that's why I quit

fighting and became a policeman," he said. "Catching criminals gives me a sense of order."

So out of tragedy, a love story has begun. But where will it end? Kay Lake says: "The important things now are my education and Lee. Happy days are here again."

And with Big Lee Blanchard on Kay's case, it looks like they're here to stay.

I closed the scrapbook. Except for the kid sister, none of it surprised me. But all of it made me think of big wrong moves: Blanchard blowing the juice from his glory case by refusing to fight smokers; a little girl obviously snuffed and dumped somewhere like garbage; Kay Lake shacking on both sides of the law. Opening the book again, I stared at the Kay of seven years before. Even at nineteen she looked way too smart to speak the words Bevo Means put in her mouth. And seeing her portrayed as naive made me angry.

I gave the scrapbooks back to the clerk and walked out of the Hearst building wondering what I'd been looking for, knowing it was more than just evidence to prove Kay's come-on was legit. Driving around aimlessly, killing time so I'd be exhausted and able to sleep through to the afternoon, it hit me: with the old man taken care of and Warrants dead, Kay Lake and Lee Blanchard were the only interesting prospects in my future, and I needed to know them past wisecracks, insinuations and the fight.

I stopped at a steak joint on Los Feliz and wolfed a king-size porterhouse, spinach and hash browns, then cruised Hollywood Boulevard and the Strip. None of the movie marquees looked inviting, and the clubs on Sunset looked too rich for a flash-in-the-pan celebrity. At Doheny the long stretch of neon ended, and I headed up into the hills. Mulholland was rife with motorcycle bulls in speed traps, and I resisted the urge to leadfoot to the beach.

Finally I got tired of driving like a law-abiding citizen and pulled over to the embankment. Movie searchlights out of Westwood Village strafed the sky just above me; I watched them swivel and pick out low cloud formations. Following the lights was hypnotic, and I let the act numb me. Cars racing by on Mulholland hardly dented my numbness, and when the lights went off I checked my watch and saw that it was past midnight.

Stretching, I looked down at the few house lights still glowing and thought of Kay Lake. Reading between the lines of the newspaper piece, I saw her servicing Bobby De Witt and his friends, maybe selling it for him, a heister's hausfrau jacked on laudanum. It read true, but ugly, like I was betraying the sparks between us. Kay's exit line started coming on as true, and I wondered how Blanchard could live with her without possessing her completely.

The house lights went off one by one, and I was alone. A cold wind blew down from the hills; I shivered and got the answer.

You come off a winning fight. Sweat-drenched, tasting blood, high as the stars, still wanting to *go*. The handbooks who made money on you bring you a girl. A pro, a semipro, an amateur tasting her own blood. You do it in the dressing room, or in a backseat too cramped for your legs, and sometimes you kick the side windows out. When you walk outside after it, people mob you and swarm to touch you, and you go high as the stars again. It becomes another part of the game, the eleventh round of a ten-round fight. And when you go back to an ordinary life, it's just a weakness, a loss. As long as he'd been away from the game, Blanchard had to know it, had to want to keep his love for Kay separate from that.

I got in the car and headed home, wondering if I would ever tell Kay that I didn't have a woman because sex tasted like blood and resin and suture scrub to me.

CHAPTER FOUR

We left our dressing rooms simultaneously, at the sound of a warning bell. Pushing out the door, I was an adrenaline live wire. I had chewed a big steak two hours before, swallowing the juice and spitting out the meat, and I could smell animal blood in my sweat. Dancing on my toes, I moved toward my corner through the most incredible fight mob I had ever seen.

The gym was packed to more than capacity, the spectators crammed together in narrow wooden chairs and bleachers. Every human being seemed to be shouting, and people in aisle seats plucked at my robe and urged me to kill. The side rings had been removed; the center ring was bathed in a perfect square of hot yellow light. Grabbing the bottom rope, I hoisted myself into it.

The referee, an old foot beat hack from Central nightwatch, was talking to Jimmy Lennon, on one-night leave from his announcer's gig at the Olympic; at ringside I saw Stan Kenton huddled with Misty June Christy, Mickey Cohen, Mayor Bowron, Ray Milland and a shitload of high brass in civvies. Kenton waved at me; I yelled "Artistry in rhythm!" at him. He laughed, and I bared my buck choppers at the crowd, who roared their approval. The roars grew to a crescendo; I turned around and saw that Blanchard had entered the ring.

Mr. Fire bowed in my direction; I saluted him with a barrage of short punches. Duane Fisk steered me to my stool; I took off my robe and leaned against the turnbuckle with my arms draped over the top rope. Blanchard moved into a similar position; we locked eyes. Jimmy Lennon waved the ref to a neutral corner, and the ring mike slinked down from a pole attached to the ceiling lights. Lennon grabbed it and shouted above the roar: "Ladies and gentlemen, policemen and supporters of LA's finest, it is time for the Fire and Ice tango!"

The crowd went batshit, howling and stomping. Lennon waited until they quieted down to a buzz, then crooned: "Tonight we have ten rounds of boxing in the heavyweight division. In the white corner, wearing white trunks, a Los Angeles policeman with a professional record of forty-three wins, four losses and two draws. Weighing two hundred and three and one half pounds, ladies and gentlemen, Big Lee Blanchard!"

Blanchard slipped off his robe, kissed his gloves and bowed in all four directions. Lennon let the spectators go nuts for a few moments, then made his amplified voice rise above it all: "And in the black corner, weighing one ninety-one, a Los Angeles policeman, undefeated with thirty-six straight pro wins—Tricky Bucky Bleichert!"

I soaked up my last hurrah, memorizing the faces at ringside, pretending I wasn't going to dive. The noise in the gym leveled off; I walked to the center of the ring. Blanchard approached; the ref mumbled words that I didn't hear; Mr. Fire and I touched gloves. I got scared shitless and moved back to my corner; Fisk slipped my mouthpiece in. Then the bell rang, and it was all over and just starting.

Blanchard charged. I met him in the middle of the ring, popping double jabs as he went into a crouch and stood in front of me weaving his head. The jabs missed, and I kept moving left, making no move to counter, hoping to sucker him into a right hand lead.

His first punch was a looping left hook to the body. I saw it coming and stepped inside, connecting with a short left cross to the head. Blanchard's hook grazed my back; it was one of the most powerful missed punches I'd ever taken. His right hand was low, and I brought in a short uppercut. It landed cleanly, and while Blanchard covered up I banged a one-two to his rib cage. Backpedaling before he could clinch or go to the body himself, I caught a left hand on the neck. It shook me, and I got up on my toes and started circling.

Blanchard stalked me. I stayed out of reach, peppering his always moving head with jabs, connecting more than half the time, reminding myself to hit low, so I wouldn't open up his scarred eyebrows. Moving from a crouch, Blanchard winged body hooks; I stepped back and countered them with on-target combinations. After a minute or so I had his feints and my jabs synchronized, and when his head snapped I dug in short right hooks to the ribs.

I danced, circled and threw punches in flurries. Blanchard stalked and looked for openings to land the big one. The round was winding down, and I realized that ceiling light glare and crowd smoke had distorted my ring bearings—I couldn't see the ropes. On reflex, I looked over my shoulder. Turning back, I caught the big one flush on the side of the head.

I staggered into the white corner turnbuckle; Blanchard was all over me. My head rang and my ears buzzed like Jap Zeros were dive-bombing inside them. I put up my hands to protect my face; Blanchard slammed pulverizing left-right hooks at my arms to bring them down. My head started clearing, and I leaped out and grabbed Mr. Fire in a bear hug clinch, holding him with all my juice, getting stronger each second as I stagger-pushed the two of us across the ring. Finally the ref intervened and yelled "Break!" I still held on, and he had to pry us apart.

I backpedaled, the dizziness and ear buzzing gone. Blanchard came at me flat-footed, wide open. I feinted with my left, and Big Lee stepped straight into a perfect overhand right. He hit the canvas flat on his ass.

I don't know who was more shocked. Blanchard sat there slack-jawed, taking the ref's count; I moved to a neutral corner. Blanchard was on his feet at seven, and this time I charged. Mr. Fire was dug in, feet planted wide apart, ready to kill or die. We were almost within swinging distance when the ref stepped between us and shouted, "The bell! The bell!"

I walked back to my corner. Duane Fisk removed my mouthpiece and doused me with a wet towel; I looked out at the fans, on their feet applauding. Every face I saw told me what *I* now knew: that I could cancel Blanchard's ticket plain and simple. And for a split second I thought that every voice was screaming for me not to throw the fight.

Fisk turned me around and popped in my mouthpiece, hissing, "Don't mix it up with him! Stay outside! Work off the jab!"

The bell rang. Fisk stepped out of the ring; Blanchard made a beeline for me. His stance was straight up now, and he threw a series of jabs that stopped just short of the money, moving in a step at a time, measuring me for a big right cross. I stayed on my toes and flicked doubled-up jabs from too far out to hurt, trying to set up a rhythm that would lull Blanchard into leaving his body open.

Most of my shots hit; Blanchard kept pressing. I banged a right to his ribs; he leaped in with a counter-right to mine. At close range, we threw body shots two handed; with no swinging room, the blows were nothing more than arm action, and Blanchard kept his chin dug into his collarbone, obviously wise to my inside uppercuts.

We stayed in close, landing only glancing blows to the arms and shoulders. I felt Blanchard's superior strength through all of it, but made no move to get out, wanting to put some hurt on him before I got back on my bicycle. I was settling into serious trench warfare when Mr. Fire got as cute as Mr. Ice at his cutest.

In the middle of a body exchange, Blanchard took one simple step backward and shot a hard left to my lower gut. The blow stung, and I backed up, getting ready to dance. I felt the ropes and brought up my guard, but before I could move sideways and away, a left-right caught me in the kidneys. My guard came down, and a Blanchard left hook connected with my chin.

I bounced off the ropes and hit the canvas on my knees. Shock waves pulsed from my jaw to my brain; I caught a jiggly picture of the referee restraining Blanchard, pointing to a neutral corner. I got up on one knee and grabbed the bottom rope, then lost my balance and flopped on my stomach. Blanchard had reached a neutral turnbuckle, and being prone took the jiggle out of my vision. I sucked in deep breaths; the new air eased the crackling feeling in my head. The ref came back and started counting, and at six I tried my legs. My knees buckled a little, but I was able to stand steady. Blanchard was blowing glove kisses to the fans, and I began hyperventilating so hard that my mouthpiece almost popped out. At eight the referee wiped my gloves on his shirt and gave Blanchard the signal to fight.

I felt out of control with anger, like a humiliated child. Blanchard came at me loose-limbed, his gloves open, like I wasn't worth a closed fist. I met him head-on, throwing a mock-woozy jab as he got into firing range. Blanchard slipped the punch easily—just like he was supposed to. He loaded up a huge right cross to finish me, and while he was rearing back I pounded a full-force counter-right at his nose. His head snapped; I followed through with a left hook to the body. Mr. Fire's guard fell; I stepped inside with a short uppercut. The bell rang just as he staggered into the ropes.

The crowd was chanting, "Buck-kee! Buck-kee! Buck-kee!" as I weaved to my corner. I spat out my mouthpiece and gasped for air; I looked out at the fans and knew that all bets were off, that I was going to pound Blanchard into dog meat and milk Warrants for every process and repo dollar I could get my hands on, put the old man in a home with *that* money and have the whole enchilada.

Duane Fisk shouted: "Box him! Box him!" The high brass judges at ringside grinned at me; I flashed them the buck-toothed Bucky Bleichert salute in return. Fisk shoved a bottle of water at my mouth, I guzzled and spat in the pail. He popped an ammonia cap under my nose and replaced my mouthpiece—then the bell rang.

Now it was straight cautious business—my specialty.

For the next four rounds I danced, feinted and jabbed from the outside, utilizing my reach advantage, never letting Blanchard tie me up or get me on the ropes. I concentrated on one target—his scarred eyebrows—and flicked, flicked, flicked my left glove at them. If the jab landed solidly and Blanchard's arms raised in reflex, I stepped inside and right-hooked to the breadbasket. Half the time Blanchard was able to counter to *my* body, and each shot that landed took a little bounce off my legs, a little *oomph* off my wind. By the end of the sixth round Blanchard's eyebrows were a gashed ridge of blood and my sides were welted from trunk line to rib cage. And we were both running out of steam.

Round seven was trench warfare fought by two exhausted warriors. I tried to stay outside and work the jab; Blanchard kept his gloves high to wipe blood out of his eyes and protect his cuts from further ripping. Every time I stepped in, firing a one-two at his gloves and gut, he nailed me to the solar plexus.

The fight had turned into a second-to-second war. Waiting for the eighth stanza, I saw that my welts were dotted with pinpoints of blood; the shouts of "Buck-kee! Buck-kee!" hurt my ears. Across the ring, Blanchard's trainer was swabbing his eyebrows with a styptic pencil and applying tiny adhesive bandages to the flaps of skin hanging loose. I slumped on my stool and let Duane Fisk feed me water and knead my shoulders, staring at Mr. Fire the whole sixty seconds, making him look like the old man so I'd have the hate juice to top out the next nine minutes.

The bell sounded. I moved toward the center of the ring on

wobbly legs. Blanchard, back in a crouch, came at me. His legs were trembling just like mine, and I saw that his cuts were closed.

I fired off a weak jab. Blanchard caught it coming in and still kept coming, muzzling my glove out of the way as my dead legs refused to backpedal. I felt the laces rip open his eyebrows; my gut caved in just as I saw Blanchard's face streaming with blood. My knees buckled; I spat my mouthpiece, toppled backward and hit the ropes. A right hand bomb was arching toward me. It looked like it was launched from miles and miles away, and I knew I'd have time to counter. I put all my hate into my own right and shot it straight at the bloody target in front of me. I felt the unmistakable crunch of nose cartilage, then everything went black and hot yellow. I looked up at blinding light and felt myself being lifted; Duane Fisk and Jimmy Lennon materialized beside me, holding my arms. I spat blood and the words "I won"; Lennon said, "Not tonight, laddie. You lost—eighth-round KO."

When it all sank in, I laughed and pulled my arms free. The last thing I thought of before passing out was that I had cut the old man loose—and *clean*.

• • •

I got ten days off from duty—at the insistence of the doctor who examined me after the fight. My ribs were bruised, my jaw was swollen to twice its normal size and the punch that did me in loosened six of my teeth. The croaker told me later that Blanchard's nose was broken, and that his cuts required twenty-six stitches. On the basis of damage inflicted, the fight was a draw.

Pete Lukins collected my winnings, and together we scouted rest homes until we found one that looked fit for human habitation—the King David Villa, a block off the Miracle Mile. For two grand a year and fifty a month deducted from his Social Security check, the old man would have his own room, three squares and plenty of "group activities." Most of the oldsters at the home were Jewish, and it pleased me that the crazy Kraut was going to be spending the rest of his life in an enemy camp. Pete and I installed him there, and when we left he was fungooing the head nurse and ogling a colored girl making up beds.

After that I stuck to my apartment, reading and listening to jazz on the radio, slopping up ice cream and soup, the only food I could handle. I felt content in knowing I had played as hard as I could—winning half the apples in the process.

The phone rang constantly; since I knew it had to be reporters or cops offering condolences, I never answered. I didn't listen to sports broadcasts and I didn't read the newspapers. I wanted a clean break with local celebrity, and holing up was the only way to accomplish it.

My wounds were healing, and after a week I was itchy to go back on duty. I took to spending afternoons on the back steps, watching my landlady's cat stalk birds. Chico was eyeing a perched bluejay when I heard a reedy voice call out, "Ain't you bored yet?"

I looked down. Lee Blanchard was standing at the foot of the steps. His eyebrows were laced with stitches and his nose was flattened and purple. I laughed and said, "Getting there."

Blanchard hooked his thumbs in his belt. "Wanta work Warrants with me?"

"What?"

"You heard me. Captain Harwell's been calling to tell you, only you were fucking hibernating."

I was tingling. "But I lost. Ellis Loew said—"

"Fuck what Ellis Loew said. Don't you read the papers? The bond issue passed yesterday, probably because we gave the voters such a good show. Horrall told Loew that Johnny Vogel was out, that you were his man. You want the job?"

I walked down the steps and stuck out my hand. Blanchard shook it and winked.

So the partnership began.

CHAPTER FIVE

Central Division Warrants was on the sixth floor of City Hall, situated between the LAPD's Homicide Bureau and the Criminal Division of the DA's Office— a partitioned-off space with two desks facing each other, two file cabinets spilling folders and a map of the County of Los Angeles covering the window. There was a pebbled glass door lettered with DEPUTY DISTRICT ATTORNEY ELLIS LOEW separating the cubicle from the Warrants boss and DA Buron Fitts—his boss—and nothing separating it from the Homicide dicks' bullpen, a huge room with rows of desks and corkboard walls hung with crime reports, wanted posters and miscellaneous memoranda. The more battered of the two desks in Warrants had a plate reading SERGEANT L.C. BLANCHARD. The desk facing it had to be mine, and I slumped into the chair picturing OFFICER D.W. BLEICHERT etched on wood next to the phone.

I was alone, the only one on the sixth floor. It was just after 7:00 A.M., and I had driven to my first day's duty early, in order to savor my plainclothes debut. Captain Harwell had called to say that I was to report to my new assignment on Monday morning, November 17, at 8:00, and that the day would begin with attending the reading of the felony summary for the previous week, which was mandatory for all LAPD personnel

41

and Criminal Division DA's. Lee Blanchard and Ellis Loew would be briefing me on the job itself later, and after that it would be the pursuit of fugitive warrantees.

The sixth floor housed the Department's elite divisions: Homicide, Administrative Vice, Robbery and Bunco, along with Central Warrants and the Central Detective Squad. It was the domain of specialist cops, cops with political juice and up-and-comers, and it was my home now. I was wearing my best sports jacket and slacks combo, my service revolver hung from a brand-new shoulder rig. Every man on the Force owed me for the 8 per cent pay raise that came with the passage of Proposition 5. My departmental juice was just starting. I felt ready for anything.

Except rehashing the fight. At 7:40 the bullpen started filling up with officers grumbling about hangovers, Monday mornings in general and Bucky Bleichert, dancemaster turned puncher, the new kid on the block. I stayed out of sight in the cubicle until I heard them filing into the hall. When the pen fell silent, I walked down to a door marked DETECTIVES' MUSTER ROOM. Opening it, I got a standing ovation.

It was applause military style, the forty or so plainclothesmen standing by their chairs, clapping in unison. Looking toward the front of the room, I saw a blackboard with "8%!!!" chalked on it. Lee Blanchard was next to the board, standing beside a pale fat man with the air of high brass. I sighted in on Mr. Fire. He grinned, the fat man moved to a lectern and banged on it with his knuckles. The claps trailed off; the men sat down. I found a chair at the back of the room and settled into it; the fat man rapped the lectern a last time.

"Officer Bleichert, the men of Central Dicks, Homicide, Ad Vice, Bunco, et cetera," he said. "You already know Sergeant Blanchard and Mr. Loew, and I'm Captain Jack Tierney. You and Lee are the white men of the hour, so I hope you enjoyed your ovation, because you won't get another one until you retire."

Everyone laughed. Tierney rapped the podium and spoke into an attached mike. "Enough horseshit. This is the felony summary for the week ending November 14, 1946. Pay close attention, it's a doozy.

"First off, three liquor store stickups, on the nights of 11/10, 11/12 and 11/13, all within ten blocks on Jefferson in University Division. Two teenaged Caucasians with sawed-offs and the heebie-jeebies, obviously hopheads. The University dicks have got no leads, and the squad boss there wants a Robbery team on it full-time. Lieutenant Ruley, see me at 0900 on this, and all you men put out the word to your snitches—hophead-heister is a bad MO.

"Moving east, we've got freelance prosties working the restaurant bars in Chinatown. They're servicing their johns in parked cars, lowballing the girls Mickey Cohen's been running there. Misdemeanor stuff so far, but Mickey C. doesn't like it and the Chinks don't like it because Mickey's girls use the hot sheet flops on Alameda—all Chink owned. Sooner or later we're looking at grief, so I want the restaurant owners pacified and forty-eight-hour detentions on every Chinatown whore we can grab. Captain Harwell's detaching a dozen nightwatch blues for a sweep later in the week, and I want the Ad Vice whore files gone through and mug shots and rap sheets pulled for every independent hooker known to work Central. I want two men from Central dicks in on this, with Ad Vice supervising. Lieutenant Pringle, see me at 0915."

Tierney paused and stretched; I looked around the room and saw that most of the officers were writing in notebooks. I was cursing myself for not bringing one when the captain slammed the lectern with two flattened palms. "Here's a collar that would please old Captain Jack no end. I'm talking about the Bunker Hill house burglaries Sergeants Vogel and Koenig have been working on. Fritzie, Bill, have you read the SID memo on it?"

Two men sitting side by side a few rows up from me called out, "No, Cap" and "Nossir." I got a good profile look at the older of them—the spitting image of Fat Johnny Vogel, only fatter.

Tierney said, "I suggest you read it immediately after this briefing. For the benefit of you men not directly involved in the investigation, the print boys found a set of latents at the last break-in, right near the silverware cupboard. They belonged to a white male named Coleman Walter Maynard, age 31, two sodomy priors. A surefire degenerate baby raper.

"County Parole's got no line on him. He was living at a transient hotel on 14th and Bonnie Brae, but he hotfooted around the time the burglaries started. Highland Park's got four sodomy unsolveds, all little boys around eight years old. Maybe it's Maynard and maybe it isn't, but between them and the B&Es we could fix him up with a nice one-way to Q. Fritzie, Bill, what else are you working on?"

Bill Koenig hunched over his notebook; Fritz Vogel cleared his throat and said, "We've been working the downtown hotels. We collared a couple of key thieves and rousted some pickpockets."

Tierney tapped the podium with one heavy knuckle. "Fritzie, were the key thieves Jerry Katzenbach and Mike Purdy?"

Vogel squirmed in his chair. "Yessir."

"Fritzie, did they snitch each other off?"

"Ah . . . yessir."

Tierney rolled his eyes up to heaven. "Let me enlighten those of you not familiar with Jerry and Mike. They're homos, and they live with Jerry's mother in a cozy little love nest in Eagle Rock. They've been bedmates since God was a pup, but every once in a while they have spats and get the urge to chase jailhouse chicken, and one rats the other off. Then the other reciprocates and they both draw a county jolt. They stool on the gangs while they're in stir, pork nancy boys and get sentence reductions for their snitch duty. This has been going on since Mae West was a virgin. Fritzie, what *else* have you been working on?"

There was a rumble of laughter throughout the room. Bill Koenig started to get up, twisting his head to see who the laughers were. Fritz Vogel pulled him back down by his coat sleeve, then said, "Sir, we've also been doing some work for Mr. Loew. Bringing in witnesses for him."

Tierney's pale face was working toward beet red. "Fritzie, I am the commander of Central Detectives, not Mr. Loew. Sergeant Blanchard and Officer Bleichert work for Mr. Loew, you and Sergeant Koenig do not. So drop what you're doing for Mr. Loew, leave the pickpockets alone and bring in Coleman Walter Maynard before he rapes any more little boys, would you please? There's a memo on his known associates on the squadroom bulletin board, and I suggest all officers acquaint themselves with it. Maynard a lamster now, and he might be holing up with one of them."

I saw Lee Blanchard leave the muster room by a side exit. Tierney leafed through some papers on the lectern and said, "Here's one that Chief Green thinks you should know about. Over the past three weeks someone's been tossing chopped-up dead cats into the cemeteries off Santa Monica and Gower. Hollywood Division's taken a half dozen reports on it. According to Lieutenant Davis at 77th Street, that's a calling card of nigger youth gangs. Most of the cats have been dumped on Thursday nights, and the Hollywood roller rink's open to shines on Thursdays, so maybe there's something to that. Ask around, talk to your informants and relay anything pertinent to Sergeant Hollander at Hollywood dicks. Now the homicides. Russ?"

A tall, gray-haired man in an immaculate double-breasted

suit took the podium; Captain Jack plopped into the nearest available chair. The tall man carried himself with an authority that was more like a judge or hotshot lawyer than a cop; he reminded me of the smooth Lutheran preacher who palled around with the old man until the Bund went on the subversive list. The officer sitting next to me whispered, "Lieutenenat Millard. Number two in Homicide, but the real boss. A real piece of velvet." I nodded and listened to the lieutenant speak in a velvet-smooth voice:

". . . and the coroner ruled the Russo-Nickerson job murder-suicide. The Bureau is handling the hit-and-run on Pico and Figueroa on 11/10, and we located the vehicle, a '39 La Salle sedan, abandoned. It's registered to a male Mexican named Luis Cruz, age 42, of 1349 Alta Loma Vista in South Pasadena. Cruz is a two-time loser with a Folsom jacket—both falls Robbery One. He's long gone, and his wife claims the La Salle was stolen in September. She says it was snatched by Cruz's cousin Armando Villareal, age 39, who's also missing. Harry Sears and I took the initial squeal on this one, and eyeball witnesses said there were two male Mexicans in the car. Have you got anything else, Harry?"

A squat, disheveled man stood up, turned around and faced the room. He swallowed a few times, then stammered, "C-C-C-Cruz's wife is sc-screwing the c-c-c-cousin. The c-c-c-car was never reported st-stolen, and the neighbors s-say the wife wants the c-cousin's parole violated so C-C-Cruz won't find out about them."

Harry Sears sat down abruptly. Millard smiled at him and said, "Thanks, partner. Gentlemen, Cruz and Villareal are now state parole absconders and priority fugitives. APBs and absconder warrants have been issued. And here's the punch line: both of these guys are boozehounds, with over a hundred plain drunks between them. Hit-and-run drunks are a damn menace, so let's get them. Captain?"

Tierney stood up and shouted, "Dismissed!" Cops swarmed me, offering hands and back slaps and chucks under the chin. I soaked it in until the muster room cleared and Ellis Loew approached, fiddling with the Phi Beta Kappa key dangling from his vest.

"You shouldn't have slugged with him," he said, twirling the key. "You were ahead on all three cards."

I held the DA's stare. "Proposition 5 passed, Mr. Loew."

"Yes, it did. But some patrons of yours lost money. Play it smarter here, Officer. Don't blow this opportunity like you did the fight."

"You ready, canvasback?"

Blanchard's voice saved me. I went with him before I did something to blow it then and there.

• • •

We headed south in Blanchard's civilian car, a '40 Ford coupe with a contraband two-way under the dashboard. Lee rambled on about the job while I looked out at the downtown LA street scene.

". . . mostly we go after priority warrantees, but sometimes we chase down material witnesses for Loew. Not too often—he's usually got Fritzie Vogel running his errands, with Bill Koenig along for muscle. Shitbirds, both of them. Anyway, we get slack periods sometimes, and we're supposed to go by the other station houses and check the squadrooms for their priority stuff—warrants filed in the regional courts. Every LAPD station has two men working Warrants, but they spend most of their time catching squeals, so we're supposed to help out. Sometimes, like today, you hear something at the felony summary or get something hot off the bulletin board. If it's *really* slow, you can serve papers for the Department 92 shysters. Three bucks a throw, chump change. The real moolah's in repos. I've got delinquent lists from H.J. Caruso Dodge and Yeakel Brothers Olds, all the nigger stiffs the credit agents are too pansy to move on. Any questions, partner?"

I resisted the urge to ask, "Why aren't you screwing Kay Lake?" and "While we're on the subject, what's the story on her?"

"Yeah. Why'd you quit fighting and join the Department? And don't tell me it was because your kid sister disappeared and catching criminals gives you a sense of order. I've heard that one twice, and I don't buy it."

Lee kept his eyes on traffic. "You got any sisters? Kid relatives you really care about?"

I shook my head. "My family's dead."

"So's Laurie. I figured it out when I was fifteen. Mom and Dad kept spending money on handbills and detectives, but I knew she was a snuff job. I kept picturing her growing up. Prom queen, straight A's, her own family. It used to hurt like a bastard, so I pictured her growing up wrong. You know, like a floozy. It was actually comforting, but it felt like I was shitting on her."

I said, "Look, I'm sorry."

Lee gave me a gentle elbow. "Don't be, because you're right. I quit fighting and joined the cops because Benny Siegel was putting the heat on me. He bought out my contract and scared off my manager, and he promised me a shot at Joe Louis if I took two dives for him. I said no and joined the Department because the Jew syndicate boys have got a rule against killing cops. I was scared shitless that he'd kill me anyway, so when I heard that the Boulevard-Citizens heisters took some of Benny's money along with the bank's, I shook down stoolies until I got Bobby De Witt on a platter. I gave Benny first crack at him. His number two man talked him out of a snuff, so I took the dope to Hollywood dicks. Benny's my pal now. Gives me tips on the ponies all the time. Next question?"

I decided not to push for information on Kay. Checking out the street, I saw that downtown had given way to blocks of small, unkempt houses. The Bugsy Siegel story stayed with me; I was running with it when Lee slowed the car and pulled to the curb.

I blurted, "What the hell"; Lee said, "This one's for my own personal satisfaction. You remember the baby raper on the felony sheet?"

"Sure."

"Tierney said there's four sodomy unsolveds in Highland Park, right?"

"Right."

"And he mentioned that there was a memo on the rape-o's KAs?"

"Sure. What—"

"Bucky, I read that memo and recognized the name of a fence—Bruno Albanese. He works out of a Mex restaurant in Highland Park. I called Highland Park dicks and got the addresses on the assaults, and two of them were within a half mile of the joint where the fence hangs out. This is his house, and R&I says he's got a shitload of unpaid traffic tickets, bench warrants issued. You want a diagram of the rest of it?"

I got out of the car and walked across a weedy front yard strewn with dog turds. Lee caught up with me at the porch and rang the bell; furious barks issued from inside the house.

The door opened, held to the frame by a chain. The barks grew to a crescendo; through the crack I glimpsed a slatternly woman. I shouted, "Police officers!" Lee wedged his foot into the space between the doorjamb and runner; I reached inside and twisted the chain off. Lee pushed the door open, and the woman ran out onto the porch. I stepped inside the house, wondering about the dog. I was eyeballing a seedy living room when a big brown mastiff leaped at me, his jaws wide open. I fumbled for my piece—and the beast started licking my face.

We stood there, the dog's front paws resting on my shoulders like we were doing the Lindy Hop. A big tongue lapped at me, and the woman yelped, "Be nice, Hacksaw! Be nice!"

I grabbed the dog's legs and lowered him to the floor; he promptly turned his attention to my crotch. Lee was talking to the slattern, showing her a mug shot strip. She was shaking her head no, hands on hips, the picture of an irate citizen. With Hacksaw at my heels, I joined them.

Lee said, "Mrs. Albanese, this man's the senior officer. Would you tell him what you just told me?"

The slattern shook her fists; Hacksaw explored Lee's crotch. I said, "Where's your husband, lady? We don't have all day."

"I told him and I'll tell you! Bruno's paid his debt to society! He doesn't fraternize with criminals and I don't know any Coleman what's his name! He's a businessman! His parole officer made him quit hanging out at that Mexican place two weeks ago, and I don't know where he is! Hacksaw, be nice!"

I looked at the real senior officer, now stagger-dancing with a two-hundred-pound dog. "Lady, your husband's a known fence with outstanding traffic warrants. I've got a hot merchandise list in the car, and if you don't tell me where he is, I'll turn your house upside down until I find something dirty. Then I'll arrest *you* for receiving stolen goods. What's it gonna be?"

The slattern beat her fists into her legs; Lee wrestled Hacksaw down to all fours and said, "Some people don't respond to civility. Mrs. Albanese, do you know what Russian roulette is?"

The woman pouted, "I'm not dumb and Bruno's paid his debt to society!" Lee pulled a .38 snubnose out of his back waistband, checked the cylinder and snapped it shut. "There's one bullet in this gun. You feeling lucky, Hacksaw?"

Hacksaw said, "Woof"; the woman said, "You wouldn't dare." Lee put the .38 to the dog's temple and pulled the trigger. The hammer clicked on an empty chamber; the woman gasped and started turning pale; Lee said, "Five to go. Prepare for doggie heaven, Hacksaw."

Lee squeezed the trigger a second time; I held in belly laughs when the hammer clicked again and Hacksaw licked his balls, bored over the whole thing. Mrs. Albanese was praying fervently with her eyes shut. Lee said, "Time to meet your maker, doggy"; the woman blurted, "No no no no no! Bruno's tending bar in Silverlake! The Buena Vista on Vendome! Please leave my baby alone!"

Lee showed me the .38's empty cylinder, and we walked back to the car with Hacksaw's happy barks echoing behind us. I laughed all the way to Silverlake.

• • •

The Buena Vista was a bar and grill shaped like a Spanish rancho—whitewashed adobe walls and turrets festooned with Christmas lights six weeks before the holiday. The interior was cool, all dark wood. There was a long oak bar just off the entrance foyer, with a man behind it polishing glasses. Lee flashed his shield at him and said, "Bruno Albanese?" The man pointed to the back of the restaurant, lowering his eyes.

The rear of the grill was narrow, with Leatherette booths and dim lighting. Wolfish eating noises led us to the last booth—the only one occupied. A thin, swarthy man was hunched over a plate piled high with beans, chili and huevos rancheros, shoveling the slop in like it was his last meal on earth.

Lee rapped on the table. "Police officers. Are you Bruno Albanese?"

The man looked up and said, "Who, me?"

Lee slid into the booth and pointed to the religious tapestry on the wall. "No, the kid in the manger. Let's make this fast, so I don't have to watch you eat. You've got outstanding warrants, but me and my partner like your dog, so we're not taking you in. Ain't that nice of us?"

Bruno Albanese belched, then said, "You mean you want some skinny?"

Lee said, "Whiz kid," and smoothed the Maynard mug shot strip on the table. "He cornholes little boys. We know he sells to you, and we don't care. Where is he?"

Albanese looked at the strip and burped. "I never seen this guy before. Somebody steered you wrong."

Lee looked at me and sighed. He said, "Some people don't respond to civility," then grabbed Bruno Albanese by the scruff of the neck and smashed his head face first into the plate of goo. Bruno sucked in grease through his mouth, nose and eyeballs, flapping his arms and banging his legs under the table. Lee held him there, intoning, "Bruno Albanese was a good man. He was a good husband and a good father to his son Hacksaw. He wasn't very cooperative with the police, but who expects perfection? Partner, can you give me a reason to spare this shitbird's life?"

Albanese was making gurgling sounds; blood was leaking into his huevos rancheros. "Have mercy," I said. "Even fences derserve a better last supper."

Lee said, "Well put," and let go of Albanese's head. He came up for air bleeding and gasping, wiping a whole Mexican cookbook off his face. When he got breath he wheezed out, "The Versailles Apartments on 6th and Saint Andrews room 803 and please don't give me a rat jacket!"

Lee said, "Bon appetit, Bruno"; I said, "You're good." We ran out of the restaurant and highballed it code three to 6th and Saint Andrews.

· · ·

The mail slots in the Versailles lobby listed a Maynard Coleman in Apartment 803. We rode the elevator up to the eighth floor and rang the buzzer; I put my ear to the door and heard nothing. Lee took a ring of skeleton keys from his pocket and worked them into the lock until one hit and the mechanism gave with a sharp click.

We entered a hot, dark little room. Lee flicked on the overhead light, illuminating a Murphy bed covered with stuffed animals—teddy bears, pandas and tigers. The crib stank of sweat and some medicinal odor I couldn't place. I wrinkled my nose, and Lee placed it for me. "Vaseline with cortisone. The homos use it for ass lube. I was gonna turn Maynard over to Captain Jack personally, but now I'm gonna let Vogel and Koenig have him first."

I moved to the bed and examined the animals; they all had ringlets of soft children's hair taped between their legs. Shivering, I looked at Lee. He was pale, his features contorted by facial tics. Our eyes met, and we silently left the room and took the elevator downstairs. On the sidewalk, I said, "What now?"

Lee's voice was shaky. "Find a phone booth and call the DMV. Give them Maynard's alias and this address and ask if they've processed any pink slips on it the past month or so. If they have, get a vehicle description and a license number. I'll meet you at the car."

I ran to the corner, found a pay phone and dialed the DMV police information line. A clerk answered, "Who's requesting?"

"Officer Bleichert, LAPD badge 1611. Auto purchase information, Maynard Coleman or Coleman Maynard, 643 South Saint Andrews, LA. Probably recent."

"Gotcha—one minute."

I waited, notebook and pen in hand, thinking of the stuffed animals. A good five minutes later, "Officer, it's a positive," jarred me.

"Shoot."

"De Soto sedan, 1938, dark green, license B as in boy, V as in Victor, 1-4-3-2 Repeat, B as in boy—"

I wrote it down, hung up and ran back to the car. Lee was scrutinizing an LA street atlas, jotting notes. I said, "Got him."

Lee closed the atlas. "He's probably a school prowler. There were elementary schools near the Highland Park jobs, and there's a half dozen of them around here. I radioed the Hollywood and Wilshire desks and told them what we've got. Patrol cars are gonna stop by the schools and put out the skinny on Maynard. What's the DMV got?"

I pointed to my notesheet; Lee grabbed the radio mike and switched on the outgoing dial. Static fired up, then the two-way went dead. Lee said, "Fuck it, let's roll."

●   ●   ●

We cruised elementary schools in Hollywood and the Wilshire District. Lee drove, I scanned curbs and school yards for green De Sotos and loiterers. We stopped once at a gamewell phone, and Lee called Wilshire and Hollywood stations with the DMV dope, getting assurances that it would be relayed to every radio car, every watch.

During those hours we hardly spoke a word. Lee gripped the wheel with white-knuckled fingers, slow lane crawling. The only time his expression changed was when we pulled over to check out kids at play. Then his eyes clouded and his hands shook, and I thought he would either weep or explode.

But he just kept staring, and the simple act of moving back into traffic seemed to calm him. It was as if he knew exactly how far to let himself go as a man before getting back to strict cop business.

Shortly after 3:00 we headed south on Van Ness, a run by Van Ness Avenue Elementary. We were a block away, going by the Polar Palace, when green De Soto BV 1432 passed us in the opposite direction and pulled into the parking lot in front of the rink.

I said, "We've got him. Polar Palace."

Lee hung a U-turn and drew to the curb directly across the street from the lot. Maynard was locking the De Soto, eyeing a group of kids skipping toward the entrance with skates slung over their shoulders. "Come on," I said.

Lee said, "You take him, I might lose my temper. Make sure the kids are out of the way, and if he pulls any hinky moves, kill him."

Solo plainclothes rousts were strictly against the book. "You're crazy. This is a —"

51

Lee shoved me out the door. "Go get him, goddamnit! This is Warrants, not a fucking classroom! Go get him!"

I dodged traffic across Van Ness to the parking lot, catching sight of Maynard entering the Polar Palace in the middle of a big throng of children. I sprinted to the front door and opened it, telling myself to go smooth and slow.

Cold air stunned me; harsh light reflecting off the ice rink stung my eyes. Shielding them, I looked around and saw papier mâché fjords and a snack stand shaped like an igloo. There were a few kids twirling on the ice, and a group of them oohing and aahing at a giant taxidermied polar bear standing on its hind legs by a side exit. There was not an adult in the joint. Then it hit me: check the men's room.

A sign pointed me to the basement. I was halfway down the stairs when Maynard started up them, a little stuffed rabbit in his hands. The stench of room 803 came back; just as he was about to pass me, I said, "Police officer, you're under arrest," and drew my .38.

The rape-o threw up his hands; the rabbit went flying. I shoved him into the wall, frisked him and cuffed his hands behind his back. Blood pounded in my head as I pushed him up the stairs; I felt something pummeling my legs. "You leave my daddy alone! Leave my daddy alone!"

The assailant was a little boy in short pants and a sailor's jumper. It took me half a second to make him as the rape-o's kid—their resemblance was bone deep. The boy attached himself to my belt and kept bawling, "Leave my daddy alone"; the father kept bawling for time to say good-bye and get a babysitter; I kept moving, up the stairs and through the Polar Palace, my gun at the rape-o's head, my other hand pushing him forward, the kid dragging behind me, yowling and punching with all his might. A crowd had formed; I shouted, "Police officer!" until they separated and gave me a shot at the door. An old geezer opened it for me, blurting, "Hey! ain't you Bucky Bleichert?"

I gasped, "Grab the kid and call for a matron"; the junior tornado was yanked off my back. I saw Lee's Ford in the parking lot, shoved Maynard all the way to it and into the backseat. Lee hit the horn and peeled; the rape-o mumbled Jesus mumbo jumbo. I kept wondering why the horn blare couldn't drown out the little boy's shrieks for his daddy.

• • •

We dropped Maynard off at the Hall of Justice jail, and Lee phoned Fritz Vogel at Central squadroom, telling him the rape-o was in custody and ready to be interrogated on the Bunker Hill burglaries. Then it was back to City Hall, a call to notify Highland Park dicks of Maynard's arrest and a call to Hollywood Juvie to ease my conscience on the kid. The matron I talked to told me that Billy Maynard was there, waiting for his mother, Coleman Maynard's ex-wife, a car hop with six hooking convictions. He was still bawling for his daddy, and I hung up wishing I hadn't called.

Three hours of report writing followed. I wrote the arresting officer's summary longhand; Lee typed it up, omitting mention of our break-in at Coleman Maynard's apartment. Ellis Loew hovered around the cubicle as we worked, muttering, "Great collar" and "I'll kill them in court with the kid angle."

We finished our paperwork at 7:00. Lee made a check mark in the air and said, "Chalk another one up for Laurie Blanchard. You hungry, partner?"

I stood up and stretched, food suddenly a great idea. Then I saw Fritz Vogel and Bill Koenig approaching the cubicle. Lee whispered, "Make nice, they've got juice with Loew."

Up close, the two resembled gone-to-seed refugees from the LA Rams' middle line. Vogel was tall and fat, with a huge flat head that grew straight out of his shirt collar and the palest blue eyes I'd ever seen; Koenig was plain huge, topping my six foot three by a couple of inches, his linebacker's body just starting to go soft. He had a broad, flattened nose, jug ears, a crooked jaw and tiny chipped teeth. He looked stupid, Vogel looked shrewd, they both looked mean.

Koenig giggled. "He confessed. The kiddie porks and the burglaries. Fritzie says we're all gonna get commendations." He stuck out his hand. "Good fight you gave blondie."

I shook the big fist, noticing fresh blood on Koenig's right shirt cuff. I said, "Thanks, Sarge," then extended my hand to Fritz Vogel. He took it for a split second, bored into me with coldly furious eyes and dropped it like it was a hot turd.

Lee slapped my back. "Bucky's aces. Smarts *and* cojones. You talked to Ellis about the confession?"

Vogel said, "He's Ellis to lieutenants and up."

Lee laughed. "I'm a privileged character. Besides, you call him kike and Jewboy behind his back, so what do you care?"

Vogel flushed; Koenig looked around with his mouth open. When he turned, I saw blood spatters on his shirtfront. Vogel said, "Come on Billy"; Koenig dutifully followed him back to the squadroom.

"Make nice, huh?"

Lee shrugged. "Shitbirds. If they weren't cops they'd be in

Atascadero. Do as I say, not as I do, partner. They're afraid of me, and you're just a rookie here."

I racked my brain for a snappy reply. Then Harry Sears, looking twice as sloppy as he did in the morning, poked his head in the doorway. "I heard something I thought you should know, Lee." The words were spoken without a trace of a stutter; I smelled liquor on the man's breath.

Lee said, "Shoot"; Sears said, "I was over at County Parole, and the supervisor told me Bobby De Witt just got an 'A' number. He'll be paroled to LA around the middle of January. Just thought you should know."

Sears nodded at me and took off. I looked at Lee, who was twitching like he did up in room 803 of the Versailles. I said, "Partner—"

Lee managed a smile. "Let's get ourselves some chow. Kay's making pot roast, and she said I should bring you home."

• • •

I tagged along for the woman and was astounded by the pad: a beige Deco-streamline house a quarter mile north of the Sunset Strip. Going in the door, Lee said, "Don't mention De Witt; it'll upset Kay." I nodded and took in a living room straight out of a movie set.

The wainscoting was polished mahogany, the furniture was Danish Modern—gleaming blond wood in a half dozen shades. There were wall prints representing hotshot twentieth-century artists, and carpets embroidered with modernistic designs, mist-hung skyscrapers or tall trees in a forest or the spires of some German Expressionist factory. A dining area adjoined the living room, and the table held fresh flowers and chafing dishes leaking the aroma of good eats. I said, "Not bad on a cop's pay. You taking a few bribes, partner?"

Lee laughed. "My fight stash. Hey babe, you here?"

Kay Lake walked in from the kitchen, wearing a floral dress that matched the tulips on the table. She took my hand and said, "Hello, Dwight." I felt like a punk kid crashing the junior prom.

"Hello, Kay."

With a squeeze she dropped my hand, ending the longest shake in history. "You and Leland partners. It makes you want to believe in fairy tales, doesn't it?"

I looked around for Lee, and saw that he'd disappeared. "No. I'm the realistic type."

"I'm not."

"I can tell."

"I've had enough reality to last me a lifetime."

"I know."

"Who told you?"

"The LA *Herald Express*."

Kay laughed. "Then you did read my press clippings. Come to any conclusions?"

"Yeah. Fairy tales don't work out."

Kay winked like Lee; I got the feeling that she was the one who taught him. "That's why you have to turn them into reality. Leland! Dinnertime!"

Lee reappeared, and we sat down to eat; Kay cracked a bottle of champagne and poured. When our glasses were full, she said, "To fairy tales." We drank, Kay refilled, Lee said, "To Bond Issue B." The second dose of bubbly tickled my nose and made me laugh; I proposed, "To the Bleichert-Blanchard rematch at the Polo Grounds, a bigger gate than Louis and Schmeling."

Lee said, "To the second Blanchard victory"; Kay said, "To a draw and no gore." We drank, and killed the bottle, and Kay retrieved another from the kitchen, popping the cork and hitting Lee in the chest. When our goblets were full, I caught my first blast of the juice and blurted, "To us." Lee and Kay looked at me in something like slow motion, and I saw that our free hands were all resting a few inches apart on the tabletop. Kay noticed me notice and winked; Lee said, "That's where I learned how." Our hands moved together into a sort of triad, and we toasted "To us" in unison.

● ● ●

Opponents, then partners, then friends. And with the friendship came Kay, never getting between us, but always filling in our lives outside the job with style and grace.

That fall of '46, we went everywhere together. When we went to the movies, Kay took the middle seat and grabbed both our hands during the scary parts; when we spent big band Friday evenings at the Malibu Rendezvous, she alternated dances with the two of us and always tossed a coin to see who got the last slow number. Lee never expressed an ounce of jealously, and Kay's come-on subsided into a low simmer. It was there every time our shoulders brushed, every time a radio jingle or a funny billboard or a word from Lee hit us the same way and our eyes met instantaneously. The quieter it got, the more available I knew Kay was—and the more I wanted her. But I let it all ride, not because it would have destroyed my partnership with Lee, but because it would have upset the perfection of the three of us.

After tours of duty, Lee and I would go to the house and find Kay reading, underlining passages in books with a yellow crayon. She'd cook dinner for the three of us, and sometimes Lee would take off to run Mulholland on his motorcycle. Then we talked.

We always spoke around Lee, as if discussing the brute center of the three of us without him present was a cheat. Kay talked about the six years of college and two master's degrees that Lee had bankrolled with his fight stash and how her work as a substitute teacher was perfect for the "overeducated dilettante" she'd become; I talked about growing up Kraut in Lincoln Heights. We never spoke of my snitching for the Alien Squad or her life with Bobby De Witt. We both sensed the other's general story, but neither of us wanted details. I had the upper hand there: the Ashida brothers and Sam Murakami were long gone and dead, but Bobby De Witt was a month away from LA parole—and I could tell Kay was afraid of his return.

If Lee was frightened, he never showed it past that moment when Harry Sears gave him the word, and it never hindered him during our best hours together—the ones spent working Warrants. That fall I learned what police work really was, and Lee was my teacher.

From mid-November through the New Year we captured a total of eleven hard felons, eighteen traffic warrantees and three parole and probation absconders. Our rousts of suspicious loiterers got us an additional half dozen arrests, all of them for narcotics violations. We worked from Ellis Loew's direct orders, the felony sheet and squadroom scuttlebutt, filtered through Lee's instincts. His techniques were sometimes cautious and roundabout and sometimes brutal, but he was always gentle with children, and when he went strong-arm to get information, it was because it was the only way to grab results.

So we became a "good guy–bad guy" interrogation team; Mr. Fire the black hat, Mr. Ice the white. Our boxing reputations gave us an added edge of respect on the street, and when Lee rabbit-punched for information and I interceded on the punchee's behalf, it got us what we wanted.

The partnership wasn't perfect. When we worked twenty-four-hour tours, Lee would shake down hopheads for Benzedrine tablets and swallow handfuls to stay alert; then every Negro roustee became "Sambo," every white man "Shitbird," every Mexican "Pancho." All his rawness came out, destroying his considerable finesse, and twice I had to hold him back for real when he got carried away with his black-hat role.

But it was a small price to pay for what I was learning. Under Lee's tutelage I got good fast, and I wasn't the only one who knew it. Even though he'd dropped half a grand on the fight, Ellis Loew warmed to me when Lee and I brought in a string of felons he was drooling to prosecute, and Fritz Vogel, who hated me for snatching Warrants from his son, reluctantly admitted to him that I was an ace cop.

And, surprisingly, my local celebrity lingered long enough to do me some extra good. Lee was a favored repo man with H.J. Caruso, the auto dealer with the famous radio ads, and when the job was slow we prowled for delinquent cars in Watts and Compton. When we found one, Lee would kick in the driver's side window and hot-wire the sled, and I would stand guard. Then we'd run a two-car convoy to Caruso's lot on Figueroa, and H.J. would slip us a double sawbuck apiece. We gabbed cops and robbers and fight stuff with him, and afterward he kicked back a good bottle of bourbon, that Lee always kicked back to Harry Sears to keep us greased up with good tips from Homicide.

Sometimes we joined H.J. for the Wednesday night fights at the Olympic. He had a specially constructed ringside booth that kept us protected when the Mexicans in the top tier tossed coins and beer cups full of piss down at the ring, and Jimmy Lennon introduced us during the prefight ceremonies. Benny Siegel stopped by the booth occasionally, and he and Lee would go off to talk. Lee always came back looking slightly scared. The man he'd once defied was the most powerful gangster on the West Coast, known to be vindictive, with a hair-trigger temper. But Lee usually got track tips—and the horses Siegel gave him usually won.

So that fall went. The old man got a pass from the rest home at Christmas, and I brought him to dinner at the house. He had recovered pretty well from his stroke, but he still had no memory of English, and rambled on in German. Kay fed him turkey and goose and Lee listened to his Kraut monologues all night, interjecting, "You tell 'em, pop" and "Crazy, man" whenever he paused for breath. When I dropped him back at the home, he gave me the fungoo sign and managed to walk in under his own steam.

On New Year's Eve, we drove down to Balboa Island to catch Stan Kenton's band. We danced in 1947, high on champagne, and Kay flipped coins to see who got last dance and first kiss when midnight hit. Lee won the dance, and I watched them swirl across the floor to "Perfidia," feeling awe for the way they had changed my life. Then it was midnight, the band fired up, and I didn't know how to play it.

Kay took the problem away, kissing me softly on the lips, whispering, "I love you, Dwight." A fat woman grabbed me and blew a noisemaker in my face before I could return the words.

We drove home on Pacific Coast Highway, part of a long stream of horn-honking revelers. When we got to the house, my car wouldn't start, so I made myself a bed on the couch and promptly passed out from too much booze. Sometime toward dawn, I woke up to strange sounds muffling through the walls. I perked my ears to identify them, picking out sobs followed by Kay's voice, softer and lower than I had ever heard it. The sobbing got worse—trailing into whimpers. I pulled the pillow over my head and forced myself back to sleep.

CHAPTER SIX

I dozed through most of the lackluster January 10 felony summary, coming awake when Captain Jack barked, "That's it. Lieutenant Millard, Sergeant Sears, Sergeant Blanchard and Officer Bleichert, go to Mr. Loew's office immediately. Dismissed!"

I walked down the corridor to Ellis Loew's inner sanctum. Lee, Russ Millard and Harry Sears were already there, milling around Loew's desk, examining a stack of morning *Herald*s.

Lee winked and handed me a copy, folded over to the local section. I saw a piece titled, "Criminal Division DA to Try for Boss's Job in '48 Republican Primary?" read three paragraphs lauding Ellis Loew and his concern for the citizens of Los Angeles and tossed the paper on the desk before I threw up. Lee said, "Here comes the man now. Hey Ellis, you going into politics? Say 'The only thing we have to fear is fear itself.' Let's see how you sound."

Lee's FDR imitation got a laugh all around; even Loew chuckled as he handed out rap sheet carbons with mug shot strips attached. "Here's the gentleman we all have to fear. Read those and find out why."

I read the sheet. It detailed the criminal career of Raymond Douglas "Junior" Nash, white male, born in Tulsa, Oklahoma, in 1908. Nash's convictions went back to 1926, and included Texas State Prison jolts for statutory rape, armed robbery, first degree mayhem and felonious assault. There were five California charges filed against him: three armed robbery warrants from up north in Oakland County and two 1944 LA papers— first degree statch rape and felony contributing to the delinquency of a minor. The rap sheet ended with notations from the San Francisco PD Intelligence Squad, stating that Nash was suspected of a dozen Bay Area stickups and was rumored to be one of the outside men behind the May '46 Alcatraz crash-out attempt. Finishing, I checked out the mug shots. Junior Nash looked like a typical inbred Okie shitkicker: long bony head, thin lips, beady eyes and ears that could have belonged to Dumbo.

I glanced at the other men. Loew was reading about himself in the *Herald*; Millard and Sears were still on the sheets, poker-faced. Lee said, "Give us the good news, Ellis. He's in LA and acting uppity, right?"

Loew fiddled with his Phi Beta Kappa key. "Eyewitnesses have made him for two market stickups in Leimert Park over the weekend, which is why he wasn't in the felony summary. He pistol-whipped an old lady during the second robbery, and she died an hour ago at Good Samaritan."

Harry Sears stammered, "Kn-kn-known as-s-sociates?"

Loew shook his head. "Captain Tierney talked to the SFPD this morning. They said Nash is a lone wolf type. Apparently he was recruited for his part in the Alcatraz thing, but that's an exception. What I—"

Russ Millard raised his hand. "Is there a common denominator in Nash's sex beefs?"

"I was getting to that," Loew said. "Nash apparently likes Negro girls. Young ones, still in their teens. All of his sex offense complainants have been colored."

Lee motioned me toward the door. "We'll hit University Station, read the dick's report and take it from there. My bet is that Nash is holing up somewhere in Leimert Park. It's white, but there's shines from Manchester on south. Lots of places to prowl for poontang."

Millard and Sears got up to leave. Loew walked up to Lee and said, "Try to avoid killing him, Sergeant. He richly deserves it, but try anyway."

Lee flashed his patented demon grin. "I'll try, sir. But you be sure to kill him in court. The voters want boys like Junior fried, makes them feel safe at night."

• • •

Our first stop was University Station. The squadroom boss showed us the Robbery reports and told us not to waste our time canvassing the area near the two markets, that Millard and Sears were doing it, concentrating on getting a better description of Nash's car, believed to be a postwar white sedan. Captain Jack had called University with word on Nash's poontang penchant, and three plainclothes Vice officers had been dispatched to check out southside whorehouses specializing in young colored girls. Newton Street and 77th Street divisions, almost entirely colored, would be sending night-watch radio cars by juke joints and playgrounds where Negro youths congregated, eyeballing for Nash and telling the kids to watch out.

There was nothing *we* could do but cruise the area on the chance that Nash was still around and put out the word to Lee's stoolies. We decided on a long Leimert Park tour and took off.

The district's main drag was Crenshaw Boulevard. Broad, running north all the way to Wilshire and south to Baldwin Hills, it spelled "postwar boom" like a neon sign. Every block from Jefferson to Leimert was lined with dilapidated, once grand houses being torn down, their facades replaced by giant billboards advertising department stores, jumbo shopping centers, kiddie parks and movie theaters. Completion dates ranging from Christmas '47 to early '49 were promised, and it hit me that by 1950 this part of LA would be unrecognizable. Driving east, we passed vacant lot after vacant lot that would probably soon spawn houses, then block after block of prewar adobe bungalows distinguished only by their color and the condition of their front lawns. Southbound, old wood frame houses took over, getting more and more unkempt.

And no one resembling Junior Nash was on the street; and every late model white sedan we saw was either driven by a woman or squarejohn type.

Nearing Santa Barbara and Vermont, Lee broke our long silence. "This grand tour stuff is the shits. I'm calling in some favors."

He pulled into a filling station, got out and hit the pay phone; I listened to calls on the two-way. I was at it for ten minutes or so when Lee came back, pale and sweating. "I got a tip. A snitch of mine says Nash is shacking with some poon in a crib near Slauson and Hoover."

I shut the radio off. "It's all colored down there. You think—"

"I think we fucking roll."

We took Vermont to Slauson, then headed east, passing storefront churches and hair-straightening parlors, vacant lots and liquor stores with no names—only neon signs blinking L-I-Q-U-O-R at one in the afternoon. Hanging a right turn on Hoover, Lee slowed the car and started scanning tenement stoops. We passed a group of three Negro men and an older white guy lounging on the steps of a particularly seedy dump; I saw the four make us as cops. Lee said, "Hopheads. Nash is supposed to run with jigs, so let's shake them. If they're dirty we'll squeeze for an address on him."

I nodded; Lee ground the car to a halt in the middle of the street. We got out and walked over; the four stuck their hands in their pockets and shuffled their feet, the dance routine of rousted hoodlums everywhere. I said, "Police. Kiss the wall nice and slow." They moved into a search position, hands above their heads, palms on the building wall, feet back, legs spread.

Lee took the two on the right; the white guy muttered, "What the—Blanchard?"

Lee said, "Shut it, shitbird," and started frisking him. I patted down the Negro in the middle first, running my hands along the arms of his suit coat, then dipping into his pockets. My left hand pulled out a pack of Luckys and a Zippo lighter; my right a bunch of marijuana cigarettes. I said, "Reefers" and dropped them to the pavement, then gave Lee a quick sidelong glance. The zoot suit Negro beside him reached toward his waistband; light gleamed on metal as his hand came away. I shouted, "Partner!" and pulled my .38.

The white man swung around; Lee shot him twice in the face point blank. The zooter got a shiv free just as I extended my gun. I fired, he dropped the knife, grabbed his neck and slammed into the wall. Wheeling, I saw the jig at the end fumbling at the front of his trousers and shot him three times. He flew backward; I heard *Bucky duck!* Hitting the cement, I got a topsy-turvy view of Lee and the last Negro drawing on each other from a couple of feet apart. Lee's three shots cut him down just as he managed to aim a tiny derringer. He fell dead, half his skull blown off.

I stood up, looked at the four bodies and blood-covered sidewalk, stumbled to the curb and vomited into the gutter until my chest ached. I heard sirens approaching, pinned my badge to my jacket front, then turned around. Lee was pulling out the stiffs' pockets, tossing shivs and reefers onto the sidewalk, away from the pools of blood. He walked over, and I was hoping he'd have a wisecrack to calm me down. He didn't; he was bawling like a baby.

•   •   •

It took the rest of the afternoon to put ten seconds down on paper.

We wrote out our reports at 77th Street Station, and were questioned by the team of Homicide dicks who investigated all officer-involved shootings. They told us that the three Negroes—Willie Walker Brown, Caswell Pritchford and Cato Early—were known grasshoppers, and that the white man—Baxter Fitch—took two strong-arm falls back in the late '20s. Since all four men were armed and harboring marijuana, they assured us that there would be no Grand Jury hearing.

I took the questioning calmly; Lee took it rough, shivering and muttering that he'd rousted Baxter Fitch for loitering a bunch of times when he worked Highland Park, and he sort of liked the guy. I stuck close to him at the station, then steered him out to his car through a throng of reporters hurling questions.

When we got to the house, Kay was standing on the front porch; one look at her gaunt face told me she already knew. She ran to Lee and embraced him, whispering, "Oh baby, oh babe." I watched them, then noticed a newspaper on the railing.

I picked it up. It was the bulldog edition of the *Mirror*, featuring a banner headline: "Boxer Cops in Gun Battle! Four Crooks Dead!!" Below were publicity stills of Fire and Ice crouched in gloves and trunks, along with mug shots of the dead men. I read a jazzed-up account of the shoot-out and a replay of October's fight, then heard Lee shout: "You'll never understand, so just leave me fucking alone!"

Lee took off running, around the driveway to the garage, Kay right behind him. I stood on the porch, amazed at the soft center in the toughest son of a bitch I'd ever known. I heard Lee's motorcycle starting up; seconds later he peeled out on it, screeching into a hard right turn, undoubtedly heading for a brutal run at Mulholland.

Kay came back just as the cycle noise died in the distance. Taking her hands, I said, "He'll get over it. He knew one of the guys, so that made it worse. But he'll get over it."

Kay looked at me strangely. "You're very calm."

"It was them or us. You look after Lee tomorrow. We're off-duty, but when we go back we're going after a real beast."

"And you look after him, too. Bobby De Witt gets out in a week or so, and he swore at his trial to kill Lee and the other

63

men who arrested him. Lee's scared, and I know Bobby. He's as bad as they come."

I put my arms around Kay and held her. "Ssssh. Fire and Ice are on the job, so rest easy."

Kay shook herself free. "You don't know Bobby. You don't know the things he made me do."

I brushed a lock of hair away from her eyes. "Yes, I do, and I don't care. I mean I do care, but—"

Kay said, "I know what you mean," and pushed me away. I let her go, knowing if I pursued it she'd tell me a shitload of things I didn't want to hear. The front door slammed, and I sat down on the steps, glad to be alone to sort things out.

Four months ago, I was a radio car hack going nowhere. Now I was a Warrants detective instrumental in passing a million-dollar bond issue, with a double shine killing on my record. Next month I would be thirty years old with five years on the job, eligible to take the Sergeant's Exam. If I passed it, then played my cards right, I could be detective lieutenant before I was thirty-five, and that was just the beginning.

I started to get itchy, so I went inside and puttered around the living room, thumbing through magazines, checking out the bookshelves for something to read. Then I heard the sound of water drumming hard, coming from the rear of the house. I walked back, seeing the wide-open bathroom door, feeling the steam, knowing it was all for me.

Kay was standing nude under the shower. Her expression stayed fixed in no expression at all, even when our eyes met. I took in her body, from freckled breasts with dark nipples to wide hips and flat stomach, then she pirouetted for me. I saw old knife scars criss-crossing her backside from thighs to spine, choked back tremors and walked away wishing she hadn't showed me on the day I killed two men.

II

39th and Norton

CHAPTER SEVEN

The phone woke me up early Wednesday morning, cutting off a dream featuring Tuesday's *Daily News* headline—"Fire and Ice Cops KO Negro Thugs"—and a beautiful blonde with Kay's body. Figuring it was the newshounds who'd been pestering me since the shoot-out, I fumbled the receiver onto the nightstand and dived back to slumberland. Then I heard, "Rise and shine, partner!" and picked it up.

"Yeah, Lee."

"You know what day this is?"

"The fifteenth. Payday. You called me up at six A.M. to—" I stopped when I caught an edge of nervous glee in Lee's voice. "Are you okay?"

"I'm swell. I ran Mulholland at a hundred ten, played house with Kay all day yesterday. Now I'm bored. Feel like doing some police work?"

"Keep going."

"I just talked to a snitch who owes me big. He says Junior Nash has got a fuck pad—a garage on Coliseum and Norton, in back of a green apartment building. Race you there? Loser buys the beer at the fights tonight?"

New headlines danced in front of my eyes. I said, "You're

on," hung up and dressed in record time, then ran out to my car
and gunned it the eight or nine miles to Leimert Park. And Lee
was already there, leaning against his Ford, parked at the curb
in front of the only structure on a huge block of vacant lots—a
puke-green bungalow court with a two-story shack at the rear.

I pulled up behind him and got out. Lee winked and said,
"You lost."

I said, "You cheated."

He laughed. "You're right, I called from a pay phone.
Reporters been bothering you?"

I gave my partner a slow eyeballing. He seemed relaxed but
itchy underneath, with his old jocular front back in place. "I
holed up. You?"

"Bevo Means came by, asked me how it felt. I told him I
wouldn't want it for a steady diet."

I pointed to the courtyard. "You talk to any of the tenants?
Check for Nash's car?"

Lee said, "No vehicle, but I talked to the manager. He's been
renting Nash that shack in the back. He's used it a couple of
times to entertain poon, but the manager hasn't seen him in a
week or so."

"You shake it?"

"No, waiting for you."

I drew my .38 and pressed it to my leg; Lee winked and aped
me, and we walked through the courtyard to the shack. Both
floors had flimsy-looking wooden doors, with rickety steps
leading to the second story. Lee tried the bottom door; it
creaked open. We pressed ourselves to the wall on opposite
sides of it, then I wheeled and entered, my gun arm extended.

No sound, no movement, only cobwebs and a wood floor
strewn with yellowed newspapers and bald tires. I backed out;
Lee took the lead up the steps, walking on his toes. At the
landing, he gave the doorknob a jiggle, shook his head no and
kicked the door in, clean off its hinges.

I ran up the stairs; Lee moved inside gun first. At the top, I
saw him reholstering his piece. He said, "Okie trash," and
made a gesture that took in the whole room. I stepped over the
door and nodded my head in agreement.

The crib reeked of rotgut wine. A bed fashioned from two
folded-out car seats took up most of the floor space; it was
covered with upholstery stuffing and used rubbers. Empty
muscatel short dogs were piled in corners, and the one window
was streaked with cobwebs and dirt. The stench got to me, so I
walked over and opened the window. Looking out, I saw a
group of uniformed cops and men in civilian clothes standing

on the sidewalk on Norton, about halfway down the block to 39th Street. All of them were staring at something in the weeds of a vacant lot; two black-and-whites and an unmarked cruiser were parked at the curb. I said, "Lee, come here."

Lee stuck his head out the window and squinted. "I think I see Millard and Sears. They were supposed to be catching squeals today, so maybe—"

I ran out of the pad, down the steps and around the corner to Norton, Lee at my heels. Seeing a coroner's wagon and a photo car screech to a halt, I sprinted. Harry Sears was knocking back a drink in full view of a half dozen officers; I glimpsed horror in his eyes. The photo men had moved into the lot and were fanning out, pointing their cameras at the ground. I elbowed my way past a pair of patrolmen and saw what it was all about.

It was the nude, mutilated body of a young woman, cut in half at the waist. The bottom half lay in the weeds a few feet away from the top, legs wide open. A large triangle had been gouged out of the left thigh, and there was a long, wide cut running from the bisection point down to the top of the pubic hair. The flaps of skin beside the gash were pulled back; there were no organs inside. The top half was worse: the breasts were dotted with cigarette burns, the right one hanging loose, attached to the torso only by shreds of skin; the left one slashed around the nipple. The cuts went all the way down to the bone, but the worst of the worst was the girl's face. It was one huge purpled bruise, the nose crushed deep into the facial cavity, the mouth cut ear to ear into a smile that leered up at you, somehow mocking the rest of the brutality inflicted. I knew I would carry that smile with me to my grave.

Looking up, I felt cold all over; my breath came in spurts. Shoulders and arms brushed me and I heard a jumble of voices: "There's not a goddamned drop of blood—" "This is *the* worst crime on a woman I've seen in my sixteen years—" "He tied her down. Look, you can see the rope burns on her ankles—" Then a long, shrill whistle sounded.

The dozen or so men quit jabbering and looked at Russ Millard. He said calmly, "Before it gets out of hand, let's put the kibosh on something. If this homicide gets a lot of publicity, we're going to get a lot of confessions. That girl was disemboweled. We need information to eliminate the loonies with, and that's it. Don't tell *anyone*. Don't tell your wives, don't tell your girlfriends, don't tell any other officers. Harry?"

Harry Sears said, "Yeah, Russ," palming his flask so the boss wouldn't see it. Millard caught the act and rolled his eyes in disgust. "No reporters are to view the body. You photo men, take your pictures *now*. You coroner's men, put a sheet over the body when they finish. You patrolmen, stake up a crime scene perimeter from the street all the way to six feet in back of the body. Any reporter who tries to cross it, you arrest immediately. When the lab men get here to examine the body, you move the reporters over to the opposite side of the street. Harry, you call Lieutenant Haskins at University Station and tell him to send over every man he can spare for canvassing."

Millard glanced around and noticed me. "Bleichert, what are you doing here? Is Blanchard here, too?"

Lee was squatting beside the stiff, writing in a pocket notebook. Pointing north, I said, "Junior Nash is renting a garage in back of that building over there. We were shaking it down when we saw the hubbub."

"Was there blood on the premises?"

"No. This isn't Nash, Lieutenant."

"We'll let the lab men be the judge of that. Harry!"

Sears was sitting in a black-and-white, talking into a radio mike. Hearing his name, he yelled, "Yeah, Russ!"

"Harry, when the lab men get here have them go up to that green building on the corner and test the garage for blood and latent prints. Then I want the street sealed—"

Millard stopped when he saw cars swinging onto Norton, beelining for the commotion; I glanced down at the corpse. The photo techs were still snapping pictures from all angles; Lee was still jotting in his notebook. The men milling around on the sidewalk kept looking at the stiff, then averting their eyes. On the street, reporters and camera jockeys were pouring out of cars, Harry Sears and a cordon of blues standing at the ready to hold them back. I got itchy to stare, and gave the girl a detailed eyeing.

Her legs were spread for sex, and from the way the knees buckled I could tell that they were broken; her jet-black hair was free of matted blood, like the killer had given her a shampoo before he dumped her. That awful death leer came on like the final brutality—it was cracked teeth poking out of ulcerated flesh that forced me to look away.

I found Lee on the sidewalk, helping string up crime scene ropes. He stared through me, like all he could see was the ghosts in the air. I said, "Junior Nash, remember?"

Lee's gaze zeroed in on me. "He didn't do this. He's trash, but he didn't do this."

Noise rose from the street as more reporters arrived and a line of blues linked arms to restrain them. I shouted to make

70

myself heard: "He beat an old woman to death! He's our priority warrantee!"

Lee grabbed my arms and squeezed them numb. "This is our priority, and we're staying! I'm senior, and I say so!" The words rumbled over the scene, causing heads to turn in our direction. I pulled my arms free and snapped to who Lee's ghost was.

"Okay, partner."

• • •

Over the next hour, 39th and Norton filled up with police vehicles, reporters and a big crowd of rubberneckers. The body was removed on two sheet-covered stretchers; in the back of the meat wagon a lab team rolled the dead girl's prints before hauling her downtown to the morgue. Harry Sears gave the press a handout that Russ Millard composed, the straight dope of everything except the gutting of the stiff. Sears drove to City Hall to check the records of the Missing Persons Bureau, and Millard stayed behind to direct the investigation.

Lab technicians were dispatched to prowl the lot for possible murder weapons and women's clothing; another forensic team was sent to check for latents and bloodstains at Junior Nash's fuck pad. Then Millard counted cop heads. There were four men directing traffic and keeping civilian ghouls in line, twelve bluesuits and five plainclothesmen, Lee and me. Millard dug a street atlas out of his cruiser and divided the entire Leimert Park area into foot beats, then assigned each man his territory and mandatory questions to be asked of every person in every house, apartment and store: Have you heard female screams at any time over the past forty-eight hours? Have you seen anyone discarding or incinerating women's clothing? Have you noticed any suspicious cars or people loitering in the area? Have *you* passed by Norton Avenue between 39th and Coliseum Streets during the past twenty-four hours, and if so, did you notice anyone in the vacant lots?

I was assigned Olmsted Avenue, three blocks east of Norton, from Coliseum south to Leimert Boulevard; Lee was given the stores and building sites on Crenshaw, from 39th north to Jefferson. We made plans to meet at the Olympic at 8:00 and split up; I started pounding pavement.

I walked, rang doorbells and asked questions, getting negative answers, writing down the addresses where no one was at home, so that the second wave of canvassing cops would have the numbers to work from. I talked to sherry-sneaking housewives and bratty little kids; to pensioners and on-leave servicemen, even an off-duty cop who worked West LA Division. I

71

threw in questions on Junior Nash and the late model white sedan and showed around his mug shots. All I got was a big fat zero; at 7:00 I walked back to my car disgusted by what I'd blundered into.

Lee's car was gone, and forensic arclights were being set up at 39th and Norton. I drove to the Olympic hoping for a good series of bouts to take the bad taste of the day out of my mouth.

H.J. Caruso had left tickets for us at the front turnstile, along with a note saying he had a hot date and wouldn't be showing up. Lee's ticket was still in the envelope; I grabbed mine and headed for H.J.'s box. The first prelim of an all-bantamweight card had already started, and I settled in to watch and wait for Lee.

The two tiny Mex warriors put on a good fight, and the crowd ate it up. Coins rained down from the top tier; shouts in Spanish and English filled the arena. After four rounds I knew that Lee wasn't going to show; the bantys, both cut bad, made me think of the butchered girl. I got up and left, knowing exactly where Lee was.

I drove back to 39th and Norton. The entire lot was lit up by arclights—as bright as day. Lee was standing just inside the crime scene rope. The night had turned cold; he was hunched into his letterman's jacket as he watched the lab techs poke around in the weeds.

I walked over. Lee saw me coming and did a quick draw, shooting me with finger pistols, his thumbs the hammers. It was a routine he pulled when he was jacked up on Benzedrine.

"You were supposed to meet me. Remember?"

Arclight glow gave Lee's raw nerved face a blue-white cast. "I said this was priority. Remember that?"

Looking off in the distance, I saw other vacant lots illuminated. "It's priority for the Bureau, maybe. Just like Junior Nash is priority for us."

Lee shook his head. "Partner, this is *big*. Horrall and Thad Green were down here a couple of hours ago. Jack Tierney's been detached to Homicide to run the investigation, with Russ Millard backstopping. You want my opinion?"

"Shoot."

"It's a showcase. A nice white girl gets snuffed, the Department goes all out to get the killer to show the voters that passing the bond issue got them a bulldog police force."

"Maybe she wasn't such a nice girl. Maybe that old lady that Nash killed was somebody's loving granny. Maybe you're taking this thing too personal, and maybe we let the Bureau handle it and get back to our job before Junior kills somebody else."

Lee balled his fists. "You got any other maybes?"

I stepped forward. "Maybe you're afraid of Bobby De Witt getting out. Maybe you're too proud to ask me for help to scare him away from the woman we both care for. Maybe we let the Bureau chalk up that dead girl for Laurie Blanchard."

Lee uncoiled his fists and turned away: I watched him rock on his heels, hoping he'd be fighting mad or wisecracking or anything but hurt when I finally saw his face. *I* made fists, then shouted: "Talk to me, goddamnit! We're partners! We killed four fucking men together, now you pull this shit on me!"

Lee turned around. He flashed his patented demon grin, but it came off nervous and sad, used up. His voice was raspy, stretched thin.

"I used to watchdog Laurie when she played. I was a scrapper, and all the other kids were afraid of me. I had a lot of girlfriends—you know, kiddie romance stuff. The girls used to tease me about Laurie, go on about how much time I spent with her, like she was my real sweetheart.

"See, I doted on her. She was pretty and she was a trouper.

"Dad used to talk about getting Laurie ballet lessons and piano lessons and singing lessons. I was gonna work goon squad at Firestone Tire like him, and Laurie was gonna be an artiste. It was just talk, but I was a kid, and it was real to me.

"Anyway, right around the time she disappeared, Dad was talking up this lesson stuff a lot, and it made me mad at Laurie. I started ditching her when she went to play after school. There was this wild girl who'd moved into the neighborhood. She was a roundheels, and she used to get tanked on bathtub and put out for all the boys. I was dicking her when Laurie got snatched, when I should have been protecting my sister."

I reached for my partner's arm to tell him I understood; Lee pushed my hand away. "Don't tell me you understand, because I'll tell you what makes it bad. Laurie got snuffed. Some degenerate strangled her or chopped her up. And when she died, I was thinking ugly things about her. About how I hated her because Dad thought she was a princess and I was a thug. I pictured my own sister cut up like that stiff this morning, and I laughed about it while I was with that floozy, screwing her and drinking her father's booze."

Lee took a deep breath and pointed to the ground a few yards away. A separate, inside perimeter had been staked, the two halves of the body marked in quicklime. I stared at the outline of the spread legs; Lee said, "I'm gonna get him. With you or without you, I'm gonna get him."

I dredged up a ghost of a smile. "See you at the Hall tomorrow."

"With you or without you."

I said, "I heard you," and walked back to my car. Hitting the ignition, I saw another empty lot a block to the north light up.

CHAPTER EIGHT

The first thing I saw when I walked into the squadroom the next morning was Harry Sears reading the *Herald* headline: "Hunt Werewolf's Den in Torture Slaying!!!"; the second thing I saw was a chain of five men— two derelicts, two squarejohn types and one in county jail demins, manacled to a bench. Harry put his paper down, stammering, "C-c-confessors. S-s-said they s-sliced the girl." I nodded, hearing screams coming from the interrogation room.

A moment later, Bill Koenig led a doubled-over fat man out the door, announcing to the bullpen at large, "He didn't do it." A couple of officers clapped satirically at their desks; a half dozen looked away, disgusted.

Koenig shoved the fat man out to the corridor. I asked Harry, "Where's Lee?"

Harry pointed to Ellis Loew's office. "W-with Loew. R-r-reporters, too."

I walked over and peered through the crack in the doorway. Ellis Loew was standing in back of his desk, playing to a score of newshounds. Lee was seated at the DA's side, dressed in his only suit. He looked tired—but nowhere near as edgy as he did last night.

Loew was sternly enunciating, ". . . and the heinous nature

of the killing deems it imperative that we make every effort to catch this fiend as soon as possible. A number of specially trained officers, including Mr. Fire and his partner Mr. Ice, have been detached from their regular duties to aid in the investigation, and with men like them on the job, I think we can expect positive results soon. Moreover . . ."

I couldn't hear for the pounding of blood in my head. I started to nudge the door open; Lee saw me, bowed to Loew and exited the office. He dogged me back to the Warrants cubicle; I wheeled around. "You got us detached, right?"

Lee put restraining hands on my chest. "Let's take this slow and easy, okay? First off, I gave Ellis a memo. It said we got verified dope Nash blew our jurisdiction."

"Are you fucking crazy!"

"Sssh. Listen, it was just to grease the skids. The APB on Nash still stands, the fuck pad is being staked out, every southside cop is out to cancel the bastard's ticket. I'm gonna stay at the pad tonight myself. I've got binoculars, and I figure between them and the arclights I'll be able to catch the plates on the cars that cruise down Norton. Maybe the killer's gonna drive by to gloat. I'll get all the license numbers, and check them against the DMV and R&I."

I sighed. "Jesus, Lee."

"Partner, all I want is a week on the girl. Nash is covered, and if he doesn't get collared by then, we go back to him as our priority warrantee."

"He's too dangerous to let go. You know that."

"Partner, *he's covered*. Now don't tell me you don't want to build on your shine killings. Don't tell me you don't know that the dead girl is a better piece of pie than Junior Nash."

I saw more Fire and Ice headlines. "One week, Lee. No more."

Lee winked. "Copacetic."

Captain Jack's voice came over the intercom: "Gentlemen, everybody to the muster room. Now."

I grabbed my notebook and walked through the bullpen. The ranks of the confessors had swollen, the new ones cuffed to radiators and heating pipes. Bill Koenig was slapping an old guy demanding to talk to Mayor Bowron; Fritzie Vogel was taking down names on a clipboard. The muster room was SRO, packed with Central and Bureau men and a shitload of plainclothes cops I'd never seen before. Captain Jack and Russ Millard were at the front, standing beside a floor microphone. Tierney tapped the mike, cleared his throat and spoke:

"Gentlemen, this is a general briefing on the 187 in Leimert

Park. I'm sure you've all read the papers and you all know it's a damn rough piece of work. It's also a damn big piece of work. The mayor's office has gotten a lot of calls, we've gotten a lot of calls, the City Council has gotten a lot of calls and Chief Horrall has gotten personal calls from a lot of people we want to keep happy. This werewolf stuff in the papers is going to get us a lot more calls, so let's get going on it.

"We'll start with the chain of command. I'm supervising, Lieutenant Millard is exec, Sergeant Sears is the runner between divisions. Deputy DA Loew is liaison to the press and civilian authorities, and the following officers are detached to Central Homicide, effective 1/16/47: Sergeant Anders, Detective Arcola, Sergeant Blanchard, Officer Bleichert, Sergeant Cavanaugh, Detective Ellison, Detective Grimes, Sergeant Koenig, Detective Liggett, Detective Navarette, Sergeant Pratt, Detective J. Smith, Detective W. Smith, Sergeant Vogel. You men see Lieutenant Millard after this briefing. Russ, they're all yours."

I got out my pen, giving the man next to me a gentle elbow to get more writing room. Every cop around me was doing the same thing; you could feel their attention rivet to the front of the room.

Millard spoke in his courtroom lawyer's voice: "Yesterday, seven A.M., Norton Avenue between 39th and Coliseum. A dead girl, naked, cut in half, right off the sidewalk in a vacant lot. Obviously tortured, but I'll hold off on that until I talk to the autopsy surgeon—Doc Newbarr's doing the job this afternoon at Queen of Angels. No reporters—there's some details we don't want them to know.

"The area has been thoroughly canvassed once—no leads so far. There was no blood where we found the body; the girl was obviously killed somewhere else and dumped in the lot. There's a number of vacant lots in the area, and they're being searched for weapons and bloodstains. An armed robbery–homicide suspect named Raymond Douglas Nash was renting a garage down the street—the place was checked for prints and bloodstains. The lab boys got zero, and Nash is not a suspect on the girl.

"There's no ID on her yet, no matchup to anyone in the Missing Persons files. Her prints have been teletyped, so we should get some kind of report soon. An anonymous call to University Station started it all, by the way. The officer who caught the squeal said it was a hysterical woman walking her little girl to school. The woman didn't give her name and hung up, and I think we can eliminate her as a suspect."

Millard switched to a patient, professorial tone. "Until the body is ID'd, the investigation has to be centered on 39th and Norton, and the next step is recanvassing the area."

A big collective groan rose. Millard scowled and said, "University Station will be the command post, and there'll be clerks there to type up and collate the field officers' reports. Clerical officers will be working up summary reports and evidence indexes. They'll be posted on the squadroom board at University, with carbons distributed to all LAPD and sheriff's divisions. You men here from other squads are to take what you hear at this briefing back to your station houses, put it on every crime sheet, every watch. Any information you get from patrolmen, you phone in to Central Homicide, extension 411. Now, I've got lists of recanvassing addresses for everyone but Bleichert and Blanchard. Bucky, Lee, take the same areas as yesterday. You men from other divisions, stand by; the rest of you men that Captain Tierney detached, see me now. That's it!"

I jockeyed out the door and took service stairs down to the parking lot, wanting to avoid Lee and put some distance between him and my okay on the Nash memo. The sky had turned dark gray, and all the way to Leimert Park I thought of thunderstorms obliterating leads in the vacant lots, washing the sliced girl investigation and Lee's grief over his little sister into the sewer until the gutters overflowed and Junior Nash popped his head out, begging to be arrested. As I parked my car, the clouds started to break up; soon I was canvassing with the sun beating down—and a new string of negative answers kiboshed my fantasies.

I asked the same questions I asked the day before, stressing Nash even harder. But this time it was different. Cops were combing the area, writing down the license numbers of parked cars and dragging sewers for women's clothing—and the locals had listened to the radio and read the papers.

One sherry-breathing hairbag held out a plastic crucifix and asked me if it would keep the werewolf away; an old geezer wearing skivvies and a clerical collar told me the dead girl was God's sacrifice because Leimert Park voted Democrat in the '46 Congressional. A little boy showed me a movie pinup of Lon Chaney, Jr. as the Wolfman and said that the vacant lot at 39th and Norton was the launching pad for his rocket ship, and a boxing fan who recognized me from the Blanchard fight asked me for my autograph, then told me straight-faced that his neighbor's bassett hound was the killer, and would I please shoot the cocksucker? The sane nos I got were as boring as the nut answers were fanciful, and I started to feel like the straight man in a monstrous comedy routine.

At 1:30, I finished and walked back to my car, thinking about lunch and checking in at University Station. There was a piece of paper stuck under the wiper blades—a sheet of Thad Green's personal stationery, with "Official Police Witness—admit this officer to autopsy of Jane Doe #31, 2:00 P.M., 1/16/47" typed in the middle of the page. Green's signature was scrawled at the bottom—and it looked suspiciously like the writing of Sergeant Leland C. Blanchard. Laughing against my will, I drove to Queen of Angels Hospital.

The corridors were crowded with nun-nurses and oldsters on gurneys. I showed an elderly sister my badge and inquired after the autopsy; she crossed herself and led me down the hall, pointing to a double-doored entranceway marked PATHOLOGY. I walked up to the patrolman standing guard and flashed my invitation; he snapped to attention and swung the doors open, and I entered a small cold room, all antiseptic white, a long metal table in the middle. Two sheet-covered objects lay on top of it. I sat down on a bench facing the slab, shivering at the thought of seeing the girl's death smile again.

The double doors opened a few seconds later. A tall old man smoking a cigar came in, along with a nun carrying a steno pad. Russ Millard, Harry Sears and Lee followed them, the Homicide exec shaking his head. "You and Blanchard keep turning up like bad pennies. Doc, can *we* smoke?"

The old man took a scalpel from his back pocket and wiped it on his trouser leg. "Sure. Won't bother the girl any, she's in dreamland for keeps. Sister Margaret, help me get that sheet off, will you?"

Lee sat down on the bench beside me; Millard and Sears lit cigarettes, then dug out pens and notebooks. Lee yawned, and asked me, "Get anything this morning?"

I saw that his Benzedrine juice was all but dead. "Yeah. A wolfman killer from Mars did the snuff. Buck Rogers is chasing him in his spaceship, and you should go home and sleep."

Lee yawned again. "Later. My best tip was the Nazis. A guy told me he saw Hitler in a bar on 39th and Crenshaw. Oh Jesus, Bucky."

Lee lowered his eyes; I looked at the autopsy slab. The dead girl was uncovered, her head lolling in our direction. I stared at my shoes while the doctor rambled on in medicalese:

"On gross pathology, we have a female Caucasian. Muscle tone indicates her age is between sixteen and thirty. The cadaver is presented in two halves, with bisection at the level of the umbilicus. On the upper half: the head is intact, with massive depressed skull fractures, facial features significantly obscured by massive ecchymoses, hematomas and edema. Downward displacement of nasal cartilage. Through-and-through laceration from both mouth corners across masseter muscles, extending through temporal mandibula joints upward to both earlobes. No visible signs of neck bruises. Multiple lacerations on anterior thorax, concentrated on both breasts. Cigarette burns on both breasts. Right breast almost completely severed from thorax. Inspection of upper half abdominal cavity reveals no free-flowing blood. Intestines, stomach, liver and spleen removed."

The doctor took an audible breath; I looked up and watched him puff on his cigar. The steno nun caught up with her note taking and Millard and Sears eyeballed the stiff deadpan while Lee stared at the floor, wiping sweat from his brow. The doc felt both breasts, then said, "Lack of hypertrophy indicates no pregnancy at time of death." He grabbed his scalpel and started poking around inside the bottom half of the corpse. I shut my eyes and listened.

"Inspection of the lower half of the cadaver reveals a midline longitudinal incision extending from the umbilicus to the symphysis pubis. Mesentery, uterus, ovaries and rectum removed, multiple lacerations on both posterior and anterior cavity walls. Large triangular gouge on left thigh. Sister, help me turn her over."

I heard the doors open; a voice called out, "Lieutenant!" I opened my eyes to see Millard getting up and the doctor and nun wrestling the stiff onto its stomach. When it was backside up, the doctor lifted the ankles and flexed the legs. "Both legs broken at the knee, and healing, light lash marks on the upper back and shoulders. Ligature marks on both ankles. Sister, hand me a speculum and swab."

Millard came back and handed Sears a piece of paper. He read it and nudged Lee. The doctor and nun turned the bottom half of the body over, spreading the legs wide. My stomach flip-flopped; Lee said, "Bingo." He stared at a teletype sheet while the doc droned on about lack of vaginal abrasions and the presence of old semen. The coldness in his voice made me angry; I grabbed the sheet and read: "Russ—she's Elizabeth Ann Short, DOB 7/29/24, Medford, Mass. Feds ID'd the prints—she was arrested in Santa Barbara 9/43. Background check in progress. Report back to Hall following autopsy. Call in all available field officers. —J.T."

The doctor said, "That's it on preliminary postmortem. Later on I'll have some more specifics, and I'll run some toxicological tests." He draped both halves of Elizabeth Ann Short and added, "Questions?" The nun headed for the door clutching her steno pad.

Millard said, "Can you give us a reconstruction?"

"Pending the test results, sure. Here's what she wasn't: she wasn't pregnant, she wasn't raped, but she had had voluntary intercourse sometime during the past week or so. She took what you might call a gentle whipping within the past week; the last marks on her back are older than the cuts on her front side. Here's what I think happened. I think she was tied down and tortured with a knife for a minimum of thirty-six to forty-eight hours. I think her legs were broken with a smooth, rounded instrument like a baseball bat while she was still alive. I think she either got beaten to death with something like a baseball bat, or she choked to death on her blood from the mouth wound. After she was dead, she was cut in half with a butcher knife or something resembling it, and the killer went in after her internal organs with something like a penknife. After *that*, he drained the blood from the body and washed it clean, my guess is in a bathtub. We took some blood samples from the kidneys, and in a few days we'll be able to tell you if she had any dope or liquor in her system."

Lee said, "Doc, did this guy know anything about medicine or anatomy? Why'd he go after that inside stuff?"

The doctor examined his cigar butt. "You tell me. The top-half organs he could have pulled out easily. The bottom organs he hacked with a knife to get at, like that was what interested him. He could have had medical training, but then again he could have had veterinary training, or taxidermist's training, or biological training, or he could have taken Physiology 104 in the LA city school system or my Pathology for Beginners class at UCLA. You tell me. I'll tell you what you've got for sure: she was dead six to eight hours before you found her, and she was killed someplace secluded that had running water. Harry, has this girl got a name yet?"

Sears tried to answer, but his mouth just fluttered. Millard put a hand on his shoulder and said, "Elizabeth Short."

The doctor saluted heaven with his cigar. "God love you, Elizabeth. Russell, when you get the son of a bitch who did this to her, give him a kick in the balls and tell him it's from Frederick D. Newbarr, M.D. Now all of you get out of here. I've got a date with a jumper suicide in ten minutes."

• • •

Walking out of the elevator, I heard Ellis Loew's voice, an octave louder and deeper than normal, echoing down the corridor. I caught "Vivisection of a lovely young woman," "Werewolf psychopath" and "My political aspirations are subservient to my desire to see justice done." Opening a connecting door into the Homicide pen, I saw the Republican bright boy emoting into radio mikes while a recording crew stood by. He was wearing an American Legion poppy on his lapel—probably purchased from the wino legionnaire who slept in the Hall of Records parking lot—a man he had once vigorously prosecuted for vagrancy.

The bullpen was taken over by ham antics, so I walked across the hall to Tierney's office. Lee, Russ Millard, Harry Sears and two old-timer cops I hardly knew—Dick Cavanaugh and Vern Smith—were huddled around Captain Jack's desk, examining a piece of paper the boss was holding up.

I looked over Harry's shoulder. Three mug shots of a showstopper brunette were taped to the page, with three-close-up face photos of the corpse at 39th and Norton affixed next to them. The slashed-mouth smile jumped out at me; Captain Jack said, "The mugs are from the Santa Barbara PD. They popped the Short girl in September '43 for underaged drinking, sent her home to her mother in Massachusetts. Boston PD contacted her an hour ago. She's flying out to ID the stiff tomorrow. The Boston cops are doing a background check back east, and all Bureau days off are cancelled. Anybody complains, I point to those pictures. What did Doc Newbarr say, Russ?"

Millard said, "Tortured for two days. Cause of death the mouth wound or the head bashing. No rape. Internal organs removed. Dead six to eight hours before the body was dumped in the lot. What else have we got on her?"

Tierney checked some papers on his desk. "Except for the juvie roust, no other record. Four sisters, parents divorced, worked in the Camp Cooke PX during the war. The father's here in LA. What's next?"

I was the only one who blinked when the big boss asked number two for advice. Millard said, "I want to recanvass Leimert Park with the mugs. Me, Harry and two other men. Then I want to go to University Station, read reports and answer calls. Has Loew given the press a look at the mugs?"

Tierney nodded. "Yeah, and Bevo Means told me the father sold the *Times and* the *Herald* some old portrait pictures of the girl. She'll be front page on the evening editions."

Millard barked, "Damn," the only word of profanity anyone ever heard him use. Seething, he said, "They'll be coming out of the woodwork to greet her. Has the father been questioned?"

Tierney shook his head and consulted some memo slips. "Cleo Short, 1020½ South Kingsley, Wilshire District. I had an officer call him and tell him to stay put, that we'd be sending some men by to talk to him. Russ, you think the strange-o's will fall in love with this one?"

"How many confessions so far?"

"Eighteen."

"Double that by morning, more if Loew got the press excited with his purple prose."

"I would say I got them motivated, Lieutenant. And I would say my prose fit the crime."

Ellis Loew was standing in the doorway, Fritz Vogel and Bill Koenig behind him. Millard locked eyes with the radio ham. "Too much publicity is a hindrance, Ellis. If you were a policeman you'd know that."

Loew flushed and reached for his Phi Beta Kappa key. "I'm a ranking civilian-police liaison officer, specially deputized by the City of Los Angeles."

Millard smiled. "You're a civilian, counselor."

Loew bristled, then turned to Tierney. "Captain, have you sent men to talk to the victim's father?"

Captain Jack said, "Not yet, Ellis. Soon."

"How about Vogel and Koenig? They'll get us what we need to know."

Tierney looked up at Millard. The lieutenant gave an almost imperceptible head shake; Captain Jack said, "Aah, Ellis, in big homicide jobs the whip assigns the men. Aah, Russ, who do you think should go?"

Millard scrutinized Cavanaugh and Smith, me trying to look inconspicuous and Lee yawning, slouched against the wall. He said, "Bleichert, Blanchard, you bad pennies question Miss Short's father. Bring your report to University Station tomorrow morning."

Loew's hands jerked his Phi Beta key clean off its chain; it fell to the floor. Bill Koenig squeezed in the doorway and picked it up; Loew about-faced into the hall. Vogel glared at Millard, then followed him. Harry Sears, breathing Old Grand Dad, said, "He sends a few niggers to the gas chamber and it goes to his head."

Vern Smith said, "The niggers must have confessed."

Dick Cavanaugh said, "With Fritzie and Bill they all confess."

Russ Millard said, "Shit-brained, grandstanding son of a bitch."

• • •

We took separate cars to the Wilshire District, rendezvousing in front of 1020½ South Kingsley at dusk. It was a garage apartment, shack sized, at the rear of a big Victorian house. Lights were burning inside; Lee, yawning, said, "Good guy—bad guy," and rang the buzzer.

A skinny man in his fifties opened the door and said, "Cops, huh?" He had dark hair and pale eyes similar to the girl in the mug shots, but that was it for familial resemblance. Elizabeth Short was a knockout; he looked like a knockout victim: bony frame in baggy brown trousers and a soiled undershirt, moles all over his shoulders, seamed face pitted with acne scars. Pointing us inside, he said, "I got an alibi, just in case you think I did it. Tighter than a crab's ass, and that is *air* tight."

Mr. White Hat to the hilt, I said, "I'm Detective Bleichert, Mr. Short. This is my partner Sergeant Blanchard. We'd like to express our condolences for the loss of your daughter."

Cleo Short slammed the door. "I read the papers, I know who you are. Neither one of you would have lasted one round with Gentleman Jim Jeffries. And as far as your condolences go, I say *c'est la vie*. Betty called the tune, so she had to pay the piper. Nothing's free in this life. You want to hear my alibi?"

I sat down on a threadbare sofa and eyeballed the room. The walls were lined floor to ceiling with shelves spilling dime novels; there was the couch, one wooden chair and nothing else. Lee got out his notebook. "Since you're so anxious to tell us, shoot."

Short slumped into the chair and ground the legs into the floor, like an animal pawing the dirt. "I was Johnny on the spot at my job from Tuesday the fourteenth at two P.M. to five P.M. Wednesday the fifteenth. Twenty-seven straight hours, time and a half for the last seventeen. I'm a refrigerator repairman, the best in the west. I work at Frost King Appliances, 4831 South Berendo. My boss's name is Mike Mazmanian. You call him. He'll alibi me up tighter than a popcorn fart, and that is *air* tight."

Lee yawned and wrote it down; Cleo Short crossed his arms over his bony chest, daring us to make something of it. I said, "When was the last time you saw your daughter, Mr. Short?"

"Betty came west in the spring of '43. Stars in her eyes and hanky-panky on her mind. I hadn't seen her since I left that dried-up old ginch of a wife of mine in Charlestown, Mass., on March 1, 1930 A.D. and never looked back. But Betty wrote me and said she needed a flop, so I—"

Lee interrupted: "Cut the travelogue, pop. When was the last time you saw Elizabeth?"

I said, "Back off, partner. The man is cooperating. Go on, Mr. Short."

Cleo Short dug in with his chair, glaring at Lee. "Before punchy here got wise, I was gonna tell you that I reached into my own savings and sent Betty a C-note to come west on, then I promised her three squares and a five-spot a week mad money if she kept the house tidy. A generous offer, if you want my opinion. But Betty had other things on her mind. She was a lousy housekeeper, so I gave her the boot on June 2, 1943 A.D., and I ain't seen her since."

I wrote the information down, then asked, "Did you know she was in LA recently?"

Cleo Short quit glaring at Lee and glared at me. "No."

"Did she have any enemies that you knew of?"

"Just herself."

Lee said, "No cute answers, Pops."

I whispered, "Let him talk," then said out loud, "Where did Elizabeth go when she left here in June of '43?"

Short jabbed a finger at Lee. "You tell your pal he calls me Pops I call him stumblebum! Tell him disrespect's a two-way street! Tell him I repaired Chief CB Horrall's Maytag 821 model myself, and I mean *air* tight!"

Lee walked into the bathroom; I saw him chasing a handful of pills with sink water. I put on my calmest white hat voice: "Mr. Short, where did Elizabeth go in June of '43?"

Short said, "That palooka lays a hand on me, I'll fix his wagon *air* tight."

"I'm sure you will. Would you ans—"

"Betty moved up to Santa Barbara, got a job at the Camp Cooke PX. She sent me a postcard in July. It said some soldier beat her up bad. That was the last I ever heard from her."

"Did the card mention the soldier's name?"

"No."

"Did it mention the names of any of her friends up at Camp Cooke?"

"No."

"Any boyfriends?"

"Hah!"

I put my pen down. "Why 'hah'?"

The old man laughed so hard that I thought his chicken chest would explode. Lee walked out of the bathroom; I gave him a sign to ease off. He nodded and sat down next to me; we waited for Short to laugh himself out. When he was down to a dry chortle, I said, "Tell me about Betty and men."

Short giggled. "She liked them and they liked her. Betty believed in quantity before quality, and I don't think she was too good at saying no, unlike her mother."

"Be specific," I said. "Names, dates, descriptions."

"You musta caught too many in the ring, Sonny, 'cause your seabag's leaky. Einstein couldn't remember the names of all Betty's boyfriends, and my name ain't Albert."

"Give us the names you do remember."

Short hooked his thumbs in his belt and rocked in the chair like a cut-rate cock of the walk. "Betty was man crazy, soldier crazy. She went for lounge lizards and anything white in a uniform. When she was supposed to be keeping house for me she was out prowling Hollywood Boulevard, cadging drinks off servicemen. When she was staying here this place was like a branch of the USO."

Lee said, "Are you calling your own daughter a tramp?"

Short shrugged. "I've got five daughters. One bad apple ain't so bad."

Lee's anger was oozing out of him; I put a restraining hand on his arm and could almost feel his blood buzzing. "What about names, Mr. Short?"

"Tom, Dick, Harry. Those punks took one look at Cleo Short and amscrayed with Betty pronto. That's as specific as I can get. You look for anything not too ugly in a uniform, you won't go wrong."

I flipped to a fresh notebook page. "What about employment? Was Betty holding down a job when she stayed here?"

The old man shouted: "Betty's job was working for me! She said she was looking for movie work, but that was a lie! All she wanted to do was parade the Boulevard in those black getups of hers and chase men! She ruined my bathtub dying her stuff black, then she took off before I could dock the damage out of her wages! Prowling the streets like a black widow spider, no wonder she got hurt! It's her mother's fault, not mine! No-cunt shanty Irish bitch! Not my fault!"

Lee drew a hard finger across his throat; we walked out to the street, leaving Cleo Short screaming at his four walls. Lee said, "Jesus fuck"; I sighed, "Yeah," thinking of the fact that we'd just been handed the entire U.S. armed forces as suspects.

I dug in my pockets for a coin. "Toss you for who writes it up?"

Lee said, "You do it, okay? I want to stick at Junior Nash's pad and get some license numbers."

"Try and get some sleep, too."

"I will."

"No, you won't."

"I can't shit a shitter. Look, will you go over to the house and keep Kay company? She's been worried about me, and I don't want her to be alone."

I thought of what I'd said at 39th and Norton last night—that statement of what all three of us knew but never talked about, that move forward that only Kay had the guts to take. "Sure, Lee."

*   *   *

I found Kay in her usual weeknight posture—reading on the living room couch. She didn't look up when I walked in, she just blew a lazy smoke ring and said, "Hi, Dwight."

I took a chair across the coffee table from her. "How'd you know it was me?"

Kay circled a passage in the book. "Lee stomps, you tread cautiously."

I laughed. "It's symbolic, but don't tell anybody."

Kay stubbed out her cigarette and put the book down. "You sound worried."

I said, "Lee's all bent out of shape on the dead girl. He got us detached to work the investigation when we should be going after a priority warrantee, and he's taking Benzedrine and starting to go a little squirrely. Has he told you about her?"

Kay nodded. "A little."

"Have you read the papers?"

"I've avoided them."

"Well, the girl is being played up as the hottest number since the atom bomb. There's a hundred men working a single homicide, Ellis Loew's looking to get fat off of it, Lee's cuckoo on the subject—"

Kay disarmed my tirade with a smile. "And *you* were front page news on Monday, but you're stale bread today. And you want to go after your big bad robber man and get yourself another headline."

"Touché, but that's only part of it."

"I know. Once you got the headline, you'd hide out and not read the papers."

I sighed. "Jesus, I wish you weren't so much smarter than me."

"And I wish you weren't so cautious and complicated. Dwight, what is going to happen with us?"

"The three of us?"

"No, *us*."

I looked around the living room, all wood and leather and Deco chromium. There was a glass-fronted mahogany cabinet; it was filled with Kay's cashmere sweaters, all the shades of the rainbow at forty dollars a pop. The woman herself, South Dakota white trash molded by a cop's love, sat across from me, and for once I said exactly what was on my mind. "You'd never leave him. You'd never leave this. Maybe if you did, maybe if Lee and I were quits as partners, maybe then we'd have a chance together. But you'd never give it all up."

Kay took her time lighting a cigarette. Exhaling a breath of smoke, she said, "You know what he's done for me?"

I said, "And for me."

Kay tilted her head back and eyed the ceiling, brushed stucco with mahogany wainscoting. Blowing smoke rings, she said, "I had such a schoolgirl crush on you. Bobby De Witt and Lee used to drag me to the fights. I brought my sketch pad so I wouldn't feel like one of those awful women buttering up their men by pretending they liked it. What I liked was you. The way you made fun of yourself with your teeth, the way you covered up so you wouldn't get hit. Then you joined the Department, and Lee told me how he heard you informed on those Japanese friends of yours. I didn't hate you for it, it just made you seem more real to me. The zoot suit thing, too. You were my storybook hero, only the stories were real, little bits and pieces here and there. Then the fight came along, and even though I hated the idea of it I told Lee to go ahead, because it seemed to mean the three of us were meant to be."

I thought of a dozen things to say, all of them true, and just about the two of us. But I couldn't, and ran to Lee for cover. "I don't want you to worry about Bobby De Witt. When he gets out, I'll lean on him. Hard. He'll never come near you or Lee."

Kay took her eyes off the ceiling and fixed me with a strange look, hard but sad underneath. "I've given up worrying about Bobby. Lee can handle him."

"I think Lee's afraid of him."

"He is. But I think it's because he knows so much about me, and Lee's afraid he'll let everyone know. Not that anyone cares."

"I care. And if I lean on De Witt, he'll be lucky to talk at all."

Kay stood up. "For a man with an up-for-grabs heart, you are such a hardcase. I'm going to bed. Good night, Dwight."

When I heard a Schubert quartet coming from Kay's bedroom, I took pen and paper from the stationery cupboard and wrote out my report on the questioning of Elizabeth Short's father. I included mention of his "air tight" alibi, his account of the girl's behavior when she lived with him in '43, the beating she got from a Camp Cooke soldier and her parade of nameless boyfriends. Padding the report with unnecessary details kept my mind most of the way off Kay, and when I finished I made myself two ham sandwiches, chased them with a glass of milk and fell asleep on the couch.

My dreams were mug shot flashes of recent bad guys, Ellis Loew representing the right side of the law with felony numbers stenciled across his chest. Betty Short joined him in black and white, full face and left profile views. Then all the faces dissolved into LAPD report forms rolling out endlessly as I tried to jot down information on Junior Nash's whereabouts in the blank spaces. I woke up with a headache, knowing I was in for a very long day.

It was dawn. I walked out to the porch and picked up the morning *Herald*. The headline was "Hunt Boyfriends in Torture Killing," a portrait photo of Elizabeth Short centered directly below it. It was captioned, "The Black Dahlia," followed by, "Authorities today were searching into the love life of 22-year-old Elizabeth Short, victim of the 'Werewolf Murder,' whose romances had changed her, according to friends, from an innocent girl to a black-clad, man-crazy delinquent known as the Black Dahlia."

I felt Kay beside me. She grabbed the paper, skimming the front page, giving a slight shudder. Handing it back, she asked, "Will all this be over soon?"

I flipped through the front section. Elizabeth Short took up six whole pages, most of the ink portraying her as a slinky femme fatale in a tight black dress. "No," I said.

CHAPTER NINE

Reporters were surrounding University Station. The parking lot was packed and the curb was lined with radio trucks, so I double-parked, stuck "Official Police Vehicle" signs under my wiper blades and pushed through the cordon of newshounds, ducking my head to avoid being recognized. It didn't work; I heard "Buck-kee!" and "Blei-chert," then hands grabbed at me. My jacket pocket was ripped loose, and I shoved myself the rest of the way inside.

The entrance hall was filled with daywatch blues going on duty; a connecting door opened up into a bustling squadroom. Cots lined the walls; I saw Lee passed out on one of them, sheets of newspaper covering his legs. Phones were ringing at desks all around me, and my headache came back, the pounding twice as bad. Ellis Loew was tacking slips of paper to a bulletin board; I tapped him hard on the shoulder.

He turned around. I said, "I want out of this circus. I'm a Warrants officer, not a Homicide dick, and I've got priority fugitives. I want to get un-detached. *Now.*"

Loew hissed, "No. You work for me, and I want you on the Short case. That's final, absolute and irrevocable. And I'll brook no prima donna demands from you, Officer. Do you understand?"

"Ellis, goddamnit!"

"You get stripes on your sleeve before you call me that, Bleichert. Until then it's Mr. Loew. Now go read Millard's summary report."

I stormed over to the rear of the squadroom. Russ Millard was asleep in a chair, his legs propped up on the desk in front of him. Four typed sheets of paper were tacked to the corkboard wall a few feet away. I read:

First Summary Report
187 P.C., Vict: Short, Elizabeth Ann, W.F.
D.O.B. 7/29/24. Filed 1/17/47 0600 Hrs.

Gentlemen—
Here's the 1st summary on E. Short, D.O.D. 1/15/47, 39th and Norton, Leimert Park.

1. 33 phony or probable phony confessions so far. Obviously innocent confessors have been released, incoherent and seriously imbalanced being held at City Jail awaiting alibi checks and sanity hearings. Known deviates being questioned by Dr. De River, consulting psychiatrist, with Det. Div. backup. Nothing solid yet.

2. Results of prlim. post mort. and follow-up: vict. choked to death on ear to ear knife slash thru mouth. No alcohol or narcotics in blood at time of death. (For det. see case file 14-187-47)

3. Boston P.D. doing background check on E. Short, family and old boyfriends and their whereabouts at time of murder. Father (C. Short) has valid alibi—he is eliminated as suspect.

4. Camp Cooke C.I.D. is checking out reports of beating E. Short received from soldier when she worked at P.X. in 9/43. E. Short arrested for underaged drinking in 9/43, C.I.D. says soldiers she was arrested with are all overseas, thus eliminated as suspects.

5. Sewers being dragged citywide for E. Short's clothing. All women's clothing found will be analyzed at Central Crime Lab. (See crime lab sum. rpts. for det.)

6. Citywide field interrogation rpts. 1/12/47—1/15/47 collated and read. One follow-up: Hollywood woman called in complaint about shouts of "weird sounding gibberish" in H.W. Hills nights of 1/13 and 1/14. Result of follow-up: put off as party revelers making noise. Field officers: disregard this occurrence.

7. From verified phone tips: E. Short lived most of 12/46 in San Diego, at home of Mrs. Elvera French. Vict. met Mrs. French's daughter, Dorothy, at movie theater where Dorothy worked, told (unverified) story about being abandoned by husband. Frenches took her in, and E. Short told them conflicting stories: she was widow of air corps major; pregnant by navy pilot; engaged to army flyer. Vict. had many dates with different men during her stay at French house. (See 14-187-47 interviews for det.)

XXXXX8. E. Short left French house on 1/9/47 in company of man she called "Red." (Desc. as: W.M., 25-30, tall, "handsome", 170-180, red hair, blue eyes.) "Red" allegedly salesman. Drives a pre-war Dodge sedan with Huntington Park tags. Vehicle cross-check initiated. A.P.B. issued on "Red".

9. Verified info: Val Gordon (W.F.) Riverside, Calif., called in, said she is sister of deceased air corps major Matt Gordon. Said: E. Short wrote to her and her parents in Fall of '46, shortly after Maj. Gordon died in plane crash. Lied about being Gordon's fiancee, requested $ from them. Parents, Miss Gordon, denied request.

10. Trunk belonging to E. Short located at Railway Express office, downtown L.A. (R.E. clerk saw vict's name and picture in papers, recalled her storing trunk in late 11/46). Trunk being gone over. Carbons of 100's of love letters to various men (mostly servicemen) found, and (many fewer) mash notes written to her. Also, many photos of E. Short with servicemen in trunk. Letters being read, names and descriptions of men being collated.

11. Verified phone info: former Air Corps Lt. J.G. Fickling called from Mobile, Ala. when he saw E. Short's name and picture in Mobile papers. Said he and vict. had "brief affair" in Boston in late '43, and "she had about 10 other boyfriends on line at all times." Fickling has verified alibi for time of murder. Eliminated as suspect, also denies ever having been engaged to E. Short.

12. Numerous tips being phoned in to all L.A.P.D. and Sheriff's divisions. Crank-sounding dismissed, others routed to applicable area squadrooms thru Cent. Homicide. All tips being cross-filed.

XXXXXX13. Address verified info: E. Short lived at these addresses in 1946. (Names following addresses are of caller or verified residents of same address. All but Linda Martin verified by D.M.V. records)
13-A-1611 N. Orange Dr., Hollywood. (Harold Costa, Donald Leyes, Marjorie Graham) 6024 Carlos Ave., Hollywood. 1842 N. Cherokee, Hollywood (Linda Martin, Sheryl Saddon) 53 Linden, Long Beach.

14. Results of SID findings in Leimert Park vact lots: no woman's clothing found, numerous knives and knife blades found, all too rusted to be murder weapon. No blood found.

15. Results of Leimert Park canvasing (with mugs of E. Short): zero (all sightings obvious crank stuff.)

In conclusion: I believe all investigatory efforts should be centered around questionings of E. Short's known associates, particularly her numerous boyfriends. Sergeant Sears and I will be going to San Diego to question her K.A.'s there. Between the APB on "Red" and the L.A. K.A. questionings we should get salient information.

Russell A. Millard, Lt.,
Badge 493, Central Homicide

I turned around to find Millard watching me. He said, "Off the top of your head, what do you think?"

I fingered my ripped pocket. "Is she worth it, Lieutenant?"

Millard smiled; I noticed that rumpled clothes and a razor stubble didn't dent his aura of class. "I think so. Your partner thinks so."

"Lee's chasing bogeymen, Lieutenant."

"You can call me Russ, you know."

"Okay, Russ."

"What did you and Blanchard get from the father?"

I handed Millard my report. "Nothing specific, just more dope on the girl as a tramp. What's with this Black Dahlia stuff?"

Millard slapped the arms of his chair. "We can thank Bevo Means for that. He went down to Long Beach and talked to the desk clerk at the hotel where the girl stayed last summer. The clerk told him Betty Short always wore tight black dresses. Bevo thought of that movie with Alan Ladd, *The Blue Dahlia*, and took it from there. I figure the image is good for at least another dozen confessions a day. As Harry says when he's had a few, 'Hollywood will fuck you when no one else will.' You're a smart bad penny, Bucky. What do you think?"

"I think I want to go back to Warrants. Will you grease it with Loew?"

Millard shook his head. "No. Will you answer my question?"

I choked down the urge to smash or beg. "She said yes or no to the wrong guy, at the wrong time, at the wrong place. And since she's had more rubber burned on her than the San Berdoo Highway, and doesn't know how to tell the truth, I'd say that finding that wrong guy is going to be a hell of a job."

Millard stood up and stretched. "Bright penny, you go up to Hollywood Station and meet Bill Koenig, then you two go question the tenants at the Hollywood addresses on my summary. Stress the boyfriend angle. Keep Koenig on a tight leash if you can, and you write the report, because Billy's practically illiterate. Report back here when you're finished."

My headache going migraine, I obeyed. The last thing I heard before hitting the street was a group of cops chortling over Betty Short's love letters.

• • •

I picked up Koenig at Hollywood Station and drove with him to the Carlos Avenue address. Parking in front of 6024, I said, "You're ranking, Sarge. How do you want to play this?"

Koenig cleared his throat loudly, then swallowed the wad of phlegm he brought up. "Fritzie does the talking, but he's home sick. How about you talk, I stand backup?" He opened his jacket to show me a leather sap stuck into the waistband. "You think it's a muscle job?"

I said, "Talk job," and got out of the car. There was an old lady sitting on the porch of 6024, a three-story brown clapboard house with a ROOMS FOR RENT sign staked on the lawn. She saw me walking over, closed her Bible and said, "I'm sorry, young man, but I only rent to career girls with references."

I flashed my shield. "We're police officers, ma'am. We came to talk to you about Betty Short."

The old woman said, "I knew her as Beth," then shot a look at Koenig, standing on the lawn surreptitiously picking his nose.

I said, "He's looking for clues."

The woman snorted, "He won't find them inside that big beak of his. Who killed Beth Short, Officer?"

I got out pen and notepad. "That's what we're here to find out. Could I have your name, please?"

"I'm Miss Loretta Janeway. I called the police when I heard Beth's name on the radio."

"Miss Janeway, when did Elizabeth Short live at this address?"

"I checked my records right after I heard that news broadcast. Beth stayed in my third-floor right-rear room from last September fourteenth to October nineteenth."

"Was she referred to you?"

"No. I remember it very well, because Beth was such a pretty girl. She knocked on the door and said she was walking up Gower when she saw my sign. She said she was an aspiring actress and needed an inexpensive room until she got her big break. I said I'd heard that one before, and told her she'd do well to lose that awful Boston accent of hers. Well, Beth just smiled and said, 'Now is the time for all good men to come to the aid of their party' with no accent at all. Then she said, 'See! See how I take direction! She was so eager to please that I rented her the room, even though my policy is not to rent to movie types."

I wrote the pertinent info down, then asked, "Was Beth a good tenant?"

Miss Janeway shook her head. "God rest her soul, but she was an awful tenant, and she made me regret bending my policy on movie picture types. She was always late on her rent, always hocking her jewelry for food money and trying to get me to let her pay by the day instead of the week. A dollar a day she wanted to pay! Can you imagine how much space my ledgers would take up if I let all my tenants do that?"

"Did Beth socialize with the other tenants?"

"Good lord, no. The third-floor right-rear room has got private steps, so Beth didn't have to come in through the front door like the other girls, and she never attended any of the coffee klatches I put on for the girls after church on Sunday.

Beth *never* went to church herself, and she told me, 'Girls are good for chitchat once in a blue moon, but give me boys any day.'"

"Here's my most important question, Miss Janeway. Did Beth have any boyfriends while she was living here?"

The old woman picked up the Bible and hugged it to herself. "Officer, if they'd come in the front door like the other girls' beaus, I would have seen them. I don't want to blaspheme the dead, so let's just say I heard lots of footsteps on Beth's stairs at the most ungodly hours."

"Did Beth ever mention any enemies? Anybody she was afraid of?"

"No."

"When was the last time you saw her?"

"Late October, the day she moved out. She said, 'I've found more simpatico digs' in her best California girl voice."

"Did she say where she was moving to?"

Miss Janeway said "No," then leaned toward me confidingly and pointed to Koenig, loping back to the car tugging at his crotch. "You should talk to that man about his hygiene. Frankly, it's disgusting."

I said, "Thank you, Miss Janeway," walked to the car and got in behind the wheel.

Koenig grunted, "What did the cooze say about me?"

"She said you're cute."

"Yeah?"

"Yeah."

"What else did she say?"

"That a man like you could make her feel young again."

"Yeah?"

"Yeah. I told her to forget it, that you're married."

"I ain't married."

"I know."

"Then why'd you tell her that?"

I pulled out into traffic. "You want her sending you mash notes at the Bureau?"

"Oh, I get it. What did she say about Fritzie?"

"Does she know Fritzie?"

Koenig looked at me like *I* was mentally defective. "Lots of people talk about Fritzie behind his back."

"What do they say?"

"Lies."

"What kind of lies?"

"Bad lies."

"For instance?"

"Lies like he got the syph fucking hooers when he worked Ad Vice. Like he got docked off a month from duty to take the mercury cure. Like he got bounced to Central dicks for it. Bad lies, even worse stuff than that."

Chills were tickling my spine. I turned onto Cherokee and said, "Such as?"

Koenig slid closer to me. "You pumping me, Bleichert? You looking for bad things to say about Fritzie?"

"No. Just curious."

"Curiosity killed the kitty cat. You remember that."

"I will. What did you get on the Sergeant's Exam, Bill?"

"I don't know."

"What?"

"Fritzie took it for me. Remember the kitty cat, Bleichert. I don't want nobody saying nothing bad about my partner."

1842, a big stucco apartment house, came into view. I pulled over and parked, muttered, "Talk job," then headed straight for the lobby.

A wall directory listed S. Saddon and nine other names—but no Linda Martin—in apartment 604. I took the elevator up to the sixth floor, walked down a hallway smelling faintly of marijuana and rapped on the door. Big band music died out, the door opened and a youngish woman in a sparkly Egyptian outfit was standing there, holding a papier mâché headdress. She said, "Are you the driver from RKO?"

I said, "Police." The door shut in my face. I heard a toilet flushing; the girl returned a moment later, and I walked into the apartment uninvited. The living room was high-ceilinged and arched; sloppily made-up bunk beds lined the walls. Suitcases, valises and steamer trunks were spilling out of an open closet door, and a linoleum table was wedged diagonally against a set of bunks without mattresses. The table was covered with cosmetics and vanity mirrors; the cracked wood floor beside it was dusted with spilled rouge and face powder.

The girl said, "Is this about those jaywalking tickets I forgot to pay? Listen, I've got three days on *Curse of the Mummy's Tomb* at RKO, and when I get paid I'll send you a check. Is that all right?"

I said, "This is about Elizabeth Short, Miss—"

The girl put out a big stage groan. "Saddon. Sheryl with a Y-L Saddon. Listen, I talked to a policeman on the phone this morning. Sergeant something or other with a bad stutter. He asked me nine thousand questions about Betty and her nine thousand boyfriends, and I told him nine thousand times that lots of girls bunk here and date lots of guys, and most of them are fly-by-nights. I told him that Betty lived here from early November to early December, that she paid a dollar a day just like the rest of us, and I didn't remember the names of any of her dates. So can I go now? The extra truck's due any minute, and I need this job."

Sheryl Saddon was out of breath and sweating from her metallic costume. I pointed to a bunk bed. "Sit down and answer my questions, or I'll roust you for the reefers you flushed down the toilet."

The three-day Cleopatra obeyed, giving me a look that would have withered Julius Caesar. I said, "First question. Does a Linda Martin live here?"

Sheryl Saddon grabbed a pack of Old Golds off the bunk and lit up. "I told Sergeant Stutter already. Betty mentioned Linda Martin a couple of times. She roomed at Betty's other place, the one over on De Longpre and Orange. And you need evidence to arrest someone, you know."

I took out my pen and notebook. "What about Betty's enemies? Threats of violence against her?"

"Betty's trouble wasn't enemies, it was too many friends, if you follow my drift. Get it? Friends like in *boy*friends?"

"Smart girl. Any of them ever threaten her?"

"Not that I know of. Listen, can we hurry this up?"

"Simmer down. What did Betty do for work while she was staying here?"

Sheryl Saddon snorted, "Comedian. Betty didn't work. She bummed change from the other girls here, and she cadged drinks and dinner off grandfather types down on the Boulevard. A couple of times she took off for two or three days and came back with money, then she told these fish stories about where it came from. She was such a little liar that nobody ever believed a word she said."

"Tell me about the fish stories. And about Betty's lies in general."

Sheryl stubbed out her cigarette and lit another one immediately. She smoked silently for a few moments, and I could tell that the actress part of her was warming to the idea of caricaturing Betty Short. Finally she said, "You know all this Black Dahlia stuff in the papers?"

"Yes."

"Well, Betty always dressed in black as a gimmick to impress casting directors when she made rounds with the other girls, which wasn't often, because she liked to sleep till noon every day. But sometimes she'd tell you she was wearing black because her father died or because she was mourning the boys who died in the war. Then the next day she'd tell you her father was alive. When she was out for a couple of days and came back flush, she'd tell one girl a rich uncle died and left her a bundle and another that she won the money playing poker in Gardena. She told everybody nine thousand lies about being married to nine thousand different war heroes. You get the picture?"

I said, "Vividly. Let's change the subject."

"Goody. How about international finance?"

"How about the movies? You girls are all trying to break in, right?"

Sheryl gave me a vamp look. "I have broken in. I was in *The Cougar Woman, Attack of the Phantom Gargoyle* and *Sweet Will Be the Honeysuckle*."

"Congratulations. Did Betty ever get any movie work?"

"Maybe. Maybe once, but then again maybe not, because Betty was such a liar."

"Go on."

"Well, on Thanksgiving all the kids on the sixth floor chipped in for a potluck supper, and Betty was flush and bought two whole cases of beer. She was bragging about being in a movie, and she was showing around this viewfinder that she said the director gave her. Now lots of girls have got chintzy little viewfinders that movie guys give them, but this was an expensive one, on a chain, with a little velvet case. I remember that Betty was on cloud nine that night, talking up a blue streak."

"Did she tell you the name of the movie?"

Sheryl shook her head. "No."

"Did she mention any names associated with the movie?"

"If she did, I don't remember."

I looked around the room, counted twelve bunk beds at a dollar a night apiece and thought of a landlord getting fat. I said, "Do you know what a casting couch is?"

The mock Cleopatra's eyes burned. "Not me, buster. Not this girl *ever*."

"Betty Short?"

"Probably."

I heard a horn honking, walked to the window and looked out. A flatbed truck with a dozen Cleopatras and pharaohs in the back was at the curb directly behind my car. I turned around to tell Sheryl, but she was already out the door.

• • •

The last address on Millard's list was 1611 North Orange Drive, a pink stucco tourist flop in the shadow of Hollywood High School. Koenig snapped out of his nose-picking reverie as I double-parked in front of it, pointing to two men perusing a stack of newspapers on the steps. "I'll take them, you take the skirts. You got names for them?"

I said, "Maybe Harold Costa and Donald Leyes. You look tired, Sarge. Don't you want to sit this one out?"

"I'm bored. What should I ask them guys?"

"I'll handle them, Sarge."

"You remember the kitty cat, Bleichert. Same thing happened to him happens to guys who try to jerk my chain when Fritzie ain't around. Now what do I roust them guys for?"

"Sarge—"

Koenig sprayed me with spittle. "I'm ranking, hotshot! You do what Big Bill says!"

Seeing red, I said, "Get alibis and ask them if Betty Short ever engaged in prostitution"; Koenig snickered in reply. I took the lawn and steps at a run, the two men moving aside to let me through. The front door opened into a shabby sitting room; a group of young people were sitting around, smoking and reading movie mags. I said, "Police. I'm looking for Linda Martin, Marjorie Graham, Harold Costa and Donald Leyes."

A honey blonde in a slacks suit dog-eared her *Photoplay*. "I'm Marjorie Graham, and Hal and Don are outside."

The rest of the people got up and fanned out into the hallway, like I was a big dose of bad news. I said, "This is about Elizabeth Short. Did any of you know her?"

I got a half dozen negative head shakes, shocked and sad looks; outside I heard Koenig shouting, "You tell me true! Was the Short bimbo peddling it?"

Marjorie Graham said, "I was the one who called the police, Officer. I gave them Linda's name because I knew she knew Betty, too."

I pointed to the door. "What about those guys outside?"

"Don and Harold? They both dated Betty. Harold called you because they knew you'd be looking for clues. Who's that man yelling at them?"

I ignored the question, sat down beside Marjorie Graham and got out my notebook. "What can you tell me about Betty that I don't know already? Can you give me *facts*? Names of other boyfriends, descriptions, specific dates? Enemies? Possible motives for somebody wanting to kill her?"

The woman flinched; I realized I was raising my voice. Keeping it low, I said, "Let's start with dates. When did Betty live here?"

"Early December," Marjorie Graham said. "I remember because there was a bunch of us sitting here listening to a radio program on the fifth anniversary of Pearl Harbor when she checked in."

"So that was December seventh?"

"Yes."

"And how long was she here?"

"No more than a week or so."

"How did she know about this place?"

"I think Linda Martin told her about it."

Millard's memo stated that Betty Short spent most of December in San Diego. I said, "But she moved out shortly afterward, right?"

"Yes."

"Why, Miss Graham? Betty lived in three places that we know of last fall—all in Hollywood. Why did she move around so much?"

Marjorie Graham took a tissue from her purse and fretted it. "Well, I don't really know for sure."

"Was some jealous boyfriend after her?"

"I don't think so."

"Miss Graham, what *do* you think?"

Marjorie sighed. "Officer, Betty used up people. She borrowed money from them and told them stories, and . . . well, a lot of pretty hard-nosed kids live here, and I think they saw through Betty pretty quick."

I said, "Tell me about Betty. You liked her, didn't you?"

"Yes. She was sweet and trusting and sort of dumb, but . . . inspired. She had this strange gift, if you want to call it that. She'd do anything to be liked, and she sort of took on the mannerisms of whoever she was with. Everybody here smokes, and Betty started smoking to be one of the kids, even though it was bad for her asthma and she hated cigarettes. And the funny thing is that she'd try to walk and talk like you, but she was always herself when she was doing it. She was always Betty or Beth or whatever nickname for Elizabeth she was going by at that moment."

I kicked the sad dope around in my head. "What did you and Betty talk about?"

Marjorie said, "Mostly I just listened to Betty talk. We used to sit here and listen to the radio, and Betty told stories. Love stories about all these war heros—Lieutenant Joe and Major Matt and on and on. I knew they were just fantasies. Sometimes she talked about becoming a movie star, like all she had to do was walk around in her black dresses and sooner or later she'd get discovered. That sort of made me mad, because I've been taking classes at the Pasadena Playhouse, and I know that acting is hard work."

I flipped to my notes from the Sheryl Saddon questioning. "Miss Graham, did Betty talk about being in a movie sometime in late November?"

"Yes. The first night she was here she was bragging about it. She said she had a co-starring role, and she showed around a viewfinder. A couple of boys pressed her for details, and she told one of them it was at Paramount, another that it was at Fox. I thought she was just fibbing to get attention."

I wrote "Names" on a clean page and underlined it three times. "Marjorie, what about names? Betty's boyfriends, people you saw her with?"

"Well, I know she went out with Don Leyes and Harold Costa, and I saw her once with a sailor, and I . . ."

Marjorie faltered; I caught a troubled look in her eyes. "What is it? You can tell me."

Marjorie's voice was stretched thin. "Right before she moved out I saw Betty and Linda Martin talking to this big older woman up on the Boulevard. She was wearing a man's suit, and she had short hair like a man. I only saw them with her that one time, so maybe it doesn't mean—"

"Are you saying the woman was a lesbian?"

Marjorie bobbed her head up and down and reached for a Kleenex; Bill Koenig stepped inside and hooked a finger at me. I walked over to him. He whispered, "Them guys talked, said the stiff peddled her twat when she got strapped bad. I called Mr. Loew. He said to keep that zipped, 'cause it's a better caper if she's a nice young cooze."

I bit off an urge to spill the dyke lead; the DA and his flunky would probably quash it, too. I said, "I've got another quick one here. Get statements from those guys, okay?"

Koenig giggled and walked outside; I told Marjorie to sit still and moved to the rear of the lobby. There was a registration desk, an open ledger on top of it. I stood at the counter and leafed through the pages until I saw a childishly scrawled "Linda Martin," with "Room 14" printed across from it.

I took the first-floor corridor back to the room, knocked on the door and waited for an answer. When none came after five seconds, I tried the knob. It gave, and I pushed the door open.

It was a cramped little room containing nothing but an unmade bed. I checked the closet; it was dead empty. The nightstand held a stack of yesterday's papers folded open to "Werewolf Murder" brouhaha; suddenly I *knew* the Martin girl was a lamster. I got down on the floor and ran a hand under the bed, brushed a flat object and pulled it out.

It was a red plastic change purse. I opened it and found two pennies, a dime and an identification card for Cornhusker High School, Cedar Rapids, Iowa. The card was made out to Lorna Martilkova, DOB 12/19/31. There was a photo of a beautiful young girl below the school's crest; in my mind I was already typing out an all-points juvie runaway warrant.

Marjorie Graham appeared in the doorway. I held out the ID card; she said, "That's Linda. God, she's only fifteen."

"Middle-aged for Hollywood. When did you see her last?"

"This morning. I told her I called the police, that they'd be coming by to talk to us about Betty. Was that the wrong thing to do?"

"You couldn't have known. And thanks."

Marjorie smiled, and I found myself wishing her a speedy one-way trip out of movieland. I kept the wish silent as I smiled back and walked outside. On the porch, Bill Koenig was standing at parade rest and Donald Leyes and Harold Costa were sprawled in lounge chairs with that green-at-the-gills look that comes with taking a few rabbit punches.

Koenig said, "They didn't do it."

I said, "No shit, Sherlock."

Koenig said, "My name ain't Sherlock."

I said, "No shit."

Koenig said, "What?"

●   ●   ●

At Hollywood Station I exercised the Warrants cops' special prerogative, issuing an all-points juvenile runaway warrant and a priority material witness warrant on Lorna Martilkova/ Linda Martin, leaving the report forms with the daywatch boss, who told me the APBs would hit the air within the hour, and that he would send officers over to 1611 North Orange Drive to question the tenants on Linda/Lorna's possible where-abouts. With that taken care of, I wrote my report on the series of questionings, stressing Betty Short as a habitual liar and the possibility that she acted in a movie sometime in November of '46. Before finishing it up, I wavered on whether to mention Marjorie Graham's lead on the old dyke. If Ellis Loew got ahold of the dope he would probably quash it along with the skinny on Betty as a part-time prostie, so I decided to omit it from the report and give the information verbally to Russ Millard.

From a squadroom phone I called the Screen Actor's Guild and Central Casting and inquired about Elizabeth Short. A clerk told me that no one by that name or any diminutive of the name Elizabeth was ever listed with them, making it unlikely that she had appeared in a legit Hollywood production. I hung up thinking of the movie as another Betty fairy tale, the viewfinder a fairy-tale prop.

It was late afternoon. Being free of Koenig felt like surviving cancer and the three interviews felt like an overdose of Betty/ Beth Short and her low-rent last months on earth. I was tired and hungry, so I drove to the house for a sandwich and a nap— and walked straight into another installment of the Black Dahlia Show.

Kay and Lee were standing around the dining room table, examining crime scene photos shot at 39th and Norton. There was Betty Short's bashed head; Betty Short's slashed breasts; Betty Short's empty bottom half and Betty Short's wide-open legs—all in glossy black and white. Kay was nervously smoking and shooting little glances at the pictures; Lee was eyeballing them, his face twitching in a half dozen directions, the Benzedrine man from outer space. Neither said a word to me; I just stood there playing straight man to the most celebrated stiff in LA history.

Finally Kay said, "Hi, Dwight," and Lee stabbed a shaky finger at a close-up of the torso mutilations. "It's not a random job, I know it. Vern Smith says some guy just picked her up on the street, took her someplace and tortured her, then dumped her in the lot. Horseshit. The guy who did this hated her for a reason and wanted the whole goddamn world to know. Jesus, two fucking days he cut her. Babe, you took pre-med classes, you think this guy had medical training? You know, like some kind of mad doctor type?"

Kay put out her cigarette and said, "Lee, Dwight's here"; Lee wheeled around.

I said, "Partner—" and Lee tried to wink, smile and speak at the same time.

It came off as one awful grimace; when he got out, "Bucky, listen to Kay, I knew all the college I bought her would do me some good," I had to look away.

Kay's voice was soft, patient. "This kind of theorizing is just nonsense, but I'll give you a theory if you'll eat something to calm yourself down."

"Theory on, teach."

"Well, it's just a guess, but maybe there were two killers, because the torture cuts are crude, while the bisection and the cut on the abdomen, which are obviously both postmortem, are neat and clean. Maybe there's just one killer though, and after he killed the girl he calmed down, then bisected her and made the abdominal cut. And anybody could have removed the internal organs with the body in two parts. I think mad doctors are only in the movies. Sweetie, *you* have to calm down. You have to quit taking those pills and you have to eat. Listen to Dwight, he'll tell you that."

I looked at Lee. He said, "I'm too hopped-up to eat," then stuck out his hand like I'd just walked in. "Hey, partner. You learn anything good about our girl today?"

I thought of telling him I learned she wasn't worth a hundred full-time cops; I thought of spilling the dyke lead and Betty Short as a sad little floozy-liar to back the claim up. But Lee's dope-juiced face made me say, "Nothing that's worth you doing this to yourself. Nothing that's worth seeing you useless when a bimbo you sent to Quentin is three days away from LA. Think of your little sister seeing you this way. Think of her—"

I stopped when tears started streaming from Lee's outer-space eyes. Now *he* just stood there like the straight man to his own blood kin. Kay moved between us, a hand on each of our shoulders. I walked out before Lee began weeping for real.

●   ●   ●

University Station was another outpost of Black Dahlia mania.

A wager pool sign-up list was posted in the locker room. It was in the form of a crudely drawn crap table felt, featuring betting spaces labeled "Solved—pay 2 to 1," "Random sex job—pay 4 to 1," "Unsolved—even money," "Boyfriend(s) pay 1 to 4," and "'Red'—no odds unless suspect captured." The "House $ man" was listed as Sergeant Shiner, and so far the big action was on "boyfriend(s)," with a dozen officers signed up, all plopping down a sawbuck to win two-fifty.

The squadroom was more comic relief. Someone had hung the two halves of a cheap black dress from the doorway. Harry Sears, half gassed, was waltzing around the Negro cleaning woman, introducing her as the real Black Dahlia, the best colored songbird since Billie Holliday. They were taking nips from Harry's flask, the cleaning lady belting gospel numbers while officers trying to talk on the phone clamped hands to their free ears.

The straight business was frenzied, too. Men were working with DMV registrations and Huntington Park street directories, trying to put together a lead on the "Red" Betty Short left San Dago with; others were reading her love letters, and two officers were on the DMV police line getting info on the license numbers Lee had gotten last night while camped out at Junior Nash's fuck pad. Millard and Loew were gone, so I dropped my questioning report and a note on the warrants I'd issued into a large tray marked FIELD DETECTIVE'S SUMMARIES. Then I took off before some ranking clown forced me to join the circus.

Being at loose ends made me think of Lee; thinking of Lee made me wish I was back at the squadroom, where at least there was a sense of humor about the dead girl. Then thinking of Lee made me mad, and I started thinking about Junior Nash, professional gunman more dangerous than fifty jealous boyfriend killers. Itchy, I went back to being a Warrants cop and prowled Leimert Park for him.

But there was no escape from the Black Dahlia.

Passing 39th and Norton, I saw rubberneckers gawking around the vacant lot while ice cream and hotdog vendors dispensed chow; an old woman was peddling Betty Short portrait glossies in front of the bar at 39th and Crenshaw, and I wondered if the charming Cleo Short had supplied the negatives for a substantial percentage cut. Pissed off, I pushed the buffoonery out of my mind and *worked*.

I spent five straight hours walking South Crenshaw and South Western, showing Nash's mug shots and talking up his MO of statch rape on young Negro tail. All I got was "No" and the question "Why ain't you after the guy who chopped up that nice Dahlia girl?" Toward mid-evening I surrendered myself to the notion that maybe Junior Nash really had blown LA. And still itchy, I rejoined the circus.

After a wolfed burger dinner, I called the night number at Administrative Vice and inquired about known lesbian gathering places. The clerk checked the Ad Vice intelligence files and came back with the names of three cocktail lounges, all on the same block of Ventura Boulevard out in the Valley: the Dutchess, the Swank Spot and La Verne's Hideaway. I was about to hang up when he added that they were out of the LAPD's jurisdiction in the unincorporated county territory patrolled by the sheriff's department, and were probably operating under their sanction—for a price.

I didn't think about jurisdictions on the ride out to the

Valley. I thought about women with women. Not lez types, but soft girls with hard edges, like my string of fight giveaways. Going over the Cahuenga Pass, I tried to put pairs of them together. All I could come up with was their bodies and the smell of liniment and car upholstery—no faces. I used Betty/ Beth and Linda/Lorna then, mug shots and high school ID combined with the bodies of the girls I remembered from my last pro fights. It got more and more graphic; then the 11000 block of Ventura Boulevard came into view and I got women- and-women for real.

The Swank Spot had a log cabin facade and double swinging doors like the saloons in western movies. The interior was narrow and poorly lit; it took long moments for my eyes to adjust to the darkness. When they did I saw a score of women trying to stare me down.

Some of them were bull dykes in khaki shirts and GI issue trousers; some were soft girls in skirts and sweaters. One hefty dagger eyed me head to toe; the girl standing next to her, a svelte redhead, put her head on her shoulder and slinked an arm around her thick waist. Feeling myself start to sweat, I looked for the bar and someone with the air of top dog. I spotted a lounge area at the back of the room, bamboo chairs and a table covered with liquor bottles, all of it encircled by wall neon blinking purple, then yellow, then orange. I walked over, arm-draped couples separated to let me through, giving me just enough room to maneuver.

The lezzie behind the serving bar poured a shot glass full of whiskey and placed it in front of me, saying, "You from the Beverage Control?" She had piercing light eyes; neon reflec- tions turned them almost translucent. I got a weird feeling that she knew what I was thinking about on the way over.

Downing the booze, I said, "LAPD Homicide"; the dyke said, "Not your bailiwick, but who got snuffed?" I fumbled for my snapshot of Betty Short and the Lorna/Linda ID card, then placed them on the bar. The whiskey lubed my hoarse voice: "Have you seen either of them?"

The woman gave the two pieces of paper, then me, a long once-over. "You tellin' me the Dahlia's a sister?"

"You tell me."

"I'll tell you I've never seen her except in the papers, and the little schoolgirl twist I've never seen, because me and my girls don't truck with underaged stuff. Capice?"

I pointed to the shot glass; the dyke refilled it. I drank; my sweat warmed, then cooled off. "Capice when your girls tell me that and I believe them."

The woman whistled, and the lounge area filled up. I grabbed the pictures and handed them to a femme draped around a lumberjack lady. They checked the photos out and shook their heads, then passed them to a woman in a Hughes Aircraft jumpsuit. She said, "No, but USDA choice tail," and gave them to a couple next to her. They muttered "Black Dahlia," real shock in their voices. Both said, "No"; the last lezzie said, "Nyet, nein, no, and not my type besides." She shoved the pictures at me, then spat on the floor. I said, "Good night, ladies," and made for the door, the word "Dahlia" whispered over and over behind me.

The Dutchess was two more free shots, a dozen more hostile looks and "No" answers, all in an old English motif. Walking into La Verne's Hideaway, I was half juiced and itchy for something I couldn't put my finger on.

La Verne's was dark inside, baby spots affixed to ceiling beams casting shadowy light on walls covered with cheap palm tree paper. Lezbo couples were cooing at each other in wraparound booths; the sight of two femmes kissing forced me to stare, then look away and seek out the bar.

It was recessed into the left wall, a long counter with colored lights reflecting off a Waikiki Beach scene. There was nobody tending it, no customers sitting on any of the stools. I walked to the back of the room, clearing my throat so the lovebirds in the booths could jump off cloud nine and return to earth. The strategy worked; clinches and kisses ended, angry and startled eyes looked up at the coming of bad news.

I said, "LAPD Homicide," and handed the pics to the nearest lezzie. "The dark-haired one is Elizabeth Short. The Black Dahlia if you've been reading the papers. The other one's her pal. I want to know if any of you have seen them, and if so who with."

The pictures made the rounds of the booths; I studied reactions when I saw that I'd have to use a bludgeon to get simple yes or no answers. Nobody said a word; all I got from reading faces was curiosity tinged with a couple of cases of lust. The photos came back to me, handed over by a diesel dagger sporting a flat top. I grabbed them and headed for the street and fresh air, stopping when I saw a woman behind the bar polishing glasses.

I moved to the bar and placed my wares on the counter, hooking a finger at her. She picked up the mug shot strip and said, "I seen her picture in the paper and that's it."

"What about this girl? She goes by the name Linda Martin."

The barmaid held up the Lorna/Linda ID card and squinted at it; I saw a flicker of recognition pass over her face. "No, sorry."

I leaned over the counter. "Don't fucking lie to me. She's fifteen fucking years old, so you come clean now, or I slap a contributing beef on you, and you spend the next five years eating pussy in Tehachapi."

The lezbo recoiled; I half expected her to go for a bottle and brain me with it. Eyes on the bar, she said, "The kid used to come in. Maybe two, three months ago. But I've never seen the Dahlia, and I think the kid liked boys. I mean, she just cadged drinks off the sisters, that was it."

Sidelong, I saw a woman just starting to sit down at the bar change her mind, grab her purse and make for the door, as if spooked by my words with the barmaid. The baby spotlight caught her face; I caught a fleeting resemblance to Elizabeth Short.

I gathered up my pictures, counted to ten and pursued the woman, getting to my car just as I saw her unlock the door of a snow-white Packard coupe parked a couple of spaces up from me. When she pulled out, I counted to five, then followed.

The rolling surveillance led me over Ventura Boulevard to the Cahuenga Pass, then down into Hollywood. Late-night traffic was scarce, so I let the Packard stay several car lengths in front of me as it headed south on Highland, out of Hollywood, into the Hancock Park District. At 4th Street, the woman turned left; within seconds we were in the heart of Hancock Park—an area Wilshire Division cops called "Pheasant Under Glass Acres."

The Packard turned the corner at Muirfield Road and stopped in front of a huge Tudor mansion fronted by a lawn the size of a football field. I continued on, my headlights picking up the car's rear plate: CAL RQ 765. Checking my rearview mirror, I saw the woman locking the driver's side door; even from a distance her trim sharkskin figure stood out.

I took 3rd Street out of Hancock Park. At Western I saw a pay phone, got out and called the DMV night line, requesting a vehicle make and criminal record check on white Packard coupe CAL RQ 765. The operator kept me waiting for close to five minutes, then returned with his read-out:

Madeleine Cathcart Sprague, white female, DOB 11/14/25, LA, 482 South Muirfield Road; no wants, no warrants, no criminal record.

Driving home, the shots of booze wore off. I started wondering if Madeleine Cathcart Sprague had anything at all to do with Betty/Beth and Lorna/Linda, or whether she was just a rich lezzie with a taste for low life. Steering with one hand, I took out my Betty Short mugs, superimposed the Sprague girl's face over them and came away with a common, everyday resemblance. Then I saw myself peeling off her sharkskin suit and knew I didn't care one way or the other.

CHAPTER TEN

I played the radio on the ride to University Station the next morning. The Dexter Gordon quartet was bebopping me into good spirits when "Billie's Bounce" quit bouncing, replaced by a feverish voice: "We interrupt our regular broadcast to bring you a bulletin. A major suspect in the investigation into the slaying of Elizabeth Short, the raven-haired party girl known as the Black Dahlia, has been captured! Previously known to the authorities only as 'Red,' the man has now been identified as Robert 'Red' Manley, age twenty-five, a Huntington Park hardware salesman. Manley was captured this morning at the South Gate home of a friend and is now being held and questioned at the Hollenbeck police station in East Los Angeles. In an exclusive handout to KGFJ, Deputy DA Ellis Loew, ace legal beagle working on the case as civilian-police liaison, said: 'Red Manley is a hot suspect. We've got him pegged as the man who drove Betty Short up from San Diego on January ninth, six days before her torture-ravaged body was found in a vacant lot in Leimert Park. This looks like the big break we've all been hoping and praying for. God has answered our prayers!'"

Ellis Loew's sentiments were replaced by a commercial for Preparation H, guaranteed to reduce the painful swelling of

111

hemorrhoids or double your money back. I flipped the radio off and changed direction, heading for Hollenback Station.

The street in front of it was blocked off with sawhorse detour signs; patrolmen were holding reporters at bay. I parked in the alley behind the station and entered through the back door to the holding tank. Drunks jabbered in cells on the misdemeanor side of the catwalk; hardcase types glowered from the felony row. It was a jailhouse full house, but there were no jailers anywhere. Opening a connecting door into the station proper, I saw why.

What looked like the entire in-station contingent was crammed into a short corridor inset with interrogation cubicles, every man straining for a look through the one-way glass of the middle room on the left side. Russ Millard's voice was coming out of a wall-mounted speaker: smooth, coaxing.

I nudged the officer nearest to me. "Has he confessed?"

The man shook his head. "No. Millard and his partner are giving him the Mutt and Jeff."

"Did he admit knowing the girl?"

"Yeah. We got him from the DMV cross-checks, and he came along peacefully. Wanna make a little bet? Innocent or guilty, take your pick. I'm feelin' lucky today."

I ignored the offer, gently elbowed my way up to the glass and peered in. Millard was seated at a battered wooden table, a handsome young guy with a carrot-hued pompadour across from him fingering a pack of cigarettes. He looked scared shitless; Millard looked like the nice-guy priest in the movies— the one who's seen it all and granted absolution for the whole enchilada.

Carrot top's voice came over the speaker. "Please, I've told it three times now."

Millard said, "Robert, we're doing this because you didn't come forward. Betty Short has been on the front page of every LA newspaper for three days now, and you knew we wanted to talk to you. But you hid out. How do you think that looks?"

Robert 'Red' Manley lit a cigarette, inhaled and coughed. "I didn't want my wife to know I was chipping on her."

"But you didn't chip on her. Betty wouldn't put out. She cock-teased you and didn't come across. That's no reason to hide from the police."

"I dated her down in Dago. I danced slow dances with her. It's the same thing as chipping."

Millard put a hand on Manley's arm. "Let's go back to the beginning. Tell me how you met Betty, what you did, what you talked about. Take your time, nobody's rushing you."

Manley stubbed out his cigarette into an overflowing ash-tray, lit another one and wiped sweat from his brow. I looked around the corridor and saw Ellis Loew leaning against the opposite wall, Vogel and Koenig flanking him like twin dogs awaiting the command to attack. A static-filtered sigh came over the loudspeaker; I turned back and watched the suspect squirm in his chair. "And this is the last time I'll have to tell it?"

Millard smiled. "That's right. Go ahead, son."

Manley got up and stretched, then paced as he talked. "I met Betty the week before Christmas, at this bar in downtown Dago. We just started gabbing, and Betty let it slip that she was sort of on her uppers, staying with this woman Mrs. French and her daughter, sort of temporarily. I bought her dinner at an Italian joint in Old Town, then we went dancing at the Sky Room at the El Cortez Hotel. We—"

Millard interrupted. "Do you always chase tail when you're out of town on business?"

Manley shouted, "I wasn't chasing tail!"

"What were you doing, then?"

"I was infatuated, that's all. I couldn't tell if Betty was a gold digger or a nice girl, and I wanted to find out. I wanted to test my loyalty to my wife and I just . . ."

Manley's voice died down; Millard said, "Son, for God's sake tell the truth. You were looking for some pussy, right?"

Manley slumped into his chair. "Right."

"Just like you always do on business trips, right?"

"No! Betty was different!"

"How was she different? Out-of-town stuff is out-of-town stuff, right?"

"No! I don't chip on my wife when I'm on the road! Betty was just . . ."

Millard's voice was so low that the loudspeaker barely picked it up. "Betty just set you off. Right?"

"Right."

"Made you want to do things you'd never done before, made you mad, made you—"

"No! No! I wanted to fuck her, I didn't want to hurt her!"

"Sssh. Sssh. Let's go back to Christmastime. You had that first date with Betty. Did you kiss her good night?"

Manley gripped the ashtray with both hands; they shook, butts spilled onto the table. "On the cheek."

"Come on, Red. No heavy pass?"

"No."

"You had a second date with Betty two days before Christmas, right?"

"Right."

"More dancing at the El Cortez, right?"

"Right."

"Soft lights, drinks, soft music, then you made your move, right?"

Goddamn you, quit saying 'Right'! I tried to kiss Betty and she gave me this song and dance about how she couldn't sleep with me because the father of her child had to be a war hero and I was only in the army band. She was goddamn nuts on the subject! All she did was talk about these horseshit war heros!"

Millard stood up. "Why do you say 'horseshit,' Red?"

"Because I knew they were lies. Betty said she was married to this guy and engaged to that guy, and I knew she was trying to make me look small because I never saw combat."

"Did she mention any names?"

"No, just ranks. Major this and Captain that, like I should be ashamed of being a corporal."

"Did you hate her for it?"

"No! Don't put words in my mouth!"

Millard stretched and sat down. "After that second date, when was the next time you saw Betty?"

Manley sighed and rested his forehead on the table. "I've told you the whole story three times."

"Son, the sooner you tell it again, the sooner you'll be able to go home."

Manley shivered and wrapped his arms around himself. "After the second date I didn't hear from Betty until January eighth, when I got this telegram at my office. The telegram said she'd like to see me when I made my next sales run down to Dago. I wired back, saying I had to be in Dago tomorrow afternoon, and I'd pick her up. Then I picked her up, and she begged me to drive her up to LA. I said—"

Millard held up a hand. "Did Betty say why she had to get to LA?"

"No."

"Did she say she was meeting somebody?"

"No."

"You agreed to do it because you thought she'd put out for you?"

Manley sighed. "Yes."

"Go ahead, son."

"I took Betty with me on my rounds that day. She stayed in the car while I called on customers. I had some calls in Oceanside the next morning, so we spent the night in a motel there, and—"

"Let's have the name of the place again, son."

"It was called the Cornucopia Motor Lodge."

"And Betty CT'd you again that night?"

"She . . . she said she had her period."

"And you fell for that old chestnut?"

"Yes."

"Did it make you mad?"

"Goddamn it, I didn't kill her!"

"Sssh. You slept in the chair and Betty slept on the bed, right?"

"Right."

"And in the morning?"

"In the morning we drove up to LA. Betty went with me on my rounds and tried to float me for a five-spot, but I turned her down. Then she handed me a cock-and-bull story about meeting her sister in front of the Biltmore Hotel. I wanted to get rid of her, so I dropped her in front of the Biltmore that night, right around five o'clock. And I never saw her again, except for all that Dahlia stuff in the papers."

Millard said, "That was five o'clock, Friday, January tenth when you last saw her?"

Manley nodded. Millard looked straight at the glass, adjusted the knot of his necktie, then stepped outside. In the corridor, officers swarmed him, hurling questions. Harry Sears slipped into the room; next to me a familiar voice rose above the commotion. "Now you'll see why Russ keeps Harry around."

It was Lee, grinning a shit-eating grin, looking like a million tax-free dollars. I cuffed him around the neck. "Welcome back to earth."

Lee cuffed me back. "It's your fault I look this good. Right after you left, Kay slipped me a Mickey Finn, some stuff she got at the drugstore. I slept seventeen hours, got up and ate like a horse."

"Your own goddamn fault for bankrolling her chemistry classes. What do you think of Red?"

"A pussy hound at worst, a divorced pussy hound by the end of the week. You agree?"

"In spades."

"You get anything yesterday?"

Seeing my best friend looking like a new man made it easy to twist the truth. "You read my FI report?"

"Yeah, at University. Good work on the juvie warrant. You get anything else?"

I lied flat-out, a trim sharkskin figure dancing in the back of my head. "No. You?"

Staring through the one-way, Lee said, "No, but what I said about getting the bastard still goes. Jesus, look at Harry."

I did. The mild-mannered stutterer was circling the interrogation room table, twirling a metal-studded sap, whacking it hard into the tabletop each time he circuited. "Ka-thack's" filled the speaker; Red Manley, arms wrapped around his chest, quivered as each blow reverberated.

Lee nudged me. "Russ has got one rule—no actual hitting. But watch how—"

I shrugged off Lee's hand and stared through the one-way. Sears was tapping the sap on the table a few inches in front of Manley, his stutterless voice dripping cold rage. "You wanted some fresh gash, and you thought Betty was easy. You came on strong, and that didn't work, so you begged. That didn't work, so you offered her money. She told you she was on the rag, and that was the final straw. You wanted to make her bleed for real. Tell me how you sliced her titties. Tell me—"

Manley screamed, "No!" Sears smashed the sap into the ashtray, the glass cracked, butts flew off the table. Red bit his lip; blood spurted out, then dribbled down his chin. Sears sapped the pile of broken glass; shards exploded all over the room. Manley whimpered, "No no no no no"; Sears hissed, "You knew what you wanted to do. You're an old cunt chaser, and you knew lots of places to take girls. You plied Betty with a few drinks, got her to talk about her old boyfriends and came on like a pal, like nice little corporal willing to leave Betty to the *real men*, the men who saw combat, who deserved to get laid with a fine cooze like her—"

"No!"

Sears hit the table, ka-thack! "*Yes*, Reddy-poo, *yes*. I think you took her to a toolshed, maybe one of those abandoned warehouses out by the old Ford plant in Pico-Rivera. There was some twine and lots of cutting tools lying around, and you got a hard-on. Then you shot your load in your pants before you could stick it in Betty. You were mad before, but now you were *really* mad. You started thinking about all the girls who laughed at that tiny little dick of yours and all the times your wife said, 'Not tonight, Reddy-poo, I've got a headache.' So you hit her and tied her down and beat her and cut her! Admit it, you fucking degenerate!"

"No!"

Ka-thack!

The table jumped off the floor from the force of the blow.

Manley almost jumped out of his chair; only Sears' hand on the back slats kept him from toppling over.

"Yes, Reddy-poo. *Yes.* You thought of every girl who said 'I don't suck,' every time your mommy spanked you, every evil eye you got from real soldiers when you played your trombone in the army band. Goldbrick, needle-dick, pussy-whipped, that's what you were thinking. That's what Betty had to pay for. Right?"

Manley dribbled blood and spittle into his lap and gurgled. "No. Please, as God is my witness, no"; Sears said, "God hates liars," and sapped the table three times—*Ka-thack! Ka-thack! Ka-thack!* Manley lowered his head and began to dry sob; Sears knelt by his chair. "Tell me how Betty screamed and begged, Red. Tell me, then tell God."

"No. No. I didn't hurt Betty."

"Did you get another hard-on? Did you come and come and come the more you cut her?"

"No. Oh God, oh God."

"That's right, Red. Talk to God. Tell God all about it. He'll forgive you."

"No, please God."

"Say it, Red. Tell God how you beat and tortured and ripped up Betty Short for three fucking days, then cut her in two."

Sears smashed the table once, twice, three times, then hurled it over onto its side. Red fumbled himself out of his chair and onto his knees. He clasped his hands and mumbled, "The Lord is my shepherd, I shall not want," then started weeping. Sears looked straight at the one-way, self-loathing etched into every plane of his flabby juicehound face. He gave the thumbs-down sign, then walked out of the room.

Russ Millard met him just outside the door and led him away from the general crowd of officers, in my direction. Eavesdropping on their whispered conversation, I picked up the gist of it: they both thought Manley was clean, but wanted to shoot him with Pentothal and give him a polygraph test to make sure. Looking back through the one-way, I saw Lee and another plainsclothesman handcuffing Red, easing him out of the interrogation room. Lee was giving the man the kid gloves treatment he usually reserved for children, talking softly to him, one hand on his shoulder. The crowd broke up when the three of them disappeared into the holding tank. Harry Sears went back into the cubicle and began cleaning up his mess; Millard turned to me. "Good report yesterday, Bleichert."

I said, "Thanks," knowing I was being sized up. We locked eyes. I asked, "What's next?"

"You tell me."

"First you send me back to Warrants, right?"

"Wrong, but keep going."

"Okay, then we canvass around the Biltmore and try to reconstruct Betty Short's movements from the tenth, when Red dropped her off, to the twelfth or thirteenth, when she got snatched. We blanket the area and collate the FIs and hope to hell the legit leads don't get lost with all phonies this publicity is getting us."

"Keep going."

"We know Betty was movie-struck and promiscuous, and that she bragged about being in a movie last November, so my bet is that she wouldn't turn down a roll on the casting couch. I think we should query producers and casting directors, see what we get."

Millard smiled. "I called Buzz Meeks this morning. He's an ex-cop, works as head of security at Hughes Aircraft. He's the Department's unofficial liaison to the studios, and he'll be asking around. You're doing well, Bucky. Run with the ball."

I wavered—wanting to impress a senior officer; wanting to roust the rich lezzie myself. Millard's pump job came on as condescending, bones of praise to keep a young cop from balking at his unwanted assignment. Madeleine Cathcart Sprague framed in my mind, I said, "All I know is that you should keep an eye on Loew and his boys. I didn't put it in my report, but Betty Short sold it outright when she needed money bad enough, and Loew's been trying to keep it kiboshed. I think he'll sit on anything that makes her look like an outright tramp. The more sympathy the public has for the girl, the more juice he gets as prosecuting attorney if this mess ever gets to court."

Millard laughed. "Bright penny, are you calling your own boss an evidence suppressor?"

I thought of myself as the same thing. "Yeah, and a shit-brained, grandstanding son of bitch."

Millard said, "Touché," and handed me a piece of paper. "Betty sightings—restaurants and bars in Wilshire Division. You can work it single or with Blanchard, I don't care."

"I'd rather canvass around the Biltmore."

"I know you would, but I want foot beat men who know the area to work there, and I need smart pennies to eliminate the phonies from the tip list."

"What are you going to be doing?"

Millard smiled sadly. "Keeping an eye on the evidence suppressor shit-brained son of a bitch and his minions to make sure they don't try to coerce a confession out of that innocent man in the holding tank."

*   *   *

I couldn't find Lee anywhere around the station, so I checked out the tip list as a single-o. The canvassing territory was centered in the Wilshire District, restaurant bars and juke joints on Western, Normandie and 3rd Street. The people I talked to were mostly barflies, daytime juicers eager to suck up to authority or gab with someone other than the usual boon acquaintances they found in gin mills. Pressing for facts, I got sincere fantasy—virtually every person had Betty Short giving them a long spiel taken from the papers and radio when she was really down in Dago with Red Manley or somewhere getting tortured to death. The longer I listened the more they talked about themselves, interweaving their sad tales with the story of the Black Dahlia, who they actually believed to be a glamorous siren headed for Hollywood stardom. It was as if they would have traded their own lives for a juicy front-page death. I included questions on Linda Martin/Lorna Martilkova, Junior Nash and Madeleine Cathcart Sprague and her snow-white Packard, but all it got me was stuporous deadpans. I decided that my FI report would consist of two words: "All bullshit."

I finished shortly after dark, and drove to the house to grab dinner.

Pulling up, I saw Kay storming out the door and down the steps, hurling an armful of paper onto the lawn, then storming back while Lee stormed beside her, shouting and waving his arms. I walked over and knelt beside the discarded pile; the papers were carbons of LAPD report forms. Sifting through them, I saw FIs, evidence indexes, questioning reports, tip lists and a complete autopsy protocol—all with "E. Short, W.F. D.O.D. 1/15/47" typed at the top. They were obviously bootlegged from University Station—and the very possession of them was enough to guarantee Lee a suspension from duty.

Kay came back with another load, shouting, "After all that's happened, all that might happen, how can you do this? It's sick and it's insane!" She dumped the papers beside the other pile; 39th and Norton glossies glinted up at me. Lee grabbed her by the arms and held her while she squirmed. "Goddamnit, you know what this is to me. You *know*. Now I'll rent a room to keep the stuff in, but babe, you stick by me on this. It's *mine*, and I need you . . . and you *know*."

They noticed me then. Lee said, "Bucky, you tell her. You reason with her."

It was the funniest Dahlia circus line I'd heard so far. "Kay's right. You've pulled at least three misdemeanors on this thing, and it's getting out—" I stopped, thinking of what *I'd* pulled, and where I was going at midnight. Looking at Kay, I shifted gears. "I promised him a week on it. That means four more days. On Wednesday it's over."

Kay sighed, "Dwight, you can be so gutless sometimes," then walked into the house. Lee opened his mouth to say something funny. I kicked a path through official LAPD paper to my car.

* * *

The snow-white Packard was in the same spot as last night. I staked it out from my car, parked directly in back of it. Huddled low in the front seat, I spent angry hours watching foot traffic enter and leave the three bars on the block—daggers, femmes and obvious sheriff's dicks with that edgy look indigenous to bagmen. Midnight came and went; the foot traffic picked up—mostly lezzies headed for the hot sheet motels across the street. Then she walked out the door of La Verne's Hideaway alone, a showstopper in a green silk dress.

I slid out the passenger side door just as she stepped off the curb, giving me a sidelong glance. "Slumming, Miss Sprague?"

Madeleine Sprague stopped; I closed the distance between us. She dug in her purse, pulling out car keys and a fat wad of cash. "So Daddy's spying again. He's on one of his little Calvinist crusades, and he said you shouldn't be subtle." She switched to a deft imitation of a Scotchman's burr: "Maddy girl, ye should not be congregating in such unsuitable places. It would not do to have ye seen by the wrong people there, lassie."

My legs were trembling, like they did while I waited for the first-round bell. I said, "I'm a police officer."

Madeleine Sprague went back to her normal voice. "Oh? Daddy's buying policemen now?"

"He didn't buy me."

She held out the cash and looked me over. "No, probably not. You'd be dressing better if you worked for him. So let's try the West Valley Sheriffs. You're already extorting La Verne, so you thought you'd try extorting her patrons."

I took the money, counted over a hundred dollars, then handed it back. "Let's try LAPD Homicide. Let's try Elizabeth Short and Linda Martin."

Madeleine Sprague's brassy act died fast. Her face scrunched up with worry, and I saw that her resemblance to Betty/Beth was more hairdo and makeup than anything else; on the whole her features were less refined than the Dahlia's, and only superficially similar. I studied that face: panicky hazel eyes caught by streetlight glow; forehead creased, like her brain was working overtime. Her hands were shaking, so I grabbed the car keys and money, stuffed them into her purse and tossed it on the hood of the Packard. Knowing I might have a major lead by the short hairs, I said, "You can talk to me here or downtown, Miss Sprague. Just don't lie. I know you knew her, so if you jerk me off on that it's the station and a lot of publicity you don't want."

The brass girl finally composed herself. I repeated, "Here or downtown?" She opened the Packard's passenger door and got in, sliding over behind the wheel. I joined her, flicking on a dashboard light so I could read her face. The smell of leather upholstery and stale perfume hit me; I said, "Tell me how long you knew Betty Short."

Madeleine Sprague fidgeted under the light. "How did you know I knew her?"

"You rabbited last night when I was questioning the barmaid. What about Linda Martin? Do you know her?"

Madeleine ran long red fingertips over the wheel. "This is all a fluke. I met Betty and Linda at La Verne's last fall. Betty said it was her first time there. I think I talked to her one time after that. Linda I talked to several times, just cocktail lounge chit-chat."

"When last fall?"

"November, I think."

"Did you sleep with either of them?"

Madeleine flinched. "No."

"Why not? That's what that dive is all about, right?"

"Not entirely."

I tapped her green silk shoulder, hard. "Are you lez?"

Madeleine went back to her father's burr. "Ye might say I take it where I can find it, laddie."

I smiled, then patted the spot I'd jabbed a moment before. "You're telling me that your sole contact with Linda Martin and Betty Short was a couple of cocktail bar conversations two months ago, right?"

"Yes. That's exatly what I'm telling you."

"Then why did you take off so fast last night?"

Madeleine rolled her eyes and rolled "Laddie," Scotch-voiced; I said, "Cut the shit and tell it straight." The brass girl spat out: "Mister, my father is Emmett Sprague. *The* Emmett

Sprague. He built half of Hollywood and Long Beach, and what he didn't build he bought. He does not like publicity, and he would not like to see 'Tycoon's Daughter Questioned in Black Dahlia Case—Played Footsie with Dead Girl at Lesbian Nightclub' in the papers. Now do you get the picture?"

I said, "In Technicolor," and patted Madeleine's shoulder.

She pulled away from me and sighed, "Is my name going into all kinds of police files where all kinds of slimy little policemen and slimy little yellow journalists will see it?"

"Maybe, maybe not."

"What do I have to do to keep it out?"

"Convince me of a few things."

"Such as?"

"Such as first you give me your impression of Betty and Linda. You're a bright kid—give me your play on them."

Madeleine stroked the wheel, then the gleaming oak dashboard. "Well, they weren't sisters, they were just using the Hideaway to cadge drinks and dinner."

"How could you tell?"

"I saw them brush off passes."

I thought of Marjorie Graham's mannish older woman. "Any passes stand out? You know, rough stuff? Bull daggers getting persistent?"

Madeleine laughed. "No, the passes I saw were very ladylike."

"Who made them?"

"Street trade I never saw before."

"Or since?"

"Yes, or since."

"What did you talk about with them?"

Madeleine laughed again, harder. "Linda talked about the boy she left behind in Hicktown, Nebraska, or wherever it was she came from and Betty talked about the latest issue of *Screenworld*. On a conversational level, they were right down there with you, only they were better looking."

I smiled and said, "You're cute."

Madeleine smiled and said, "You're not. Look, I'm tired. Aren't you going to ask me to prove I didn't kill Betty? Since I can prove it, won't that put an end to this farce?"

"I'll get to that in a minute. Did Betty ever talk about being in a movie?"

"No, but she was movie-struck in general."

"Did she ever show you a movie viewfinder? A lens gadget on a chain?"

"No."

"What about Linda? Did she talk about being in a movie?"

"No, just her hicktown sweetheart."

"Do you have any idea where she'd go if she was on the lam?"

"Yes. Hicktown, Nebraska."

"Besides there."

"No. Can I—"

I touched Madeleine's shoulder, more of a caress than a pat. "Yeah, tell me your alibi. Where were you and what were you doing from last Monday, January thirteenth, through to Wednesday the fifteenth."

Madeleine cupped her hands to her mouth and blew a horn fanfare, then rested them on the seat by my knee. "I was at our house in Laguna from Sunday night through Thursday morning. Daddy and Mommy and sister Martha were there with me, and so were our live-in servants. If you want verification, call Daddy. Our number is Webster 4391. But be discreet. Don't tell him where you met me. Now, do you have any other questions?"

My private Dahlia lead was blown, but it gave me the green light in another direction. "Yeah. You ever do it with men?"

Madeleine touched my knee. "I haven't met any lately, but I'll do it with you to keep my name out of the papers."

My legs were Jell-O. "Tomorrow night?"

"All right. Pick me up at eight, like a gentleman. The address is 482 South Muirfield."

"I know the address."

"I'm not surprised. What's your name?"

"Bucky Bleichert."

Madeleine said, "It goes with your teeth."

I said, "Eight o'clock," and got out of the Packard while my legs could still function.

CHAPTER ELEVEN

Lee said, "You want to catch the fight films at the Wiltern tonight? They're showing oldies—Dempsey, Ketchel, Greb. What do you say?"

We were sitting at desks across from each other in the University squadroom, manning telephones. The clerical flunkies assigned to the Short case had been given Sunday off, so regular field dicks were doing the drudge work, taking down tips, then writing out slips assessing the tipsters and routing possible follow-ups to the nearest detective division. We'd been at it for an hour without interruption, Kay's "gutless" remark hanging between us. Looking at Lee, I saw that his eyes were just starting to pin, a sign that he was coming on to a fresh Benzie jolt. I said, "I can't."

"Why not?"

"I've got a date."

Lee grinned-twitched. "Yeah? Who with?"

I changed the subject. "Did you smooth it out with Kay?"

"Yeah, I rented a room for my stuff. The El Nido Hotel, Santa Monica and Wilcox. Nine scoots a week, chump change if it makes her feel good."

"De Witt gets out tomorrow, Lee. I think I should lean on him, maybe get Vogel and Koenig to do it."

Lee kicked at a wastebasket. Paper wads and empty coffee cups flew out; heads darted up from other desks. Then his phone rang.

Lee picked it up. "Homicide, Sergeant Blanchard speaking."

I stared at my routing slips; Lee listened to his caller. Wednesday, Dahlia kiss-off time, came into focus as an eternity away, and I wondered if he'd need weaning off the Benzedrine. Madeleine Sprague jumped into my mind—her nine millionth jump since she said, "I'll do it with you to keep my name out of the papers." Lee had been on his call for a long time without interjecting comments or questions; I started wishing that my phone would ring and make Madeleine jump away.

Lee put down the receiver. I said, "Anything interesting?"

"Another loony. Who's your date tonight?"

"A neighbor girl."

"Nice girl?"

"A honey. Partner, if I find you hopped-up after Tuesday, it's the Bleichert-Blanchard rematch."

Lee gave me an outer space grin. "It's Blanchard-Bleichert, and you'd lose again. I'm getting coffee. You want some?"

"Black, no sugar."

"Coming up."

* * *

I logged in a total of forty-six phone tips, about half of them reasonably coherent. Lee took off in the early afternoon, and Ellis Loew stuck me with the job of typing up Russ Millard's new summary report. It stated that Red Manley had been released to his wife after conclusively passing lie detector and Pentothal tests, and that Betty Short's love letters had been thoroughly gone through. A number of her swains had been ID'd and cleared as suspects, as had most of the guys who appeared in her photographs. Efforts to identify the remaining men were continuing, and the Camp Cooke MPs had called in with the word that the soldier who beat up Betty in '43 was killed in the Normandy Invasion. As for Betty's many marriages and engagements, a forty-eight-state capital record check revealed that no marriage licenses had ever been issued to her.

The report went downhill from there. The license numbers that Lee had glommed from the window of Junior Nash's fuck pad had yielded zero; over three hundred Dahlia sightings a day were flooding LAPD and Sheriff's Department switchboards. There had been ninety-three phony confessions so far, with four seriously cracked loonies without alibis held at the

Hall of Justice Jail, awaiting sanity hearings and probable shipment to Camarillo. Field interrogations were still going full speed—190 full-time men now on the case. The only ray of hope was the result of my 1/17 FI questionings: Linda Martin/ Lorna Martilkova was spotted in a couple of Encino cocktail lounges, and a big push to grab her was being centered in that area. I finished up the typing job gut certain that Elizabeth Short's killer was never going to be found, and put money on it—a double sawbuck on "Unsolved-pay 2 to 1" in the squad-room pool.

· · ·

I rang the doorbell of the Sprague mansion at exactly 8:00. I was dressed in my best outfit—blue blazer, white shirt and gray flannels—and put money on myself as a fool for kowtowing to the surroundings—I'd be taking the clothes off as soon as Madeleine and I got to my place. The ten hours of phone work stuck with me despite the shower I'd taken at the station, I felt even more out of place than I should have and my left ear still ached from the barrage of Dahlia talk.

Madeleine opened the door, a knockout in a skirt and a tight cashmere sweater. She once-overed me, took my hand and said, "Look, I hate to pull this, but Daddy has heard about you. He insisted you stay for dinner. I told him we met at that art exhibit at Stanley Rose's Bookshop, so if you have to pump everybody for my alibi, try to be subtle about it. All right?"

I said, "Sure," let Madeleine link her arm through mine and lead me inside. The entrance foyer was as Spanish as the outside of the mansion was Tudor: tapestries and crossed wrought-iron swords on the whitewashed walls, thick Persian carpets over a polished wood floor. The foyer opened into a giant living room with a men's club atmosphere—green leather chairs arranged around low tables and settees; huge stone fireplace; small Oriental throw rugs, multicolored, placed together at different angles, so that just the right amount of oak floor bordered them. The walls were cherrywood, and featured framed sepias of the family and their ancestors.

I noticed a stuffed spaniel poised by the fireplace with a yellowed newspaper rolled into its mouth. Madeleine said, "That's Balto. The paper is the LA *Times* for August 1, 1926. That's the day Daddy learned he'd made his first million. Balto was our pet then. Daddy's accountant called up and said, 'Emmett, you're a millionaire!' Daddy was cleaning his pistols, and Balto came in with the paper. Daddy wanted to consecrate the moment, so he shot him. If you look closely, you can see the bullet hole in his chest. Hold your breath, lovey. Here's the family."

Slack-jawed, I let Madeleine point me into a small sitting room. The walls were covered with framed photographs; the floor space was taken up by the three other Spragues in matching easy chairs. They all looked up; nobody stood up. Smiling without exposing my teeth, I said, "Hello." Madeleine made the introductions while I gawked down at the still-life ensemble.

"Bucky Bleichert, may I present my family. My mother, Ramona Cathcart Sprague. My father, Emmett Sprague. My sister, Martha McConville Sprague."

The ensemble came to life with little nods and smiles. Then Emmett Sprague beamed, got to his feet and stuck out his hand. I said, "A pleasure, Mr. Sprague," and shook it, eyeing him while he eyed me. The patriarch was short and barrel-chested, with a cracked, sun-weathered face and a full head of white hair that had probably once been sandy colored. I placed his age as somewhere in his fifties, his handshake as the grip of someone who'd done a good deal of physical labor. His voice was cut-glass Scottish, not the broad burr of Madeleine's imitation: "I saw you fight Mondo Sanchez. You boxed the pants off him. Another Billy Conn you were."

I thought of Sanchez, a built-up middleweight stiff I'd fought because my manager wanted me to get a rep for creaming Mexicans. "Thanks, Mr. Sprague."

"Thank you for giving such a dandy performance. Mondo was a good boy, too. What happened to him?"

"He died from a heroin overdose."

"God bless him. Too bad he didn't die in the ring, it would have spared his family a lot of grief. Speaking of families, please shake hands with the rest of mine."

Martha Sprague stood up on command. She was short, plump and blonde, with a tenacious resemblance to her father, blue eyes so light that it looked like she sent them out to be bleached and a neck that was acned and raw from scratching. She looked like a teenaged girl who'd never outgrow her baby fat and mature into beauty. I shook her firm hand feeling sorry for her; she caught what I was thinking immediately. Her pale eyes fired up as she yanked her paw away.

Ramona Sprague was the only one of the three who looked like Madeleine; if not for her I would have thought the brass girl was adopted. She possessed a pushing-fifty version of Madeleine's lustrous dark hair and pale skin, but there was nothing else attractive about her. She was fat, her face was flaccid, her rouge and lipstick were applied slightly off center, so that her face was weirdly askew. Taking her hand, she said, "Madeleine has said so many nice things about you," with a trace of a slur. There was no liquor on her breath; I wondered if she was jacked on drugstore stuff.

Madeleine sighed, "Daddy, can we eat? Bucky and I want to catch a nine-thirty show."

Emmett Sprague slapped me on the back. "I always obey my eldest. Bucky, will you entertain us with boxing and police anecdotes?"

"Between mouthfuls," I said.

Sprague slapped my back again, harder. "I can tell you didn't catch too many in the cabeza. Like Fred Allen you are. Come on, family. Dinner is served."

We filed into a large, wood-paneled dining room. The table in the middle of it was small, with five place settings already laid down. A serving cart was stationed by the door, leaking the unmistakable aroma of corned beef and cabbage. Old Man Sprague said, "Hearty fare breeds hearty people, haute cuisine breeds degenerates. Dig in, lad. The maid goes to her voodoo revival meetings on Sunday nights, so there's no one here but us white folks."

I grabbed a plate and piled it with food. Martha Sprague poured the wine and Madeleine dished herself out a small portion of each item and sat down at the table, motioning for me to sit beside her. I did, and Martha announced to the room: "I want to sit opposite Mr. Bleichert so I can draw him."

Emmett caught my eye and winked. "Bucky, you are in for a cruel caricaturing. Martha's pencil never flinches. Nineteen years old she is, and a high-paid commercial artist already. Maddy's my pretty one, but Martha's my certified genius."

Martha winced. She placed her plate directly across from me and sat down, arraying a pencil and a small sketch pad beside her napkin. Ramona Sprague took the adjoining seat and patted her arm; Emmett, standing by his chair at the head of the table, proposed a toast: "To new friends, prosperity and the great sport of boxing."

I said, "Amen," forked a slice of corned beef into my mouth and chewed it. It was fatty and dry, but I put on a yum-yum face and said, "This is delicious."

Ramona Sprague gave me a blank look; Emmett said, "Lacey, our maid, believes in voodoo. Some sort of Christian variation on it. She probably put a spell on the cow, made a pact with her nigger Jesus so the beast would be nice and juicy.

Speaking of our colored brethren, how did it feel to shoot those two jigaboos, Bucky?"

Madeleine whispered, "Humor him."

Emmett caught the aside and chuckled. "Yes, lad, humor me. In fact, you should humor all rich men pushing sixty. They might go senile and confuse you with their heirs."

I laughed, exposing my choppers; Martha reached for her pencil to capture them. "I didn't feel much of anything. It was them or us."

"And your partner? That blond lad you fought last year?"

"Lee took it a bit harder than I did."

Emmett said, "Blonds are overly sensitive. Being one, I know. Thank God I've two brownies in the family to keep us pragmatic. Maddy and Ramona have that bulldog tenacity that Martha and I lack."

Only the food I was chewing kept me from braying outright. I thought of the spoiled sewer crawler I was going to screw later that night and her mother smiling numbly across the table from me. The impulse to laugh came on stronger and stronger; I finally got my mouthful swallowed, belched instead of howled and raised my glass. "To you, Mr. Sprague. For making me laugh for the first time in a week."

Ramona gave me a disgusted look; Martha concentrated on her artwork. Madeleine played footsie with me under the table and Emmett toasted me back. "Rough week you had, lad?"

I laughed. "In spades. I've been detached to Homicide to work on the Black Dahlia thing. My days off have been cancelled, my partner's obsessed with it, and the crazies have been coming out of the woodwork. There's two hundred cops working a single case. It's absurd."

Emmett said, "It's tragic, is what it is. What's your theory, lad? Who on God's earth could have done a thing like that to another human being?"

I knew then that the family didn't know about Madeleine's tenuous connection to Betty Short, and decided not to press for her alibi. "I think it's a random job. The Short girl was what you might call easy. She was a compulsive liar with a hundred boyfriends. If we get the killer, it'll be a fluke."

Emmett said, "God bless her, I hope you get him and I hope he gets a hot date with that little green room up at San Quentin."

Running her toes up my leg, Madeleine pouted, "Daddy, you're monopolizing the conversation and you're making Bucky sing for his supper."

"Shall I sing for mine, lassie? Even though I'm the bread-winner?"

Old Man Sprague was angry—I could see it in his rising color and the way he hacked at his corned beef. Curious about the man, I said, "When did you come to the United States?"

Emmett beamed. "I'll sing for anyone who wants to hear my immigrant success story. What kind of name is Bleichert? Dutch?"

"German," I said.

Emmett raised his glass. "A great people, the Germans. Hitler was a bit excessive, but mark my words that someday we'll regret not joining forces with him to fight the Reds. Where in Germany are your people from, lad?"

"Munich."

"Ah, München! I'm surprised they left. If I'd grown up in Edinburgh or some other civilized place I'd still be wearing kilts. But I came from godawful Aberdeen, so I came to America right after the first war. I killed a lot of your fine German countrymen during that war, lad. But they were trying to kill me, so I felt justified. Did you meet Balto out in the parlor?"

I nodded; Madeleine groaned, Ramona Sprague winced and speared a potato. Emmett said, "My old dreamer friend Georgie Tilden taxidermied him. Scads of odd talents dreamer Georgie had. We were in a Scots regiment together during the war, and I saved Georgie's life when a bunch of your fine German countrymen got obstreperous and charged us with bayonets. Georgie was enamored of the flickers; he loved a good nickelodeon show. We went back to Aberdeen after the armistice, saw what a dead dog town it was, and Georgie persuaded me to come to California with him—he wanted to work in the silent flicker business. He was never worth a damn unless I was there to lead him around by the snout, so I looked around Aberdeen, saw that it was a third-class destiny and said, 'Aye, Georgie, California it is. Maybe we'll strike rich. And if we don't, we'll fail where the sun always shines.'"

I thought of my old man, who came to America in 1908 with big dreams—but married the first German emigrant woman he met and settled for wage slavery with Pacific Gas and Electric. "What happened then?"

Emmett Sprague rapped the table with his fork. "Knock wood, it was the right time to arrive. Hollywood was a cow pasture, but the silents were moving into their heyday. Georgie got work as a lighting man, and I found work building damn good houses—damn good and cheap. I lived outdoors and put every damn good dime back into my business, then took out loans from every bank and shylock willing to lend money and bought damn good property—damn good and cheap. Georgie introduced me to Mack Sennett, and I helped him build sets out at his studio in Edendale, then touched him for a loan to buy more property. Old Mack knew a lad on the make when he saw one, being one himself. He gave me the loan on the proviso that I help him with that housing project he was putting up— Hollywoodland—underneath that godawful hundred-foot sign he erected on Mount Lee to ballyhoo it. Old Mack knew how to squeeze a dollar dry, he did. He had extras moonlighting as laborers and vice versa. I'd drive them over to Hollywoodland after ten or twelve hours on a Keystone Kops flicker, and we'd put in another six hours by torchlight. I even got an assistant director's credit on a couple of movies, old Mack was so grateful for the way I squeezed his slaves."

Madeleine and Ramona were picking at their food with sullen faces, like they'd been captive audiences to the story before; Martha was still drawing, staring intently at me, *her* captive. "What happened to your friend?" I asked.

"God bless him, but for every story of success there's a corresponding one of failure. Georgie didn't butter up the right people. He didn't have the drive to complement his God-given talent, and he just fell by the wayside. He was disfigured in a car crash back in '36, and now he's what you might call a never was. I give him odd jobs tending some of my rental property and he does some rubbish hauling for the city—"

I heard a sharp screechy sound, and looked across the table. Ramona had missed stabbing a potato, and her fork had slid off the plate. Emmett said, "Mother, are you feeling well? Is the food to your liking?"

Ramona stared in her lap and said, "Yes, Father"; it looked like Martha was bracing her elbow. Madeleine went back to playing footsie with me; Emmett said, "Mother, you and our certified genius have not been doing a very good job of entertaining our guest. Would you care to participate in the conversation?"

Madeleine dug her toes into my ankle—just as I was about to try to lighten things up with a joke. Ramona Sprague forked herself a small mouthful of food, chewed it daintily and said, "Did you know that Ramona Boulevard was named after me, Mr. Bleichert?"

The woman's out-of-kilter face congealed around the words; she spoke them with a strange dignity. "No, Mrs. Sprague, I didn't know that. I thought it was named after the Ramona Pageant."

"I was named after the pageant," she said. "When Emmett married me for my father's money he promised my family that he would use his influence with the City Zoning Board to have a street named after me, since all his money was tied up in real estate and he couldn't afford to buy me a wedding ring. Father assumed it would be a nice residential street, but all Emmett could manage was a dead-end block in a red light district in Lincoln Heights. Are you familiar with the neighborhood, Mr. Bleichert?" Now the doormat's voice held an edge of fury.

"I grew up there," I said.

"Then you know that Mexican prostitutes expose themselves out of windows to attract customers. Well, after Emmett succeeded in getting Rosalinda Street changed to Ramona Boulevard he took me for a little tour there. The prostitutes greeted him by name. Some even had anatomical nicknames for him. It made me very sad and very hurt, but I bided my time and got even. When the girls were small I directed my own little pageants, right outside on our front lawn. I used the neighbor's children as extras and reenacted episodes out of Mr. Sprague's past that he would rather forget. That he would—"

The head of the table was slammed; glasses toppled and plates rattled. I stared at my lap to give the family infighters back some of their dignity and saw that Madeleine was gripping her father's knee so hard that her fingers were blue-white. She grabbed my knee with her free hand—with ten times the strength I thought she'd be capable of. An awful silence stretched, then Ramona Cathcart Sprague said, "Father, I'll sing for my supper when Mayor Bowron or Councilman Tucker comes to dinner, but not for Madeleine's male whores. A common policeman. My God, Emmett, how little you think of me."

I heard chairs scraping the floor, knees bumping the table, then footsteps moving out of the dining room; I saw that my hand was gripping Madeleine's the same way I curled it into an eight-ounce glove. The brass girl was whispering, "I'm sorry, Bucky. I'm sorry." Then a cheery voice said, "Mr. Bleichert?" and I looked up because it sounded so happy and sane.

It was Martha McConville Sprague, holding out a piece of paper. I took it with my free hand; Martha smiled and walked away. Madeleine was still muttering apologies when I looked at the picture. It was the two of us, both naked. Madeleine had her legs spread. I was between them, gnawing at her with giant Bucky Bleichert teeth.

• • •

We took the Packard down to hot sheet row on South La Brea. I drove, and Madeleine had the smarts not to talk until we passed a cinderblock auto court called the Red Arrow Inn. Then she said, "Here. It's clean."

I parked beside a line of pre-war jalopies; Madeleine went to the office and returned with the key to room eleven. She opened the door; I flicked on the wall light.

The flop was done up in dreary shades of brown and reeked of its previous inhabitants. I heard a dope sale being transacted in number twelve; Madeleine started to look like the caricature in her sister's drawing. I reached for the light switch to blot it all out. She said, "No. Please, I want to see you."

The narco sale burst into an argument. I saw a radio on the dresser and turned it on; an ad for Gorton's Slenderline Shop ate up the angry words. Madeleine pulled off her sweater and removed her nylons standing up; she was down to her undergarments before I began fumbling at my clothes. I snagged the zipper stepping out of my trousers; I ripped a shirt seam unhitching my shoulder holster. Then Madeleine was naked on the bed—and the kid sister's picture was obliterated.

I was nude inside of a second and joined with the brass girl inside of two. She muttered something like, "Don't hate my family, they're not bad," and I silenced her with a hard kiss. She returned it; our lips and tongues played until we had to break for breath. I ran my hands down to her breasts, cupping and kneading; Madeleine gasped little words about making up for the other Spragues. The more I kissed and felt and tasted her and the more she loved it, the more she murmured about *them*—so I grabbed her hair and hissed, "Not them, *me*. Do *me*, be with *me*."

Madeleine obeyed, going between my legs like a reverse of Martha's drawing. Captured that way, I felt myself getting ready to burst. I pushed Madeleine away so as not to explode, whispering, "Me, not them," stroking her hair, trying to concentrate on an inane radio jingle. Madeleine held me harder than any fight giveaway girl ever did; when I was cooled down and ready, I eased her onto her back and pushed myself inside her.

Now it was no common policeman and rich girl slut. It was us together, arching, shifting and moving, hard, but with all the time in the world. We moved together until the dance music and jingles ended and the radio dial tone came and went, the cinderblock rutting room silent except for us. Then we ended it—perfectly, together.

We held each other afterward, pockets of sweat binding us head to toe. I thought of going on duty in less than four hours and groaned; Madeleine broke our embrace and aped my trademark, flashing her perfect teeth. Laughing, I said, "Well, you kept your name out of the papers."

"Until we announce the Bleichert-Sprague nuptials?"

I laughed harder. "Your mother would love that."

"Mother's a hypocrite. She takes pills that the doctor gives her, so she's not a hophead. I fool around, so I'm a whore. She's sanctioned, I'm not."

"Yes, you are. You're my—" I couldn't quite say, "whore."

Madeleine tickled my ribs. "Say it. Don't be a cop from squaresville. *Say it.*"

I grabbed her hand before the tickling made me helpless. "You're my paramour, you're my inamorata, you're my sweetheart, you're the woman I suppressed evidence for—"

Madeleine bit my shoulder and said, "I'm your whore."

I laughed. "Okay, you're my violator of 234-A PC."

"What's that?"

"The California penal code designation for prostitution."

Madeleine waggled her eyebrows. *"Penal* code?'

I put up my hands. "You got me there."

The brass girl nuzzled me. "I like you, Bucky."

"I like you, too."

"You didn't start out liking me. Tell true—at first you just wanted to screw me."

"That's true."

"Then when did you start liking me?"

"The moment you took off your clothes."

"Bastard! You want to know when I started liking you?"

"Tell true."

"When I told Daddy I met this nice policeman Bucky Bleichert. Daddy's jaw dropped. He was impressed, and Emmett McConville Sprague is a very hard man to impress."

I thought of the man's cruelty to his wife and made a neutral comment: "He's an impressive man."

Madeleine said, "Diplomat. He's a hardcase, tightwad Scotchman son of a bitch, but he's a man. You know how he really made his money?"

"How?"

"Gangster kickbacks and worse. Daddy bought rotten lumber and abandoned movie facades from Mack Sennett and built houses out of them. He's got firetraps and dives all over

LA, registered to phony corporations. He's friends with Mickey Cohen. His people collect the rents."

I shrugged. "The Mick's thick with Bowron and half the Board of Supervisors. You see my gun and handcuffs?"

"Yes."

"Cohen paid for them. He put up the dough for a fund to help junior officers pay for their equipment. It's good public relations. The city tax assessor never checks his books, because the Mick pays for the gas and oil on all his field agent's cars. So you're not exactly shocking me."

Madeleine said, "Do you want to hear a secret?"

"Sure."

"Half a block of Daddy's Long Beach houses collapsed during the '33 earthquake. Twelve people were killed. Daddy paid money to have his name expunged from the contractor's records."

I held Madeleine out at arm's length. "Why are you telling me these things?"

Caressing my hands, she said, "Because Daddy's impressed with you. Because you're the only boy I've ever brought home that he thought was worth spit. Because Daddy worships toughness and he thinks you're tough, and if we get serious he'd probably tell you himself. Those people weigh on him, and he takes it out on Mother because it was her money he built that block with. I don't want you to judge Daddy by tonight. First impressions last, and I like you and I don't want—"

I pulled Madeleine to me. "Be still, babe. You're with me now, not your family."

Madeleine held me tightly. I wanted to let her know things were copacetic, so I tilted her chin up. Tears were in her eyes; she said, "Bucky, I didn't tell you all of it about Betty Short."

I gripped her shoulders. "What?"

"Don't be mad at me. It's nothing, I just don't want to keep it a secret. I didn't like you at first, so I didn't—"

"Tell me *now*."

Madeleine looked at me, a stretch of sweat-stained bedsheet separating us. "Last summer I was bar hopping a lot. Straight bars in Hollywood. I heard about a girl who was supposed to look a lot like me. I got curious about her and left notes at a couple of places—'Your lookalike would like to meet you' and my private number at the house. Betty called me, and we got together. We talked, and that was it. I ran into her again with Linda Martin at La Verne's last November. It was just a coincidence."

"And that's all of it?"

"Yes."

"Then babe, you'd better prepare yourself. There's fifty-odd cops canvassing bars, and if even one of them gets hold of your little lookalike number, you're headed for a trip across page one. There's not a goddamned thing I could do about it, and if it happens, don't ask me—because I've done all I'm going to."

Drawing away from me, Madeleine said, "I'll take care of it."

"You mean your Daddy will?"

"Bucky lad, are ye telling me you're jealous of a man twice your age and half your size?"

I thought of the Black Dahlia then, her death eclipsing my shoot-out headlines. "Why did you want to meet Betty Short?"

Madeleine shivered; the red neon arrow that gave the flop its name blinked through the window and across her face. "I've worked hard at being loose and free," she said. "But the way people described Betty it sounded like she was a natural. A real wild girl from the gate."

I kissed my wild girl. We made love again, and I pictured her coupled with Betty Short the whole time—both of them naturals.

CHAPTER TWELVE

Russ Millard took in my rumpled clothes and said, "A ten-ton truck or a woman?"

I looked around at University squadroom starting to fill up with daywatch dicks. "Betty Short. No phone work today, okay, boss?"

"In the mood for some fresh air?"

"Keep talking."

"Linda Martin was spotted last night out in Encino, trying to get served at a couple of bars. You and Blanchard go out to the Valley and look for her. Start at the twenty-thousand block of Victory Boulevard and work west. I'll be sending some other men as soon as they report in."

"When?"

Millard checked his watch. "Immediately, if not sooner."

I eyeballed for Lee and didn't see him, nodded assent and reached for the phone on my desk. I called the house, the City Hall Warrants office and Information for the number of the El Nido Hotel. I got a no answer for the first call and two no Blanchards for the others. Then Millard came back, with Fritz Vogel and—amazingly—Johnny Vogel in plainclothes.

I stood up. "I can't find Lee, Skipper."

Millard said, "Go with Fritzie and John. Take an unmarked

radio car so you can keep in touch with the other men out there."

The fat Vogel boys stared at me, then at each other. The look they exchanged said my unkempt state was a Class B Felony. "Thanks, Russ," I said.

• • •

We drove to the Valley, the Vogels in the front seat, me in the back. I tried to doze, but Fritzie's monologue on hooers and woman killers made it impossible. Johnny nodded along; every time his father paused for breath, he said, "Right, Dad." Going over the Cahuenga Pass, Fritzie ran out of verbal steam; Johnny's yes-man act fell silent. I closed my eyes and leaned against the window. Madeleine was doing a slow striptease in concert with motor hum when I heard the Vogels whispering.

". . . he's alseep, Daddy."

"Don't call me 'Daddy' on the job, I've told you a million goddamn times. It makes you sound like a nancy boy."

"I proved I'm not no nancy boy. Homos couldn't do what I did. I'm not cherry no more, so don't say nancy boy."

"Be still, damn you."

"Daddy, I mean Dad—"

"I said be still, Johnny."

The fat braggart cop reduced to a child grabbed my interest; I faked a snore-wheeze so the two would keep it up. Johnny whispered, "See, Dad, he's asleep. And he's the nance, not me. I proved it. Buck-tooth bastard. I could take him, Dad. You know I could. Job-stealing bastard, I had Warrants in the bag until—"

"John Charles Vogel, you hush this instant or I'll take a strap to you, twenty-four-year-old policeman or not."

The radio started barking then; I faked a big yawn. Johnny turned around and smiled. He said, "Catch up on your beauty sleep?" wafting his legendary halitosis.

My first instinct was to call him on his crack about taking me—then my sense of squadroom politics took over. "Yeah, I had a late night."

Johnny winked ineffectually. "I'm a quiff hound myself. I go a week without it, I'm climbing the walls."

The dispatcher droned, ". . . repeat, 10-A-94, roger your location."

Fritzie grabbed the mike. "10-A-94, rogering at Victory and Saticoy."

The dispatcher replied, "See the barman at the Caledonia

Lounge, Victory and Valley View. Warrantee Linda Martin reported there now. Code three."

Fritzie hit the siren and punched the gas. Cars pulled to the curb; we shot forward in the middle lane. I sent one up to the Calvinist God I believed in as a kid: don't let the Martin girl mention Madeleine Sprague. Valley View Avenue appeared in the windshield; Fritzie hung a hard right turn, killing the siren in front of a mock-bamboo hut.

The bar's mock-bamboo door burst open; Linda Martin/ Lorna Martilkova, looking as fresh-scrubbed as her picture, burst out. I tumbled from the car and hit the sidewalk running, Vogel and Vogel huffing and puffing behind me. Linda/Lorna ran like an antelope, clutching an oversized purse to her chest; I closed the distance between us by sprinting flat-out. The girl reached a busy side street and darted into traffic; cars swerved to avoid hitting her. She looked over her shoulder then; I dodged a beer truck and motorcycle on a collision course, sucked wind and *hauled*. The girl stumbled over the opposite curb, her purse went flying, I made a final leap and grabbed her.

She came up off the pavement spitting and beating at my chest; I grabbed her tiny fists, twisted them behind her back and cuffed her wrists. Lorna tried kicking then, well-aimed little shots at my legs. One kick connected with my shinbone; the girl, off balance from the cuffs, hit the ground ass-first. I helped her up, catching a wad of spittle on my shirtfront. Lorna yelped, "I'm an emancipated minor and if you touch me without a matron present I can sue you!" Catching my breath, I push-pulled her over to where her purse was lying.

I picked it up, surprised by the bulk and weight. Looking inside, I saw a small metal film can. I said, "What's the movie about?" The girl stammered, "P-P-Please, mister, my p-p-parents."

A horn tooted; I saw Johnny Vogel leaning out the window of the cruiser. "Millard said to bring the girl to Georgia Street juvie."

I hauled Lorna over and shoved her into the backseat. Fritzie hit the siren, and we leadfooted.

* * *

The run to downtown LA took thirty-five minutes.

Millard and Sears were waiting for us on the steps of Georgia Street Juvenile Hall. I led the girl in while Vogel and Vogel strode ahead. Court matrons and juvie dicks cleared a path for us inside; Millard opened a door marked DETENTION INTER-

VIEWS. I removed Lorna's cuffs, Sears walked into the room, pulled out seats and arranged ashtrays and notepads. Millard said, "Johnny, you go back to University and work the phones."

Fat Boy started to protest, then looked at his father. Fritzie nodded yes; Johnny exited, looking wounded. Fritzie announced, "I'm gonna call Mr. Loew. He should be in on this."

Millard said, "No. Not until we have a statement."

"Give her to me, I'll get you a statement."

"A voluntary statement, Sergeant."

Fritzie flushed. "I consider that a goddamn insult, Millard."

"You consider it what you damn well like, but you do what I damn well say, Mr. Loew or no Mr. Loew."

Fritz Vogel stood perfectly still. He looked like a human A-bomb about to explode, his voice the fuse: "You whored with the Dahlia, didn't you, girlie? You peddled your little twat with her. Tell me where you were during her lost days."

Lorna said, "Screw you, Charlie."

Fritzie stepped toward her; Millard moved between them. "I'll ask the questions, Sergeant."

You could have heard a pin drop. Vogel stood toe to toe with Millard. Seconds stretched, and then Fritzie squeaked, "You're a goddamned bleeding heart Bolshevik."

Millard took one step forward; Vogel took one step back. "Get out, Fritzie."

Vogel took three steps backward. His heels hit the wall, and he pivoted out the door, slamming it. The echo reverberated; Harry disarmed the remnants of the bomb: "How does it feel to be the object of such a fuss, Miss Martilkova?"

The girl said, "I'm Linda Martin," and tugged at the pleats of her skirt.

I took a seat, caught Millard's eye and pointed to the purse resting on the table, the film can poking out. The lieutenant nodded and sat down next to Lorna. "You know this is about Betty Short, don't you, sweetheart?"

The girl lowered her head and began sniffling; Harry handed her a Kleenex. She tore it into strips and smoothed them out on the table. "Does this mean I'll have to go back to my folks?"

Millard nodded. "Yes."

"My dad hits me. He's a dumb Slovak, and he gets drunk and hits me."

"Sweetheart, when you get back to Iowa you'll be on non-court probation. You tell your probation officer your father hits you and he'll put a stop to it damn quick."

"If my dad finds out what I did in LA, he'll hit me bad."

"He won't find out, Linda. I told those other two officers to leave to make sure what you say stays confidential."

"If you send me back to Cedar Rapids, I'll just run away again."

"I'm sure you will. Now the sooner you tell us what we want to know about Betty and the sooner we believe you, the sooner you'll be on the train and able to escape. So that gives you a good reason to be truthful with us, doesn't it, Linda?"

The girl went back to playing with her Kleenex. I sensed a jaded little brain considering all the angles, all the possible outs. Finally she sighed, "Call me Lorna. If I'm going back to Iowa I should get used to it."

Millard smiled; Harry Sears lit a cigarette and poised his pen over his steno pad. My blood pressure zoomed to the tune of "No Madeleine, no Madeleine, no Madeleine."

Russ said, "Lorna, are you ready to talk to us?"

The former Linda Martin said, "Shoot."

Millard asked, "When and where did you meet Betty Short?"

Lorna mussed up her Kleenex strips. "Last fall, at this career girl's place on Cherokee."

"1842 North Cherokee?"

"Uh-huh."

"And you became friends?"

"Uh-huh."

"Say yes or no please, Lorna."

"Yes, we became friends."

"What did you do together?"

Lorna bit at her cuticles. "We talked girl talk, we made casting rounds, we bummed drinks and dinner at bars—"

I interrupted: "What kind of bars?"

"What do you mean?"

"I mean nice places? Dives? Servicemen's hangouts?"

"Oh. Just places in Hollywood. Places where we figured they wouldn't ask me for ID."

My blood pressure decelerated. Millard said, "You told Betty about the rooming house on Orange Drive, the place where you were staying, right?"

"Uh-huh. I mean yes."

"Why did Betty move out of the place on Cherokee?"

"It was too crowded, and she'd tapped all the girls for a dollar here, a dollar there, and they were mad at her."

"Were any of them particularly mad?"

"I don't know."

"Are you sure Betty didn't move out because of boyfriend trouble?"

"I'm sure."

"Do you recall the names of any of the men Betty went out with last fall?"

Lorna shrugged. "They were just pickups."

"What about names, Lorna?"

The girl counted on her fingers, stopping when she got to three. "Well, there were these two guys at Orange Drive, Don Leyes and Hal Costa, and a sailor named Chuck."

"No last name on Chuck?"

"No, but I know he was a gunnery mate second class."

Millard started to ask another question, but I held up my hand to cut him off. "Lorna, I talked to Marjorie Graham the other day, and she said she told you the police were coming by Orange Drive to talk to the tenants about Betty. You ran then. Why?"

Lorna bit a hangnail off and sucked at the wound. "Because I knew that if my picture got in the papers as Betty's friend my parents would see it and make the police send me home."

"Where did you go when you rabbited?"

"I met a man in a bar and got him to rent me a room at an auto court in the Valley."

"Did you—"

Millard silenced me with a chopped hand gesture. "You said you and Betty made casting rounds together. Did you ever get any movie work?"

Lorna twisted her fingers together in her lap. "No."

"Then could you tell me what's in that film can in your purse?"

Eyes on to the floor and dripping tears, Lorna Martilkova whispered, "It's a movie."

"A dirty movie?"

Lorna nodded mutely. The girl's tears were rivers of mascara now; Millard handed her a handkerchief. "Sweetheart, you have to tell us all of it, from the beginning. So think it all out, and take your time. Bucky, get her some water."

I left the room, found a drinking fountain and cup dispenser in the hall, filled a large paper container and returned with it. Lorna was speaking softly when I placed the cup on the table in front of her.

". . . and I was cadging at this bar in Gardena. This Mexican man—Raoul or Jorge or something—started talking to me. I thought I was pregnant, and I was desperate wicked bad for money. He said he'd give me two hundred dollars to act in a nudie film."

Lorna stopped, slugged down the water, took a deep breath

and kept going. "The man said he needed another girl, so I called Betty at the Cherokee place. She said yes, and the Mexican man and me picked her up. He got us hopped on reefers, I think 'cause he was afraid we'd get scared and back out. We drove down to Tijuana, and we made the movie at this big house outside town. The Mex man worked the lights and ran the camera and told us what to do and drove us back to LA, and that's *all of it, from the beginning,* so will you call my folks now?"

I looked at Russ, then Harry; they were staring at the girl impassively. Wanting to fill in the blank spaces of my own private lead, I asked, "When did you make the film, Lorna?"

"Around Thanksgiving."

"Can you give us a description of the Mexican man?"

Lorna stared at the floor. "Just a greasy Mex. Maybe thirty, maybe forty, I don't know. I was on hop, and I don't remember too good."

"Did he seem particulary interested in Betty?"

"No."

"Did he touch either of you? Get rough with you? Make passes?"

"No. He just moved us around."

"Together?"

Lorna whimpered, "Yes"; my blood buzzed. My voice sounded weird to my own ears, like I was some ventriloquist's puppet. "Then this wasn't just nudie stuff? This was you and Betty playing lez?"

Lorna gave a little dry sob and nodded; I thought of Madeleine and pushed ahead, oblivious to where the girl might take it: "You lez? Was Betty lez? You do any *lez* pub crawling?"

Millard barked, "Bleichert, can it!" Lorna leaned forward in her chair, grabbed the soft daddy cop and hugged him fiercely. Russ looked at me and brought a flat palm slowly down, like a conductor asking the orchestra for a hush. He stroked the girl's head with his free hand, then cocked a finger at Sears.

The girl moaned, "I'm not lez, I'm not lez, it was just that one time"; Millard cradled her like a baby.

Sears asked, "Was Betty a lesbian, Lorna?"

I held my breath. Lorna wiped her eyes on Millard's coat front and looked at me. She said, "I'm not lezzie, and Betty wasn't, and we only bummed at normal-type bars, and it was just that one time in the movie because we were broke and on hop, and if this gets in the papers my daddy'll kill me."

I glanced at Millard, sensed that he bought it, and got a strong instinct that the whole dyke offshoot of the case was a fluke. Harry asked, "Did the Mexican man give Betty a viewfinder?"

Lorna muttered "Yes," her head on Millard's shoulder.

"Do you remember his car? The make, the color?"

"I . . . I think it was black and old."

"Do you remember the bar where you met him?"

Lorna lifted her head; I saw that her tears had dried. "I think it was on Aviation Boulevard, near all those aircraft plants."

I groaned; that part of Gardena was a solid mile of juke joints, poker parlors and cop-sanctioned whorehouses. Harry said, "When did you see Betty last?"

Lorna moved back to her own chair, clenching herself against another display of emotion—a hardcase reaction for a fifteen-year-old kid. "The last time I saw Betty was a couple of weeks later. Right before she moved out of the Orange Drive place."

"Do you know if Betty ever saw the Mexican man again?"

Lorna picked at the chipped polish on her nails. "The Mex was a fly-by-nighter. He paid us, drove us back to LA and left."

I butted in: "But you saw him again, right? There's no way he could have made a copy of the movie before you all drove back from TJ."

Lorna studied her nails. "I went looking for him in Gardena, when I read in the papers about Betty. He was about to go back to Mexico, and I conned him out of a print of the movie. See . . . he didn't read the papers, so he didn't know that all of a sudden Betty was famous. See . . . I figured that a Black Dahlia stag film was a collector's item, and if the police tried to ship me back to my folks I could sell it and hire a lawyer to fight my extradition. You'll give it back to me, won't you? You won't let people look at it?"

Out of the mouths of babes. Millard said, "You went back to Gardena and found the man again?"

"Uh-huh. I mean yes."

"Where?"

"At one of those bars on Aviation."

"Can you describe the place?"

"It was dark, with flashing lights out front."

"And he willingly gave you a copy of the film? For nothing?"

Lorna eyed the floor. "I did him and his friends."

"Can you improve on your description of him, then?"

"He was fat and he had a tiny little pecker! He was ugly and so were his friends!"

Millard pointed Sears to the door; Harry tiptoed quietly out. Russ said, "We'll try to keep this out of the papers, and we'll destroy the film. One question before the matron takes you up to your room. If we take you down to Tijuana, do you think you could find the house where the movie was shot?"

Shaking her head, Lorna said, "No. I don't want to go down to that awful place. I want to go home."

"So your father can hit you?"

"No. So I can get out again."

Sears returned with a matron; the woman led hard/soft/pathetic/feisty Linda/Lorna away. Harry, Russ and I looked at one another; I felt the girl's sadness smothering me. Finally the senior man said, "Comments?"

Harry kicked in first. "She's hedging on the Mex and the pad in TJ. He probably beat her up and screwed her, and she's afraid of reprisals. Aside from that, I buy her story."

Russ smiled. "What about you, bright penny?"

"She's covering on the Mex angle. I think she might have been screwing him regularly, and now she's protecting him from a smut rap. I'd also lay odds the guy is white, that the Mex routine is a cover-up to go along with the TJ stuff—which I do buy—because that place is a cesspool, and most of the smuthounds I rousted working Patrol got their stuff there."

Millard winked à la Lee Blanchard. "Bucky, you are a very bright penny today. Harry, I want you to talk to Lieutenant Waters here. Tell him to hold the girl incommunicado for seventy-two hours. I want a private cell for her, and I want Meg Caulfield detached from Wilshire Clerical to play cellmate. Tell Meg to give her a good pumping and report in every twenty-four hours.

"When you finish that, call R&I and Ad Vice for the rap sheets on white and Mexican males with pornography convictions, then call Vogel and Koenig and send them down to Gardena to check the bars for Lorna's movie man. Call the Bureau too, and tell Captain Jack we've got a little Dahlia film to look at. Then call the *Times* and give them the smut lead before Ellis Loew sits on it. Give them a Jane Doe for Lorna, have them add an appeal for pornography tips and pack a bag, because we're going down to Dago and TJ later tonight."

I said, "Russ, you know this is a long shot."

"The biggest one since you and Blanchard beat the crap out of each other and became partners. Come on, bright penny. It's blue movie night at City Hall."

• • •

A projector and screen had already been set up in the muster room; an all-star cast was awaiting the all-star smut movie.

Lee, Ellis Loew, Jack Tierney, Thad Green and Chief of Police
C.B. Horrall himself were seated in front of the screen; Millard
handed the film can to the clerical stooge manning the
projector, muttering, "Where's the popcorn?"

The big chief walked over and gave me a gladhander's shake.
"A pleasure, sir," I said.

"A mutual pleasure, Mr. Ice, and my wife sends her belated
regards for the pay raise you and Mr. Fire got us." He pointed
to a seat next to Lee. "Lights! Camera! Action!"

I sat down beside my partner. Lee looked drawn, but not
dope-juiced. A *Daily News* was unfolded on his lap; I saw
"Boulevard-Citizens Mastermind to be Released Tomorrow—
LA Bound After 8 Years in Custody." Lee checked out my
raggedy state and said, "Getting any?"

I was about to respond when the lights went off. A blurred
image hit the screen; cigarette smoke wafted into it. A title
flashed—*Slave Girls From Hell*—then a big, high-ceilinged
room with Egyptian hieroglyphics on the walls came into view
in grainy black and white. Pillars shaped like coiled serpents
were stationed throughout the room; the camera zoomed in for
a close-up of two inset plaster snakes swallowing each other's
tails. Then the snakes dissolved into Betty Short, wearing only
stockings, doing an inept hoochie-koochie dance.

My groin clenched; I heard Lee draw a sharp breath. An arm
entered the screen, passing a cylindrical object to Betty. She
took it; the camera moved in. It was a dildo, scales covering the
shaft, fangs extending from the large circumcised head. Betty
put it in her mouth and sucked it, eyes wide open and glassy.

There was an abrupt cut, then Lorna, naked, was lying on a
divan, her legs spread. Betty entered the picture. She knelt
between Lorna's legs, stuck the dildo inside her and simulated
sex with it. Lorna buckled and rotated her hips, the screen
went out of focus, then blipped to a close-up—Lorna writhing
in phony ecstasy. Even a two-year-old could tell she was
contorting her face to hold back screams. Betty re-entered the
frame, poised between Lorna's thighs.

She looked up at the camera, mouthing, "No, please." Then
her head was shoved down, and she worked her tongue next to
the dildo in a shot so close in that every ugly detail seemed to
be magnified ten million times.

I wanted to shut my eyes, but couldn't. Next to me, Chief
Horrall said calmly, "Russ, what do you think? You think this
has got anything to do with the girl's murder?"

Millard answered with a hoarse voice. "It's a long shot, Chief.
The movie was made in November and from what the Martil-

kova girl said, the Mexican doesn't play as a killer. It's got to be checked out, though. Maybe the Mex showed the movie to somebody, and *he* got a case on Betty. What I—"

Lee kicked his chair over and shouted: "Who gives a fuck if he didn't kill her! I've sent Boy Scouts to the green room for less than that! So if you won't do something about it, I will!"

Everyone sat there, shock-stilled. Lee stood in front of the screen, blinking from the hot white light in his eyes. He wheeled and ripped the obscenity down; the screen and tripod hit the floor with a crash. Betty and Lorna continued their sex on a chalked-up blackboard; Lee took off running. I heard the projector knocked over in back of me; Millard yelled, "Bleichert, get him!"

I got up, tripped, got up again and tore out of the muster room, catching sight of Lee stepping into the elevator at the end of the hall. When the doors shut and the elevator descended, I ran for the stairs, hurtled down six flights and out into the parking lot just in time to see Lee peeling rubber northbound on Broadway. There was a string of unmarked cruisers lined up on the Department's side of the lot; I jogged over and checked under the driver's seat of the nearest one. The keys were right there. I hit the ignition, then the gas, and took off.

I gained ground quickly, coming up behind Lee's Ford as he swerved into the middle lane on Sunset, heading west. I gave him three short horn blasts; he responded by tapping his horn in the LAPD semaphore that meant "Officer in Pursuit." Cars pulled over to let him through—there was nothing I could do but hit my own horn and stay glued to his tail.

We hauled ass out of downtown, through Hollywood and over the Cahuenga Pass to the Valley. Turning onto Ventura Boulevard, I got spooked by the proximity of the lez bar block; when Lee ground his Ford to a halt smack in the middle of it, I choked on a wave of panic and thought: *He can't know about my brass girl, there's no way; the lezzie film must have flipped his switch.* Then Lee got out and pushed through the door of La Verne's Hideaway. Worse panic made me stomp the brakes and fishtail the cruiser into the sidewalk; thoughts of Madeleine and evidence suppression raps propelled me into the dive after my partner.

Lee was facing off booths full of daggers and femmes, shouting curses. I flailed with my eyes for Madeleine and the barmaid I'd rousted; not seeing them, I got ready to cold cock my best friend.

"You fucking quiff divers seen a little movie called *Slave Girls*

From Hell? You buy your stag shit from a fat Mex about forty? You—"

I grabbed Lee from behind in a full nelson and spun him around toward the door. His arms were clenched and his back was arched, but I was able to use his weight against him. We stumbled outside, then tripped together in a jumble of arms and legs and hit the pavement. I kept the hold clamped on with all my strength, then heard a siren approaching and snapped that Lee wasn't resisting—he was just lying there, muttering "Partner" over and over.

The siren wailed louder, then died; I heard car doors slamming. I extricated myself from Lee and helped him, rag doll limp, to his feet. And Ellis Loew was right there.

Loew had murder in his eyes. It hit me that Lee's explosion came from his weird chastity, a week of death and dope and its pornographic capper. Safe myself, I put an arm around my partner's shoulders. "Mr. Loew, it was just that goddamn movie. Lee thought the dykes here could give us a lead on the Mex."

Loew hissed, "Bleichert, shut up," then turned his velvet rage on Lee: "Blanchard, I got you Warrants. You're *my* man, and you made *me* look like a fool in front of the two most powerful men in the Department. This is no lesbian killing, those girls were on drugs and hated it. Now I covered for you with Horrall and Green, but I don't know how much good that will do you in the long run. If you weren't *Mr. Fire, Big Lee Blanchard*, you'd be suspended from duty already. You've gotten personally involved in the Short case, and that's an unprofessionalism I will not tolerate. You're back on Warrants duty as of tomorrow morning. Report to me at 0800, and bring in formal letters of apology to Chief Horrall and Chief Green. For the sake of your pension, I advise you to grovel."

Lee, his body limp, said, "I want to go to TJ to look for the smut man."

Loew shook his head. "Under the circumstances, I would call that request ridiculous. Vogel and Koenig are going to Tijuana, you're back on Warrants, and Bleichert, you're to remain on the Short case. Good day, Officers."

Loew stormed over to his black-and-white; the patrolman driver hung a U-turn out into traffic. Lee said, "I have to talk to Kay." I nodded, and a sheriff's patrol car cruised by, the passenger cop blowing kisses to the lezzies in the doorway. Lee walked to his car murmuring, "Laurie. Laurie, oh babe."

CHAPTER THIRTEEN

I showed up at the Bureau at 8:00 the next morning, wanting to ease Lee through the ignominy of his return to Warrants and share the diet of crow Ellis Loew would undoubtedly be feeding him. Identical memo slips from Chief Green were on both of our desks: "Report to my office tomorrow, 1/22/47, 6:00 P.M." The handwritten words looked ominous.

Lee did not report in at 8:00; I sat at my desk for the next hour, picturing him fretting over Bobby De Witt's release, a captive of his ghosts, his ghost chaser redemption gone now that he was off the Dahlia case. Across the partition in the DA's office, I heard Loew barking and pleading on the phone to the city editors of the *Mirror* and *Daily News*—Republican rags rumored to be sympathetic to his political aspirations. The gist of his talk was that he would help them cutthroat the *Times* and *Herald* with inside Dahlia info on the proviso that they soft-pedal their coverage of Betty Short's roundheeled ways and portray her as a sweet but misguided young girl. From the hotshot's self-satisfied farewells, I could tell that the newsmen went for it, buying Loew's line that "The more sympathy we attract for the girl, the more juice we get when I prosecute the killer."

When Lee didn't show up by 10:00, I went into the muster room and read through the bulging E. Short case file, wanting to satisfy myself that Madeleine's name wasn't in it. Two hours and two hundred form pages later I was satisfied—her name was not listed among the hundreds of people questioned, nor was she fingered by tipsters. The only mention of lesbians was obvious nut case stuff—religious crackpots calling in poison phone clues, informing on rival sect members as "Nun dykes sacrificing the girl to Pope Pius XII" and "Lezbos performing communistic anti-Christ rituals."

By noon, Lee still hadn't put in an appearance. I called the house, University squadroom and the El Nido Hotel, with no success. Wanting to look busy so that no one would put me to work, I prowled the bulletin boards reading summary reports.

Russ Millard had compiled a new update before leaving for San Diego and Tijuana last night. It stated that he and Harry Sears would be checking the R&I and Ad Vice files for convicted and suspected pornographers, and would be searching for the smut movie filming site down in TJ. Vogel and Koenig had been unable to locate Lorna Martilkova's "Mexican man" in Gardena, and were also going to Tijuana to work on the stag film angle. The coroner's inquest had been held yesterday; Elizabeth Short's mother was present, and identified her remains. Marjorie Graham and Sheryl Saddon testified about Betty's life in Hollywood, Red Manley as to how he drove Betty up from Dago and dropped her off in front of the Biltmore Hotel on January tenth. Intensive canvassing of the area around the Biltmore had thus far yielded no verified sightings, the records of convicted sex loonies and registered sex offenders were still being combed, the four drool case confessors were still being held at City Jail awaiting alibi checks, sanity hearings and further questioning. The circus was continuing, phone tips flooding in, resulting in third-, fourth- and fifth-hand questionings—officers talking to people who knew people who knew people who knew the exalted Dahlia. Needle in a haystack stuff straight down the line.

I was getting goldbrick looks from the men working at their desks, so I went back to my cubicle. Madeleine jumped into my head; I picked up the phone and called her.

She answered on the third ring: "Sprague residence."

"It's me. You want to get together?"

"When?"

"Now. I'll pick you up in forty-five minutes."

"Don't come here, Daddy's having a business soiree. Meet you at the Red Arrow?"

I sighed. "I've got an apartment, you know."

"I only rut in motels. One of my rich girl idiosyncrasies. Room eleven at the Arrow in forty-five?"

I said, "I'll be there," and hung up. Ellis Loew tapped the partition. "Go to work, Bleichert. You've been skating all morning, and it's getting on my nerves. And when you see your phantom partner, tell him his little no-show has cost him three days' pay. Now check out a radio car and roll."

•   •   •

I rolled straight to the Red Arrow Motel. Madeleine's Packard was parked in the alley behind the bungalows; the door to room eleven was unlocked. I walked in, smelled her perfume and squinted into the darkness until I was rewarded with a giggle. Undressing, my eyes got accustomed to the lack of light; I saw Madeleine—a nude beacon on a tattered bedspread.

We joined so strongly that the bedsprings banged the floor. Madeleine kissed her way down to between my legs, made me hard, then did a quick turn onto her back. I went in her thinking of Betty and the snake shaft thing, then blotted it out by concentrating on the ripped wallpaper in front of my eyes. I wanted to go slow, but Madeleine gasped, "Don't hold back, I'm ready." I pushed hard, slamming the two of us together, my hands braced on the bed rail. Madeleine locked her legs around my back, grabbed the rail over her head and pushed, pulled and gyrated against me. We came seconds apart, moving in a stretching, slamming counterpoint; when my head hit the pillow, I bit at it to stanch my tremors.

Madeleine slid out from under me. "Sugar, are you all right?"

I was seeing the snake thing. Madeleine tickled me; I twisted around and looked at her to make it go away. "Smile at me. Look soft and sweet."

Madeleine gave me a Pollyanna grin. Her smeared red lipstick reminded me of the Dahlia's death smile; I shut my eyes and grabbed her hard. She stroked my back softly, murmuring, "Bucky, what is it?"

I stared at the curtains on the far wall. "We picked up Linda Martin yesterday. She had a print of a stag movie in her purse, her and Betty Short playing lez. They filmed it down in TJ, and there was all this spooky stuff in it. It spooked me, and it spooked my partner bad."

Madeleine stopped her caresses. "Did Linda mention me?"

"No, and I checked through the case file. There's no mention of that note-leaving number you pulled. But we've got a policewoman planted in the girl's cell to pump her, and if she blabs, you're sunk."

"I'm not worried, sugar. Linda probably doesn't even remember me."

I slid over to where I could eyeball Madeleine up close. Her lipstick was a bloody disarray, and I daubed at it with the pillow. "Babe, I'm withholding evidence for you. It's a fair trade for what I'm getting, but it still spooks me. So you be damn sure you come clean. I'll ask you one time. Is there anything you haven't told me about you and Betty and Linda?"

Madeleine ran her fingers down my rib cage, exploring the welt scars I'd gotten in the Blanchard fight. "Sugar, Betty and I made love once, that one time we met last summer. I just did it to see what it would be like to be with a girl who looked so much like me."

I felt like I was sinking; like the bed was dropping out from under me. Madeleine looked like she was at the end of a long tunnel, captured by some kind of weird camera trick. She said, "Bucky, that's all of it, I swear that's all of it," her voice wobbling from deep nowhere. I got up and dressed, and it was only when I strapped on my .38 and cuffs that I felt like I'd quit treading quicksand.

Madeleine pleaded, "Stay, sugar, stay"; I went out the door before I could succumb. In my cruiser, I flipped on the two-way, looking for good sane cop noise to distract me. The dispatcher barked, "Code four all units at Crenshaw and Stocker. Clear robbery scene, two dead, suspect dead, unit 4-A-82 reports suspect is Raymond Douglas Nash, white male, object fugitive warrant number—"

I yanked the radio cord and hit the ignition, gas and siren in what felt like a single swipe. Pulling out, I heard Lee pacifying me with "Don't tell me you don't know the dead girl is a better piece of pie than Junior Nash"; speedballing downtown, I saw myself kowtowing to my partner's ghosts even though I knew the Okie killer was a real live killer bogeyman. Jamming into the Hall parking lot, I saw Lee cajoling, wheedling, pushing, pulling and twisting at me to get his way; running up to the Bureau, I saw red.

I came out of the stairway yelling, "Blanchard!" Dick Cavanaugh, walking out of the bullpen, pointed to the bathroom. I kicked in the door; Lee was washing his hands in the sink.

He held them up to show me, blood oozing from cuts on the knuckles. "I beat up a wall. Penance for Nash."

It wasn't enough. I let the crimson loose all the way, smashing my best friend until my own hands were ruined and he was senseless at my feet.

CHAPTER FOURTEEN

Losing the first Bleichert-Blanchard fight got me local celebrity, Warrants and close to nine grand in cash; winning the rematch got me a sprained left wrist, two dislocated knuckles and a day in bed, woozy from an allergic reaction to the codeine pills Captain Jack gave me when he got word of the punch-out and saw me in my cubicle trying to tape up my fist. The only thing good that came of my "victory" was a twenty-four-hour respite from Elizabeth Short; the worst was yet to come—bracing Lee and Kay to see if I could salvage the three of us, without giving up my balls.

I drove to the house Wednesday afternoon, Dahlia kiss-off day and the one-week anniversary of the celebrity stiff's first appearance. The confab with Thad Green was scheduled for 6:00 that evening, and if there was any way to work a patch job with Lee before then, it had to be tried.

The front door was standing open; the coffee table held a copy of the *Herald*, folded open to pages two and three. The detritus of my messy life was smeared all over it—the Dahlia, hatchet-faced Bobby De Witt homeward bound, Junior Nash shot by an off-duty sheriff's dick after he knocked off a Jap greengrocer, killing the proprietor and his fourteen-year-old son.

154

"We're famous, Dwight."

Kay was standing in the hallway. I laughed; my bad knuckles throbbed. "Notorious, maybe. Where's Lee?"

"I don't know. He left yesterday afternoon."

"You know he's in trouble, don't you?"

"I know you beat him up."

I walked over. Kay's breath reeked of cigarettes, her face was mottled from crying. I held her; she held me back and said, "I don't blame you for it."

I nuzzled her hair. "De Witt's probably in LA by now. If Lee isn't back by tonight, I'll come and stay with you."

Kay pulled away. "Don't come unless you want to sleep with me."

I said, "Kay, I can't."

"Why? Because of that neighbor girl you're seeing?"

I remembered my lie to Lee. "Yes . . . no, not that. It's just that . . ."

"It's just *what*, Dwight?"

I grabbed Kay so she wouldn't be able to look in my eyes and know that half of what I was saying made me a child, half made me a liar. "It's just that you and Lee are my family, and Lee's my partner, and until we get this trouble he's in settled and see if we're still partners then you and me together is just no damn good. The girl I've been seeing is nothing. She doesn't really mean a thing to me."

Kay said, "You're just frightened of anything that doesn't involve fighting and cops and guns and all that," and tightened her grip. I let myself be held, knowing she'd nailed me clean. Then I broke it off and drove downtown to "All That."

• • •

The clock in Thad Green's waiting room hit 6:00, and there was no Lee; at 6:01 Green's secretary opened his door and ushered me in. The Chief of Detectives looked up from his desk. "Where's Blanchard? He's the one I really wanted to see."

I said, "I don't know, sir," and stood at parade rest; Green pointed me to a chair. I sat down, and the COD fixed me with a hard stare. "You've got fifty words or less to explain your partner's behavior Monday night. Go."

I said, "Sir, Lee's little sister was murdered when he was a kid, and the Dahlia case is what you might call an obsession with him. Bobby De Witt, the man he sent up on the Boulevard-Citizens job, got out yesterday, and a week ago we killed those four hoods. The stag film was the capper. It set Lee off, and he pulled that stunt at the dyke bar because he thought he could get a lead on the guy who made the film."

Green quit nodding along. "You sound like a shyster trying to justify his client's actions. In my police department, a man checks his emotional baggage when he pins on his badge, or he checks out. But just to let you know that I'm not entirely unsympathetic, I'll tell you this. I'm suspending Blanchard for a trial board, but not for his Monday night tantrums. I'm suspending him for a memo he submitted stating that Junior Nash blew our jurisdiction. I think it was a phony. What do you think, Officer?"

I felt my legs fluttering. "I believed it, sir."

"Then you're not as intelligent as your Academy scores led me to believe. When you see Blanchard, tell him to turn in his gun and badge. You stay on the Short investigation, and kindly refrain from fisticuffs on city property. Good night, Officer."

I stood up, saluted and about-faced out of the office, maintaining my military gait until I was down the hall in the muster room. Grabbing a desk phone, I called the house, University squadroom and the El Nido Hotel—all with zero results. Then a dark thought crossed my mind, and I dialed the number of the County Parole office.

A man answered: "Los Angeles County Parole, may I help you?"

"This is Officer Bleichert, LAPD. I need the disposition on a recent parolee."

"Shoot, Officer."

"Robert 'Bobby' De Witt. Came out of Quentin yesterday."

"That's easy. He hasn't reported to his PO yet. We called the bus depot at Santa Rosa, and found out that De Witt didn't buy a ticket for LA, he bought one for San Diego, with a transfer to Tijuana. We haven't issued an absconder warrant yet. De Witt's PO figured he might have gone down to TJ to get laid. He's giving him until tomorrow morning to show up."

I hung up, relieved that De Witt didn't head straight for LA. Thinking of prowling for Lee, I took the elevator down to the parking lot and saw Russ Millard and Harry Sears walking toward the back stairs. Russ noticed me and hooked a finger; I trotted over.

I said, "What happened in TJ?"

Harry, breathing Sen-Sen, answered: "Goose egg on the stag movie. We checked for the pad and couldn't find it, rousted some smut peddlers. Double goose egg. We checked some of the Short girl's acquaintances in Dago—triple gooser. I—"

Millard put a hand on his partner's shoulder. "Bucky,

156

Blanchard's down in Tijuana. A border patrolman we talked to saw him, recognized him from all the fight publicity. He was hobnobbing with a bad-looking bunch of Rurales."

I thought of De Witt TJ bound and wondered why Lee would be talking to the Mex state police. "When?"

Sears said, "Last night. Loew and Vogel and Koenig are down there too, at the Divisidero Hotel. They've been talking to the TJ cops. Russ thinks they're measuring spics for a frame on the Dahlia."

Lee chased smut demons through my mind; I saw him bloody at my feet and shivered. Millard said, "Which is crap, because Meg Caulfield got the straight dope on the smut man out of the Martilkova girl. He's a white guy named Walter "Duke" Wellington. We checked his Ad Vice jacket, and he's got a half dozen pandering and pornography beefs. All well and good, except Captain Jack got a letter from Wellington, postmarked three days ago. He's hiding out, gun-shy from all the Dahlia publicity, and he copped to making the film with Betty Short and Lorna. He was afraid of getting tagged for the snuff, so he sent in a detailed alibi for Betty's missing days. Jack checked it out personally, and it's ironclad. Wellington sent a copy of the letter to the *Herald*, and they're publishing it tomorrow."

I said, "So Lorna was lying to protect him?"

Sears nodded. "That looks like the picture. Wellington's still on the lam from old pimping warrants, though, and Lorna clammed up when she got wise to Meg. And here's the kicker: we called Loew to tell him the Mex man was horseshit, but a Rurale buddy of ours says that Vogel and Koenig are still rousting spics."

The circus was turning into a farce. I said, "If the newspaper letter kiboshes their Mex job, they'll be looking for patsies up here. We should hold our info back from them. Lee's on suspension, but he made carbons from the case file, and he's got them stored in a hotel room in Hollywood. We should hold on to it, use it to store our stuff."

Millard and Sears nodded slowly; the real kicker kicked me. "County Parole said Bobby De Witt bought a ticket for TJ. If Lee's down there too, it could be trouble."

Millard shivered. "I don't like the feel of it. De Witt's a bad piece of work, and maybe he found out that Lee was headed down there. I'll call the Border Patrol and have them put out a detain order on him."

Suddenly I knew it all came down to me. "I'm going."

CHAPTER FIFTEEN

I crossed the border at dawn. Tijuana was just coming awake as I turned onto Revolución, its main drag. Child beggars were digging for breakfast in trash cans, taco venders were stirring pots of dog-meat stew, sailors and marines were being escorted out of whorehouses at the end of their five-spot all-nighters. The smarter ones stumbled over to Calle Colon and the penicillin pushers; the stupidos hotfooted toward East TJ, the Blue Fox and Chicago Club—no doubt eager to catch the early morning donkey show. Tourist cars were already lined up outside the cut-rate upholstery joints; Rurales driving prewar Chevys cruised like vultures, wearing black uniforms that looked almost like Nazi issue.

I cruised myself, looking for Lee and his '40 Ford. I thought about stopping at the Border Patrol hut or Rurale substation to seek help, then remembered my partner was suspended from duty, illegally armed and probably stretched so thin that words from the wrong greaser would provoke him to God knows what. Recalling the Divisidero Hotel from my high school excursions south, I drove to the edge of town to seek American aid.

The pink Art Deco monstrosity stood on a bluff overlooking a tin roof shantytown. I intimidated the desk clerk; he told me the "Loew party" was in suite 462. I found it on the ground floor rear, angry voices booming on the other side of the door.

Fritzie Vogel was yelling, "I still say we get ourselves a spic! The letter to the *Herald* didn't say stag movie, it just said Wellington saw the Dahlia and the other girlie in November! We can still—"

Ellis Loew shouted back: "We *can't* do that! Wellington admitted making the movie to Tierney! He's the supervising officer, and we can't go over his head!"

I opened the door and saw Loew, Vogel and Koenig huddled in chairs, all of them holding eight-star *Herald*'s obviously hot off the presses. The framing session fell silent; Koenig gawked; Loew and Vogel muttered, "Bleichert," simultaneously.

I said, "Fuck the fucking Dahlia. Lee's down here, Bobby De Witt's here and it's got to go bad. You—"

Loew said, "Fuck Blanchard, he's suspended"; I beelined for him. Koenig and Vogel formed a wedge between us; trying to move through them was like bucking a brick wall. The DA backed off to the other side of the room, Koenig grabbed my arms, Vogel put his hands on my chest and pushed me outside. Loew evil-eyed me from the doorway, then Fritzie chucked my chin. "I've got a soft spot for light heavyweights. If you promise not to hit Billy, I'll help you find your partner."

I nodded, and Koenig let me go. Fritzie said, "We'll take my car. You don't look fit to drive."

• • •

Fritzie drove; I eyeballed. He kept up a stream of chatter on the Short case and the lieutenancy it was going to get him; I watched beggars swarm turistas, hookers dispense front seat blow jobs and zoot suit youths prowl for drunks to roll. After four fruitless hours the streets became too car-choked to manuever in, and we got out and walked.

On foot, the squalor was worse. The kiddie beggars got right up in your face, jabbering, shoving crucifixes at you. Fritzie swatted and kicked them away, but their hunger-ridden faces got to me, so I changed a fiver into pesos and tossed handfuls of coins into the gutter whenever they converged. It spawned scratching, biting and gouging free-for-alls, but it was better than looking into sunken eyes and seeing nada.

An hour of prowling two abreast got us no Lee, no Lee's '40 Ford and no gringos resembling Bobby De Witt. Then a Rurale in black shirt and jackboots, lounging in a doorway, caught my eye. He said, "Policia?" and I stopped and flashed my badge in answer.

The cop dug in his pockets and pulled out a teletype photo strip. The picture was too blurred to identify, but the "Robert Richard De Witt" was plain as day. Fritzie patted the cop's epaulets. "Where, Admiral?"

The Mex clicked his heels and barked, "Estación, vamanos!" He marched ahead of us, turning into an alley lined with VD clinics, pointing to a cinderblock hut fenced in with barbed wire. Fritzie handed him a dollar; the Mex saluted like Mussolini and about-faced away. I strode for the station, forcing myself not to run.

Rurales holding tommy guns flanked the doorway. I showed my badge; they heel clicked and let me in. Fritzie caught up with me inside; dollar bill in hand, he went straight for the front desk. The desk cop grabbed the buck and Fritzie said, "Fugitivo? Americano? De Witt?"

The deskman smiled and hit a switch beside his chair, barred doors in the side wall clicked open. Fritzie said, "Precisely what is it we want this scum to tell us?"

I said, "Lee's down here, probably chasing smut leads on his own. De Witt came here directly from Quentin."

"Without checking in with his PO?"

"Right."

"And De Witt has a hard-on for Blanchard from the Boulevard-Citizens job?"

"Right."

"Enough said."

We walked down a corridor lined with cells. De Witt was alone in the last lock-up, sitting on the floor. The door buzzed open; Kay Lake's defiler stood up. The years in stir had not been kind to him: the hatchet-faced tough of the '39 newspaper pictures was now a well-used piece of work, bloated in the body, grizzled in the face, his pachuco haircut as outdated as his Salvation Army suit.

Fritzie and I walked in. De Witt's greeting was con bravado tinged with just the right amount of subservience. "Cops, huh? Well, at least you're Americans. Never thought I'd be glad to see you guys."

Fritzie said, "Why start now?" and kicked De Witt in the balls. He doubled over; Fritzie grabbed his duck's ass scruff and gave him a hard backhand. De Witt started to foam at the mouth; Fritzie let go of his neck and wiped pomade on his sleeve. De Witt hit the floor, then crawled over to the commode and vomited into it. When he tried to get himself upright, Fritzie pushed his head back into the bowl and held it there with a big spit-shined wing-tip brogue. The ex-bank-robber-pimp drank piss water and puke.

Vogel said, "Lee Blanchard's here in TJ, and you came here flush out of Big Q. That's a goddamned strange coincidence, and I don't like it. I don't like you, I don't like the syphilitic whore you were born out of, I don't like being down here in a rat-infested foreign country when I could be at home with my family. I *do* like inflicting pain on criminals, so you had better answer my questions truthfully, or I'll hurt you bad."

Fritzie released his foot; De Witt came up gasping for air. I picked a soiled skivvy shirt up off the floor, and was about to hand it to him when I remembered the lash scars on Kay's legs. The image made me throw the shirt at De Witt, then grab a chair from the catwalk and reach for my handcuffs. Fritzie swabbed the ex-con's face, I shoved him into the seat and cuffed his wrists to the back slats.

De Witt looked up at us; his trouser legs darkened as his bladder went. Fritzie said, "Did you know that Sergeant Blanchard is here in Tijuana?"

De Witt shook his head back and forth, spraying off the remnants of his toilet dip. "I ain't seen Blanchard since my fucking trial!"

Fritzie shot him a little backhand, his Masonic ring severing a cheek vein. "Don't use profanity with me, and address me as sir. Now, did you know that Sergeant Blanchard is here in Tijuana?"

De Witt blubbered, "No"; Fritzie said, "No, *sir*," and slapped him. De Witt hung his head, lolling his chin on his chest. Fritzie prodded it up with one finger. "No, what?"

De Witt screeched, "No, sir!"

Even through my hate haze I could tell he was coming clean. I said, "Blanchard's afraid of you. Why?"

Twisting in the chair, greasy pompadour wilted over his forehead, De Witt laughed. Wild laughter, the kind that cuts through pain, then makes it worse. Livid, Fritzie balled a fist to punish him; I said, "Let him be." Vogel relented; De Witt's loony chuckles trailed off.

Sucking in breath, De Witt said, "Man o Manieschewitz, what a laugh. Lee beauty gotta be scared of me 'cause of how I flapped my trap at the trial, but all I know is what I read in the papers, and I gotta tell you that little reefer roust put the fear of God into me, if I'm lyin', I'm flyin'. Maybe I was thinkin' revenge up to then, maybe I was talkin' trash to my cellies, but when Lee beauty killed them niggers and—"

Vogel right hooked De Witt, toppling him, chair and all, to

the floor. Spitting blood and teeth, the aging lounge lizard moaned and laughed at the same time; Fritzie knelt beside him and pinched his carotid artery, shutting off the blood to his brain. "Bobby boy, I do not like Sergeant Blanchard, but he is a fellow officer, and I will not have syphilitic scum like you defaming him. Now you risked a parole violation and a trip back to Q for a trip down here. When I let go of your neck you will tell me why, or I will pinch your neck again until your gray cells go snap, crackle and pop like Kellogg's Rice Krispies."

Fritzie released the hold; De Witt's face went from blue to dark red. With one hand, Vogel grabbed suspect and chair and placed them upright. Lounge lizard Bobby started to laugh again, then sputtered blood and stopped. Looking up at Fritzie, he reminded me of a dog who loves his cruel master because it's the only one he's got. His voice was a beaten dog whimper: "I came down to cop some horse and bring it back to LA before I reported in to my PO. The guy I got is supposed to be a softie, you tell him 'Gee, sir, I been in stir eight years and I hadda get my ashes hauled,' and he don't violate you for bein' late."

De Witt took a deep breath; Fritzie said, "Snap, crackle, pop." Bobby boy dog whimpered the rest of his confession rapidamente: "The man down here is this cholo named Felix Chasco. He's supposed to meet me at the Calexico Gardens Motel tonight. The LA man's the brother of this guy I knew at Quentin. I ain't met him and please don't hurt me no more."

Fritzie let out a huge whoop and ran out of the cell to report his booty; De Witt licked blood off his lips and looked at me, his dog master now that Vogel was gone. I said, "Finish up on you and Lee Blanchard. And don't get hysterical this time."

De Witt said, "Sir, all that's between me and Blanchard is that I fucked this cunt Kay Lake."

I remember moving toward him and I remember picking him up two-handed by the neck, wondering how hard you had to squeeze a dog's throat to make its eyeballs pop out. I remember him changing color and voices in Spanish, and Fritzie shouting, "His story checks." Then I remember being hurled backward, thinking, so that's what bars feel like. Then I remember nothing.

• • •

I came to thinking I'd been knocked down in a third Bleichert-Blanchard fight, wondering how much hurt I'd put on my partner. I babbled, "Lee? Lee? Are you all right?" then sighted in on two greaser cops with ridiculous dime store regalia on their blackshirts. Fritzie Vogel towered over them, saying, "I let Bobby boy go so we could tail him to his pal. But he blew the tail while you were catching up on your beauty sleep, which was too bad for him."

Someone hugely strong lifted me up off the cell floor; coming out of my haze I knew it had to be Big Bill Koenig. Woozy and rubberlegged, I let Fritzie and the Mex cops lead me through the station and outside. It was dusk, and the TJ sky was already lit with neon. A Studebaker patrol car pulled up; Fritzie and Bill ushered me into the backseat. The driver hit the loudest siren the world had ever heard, then gunned it.

We drove west out of town, stopping in the gravel center of a horseshoe-shaped auto court. TJ cops in khakis and jodhpurs were standing guard in front of a back unit, holding pump shotguns. Fritzie winked and offered me his arm to lean on; I spurned it and got out of the car under my own steam. Fritzie led the way over; the cops saluted us with their gun barrels, then opened the door.

The room was a cordite-reeking slaughterhouse. Bobby De Witt and a Mexican man lay dead on the floor, bullet holes oozing blood all over them. Brain spatters leaking fluid covered one entire wall; De Witt's neck was bruised from where I'd been throttling him. My first coherent thought was that I'd done it during my blackout, vigilante vengeance to protect the only two people I loved. Fritzie must have been a mind reader, because he laughed and said, "Not you, boyo. The spic is Felix Casco, a known dope trafficker. Maybe it was other dope scum, maybe it was Lee, maybe it was God. I say let our Mexican colleagues handle their own dirty laundry and let's us go back to LA and get the son of a bitch who sliced the Dahlia."

CHAPTER SIXTEEN

Bobby De Witt's murder got a half column in the LA *Mirror*, I got a day off from a surprisingly solicitious Ellis Loew, Lee's disappearance got a squad of Metropolitan Division cops full-time.

I spent most of the day off in Captain Jack's office, being interrogated by them. They asked me hundreds of questions about Lee—from the reasons for his outbursts at the stag film and La Verne's Hideaway, to his obsession with the Short case, to the Nash memo and his shack job with Kay. I played fast and loose with facts, and lied by omission—keeping it zipped about Lee's Benzedrine use, his file room at the El Nido Hotel and the fact that his cohabitation was chaste. The Metro bulls repeatedly asked me if I thought Lee killed Bobby De Witt and Felix Chasco; I repeatedly told them he wasn't capable of murder. Asked for an interpretation of my partner's flight, I told them about beating Lee up over the Nash job, adding that he was an ex-boxer, maybe soon to be an ex-cop, too old to go back to fighting, too volatile to live a squarejohn life—and the Mexican interior was probably as good a place as any for a man like that. As the interrogation wound down, I sensed that the officers weren't interested in securing Lee's safety—they were building a case for his LAPD expulsion. I was repeatedly told not to stick my nose in their investigation and each time I agreed I dug my fingers into my palms to keep from hurling insults and worse.

From City Hall I went to see Kay. Two Metro goons had already paid her a visit, putting her through the wringer about her life with Lee, rehashing her old life with Bobby De Witt. The iceberg look she gave me said I was slime for belonging to the same police department; when I tried to comfort her and offer words of encouragement about Lee's return, she said, "And all that," and pushed me away.

I checked out room 204 of the El Nido Hotel then, hoping for some kind of message, some kind of clue that said, "I'll be back, and the three of us will keep going." What I found was a shrine to Elizabeth Short.

The room was a typical Hollywood bachelor flop: Murphy bed, sink, tiny closet. But the walls were adorned with Betty Short portrait pictures, newspaper and magazine photos, horror glossies from 39th and Norton, dozens of them enlarged to magnify every gruesome detail. The bed was covered with cardboard boxes—an entire detective's case file, with carbons of miscellaneous memos, tip lists, evidence indexes, FIs and questioning reports all cross-filed alphabetically.

Having nothing to do and no one to do it with, I leafed through the folders. The bulk of the information was staggering, the manpower behind it more staggering, the fact that it was all over one silly girl the most staggering of all. I didn't know whether to toast Betty Short or rip her off the walls, so I badged the desk clerk on my way out, paid him a month's rent in advance and kept the room like I promised Millard and Sears—even though I was really holding it for Sergeant Leland C. Blanchard.

Who was somewhere out there in the Big Nowhere.

I called up the classified desks of the *Times*, *Mirror*, *Herald* and *Daily News*, placing a personals ad to run indefinitely: "Fire—Nightflower room will remain intact. Send me a message—Ice." With that behind me, I drove to the only place I could think of to send him one.

39th and Norton was just a block of empty lots now. No arclights, no police cars, no nighttime gawkers. A Santa Ana wind blew in while I stood there, and the more I pulled for Lee to come back to me the more I knew my hotshot cop life was as gone as everybody's favorite dead girl.

CHAPTER SEVENTEEN

In the morning I sent the big boys a message. Hiding out in a storage room down the hall from my cubicle, I typed copies of a transfer request letter, one each for Loew, Russ Millard and Captain Jack. The letter read:

I request to be detached from the Elizabeth Short investigation immediately, and returned to my duties at Central Division Warrants. I feel that the Short case is more than adequately staffed, by far more experienced officers than myself, and that I could more effectively serve the Department working Warrants. Moreover, with my partner, Sergeant L.C. Blanchard, missing, I will be in the position of Senior Officer, and I will need to break in a replacement at a time when there is most likely a large backlog of priority papers. In preparation for my duties as Senior Warrants officer, I have been studying for the Sergeant's Examination, and expect to take it at the next promotion board this spring. This, I feel, will give me leadership training, and will make up for my relative lack of experience as a plainclothes field officer.

Respectfully,
Dwight W. Bleichert, Badge 1611,
Central Detectives

Finishing, I read the letter over, deciding that it worked in just the right blend of respect and exasperation, with the half-truth about the Sergeant's Exam a good closing line. I was signing the copies when I heard a tremendous ruckus coming from the bullpen.

I folded the pages into my jacket pocket and went to investigate. A group of detectives and crime lab techs in white smocks were surrounding a table, looking down at it, jabbering and gesturing away. I joined the throng, muttering "Holy fuck," when I saw what was jazzing them.

An envelope was lying on a metal evidence tray. It was stamped and postmarked and smelled faintly of gasoline. The front of it was covered with letters clipped from newspapers and magazines, glued to the plain white surface. The words spelled out:

TO THE HERALD AND OTHER LA PAPERS.
HERE IS DAHLIA'S BELONGINGS.
LETTER TO FOLLOW.

A lab man wearing rubber gloves slit the envelope and pulled out the contents—a little black address book, a plastic-sheathed Social Security card and a thin stack of photographs. Squinting, I read the name on the card—Elizabeth Ann Short—and knew the Dahlia case had blown wide open. The man next to me was talking the delivery up—a postal carrier found the envelope in a mailbox near the downtown library, almost keeled from a heart attack, then grabbed a pair of radio car bulls, who code three'd the booty over.

Ellis Loew pushed his way up against the lab techs, Fritzie Vogel at his heels. The head tech flailed his hands in anger; a cacophony of speculation hit the pen. Then there was a loud whistle, and Russ Millard yelled, "Damnit, back off and let them work. And give them some quiet."

We did.

The techs descended on the envelope, dusting it with print powder, leafing through the address book, examining the snapshots and calling out their findings like surgeons at an operating table:

"Two partial latents on the back flap, smudged, no more than one or two comparison points, not enough to run a make on, maybe enough to compare to incoming suspects—"

"No prints on Social Security card—"

"Pages of address book readable, but gasoline saturated, no chance of sustaining latents. Names and phone numbers mostly men, not listed alphabetically, some pages ripped out—"

"Photographs are of Short girl with servicemen in uniform, the men's faces crossed out—"

Stunned, I wondered: *Would* a letter follow? Was my random snuff theory blown? Since the stuff was obviously sent in by the killer, was *he* one of the servicemen in the pictures? Was the mailing cat and mouse, or the precursor to surrender and confession? All around me, other officers were running with the same dope, the same questions, talking in knots of two and three, or looking rapt, like they were talking with themselves. The lab techs took off with the plethora of new leads, cradling them in rubber-gloved hands. Then the only calm man in the room whistled again.

And again the commotion froze. Russ Millard, poker-faced, counted the heads and pointed us over to the rear bulletin board. We lined up there; he said, "I don't know what it means, except I'm pretty sure the killer sent the stuff. The lab boys are going to need more time on the envelope, then they'll photograph the pages and give us a list of names to do interviews from."

Dick Cavanaugh said, "Russ, he's playing with us. Some of the pages were ripped out, and I'll lay you ten to one his name was on one of them."

Millard smiled. "Maybe, maybe not. Maybe he's crazy and wants to get caught, maybe some of the people in the book know him. Maybe the techs will get latents off the photos or be able to identify some of the men from the insignia of their uniforms. Maybe the bastard *will* send a letter. That's a lot of maybes, so I'll tell you what we've got for sure: all eleven of you are going to drop what you're doing and canvass the area around the mailbox where that envelope was found. Harry and I will be going over the case file to see if any of our previous suspects live or work around there. *Then*, when we've got the list of names from the book, we'll go at it *discreetly*. Betty spread herself pretty thin with men, and homewrecking isn't my style. Harry?"

Sears was standing by the wall map of downtown LA, holding a pen and clipboard. He stuttered, "W-w-we'll do f-f-foot beats." I saw my transfer request stamped "Rejected." Then I heard an argument on the opposite side of the squad-room.

The arguers were Ellis Loew and Jack Tierney, both of them trying to score points and keep it sotto voce. They ducked behind a wall post for privacy, I ducked over to an adjacent phone cubicle to eavesdrop—hoping for skinny on Lee.

It wasn't about Lee—it was about *Her*.

". . . Jack, Horrall wants to take three quarters of the men off the investigation. Bond issue or no bond issue, he thinks he's given the voters enough of a show. We can get around him by going at the names in the book a hundred percent. The more publicity the case gets, the more truck we've got with Horrall—"

"Goddamn it, Ellis—"

"No. Just listen to me. Before, I wanted to downplay the girl as a floozy. The way I see it now is that it's too far out in the open already to sit on. We know what she was, and we'll get it confirmed a couple of hundred times by the men in that little black book. We keep our men questioning them, I'll keep feeding the names to my newspaper contacts, we'll keep a head of steam on this thing until we get the killer."

"It's a sucker play, Ellis. The killer's name probably isn't in the book. He's a psycho, and he's showing us his backside and saying, 'Make something out of it.' The girl's a gravy train, Ellis. I've known it from the beginning, just like you. But this has got to backfire on us. I'm working a half dozen other homicides with skeleton crews, and if the married men in that book get their names in the paper, then their lives will be shot to shit because they copped Betty Short for a quick piece of tail."

There was a long stretch of silence. Then Loew said, "Jack, you know I'll be DA sooner or later. If not next year, in '52. And you know that Green will be retiring in a few years, and you know who I want to replace him. Jack, I'm thirty-six and you're forty-nine. I may get another shot at something this big. You won't. For God's sake take the farsighted view on it."

More silence. I pictured Captain Jack Tierney weighing the pros and cons of selling his soul to Satan with a Phi Beta Kappa key and a hard-on for the City of Los Angeles. When he said, "Okay, Ellis," I tore up my transfer request and walked back to rejoin the circus.

CHAPTER EIGHTEEN

Over the next ten days the circus turned into wholesale farce, with an occasional tragedy thrown in.

No other leads were gleaned from the "Death Letter," and the 243 names in the book were divvied up between four detective teams, the low number of cops Jack Tierney's ploy aimed at padding that part of the investigation into extended newspaper and radio juice. Russ Millard argued for twenty teams and a fast, clean sweep; Captain Jack, backstopped by the DA Satan, refused. When Big Bill Koenig was deemed too combustible to work the questionings and was given clerical duties, I was paired with Fritz Vogel. Together, we questioned fifty-odd people, mostly men, about their association with Elizabeth Short. We heard predictable stories of them meeting Betty in bars and buying her drinks and dinner, listening to her fantasies of being the bride or widow of war heros, bedding or not bedding her. A number of the men did not even know the notorious Dahlia—they were "friends of friends," their names passed on out of pussy hound camaraderie.

Of our parcel of names, sixteen of the guys were what Fritzie labeled "Certified Dahlia Fuckers." They were mostly lower-echelon movie minions: agents, talent scouts and casting directors who hung out at Schwab's Drugstore chasing gullible would-be starlets, empty promises on their lips, Trojan "value packs" in their pockets. They told proud or shamefaced casting couch stories every bit as sad as Betty's tales of bliss with studs in uniform. Finally, the men in Elizabeth Short's little black book had two things in common—they got their names in the LA dailies and they coughed up alibis that eliminated them as suspects. And word filtered back to the squadroom that the publicity eliminated more than a few of them as husbands.

The women were a mixed bag. Most were just pals—girl talk acquaintances, fellow cocktail lounge cadgers and aspiring actresses heading nowhere. A dozen or so were hookers and semi-pro B girls, instant soulmates that Betty met in bars. They gave us leads that petered out on follow-up investigation—basically, the word that Betty sold herself freelance to conventioneers at several lower-class downtown hotels. They hedged that Betty rarely peddled it, and could not identify any of her tricks by name; Fritzie's canvassing of the hotels got him an angry zero, and the fact that several other women—R&I confirmed as prostitutes—couldn't be located, pissed him off even more.

Madeleine Sprague's name did not appear in the book, nor did it turn up in any of my subsequent questionings. No dyke or dyke bar leads came out of the 243 names, and every night I checked the University squadroom bulletin boards to see if any of the other teams had latched on to her monicker. None of them did, and I started to feel very safe regarding my evidence suppression tango.

While the book queries got most of the headlines, the rest of the circus continued on: tips, tips and more tips wasted thousands of police man-hours; poison phone and poison pen communiques had local squadroom dicks bracing spiteful loonies implicating their enemies for hundreds of major and minor grievances. Discarded women's garments were sifted through at the Central crime lab, and every piece of size eight black female apparel that was found launched another extensive neighborhood run-through.

The biggest surprise of my little black book tour was Fritz Vogel. Free of Bill Koenig, he possessed a surprising wit, and in his muscle fashion he was as adept an interrogator as Russ Millard. He knew when to punch for information, hitting fast and hard, fueled by personal rancor but capable of putting it out of his mind when the interrogee coughed up what we wanted. Sometimes I sensed that he was holding back out of respect for my nice guy questioning style, that the pragmatist in him knew it was the best way to get results. We became an effective Mutt and Jeff duo fast, and I could tell that I was a restraining influence on Fritzie, a check and balance on his admitted fondness for hurting criminals. He gave me a wary respect for the hurt I'd put on Bobby De Witt, and a few days into the temporary partnership we were bullshitting in broken German, a way to kill time driving to and from questionings. With me, Fritzie spoke less in tirades and came across as one of the guys—with a mean streak. He talked up the Dahlia and his coveted lieutenancy, but didn't talk frames, and since he never tried to pull any railroad jobs around me and was straight in his FI reports, I got the notion that Loew had either given up the idea or was biding his time. I could also tell that Fritzie was constantly sizing me up, that he knew Koenig wouldn't cut it as partner to Detective Division brass, but with Lee gone, I would. The appraisal process flattered me, and I kept myself razor sharp during interrogations. I had played second banana to Lee working Warrants, and if Fritzie and I partnered up I wanted him to know that I wouldn't play stooge—or lacky—like Harry Sears to Russ Millard.

Millard, Fritzie's cop antithesis, exerted his own pull on me. He took to using Room 204 at the El Nido as his field office, going there at end of watch to read Lee's superbly cross-filed collection of paper. With Lee gone, time weighed heavy on me, so I joined him most evenings. When he looked at the Dahlia horror pictures, he always made the sign of the cross and murmured "Elizabeth" with reverence; walking out, he said, "I'll get him, dear." He always left at 8:00 on the dot, to go home to his wife and sons. That a man could care so deeply yet put it aside so casually amazed me. I asked him about it; he said, "I will not let brutality rule my life."

From 8:00 on, my own life was ruled by two women, a crossfire of their strange, strong wills.

From the El Nido, I'd go to see Kay. With Lee gone and no longer footing the bills, she had to find full-time work, and she did—getting a job teaching sixth grade at an elementary school a few blocks off the Strip. I'd find her grading book reports and perusing kiddie artwork stoically, glad to see me, but caustic underneath, like maintaining a business-as-usual front would keep her grief over Lee's absence and her contempt for my reluctance at bay. I tried denting the front by telling her I wanted her, but would only move on it when Lee's vanishing act was resolved; she answered with overeducated psychological claptrap about our missing third, turning the education he bought her around, using it as a weapon against him. I

exploded at phrases like "paranoid tendencies" and "patholog-
ical selfishness," coming back with "he *saved* you, he *made*
you." Kay's comeback for that was, *"He only helped me."* I had
no comeback for the truth behind the jargon and the fact that
without Lee as a centerpiece, the two of us were loose ends, a
family sans patriarch. It was that stasis that drove me out the
door ten nights running—straight to the Red Arrow Motel.

So I brought Kay with me to Madeleine.

We'd rut first thing, talk later. The talk was always of
Madeleine's family, followed by fantasies that I concocted so as
not to feel impoverished in the wake of her tales. The brass girl
had robber baron Daddy, *the* Emmett Sprague, confrere of
Mack Sennett in the Hollywood salad days; art poseur and
elixir-guzzling Mommy, a direct descendant of *the* California
land grant Cathcarts; genius sister Martha, hotshot commercial artist, rising star on Ad Agency Row downtown. For a
supporting cast there was Mayor Fletcher Bowron, public
relations–minded thug Mickey Cohen, "Dreamer" Georgie
Tilden, Emmett's former stooge, the son of a famous Scottish
anatomist and wastrel nickolodeon artiste. The Dohenys and
Sepulvedas and Mulhollands were also close friends, as were
Governor Earl Warren and DA Buron Fitts. Having only senile
Dolph Bleichert, the late Greta Heilbrunner Bleichert, the Japs
I snitched off and fight acquaintances, I spun yarns out of thin
air: scholastic medals won and proms attended; bodyguarding
FDR in '43. I dissembled away until it was time to rut again,
grateful that we always kept the lights off between bouts, so
Madeleine couldn't read my face and know I was coming from
hunger.

Or from the Dahlia.

The first time it happened accidentally. We were making
love, both of us close to peaking. My hand slipped off the bed
rail and hit the light switch on the wall, illuminating Betty
Short below me. For just a few seconds I believed it was her,
and I called out for Lee and Kay to help me. When my lover
was Madeleine again, I reached for the switch, only to have her
grab my wrist. Moving hard, springs creaking, light glaring, I
made Madeleine Betty—made her eyes blue instead of hazel,
made her body Betty's body from the stag film, made her
silently mouth, "No, please." Coming, I knew it could never be
that good with just plain Madeleine; when the brass girl
whispered, "I knew she'd get to you sooner or later," I dry
sobbed that all my pillow stories were lies and poured out the
nonstop true story of Lee and Kay and Bucky, straight through
to Mr. Fire's fix on the dead girl and his jump off the face of the

earth. When I finished, Madeleine said, "I'll never be a schoolteacher from Sioux Falls, South Dakota, but I'll be Betty or anyone else you want me to be." I let her stroke my head, grateful not to have to lie anymore, but sad that she—and not Kay—was my confessor.

So Elizabeth Short and I were formally joined.

CHAPTER NINETEEN

Lee stayed gone and Madeleine stayed Betty, and there was nothing I could do about either transformation. Heeding the Metro goons' warning, I kept my nose out of their investigation, constantly wondering if Mr. Fire took his powder preplanned or accidentally. I did check his bank records, finding an $800 balance with no recent withdrawals, and when I heard that a nationwide and Mexico APB had been issued on Lee and his '40 Ford, yielding goose egg, my instincts told me he had fled way south of the border, where the Rurales used gringo police bulletins as toilet paper. Russ Millard told me that two Mexican men, both well-known dope traffickers, had been arrested in Juarez for the murder of Bobby De Witt and Felix Chasco, which eased my mind on Metro making Lee for the job—but then scuttlebutt filtered down from high, high brass circles. Chief Horrall had rescinded the APB and decreed, "Let sleeping dogs lie." Thad Green's secretary told Harry Sears that she had heard Lee was going to be dismissed from the LAPD if he did not show up within thirty days of the time he vanished.

January dwindled out, rainy days with only one spark of excitement. An envelope arrived by mail at the Bureau. It had a clipped word address, with a clipped word letter on plain bond paper inside:

HAVE CHANGED MY MIND.
YOU WOULD NOT GIVE ME A SQUARE DEAL.
DAHLIA KILLING JUSTIFIED
—BLACK DAHLIA AVENGER.

Taped to the page was a photograph of a short, heavyset man wearing a business suit, his face scratched out. No prints or other forensic leads were gleaned from the snapshot or envelope, and since the servicemen pics from the first letter had been withheld from the press as a suspect elimination device, we knew letter number two was legit. The Bureau consensus was that the photo was of the killer, symbolically eliminating himself from the overall "picture."

With the death letter and stag film leads ground to dust, a second consensus took over: we were never going to get the bastard. The odds on "Unsolved" dropped to even money in the squadroom pool; Thad Green told Russ and Captain Jack that Horrall was going to pull the chain on the Dahlia mess on February 5, returning a large number of officers to their normal duties. Rumor had it that I would be one of the returnees, breaking in Johnny Vogel as my partner. Bad Breath Johnny rankled, but going back to Warrants came on as Paradise regained. Betty Short would then exist the only place I wanted her to—as the spark point of my imagination.

CHAPTER TWENTY

"The following Central Division and Detective Bureau officers temporarily assigned to the E. Short investigation are to return to their normal assignments, effective tomorrow, 2/6/47:

Sgt. T. Anders - ret. to Central Bunco.

Det. J. Arcola - ret. to Central Burglary.

Sgt. R. Cavanaugh - ret. to Central Robbery.

Det. G. Ellison - ret. to Central Detectives.

Det. A. Grimes - ret. to Central Detectives.

Det. C. Ligget - ret. to Central Juvenile.

Det. R. Navarette - ret. to Central Bunco.

Sgt. J. Pratt - ret. to Central Homicide. (See Lt. Ruley for assignment.)

Det. J. Smith - ret. to Central Homicide. (See Lt. Ruley.)

Det. W. Smith - ret. to Central Detectives.

Chief Horrall and Deputy Chief Green wish me to thank you for your help on this investigation, most especially the many overtime hours logged in. Commendation letters will be sent to all of you.

My thanks also—

Capt. J.V. Tierney, Commander, Central Detectives.

The distance between the bulletin board and Millard's office was about ten yards; I covered it in about a tenth of a second. Russ looked up from his desk. "Hi, Bucky. How's tricks?"

"Why wasn't I on that transfer list?"

"I asked Jack to keep you on the Short case."

"Why?"

"Because you're getting to be a damn good detective, and Harry's retiring in '50. Want more?"

I was wondering what to say when the phone rang. Russ picked it up and said, "Central Homicide, Millard," then listened for a few moments and pointed to the extension on the desk across from him. I grabbed the receiver, catching a deep male voice in mid-sentence:

". . . attached to the CID unit here at Fort Dix. I know you've had a lot of confessions peter out on you, but this one sounds good to me."

Russ said, "Go on, Major."

"The soldier's name is Joseph Dulange. He's an MP, attached to the headquarters company at Dix. He made the confession to his CO, coming off a bender. His buddies say he carries a knife, and he flew to Los Angeles on furlough on January eighth. On top of that, we found bloodstains on a pair of his trousers—too small an amount to type. Personally, I think he's a bad apple. He got in a lot of brawls overseas, and his CO says he's a wife beater."

"Major, is Dulange near you right now?"

"Yes. He's in a cell across the hall."

"Do this for me, please. Ask him to describe Elizabeth Short's birthmarks to you. If he does it accurately, my partner and I will be on the next transport flight out of Camp MacArthur."

The major said, "Yes, sir"; the Fort Dix half of the conversation broke off. Russ said, "Harry's got the flu. Feel like a trip to New Jersey, bright penny?"

"Are you serious?"

"If that soldier comes up with the moles on Elizabeth's rear end, I am."

"Ask him about the slash marks, the stuff that didn't make the papers."

Russ shook his head. "No. It might excite him too much. If this is legit, we're flying out on the QT and reporting in from Jersey. If Jack or Ellis get hold of this they'll send Fritzie, and he'll have that soldier in the electric chair by morning, guilty or otherwise."

The Fritzie crack irked me. "He's not that bad. And I think Loew's given up on the frame idea."

"You're an impressionable penny, then. Fritzie's as bad as they get, and Ellis—"

The major came back on the line: "Sir, Dulange said the girl had three little dark moles on the left cheek of her, uh . . . derriere."

"You could have said ass, Major. And we're on our way."

* * *

Corporal Joseph Dulange was a tall, hard-muscled man of twenty-nine, dark-haired, horse-faced, with a pencil-thin mustache. Dressed in olive drab fatigues, he sat across a table from us in the Fort Dix provost marshal's office, looking incorrigibly mean. A judge advocate captain sat beside him, probably to make sure Russ and I didn't try the civilian third degree. The eight-hour plane ride had been bumpy; at 4:00 A.M. I was still on LA time, exhausted but keyed-up. On the ride over from the airstrip, the CID major we'd talked to on the phone had briefed us on Dulange. He was a twice-married combat vet, a boozehound, a feared brawler. His statement was incomplete, but buttressed by two hard facts: he flew to LA on January eighth, and was arrested for Plain Drunk in New York City's Pennsylvania Station on January seventeenth.

Russ kicked it off. "Corporal, my name is Millard, and this is Detective Bleichert. We're from the Los Angeles Police Department, and if you convince us you killed Elizabeth Short, we'll arrest you and take you back with us."

Dulange shifted in his chair and said, "I sliced her," his voice high and nasal.

Russ sighed. "A lot of other people have told us that."

"I fucked her, too."

"Really? You cheat on your wife?"

"I'm a Frenchman."

I moved into my bad guy role. "I'm a German, so who gives a shit? What's that have to do with you cheating on your wife?"

Dulange flicked his tongue like a reptile. "I give it the French way. My wife don't like it like that."

Russ elbowed me. "Corporal, why did you take your furlough in Los Angeles? What were you interested in?"

"Cunt. Johnnie Red Label. Excitement."

"You could have found that across the river in Manhattan."

"Sunshine. Movie stars. Palm trees."

Russ laughed. "LA's got all of that. It sounds like your wife gives you a long leash, Joe. You know, furlough all by yourself."

"She knows I'm a Frenchman. I give it to her good when I'm home. Missionary style, ten inches. She got no complaints."

179

"What if she did complain, Joe? What would you do to her?"

Deadpan, Dulange said, "One complaint, I use my fists. Two complaints, I slice her in half."

I broke in: "Are you telling me you flew three thousand miles to eat some pussy?"

"I'm a Frenchman."

"You look like a homo to me. Gash divers are all repressed fruits, it's been proven. You got an answer for that, shitbird?"

The soldier-lawyer got up and whispered in Russ's ear; Russ nudged me under the table. Dulange cracked his deadpan into a big grin. "I got my answer hangin' ten hard, flatfoot."

Russ said, "You'll have to excuse Detective Bleichert, Joe. He's got a short fuse."

"He's got a short pecker. All Krauts do. I'm a Frenchman, I know."

Russ laughed uproariously, like he'd just heard a real knee-slapper at the Elks Club. "Joe, you're a pisser."

Dulange waggled his tongue. "I'm a Frenchman."

"Joe, you're a hot sketch, and Major Carroll told me you're a wife beater. Is that true?"

"Can niggers dance?"

"They certainly can. Do you enjoy hitting women, Joe?"

"When they ask for it."

"How often does your wife ask for it?"

"She asks for the big tensky every night."

"No. Asks to get hit, I mean."

"Every time I'm pallin' with Johnnie Red and she cracks wise, then she's askin' for it."

"You and Johnnie go back a ways?"

"Johnnie Red's my best friend."

"Did Johnnie go with you to LA?"

"In my pocket."

Sparring with a psycho drunk was wearing me down; I thought of Fritzie and the direct approach. "Are you having the DTs, shitbird? You want a little rap in the cabeza to clear things up for you?"

"Bleichert, enough!"

I shut up. The JA man glared at me; Russ straightened the knot in his necktie—the signal for me to keep it zipped. Dulange cracked the knuckles on his left hand one by one. Russ tossed a pack of cigarettes on the table, the oldest "I'm your pal" ploy in the book.

The Frenchman said, "Johnnie Red don't like me to smoke 'cept in his company. You bring Johnnie in, I'll smoke. I confess better in Johnnie's company, too. Ask the Catholic chaplain at

North Post. He told me he always smells Johnnie when I go to confession."

I started smelling Corporal Joseph Dulange as an attention-seeking drool case. Russ said, "Booze confessions aren't valid in court, Joe. But I'll tell you what. You convince me you killed Betty Short, and I'll make sure Johnnie comes back to LA with us. A nice eight-hour flight would give you plenty of time to renew your acquaintance with him. What do you say?"

"I say I chopped the Dahlia."

"I say you didn't. I say you and Johnnie are going to stay parted for a while."

"I chopped her."

"How?"

"On her titties, ear to ear and in half. Chop. Chop. Chop."

Russ sighed. "Let's backtrack, Joe. You flew out of Dix on Wednesday, January eighth, you landed at Camp MacArthur that night. You and Johnnie are in LA, anxious to sow some wild oats. Where did you go first? Hollywood Boulevard? Sunset Strip? The beach? Where?"

Dulange cracked his knuckles. "Nathan's Tattoo Parlor, 463 North Alvarado."

"What did you do there?"

Crazy Joe rolled up his right sleeve, revealing a forked snake's tongue with "Frenchy" emblazoned below it. Flexing his bicep, the tattoo stretched. Dulange said, "I'm a Frenchman."

Millard pulled his patented reversal. "I'm a cop, and I'm getting bored. When I get bored, Detective Bleichert takes over. Detective Bleichert was once the tenth-ranked light heavyweight in the world, and he is not a nice man. Right, partner?"

I balled my fists. "I'm a German."

Dulange laughed. "No tickee, no washee. No Johnnie, no story."

I almost leaped across the table at him. Russ grabbed my elbow and held it, viselike, while he bargained. "Joe, I'll make you a deal. First you convince us you *knew* Betty Short. Give us some facts. Names, dates, descriptions. You do that, and when we take our first break, you and Johnnie can go back to your cell and get reacquainted. What do you say?"

"Johnnie pint?"

"No, his big brother Johnnie fifth."

The Frenchman grabbed the pack of butts and shook one loose; Russ had his lighter out and extended. Dulange took a monumental drag, exhaling a rush of words along with the smoke:

"After the tattoo joint, me and Johnnie got a cab downtown and got a room. Havana Hotel, Ninth and Olive, deucesky a night, big cockroaches. They started makin' a ruckus, so I put out mousetraps. That killed 'em. Me and Johnnie slept it off, then the next day we went cunt chasin'. No luck. Next day I get me this Filipino cunt at the bus depot. She says she needs bus fare to Frisco, so I offer her a fivesky to take on me and Johnnie. She says tensky minumum for two guys. I say Johnnie's hung like Jesus, she should pay me. We go back to the hotel, all the cockroaches got loose from the traps. I introduce her to Johnnie, tell her he goes first. She gets scared, says, 'You think you're Fatty Arbuckle?' I tell her I'm a Frenchman, who does she think she is, thinks she can high-hat Johnnie Red?

"Cockroaches start howlin' like niggers. The Filipino says Johnnie's got sharp teeth, no sir. She runs like sixty, me and Johnnie hole up till late Saturday. We want cunt bad. We go by this army-navy on Broadway, and I get me some ribbons for my Ike jacket. DSC with oak leaf, silver star, bronze star, ribbons for all the Jap campaigns. I look like George S. Patton, only hung bigger. Me and Johnnie go to this bar called the Night Owl. Dahlia sashays in, Johnnie says, 'Yes sir, that's my baby, no sir, don't mean maybe, yes sir, that's my baby now.'"

Dulange stubbed out his cigarette and reached for the pack. Russ jotted notes; I figured time and location, remembering the Night Owl from my days working Central Patrol. It was on 6th and Hill—two blocks from the Biltmore Hotel, where Red Manley dropped Betty Short on Friday, January tenth. The Frenchman, DT recollections notwithstanding, had gained another notch of credibility.

Russ said, "Joe, this was Saturday the eleventh into Sunday the twelfth you're talking about?"

Dulange fired up another cigarette. "I'm a Frenchman, not a calendar. Sunday follows Saturday, you figure it out."

"Go on."

"Anyhow, Dahlia, me and Johnnie have a little chat, and I invite her over to the hotel. We get there and the cockroaches are loose, singin' and bitin' at the woodwork. Dahlia says she won't spreadsky 'less I kill 'em. I grab Johnnie and start boppin' 'em with him, Johnnie told me it don't hurt. But the Dahlia cunt won't spreadsky till the roaches are disposed of scientific style. I go down the street and get this doctor. He gives the roaches poison injections for a fivesky. Me and Dahlia fuck like bunnies, Johnnie Red watches. He's mad, 'cause Dahlia's so good I don't want to give him none."

I threw in a cut-the-shit question: "Describe her body. Do a good job, or you won't see Johnnie Red until you get out of the stockade."

Dulange's face went soft; he looked like a little kid threatened with the loss of his teddy bear. Russ said, "Answer the man's question, Joe."

Dulange grinned. "Till I cut 'em off, she had perky little titties with pink nipples. Kinda thick legs, nice bush. She had them moles I told Major Carroll about, and she had these scratches on her back, real fresh, like she'd just took a whippin'."

I tingled, remembering the "soft lash marks" the coroner mentioned at the autopsy. Russ said, "Go on, Joe."

Dulange ghoul grinned. "Then Dahlia starts actin' nutso, sayin', 'How come you're only a corporal if you won all them medals?' She starts callin' me Matt and Gordon and keeps talkin' about our baby, even though we just did it once, and I wore a safe. Johnnie gets spooked, and him and the cockroaches start singin', 'No sir, that *ain't* my baby.' I want more cuntsky, so I take Dahlia down the street to see the roach doctor. I slip him a tensky, and he gives her a fake examination and tells her, 'The baby will be healthy and arrive in six months.'"

More confirmation, smack in the middle of a DT haze—the Matt and Gordon were obviously Matt Gordon and Joseph Gordon Fickling, two of Betty Short's fantasy husbands. I thought 50-50, let's close it out for Big Lee Blanchard; Russ said, "Then what, Joe?"

Dulange looked genuinely puzzled—past bravado, boozebrain memories and a desire to be reunited with Johnnie Red. "Then I sliced her."

"Where?"

"In half."

"No, Joe. Where did you perform the murder?"

"Oh. At the hotel."

"What room number?"

"116."

"How'd you get the body to 39th and Norton?"

"I stole a car."

"What kind of car?"

"A Chevy."

"Make and model?"

" '43 sedan."

"American cars weren't manufactured during the war, Joe. Try again."

" '47 sedan."

"Somebody left the keys in a nice new car like that? In downtown LA?"

"I hot-wired it."

"How do you hot-wire a car, Joe?"

"What?"

"Explain the procedure to me."

"I forgot how I did it. I was drunk."

I cut in: "Where's 39th and Norton?"

Dulange toyed with the cigarette pack. "It's near Crenshaw Boulevard and Coliseum Street."

"Tell me something that wasn't in the papers."

"I cut her to ear to ear."

"Everybody knows that."

"Me and Johnnie raped her."

"She wasn't raped, and Johnnie would have left marks. There weren't any. Why'd you kill her?"

"She was a bad fuck."

"Bullshit. You said Betty fucked like a rabbit."

"A bad rabbit."

"All cats are gray in the dark, shitbird. Why'd you kill her?"

"She wouldn't go French."

"That's no reason. You can get French at any five-dollar whorehouse. A Frenchman like you should know that."

"She gave bad French."

"There's no such thing, shitbird."

"I chopped her!"

I slammed the tabletop à la Harry Sears. "You're a lying frog son of a bitch!"

The JA man got to his feet; Dulange bawled, "I want my Johnnie."

Russ told the captain, "Have him back here in six hours," and smiled at me—the softest smile I'd ever seen him give.

•   •   •

So we left it at 50-50 moving toward 75-25 against. Russ left to call in his report and dispatch an SID team over to Room 116 of the Havana Hotel to check for bloodstains; I went to sleep in the BOQ room Major Carroll assigned us. I dreamed of Betty Short and Fatty Arbuckle in black and white; when the alarm went off I reached for Madeleine.

Opening my eyes, I saw Russ, dressed in a clean suit. He handed me a newspaper and said, "Never underestimate Ellis Loew."

It was a Newark tabloid job bearing the headline: "Fort Dix Soldier Culprit in Sinsational Los Angeles Murder!" Below the banner print were side-by-side photos of Frenchman Joe Dulange and Loew, posed theatrically behind his desk. The text read:

In a scoop to our sister publication the Los Angeles *Mirror*, Los Angeles Deputy District Attorney Ellis Loew, Chief Legal Officer on the mystifying "Black Dahlia" murder case, announced a major break-through last night. "I have just been informed by two of my closest colleagues, Lieutenant Russell Millard and Officer Dwight Bleichert, that Fort Dix, New Jersey Corporal Joseph Dulange has confessed to the murder of Elizabeth Short, and that the confession has been validated by facts that only the killer would know. Corporal Dulange is a known degenerate, and I will be supplying the press with more facts on the confession as soon as my men return Dulange to Los Angeles for arraignment."

The Elizabeth Short case has baffled authorities since the morning of January 15, when Miss Short's nude, mutilated body, cut in half at the waist, was found in a vacant lot in Los Angeles. Deputy DA Loew would not reveal the details of Corporal Dulange's confession, but he did say that Dulange was a known intimate of Miss Short. "Details will be forthcoming," he said. "The important thing is that this fiend is in custody, where he will not kill again."

I laughed. "What did you really tell Loew?"

"Nothing. When I talked to Captain Jack the first time, I told him Dulange was a strong possible. He bawled me out for not reporting before we left, and that was it. The second time I called I told him Dulange was starting to look like another crazy. He got very upset, and now I know why."

I stood up and stretched. "Let's just hope he really killed her."

Russ shook his head. "SID said there's no bloodstains in the hotel room, and no running water to drain the body. And Carroll had a tri-state bulletin out on Dulange's whereabouts January tenth through the seventeenth—drunk tanks, hospitals, the works. We just got a kickback: Frenchy was in the jail ward of St. Patrick's Hospital in Brooklyn January fourteenth to the seventeenth. Severe DTs. He was released that morning and picked up in Penn Station two hours later. *The man is clean.*"

I didn't know who to be mad at. Loew and company wanted to clear the slate any way possible, Millard wanted justice, I was going home to headlines that made me look like a fool.

"What about Dulange? You want to brace him again?"

"And hear about more singing cockroaches? No. Carroll confronted him with the kickback. He said he made up the killing story to get publicity. He wants to reconcile with his first wife, and he thought the attention would get him some sympathy. I talked to him again, and it was nothing but DT stuff. There's nothing more he can tell us."

"Jesus Christ."

"The savior indeed. Joe's getting a quickie discharge and we're getting a flight back to LA in forty-five minutes. So get dressed, partner."

I put on my stale clothes, then Russ and I walked out to the sallyport to wait for the jeep that would take us to the airstrip. In the distance, I could see a tall uniformed figure approaching. I shivered against the cold; the tall man got closer. I saw that it was none other than Corporal Joseph Dulange.

Reaching the sallyport, he held out a morning tabloid and poked at his picture on the front page. "I got the whole hog, you're small print where Krauts belong."

I smelled Johnnie Red on his breath and sucker-punched him square in the chops. Dulange went down like a ton of bricks; my right hand throbbed. Russ Millard's look reminded me of Jesus getting ready to rebuke the heathens. I said, "Don't be so goddamn proper. Don't be such a fucking saint."

CHAPTER TWENTY-ONE

Ellis Loew said, "I called this little meeting for several reasons, Bucky. One is to apologize for jumping the gun on Dulange. I was precipitious in talking to my newspaper people, and you got hurt. I apologize for that."

I looked at Loew, and at Fritz Vogel sitting beside him. The "little meeting" was in the living room of Fritzie's house; the two days of Dulange headlines portrayed me as no worse than an overeager cop on a wild goose chase. "What do you want, Mr. Loew?"

Fritzie laughed; Loew said, "Call me Ellis."

The setup hit a new bottom in the sublety department—way below the highballs and bowl of pretzels Fritzie's hausfrau had served as amenities. I was supposed to meet Madeleine in an hour—and off-duty fraternizing with my boss was the last thing in the world I wanted. "Okay, Ellis."

Loew bristled at my tone. "Bucky, we've clashed a number of times in the past. Maybe we're even clashing now. But I think we agree on a few things. We'd both like to see the Short case closed out and get back to normal business. You want to go back to Warrants, and as much as I would like to prosecute the killer, my part in the investigation has gotten out of hand, and it's time that I returned to the old cases on my docket."

I felt like a bush league cardsharp holding a royal flush. "What do you want, Ellis?"

"I want to return you to Warrants tomorrow, and I want to give the Short case a last go before I return to my old caseload. We're both comers, Bucky. Fritzie wants you for his partner when he gets his lieutenancy, and—"

"Russ Millard wants me when Harry Sears retires."

Fritzie took a belt of his highball. "You're too raw for him, boyo. He's told people you can't control your temper. Old Russ is a sob sister, and I'm much more your type."

It was a good wild card; I thought of the disgusted look Russ gave me after I coldcocked Joe Dulange. "What do you want, *Ellis?*"

"Very well, *Dwight*, I'll tell you. There are four confessors still being held at City Jail. They've got no alibis for Betty Short's missing days, they weren't coherent when they were first questioned, and they are all violent, frothing-at-the-mouth lunatics. I want them reinterrogated, with what you might call 'appropriate props.' It's a muscle job, and Fritzie wanted Bill Koenig for it, but he's a bit too enamored of violence, so I picked you. So, *Dwight*, yes or no. Back to Warrants or Homicide shitwork until Russ Millard gets tired of you? Millard is a patient, forbearing man, *Dwight*. That might be a long time."

My royal flush collapsed. "Yes."

Loew beamed. "Go to the city jail now. The night jailer has released waivers for the four men. There's a drunk wagon in the nightwatch lot, keys under the mat. Drive the suspects to 1701 South Alameda, meet Fritzie. Welcome back to Warrants, *Dwight*."

I stood up. Loew took a pretzel from the bowl and nibbled it daintily; Fritzie drained his glass, his hands shaking.

• • •

The loonies were waiting for me in a holding tank, wearing jail denims, chained together and manacled at the ankles. The waivers the jailer had given me came with mug shots and rap sheets carbons attached; when the cell door was racked electronically, I matched pictures to faces.

Paul David Orchard was short and burly, with a flat nose spread across half his face and long, pomade-lacquered blond hair; Cecil Thomas Durkin was a fiftyish mulatto, bald, freckled, close to six and a half feet tall. Charles Michael Issler had enormous sunken brown eyes, and Loren (NMI) Bidwell was a frail old man, shaking from palsy, liver spots covering his skin. He looked so pathetic that I double-checked his sheet to make sure I had the right man; child molesting beefs running back to 1911 told me I did. "Out in the catwalk," I said. "Roll it up now."

The four shuffled out, scissor-walking sideways, their chains dragging the floor. I pointed them to a side exit adjoining the catwalk; the jailer opened the door from outside. The loony conga line scissored into the parking lot; the jailer held a bead on them while I found the drunk wagon and backed it up.

The jailer opened the wagon's back door; I checked the rear-view mirror and watched my cargo climb aboard. They were whispering among themselves, taking gulps of the crisp night air as they stumbled up and in. The jailer locked the door behind them and signaled me with his gun barrel; I took off.

1701 South Alameda was in the East LA Industrial District, about a mile and a half from the city jail. Five minutes later, I found it—a giant warehouse smack in the middle of a block of giant warehouses, the only one with its street facade illuminated: KOUNTY KING LUNCH MEAT—SERVING LOS ANGELES COUNTY WITH INSTITUTIONAL FOOD SINCE 1923. I tapped the horn as I parked; a door beneath the sign opened up, the light went off, Fritzie Vogel was standing there with his thumbs hooked in his belt.

I got out and unlocked the back door. The loonies stumbled into the street; Fritzie called, "This way, gentlemen." The four scissor-walked in the direction of the voice; a light went on in back of Fritzie. I secured the van and walked over.

Fritzie ushered the last loony in and greeted me in the doorway. "County kickbacks, boyo. The man who owns this place owes Sheriff Biscailuz, and he's got a plainclothes lieutenant who's got a doctor brother who owes me. You'll see what I'm talking about in a while."

I shut the door and bolted it; Fritzie led me past the scissor-walkers and down a hall reeking of meat. At the end, it opened into a huge room—sawdust-covered cement floors, row after row of rusted meathooks hanging from the ceiling. Sides of beef dangled from over half of them, in the open at room temperature while horseflies feasted. My stomach looped; then, at the rear, I saw four chairs stationed directly beneath four unused hooks and got the picture for real.

Fritzie was unlocking the loonies' manacles and cuffing their hands in front of them. I stood by and gauged reactions. Old Man Bidwell's palsy was going into overdrive, Durkin was humming to himself, Orchard sneered, his head cocked to one side, like his butch-waxed pompadour was weighing it down.

Only Charles Issler looked lucid enough to be concerned—he was fretting his hands and looking from Fritzie to me, his eyes constantly darting.

Fritzie took a roll of tape from his pocket and tossed it to me. "Tape the rap sheets to the wall next to the hooks. Alphabetically, straight across."

I did it, noticing a sheet-draped table wedged diagonally into a connecting doorway a few feet away. Fritzie led the prisoners over and made them stand on the chairs, then dangle their handcuff chains loosely over the meathooks. I skimmed the rap sheets, hoping for facts that would make me hate the four enough to get me through the night and back to Warrants.

Loren Bidwell was a three-time Atascadero loser, the falls for aggravated sexual assault on minors. Between prison jolts, he confessed to all the big sex crimes, and was even a major suspect in the Hickman child snuff case back in the '20s. Cecil Durkin was a hophead, a knife fighter and a jailhouse rape-o who played jazz drums with some good combos; he took two Quentin jolts for Arson and was caught masturbating at the scene of his last torch—the home of a bandleader who had allegedly stiffed him on payment for a nightclub gig. That fall cost him twelve years in stir; since his release he'd been working as a dishwasher, living at a Salvation Army domicile.

Charles Issler was a pimp and career confessor specializing in copping to hooker homicides. His three procuring beefs had netted him a year county jail time; his phony confessions two ninety-day observation stints at the Camarillo nut farm. Paul Orchard was a jack roller, a male prostitute, and a former San Bernardino County deputy sheriff. On top of his vice beefs, he had two convictions for grievous aggravated assault.

A little surge of hate juice entered me. It felt tenuous, like I was about to go into the ring against a guy I wasn't sure I could take. Fritzie said, "A charming quartet, huh, boyo?"

"Real choirboys."

Fritzie curled a come-hither finger at me; I walked over and faced the four suspects. My hate juice was holding as he said, "You all confessed to killing the Dahlia. We can't prove you did, so it's up to you to convince us. Bucky, you ask questions about the girlie's missing days. I'll listen in until I hear syphilitic lies."

I braced Bidwell first. His palsy spasms had the chair rocking underneath him; I reached up and grabbed the meat hook to hold him steady. "Tell me about Betty Short, pops. Why'd you kill her?"

The old man beseeched me with his eyes; I looked away.

Fritzie, perusing the rap sheets on the wall, picked up on the silence. "Don't be timid, boyo. That bird made little boys suck his hog."

My hand twitched and jerked the hook. "Come clean, pop. Why'd you snuff her?"

Bidwell answered in a breathless geezer's voice: "I didn't kill her, mister. I just wanted a ticket to the honor farm. Three hots and a cot's all I wanted. Please, mister."

The geez didn't look strong enough to *lift* a knife, let alone tie a woman down and carry the two halves of her stiff out to a car. I moved to Cecil Durkin.

"Tell me about it, Cecil."

The hepcat mocked me. "Tell you about it? You get that line from *Dick Tracy* or *Gangbusters*?"

Out of the corner of my eye I saw Fritzie watching, measuring me. "One more time, shitbird. Tell me about you and Betty Short."

Durkin giggled. "I fucked Betty Short and I fucked your mama! I'm your daddy!"

I one-two'd him in the solar plexus, hard little shots. Durkin's legs buckled, but he kept his feet on the chair. He gasped for breath, got a lungful and went back to bravado: "You think you clever, don't you? You the bad guy, your buddy the nice guy. You gonna hit me, he gonna rescue me. Don't you clowns know that bit went out with vaudeville?"

I massaged my right hand, still bone bruised from Lee Blanchard and Joe Dulange. "I'm the nice guy, Cecil. Keep that in mind."

It was a good line. Durkin fumbled for a comeback; I turned my attention to Charles Michael Issler.

He looked down and said, "I didn't kill Liz. I don't know why I do these things, and I apologize. So please don't let that man hurt me."

His manner was quietly sincere, but something about him put me off. I said, "Convince me."

"I . . . I can't. I just didn't."

I thought of Issler as a pimp, Betty as a part-time prostie, and wondered if there was a possible connection between them—then remembered that the hookers in the little black book questionings said she always worked freelance. I said, "Did you know Betty Short?"

"No."

"Did you know of her?"

"No."

"Why'd you confess to her murder?"

"She . . . she looked so sweet and pretty and I felt so bad when I saw her picture in the paper. I . . . I always confess to the pretty ones."

"Your rap sheet says you only cop to hooker snuffs. Why?"

"Well, I . . ."

"You hit your girls, Charlie? You get them gone on hop? You make them service your pals—"

I stopped, thinking of Kay and Bobby De Witt. Issler bobbed his head up and down, slowly at first, then harder and harder. Soon he was sobbing, "I do such bad things, nasty, nasty things. Nasty, nasty, nasty."

Fritzie walked over and stood beside me, brass knuckles coiled in both fists. He said, "This kid gloves routine is getting us nowhere," and kicked Issler's chair out from under him. The confessor-pimp screamed and flopped like an impaled fish; bones snapped as the cuffs caught the brunt of his weight. Fritzie said, "Watch, boyo."

Shouting, "Jack Roller!" "Nigger!" "Baby fucker!" he kicked the other three chairs to the floor. Now there were confessors dangling four abreast, shrieking, grabbing at one another with their legs, an octopus in county jail denim. The screams sounded like one voice—until Fritzie zeroed in on Charles Michael Issler.

He roundhoused the knuckle dusters into his midsection, left-right, left-right, left-right. Issler screamed and gurgled; Fritzie yelled, "Tell me about the Dahlia's missing days you syphilitic whoremonger!"

My legs felt like they were about to go. Issler screeched, "I . . . don't . . . know . . . anything." Fritzie shot him an uppercut to the crotch.

Tell me what you know!

"I knew you at Ad Vice!"

Fritzie winged rabbit punches. "Tell me what you know! Tell me what your girls told you, you syphilitic whoremonger!"

Issler retched; Fritzie moved in close and worked his body. I heard ribs cracking, then stared off to my left, to a burglar alarm lever on the wall by the connecting doorway. I stared and stared and stared; Fritizie ran into my field of vision and wheeled over the sheet-covered table I'd noticed before.

The loonies flopped on their hooks, moaning low. Fritzie got right up next to me, cackled in my face, then whipped off the sheet.

The table held a naked female corpse, cut in half at the waist—a pudgy girl coiffed and made up to look like Elizabeth Short. Fritzie grabbed Charlie Issler by the scruff of the neck, hissing, "For your cutting pleasure, may I present Jane Doe number forty-three. You're all going to slice her, and the best slicer buys the ticket!"

Issler shut his eyes and bit through his lower lip. Old Man Bidwell went purple, starting to foam at the mouth. I smelled loosed feces on Durkin and saw Orchard's wrists broken, twisted to right angles, bones and tendons exposed. Fritzie pulled out a pachuco toad stabber and popped the blade. "Show me how you did it, you filths. Show me what didn't get in the papers. Show me and I'll be nice to you and make alllll your hurt go away. Bucky, take off their cuffs."

My legs went. I stumbled into Fritzie, hurled him to the floor, ran for the alarm and pulled the lever. A code three response siren went off so good, so loud, so hard that it felt like its sound waves were what propelled me out of the warehouse and into the drunk wagon and all the way to Kay's door with no excuses and words of loyalty for Lee.

So were Kay Lake and I formally joined.

CHAPTER TWENTY-TWO

Tripping that alarm was the costliest act of my life.

Loew and Vogel succeeded in putting the hush on it. I was booted off Warrants and back into uniform—swingwatch foot patrol out of Central Station, my old home. Lieutenant Jastrow, the watch boss, was thick with the demon DA. I could tell he was checking out my every act—waiting for me to snitch or rabbit or somehow follow up on the big wrong move I had to make.

I did nothing about it. It was the word of a five-year officer versus a twenty-two-year man and the city's future District Attorney, backed by their hole card: the radio car officers who responded to the alarm were made the new Central Division Warrants team, a piece of serendipity guaranteed to keep them quiet and happy. Two consolations kept me from going crazy: Fritzie didn't kill anybody, and when I checked the city jail release records I learned that the four confessors had been treated for "car crash injuries" at Queen of Angels and shipped to different state ding farms for "observation." And my horror pushed me where I'd been too scared and stupid to go for a long, long time.

Kay.

That first night she was as much my grief catcher as my lover. I was afraid of noise and abrupt movement, so she undressed me and made me be still, murmuring, "And all that," every time I tried to talk about Fritzie or the Dahlia. She touched me so softly that it was hardly touching at all; I touched every whole and healthy part of her until I felt my own body cease to be fists and cop muscle. Then we roused each other slowly and made love, with Betty Short far away.

A week later I broke it off with Madeleine, the "neighbor girl" whose identity I had kept secret from Lee and Kay. I didn't offer a reason, and the rich gutter crawler aced me as I was about to hang up the phone. "Find somebody *safe*? You'll be back, you know. I look like her."

Her.

A month passed. Lee didn't return, the two dope traffickers were convicted and hanged for the De Witt–Chasco killings, my Fire and Ice ad continued to run in all four LA dailies. The Short case moved from headlines to back pages, tips fell off to almost zero, everyone but Russ Millard and Harry Sears went back to their regular assignments. Still assigned to *Her*, Russ and Harry kept putting in straight eights at the Bureau and in the field, spending evenings at the El Nido, going over the master file. When I got off duty at 9:00, I'd visit for a while on my way to see Kay, quietly amazed at how obsessed Mr. Homicide was becoming, his family neglected as he prowled paper until midnight. The man inspired confession; when I told him the story of Fritzie and the warehouse, his absolution was a fatherly embrace and the admonishing, "Take the Sergeant's Exam. In a year or so I'll go to Thad Green. He owes me one, and when Harry retires you'll be my partner."

It was a promise to build on, and it kept bringing me back to the file. With my days free and Kay at work, I had nothing to do, so I read it over and over. The "R," "S," and "T" folders were missing, which was an annoyance, but other than that it was perfection. My real woman had Betty Short pushed back across a Maginot Line into professional curiosity, and I kept reading, thinking and hypothesizing from the standpoint of becoming a good detective—the road I was on until I tripped that alarm. Sometimes I felt connections begging to be made, sometimes I cursed myself for not having ten percent more gray matter, sometimes the report carbons just made me think of Lee.

I continued with the woman he saved from a nightmare. Kay and I played house three and four times a week, the hours late now that I was working swingwatch. We made our tender kind of love and talked around the bad events of the past months, and as gentle and good as I was, I kept churning inside for an outside conclusion—Lee back, the Dahlia killer on a platter, one more Red Arrow shack with Madeleine or Ellis Loew and Fritzie Vogel nailed to a cross. What always came with it was a big, ugly replay of me hitting Cecil Durkin, followed by the question: how far would you have gone that night?

The beat was where it ate at me the most. I worked East 5th Street from Main to Stanford, skid row. Blood banks, liquor stores selling half pints and short dogs exclusively, fifty-cent-a-night flophouses and derelict missions. The unspoken rule down there was that foot beat hacks worked strong-arm. You broke up bottle gangs by whacking winos with your billy club; you hauled jigs out of the day labor joints when they insisted on getting hired. You rounded up drunks and ragpickers indiscriminately to meet the city quota, beating them down if they tried to run from the drunk wagon. It was attrition duty, and the only officers good at it were the transplanted Okie shitkickers hired in the manpower shortage during the war. I patrolled half-heartedly: little jabs with my stick, handing winos dimes and quarters to get them off the street and into the wine bars where I wouldn't have to roust them, low quotas on my drunk sweeps. I got a rep as the Central swingwatch "sob sister"; twice Johnny Vogel saw me passing out chump change and hooted uproariously. Lieutenant Jastrow gave me a Class D fitness report my first month back in uniform—a clerical aide told me he cited my "Reluctance to employ sufficient force with recalcitrant misdemeanants." Kay got a kick out of the line, but I saw a stack of bum paper building up so high that all Russ Millard's juice wouldn't be able to return me to the Bureau.

So I was back where I was before the fight and the bond issue, only further east and on foot. Rumors raged on my way up to Warrants; now speculation centered on my fall. One story had me shitcanned for beating up Lee, others had me infringing on East Valley Division's process-serving territory, punking out on a bout with the 77th Street rookie who won the '46 Golden Gloves, incurring Ellis Loew's wrath by leaking Dahlia info to a radio station opposed to his upcoming DA candidacy. Every rumor portrayed me as a backstabber, a Bolshevik, a coward and a fool; when my second month's fitness report ended with the line, "This officer's passive patrol behavior has earned him the enmity of every enforcement-minded policeman on his watch," I started thinking of handing out five-spots to the winos and beatings to every bluesuit who looked at me even slightly hinky.

Then *she* came back.

I never thought about her on the beat; when I studied the file, it was just detective drudge work, facts and theorizing on a common DOA. When my lovemaking with Kay got too involved in affection, she came to help, served her purpose and was banished as soon as we finished. It was when I was asleep and helpless that she lived.

It was always the same dream. I was at the warehouse with Fritz Vogel, beating Cecil Durkin to death. She watched, screaming that none of the drool cases killed her, promising to love me if I made Fritzie quit hitting Charlie Issler. I stopped, wanting the sex. Fritzie continued his carnage, and Betty wept for Charlie while I had her.

I always woke up grateful for daylight, especially when Kay was beside me.

On April 4, almost two and a half months after Lee's disappearance, Kay got a letter on official LAPD stationery:

4/3/47

Dear Miss Lake-

This is to inform you that Leland C. Blanchard has been formally dismissed from the Los Angeles Police Department on grounds of moral turpitude, effective 3/15/47. You were the beneficiary of his Los Angeles City Credit Union account, and since Mr. Blanchard remains out of touch, we feel it is only fair to send you the existing balance.

Best wishes,
Leonard V. Strock,
Sergeant,
Personnel Division

A check for $14.11 was included. It made me killing mad, and I attacked the master file so I wouldn't attack my new enemy— the bureaucracy that owned me.

CHAPTER TWENTY-THREE

Two days later the connection jumped up off the carbon and grabbed me by the balls.

It was my own FI report, filed on 1/17/47. Under "Marjorie Graham," I had written: "M.G. stated E. Short used nickname variations of 'Elizabeth' according to the company she was with."

Bingo.

I had heard Elizabeth Short called "Betty," "Beth," and once or twice "Betsy," but *only* Charles Michael Issler, a *pimp*, referred to her as "Liz." At the warehouse he had denied knowing her. I recalled that he didn't impress me as a killer, but that I still found him hinky. When I'd thought about the warehouse before, it was Durkin and the stiff that came on strong; now I replayed it strictly for facts:

Fritzie had beat Issler half to death, ignoring the other three loonies;

He had stressed side issues, shouting: "Tell me what you know about the Dahlia's missing days," "Tell me what *you* know," "Tell me what your girls told you."

Issler had answered back, "I knew you at Ad Vice."

I thought of Fritzie's hands shaking earlier that night; I remembered him shouting at Lorna Martilkova: "You whored with the Dahlia, didn't you, girlie? *Tell me where you were during her lost days.*" Then the finale hit: Fritzie and Johnny Vogel whispering on the ride out to the Valley.

"*I proved I'm not no nancy boy. Homos couldn't do what I did.*"

"*Be still, damn you!*"

I ran out to the hall, fed the pay phone a nickel and dialed Russ Millard's number at the Bureau.

"Central Homicide, Lieutenant Millard."

"Russ, it's Bucky."

"Something wrong, bright penny? You sound shaky."

"Russ, I think I've got something. I can't tell you now, but I need two favors."

"This is about Elizabeth?"

"Yes. Goddamnit, Russ—"

"Hush, and tell me."

"I need you to get me the Ad Vice file for Charles Michael Issler. He's got three pimping priors, so I know he'll have one."

"And?"

I dry swallowed. "I want you to check on Fritz Vogel's and John Vogel's whereabouts January tenth through fifteenth."

"Are you telling me—"

"I'm telling you maybe. I'm telling you maybe real strong."

There was a long silence, then: "Where are you?"

"The El Nido."

"Stay there. I'll call you back inside of half an hour."

I hung up and waited, thinking of a sweet package of glory and revenge. Seventeen minutes later the phone rang; I pounced on it. "Russ, what—"

"The file's missing. I checked the 'I's' myself. They were all put back unevenly, so my guess is that it was snatched recently. On the other, Fritzie was on duty at the Bureau straight through those days, racking up overtime on old cases, and Johnny was on vacation leave, where I don't know. Now, will you explain all this?"

I got an idea. "Not now. Meet me here tonight. *Late.* If I'm not here, wait for me."

"Bucky—"

"Later, padre."

• • •

I called in sick that afternoon; that night I committed two felony B & E's.

My first victim was working swingwatch; I called Personnel Division and impersonated a city payroll clerk to get his home address and phone number. The catching officer kicked loose; at dusk I parked across the street and eyeballed the apartment house that John Vogel called home.

It was a stucco four flat on Mentone near the LA–Culver City border, a salmon-pink structure flanked by identical buildings painted light green and tan. There was a pay phone at the corner; I used it to dial Bad Breath Johnny's number, an extra precaution to make sure the bastard wasn't in. Twenty rings went unanswered. I walked calmly over, found a bottom floor door with "Vogel" on the mail slot, worked a double-over hairpin into the keyhole and let myself in.

Inside, I held my breath, half expecting a killer dog to leap at me. I checked the luminous dial on my watch, decided ten minutes was tops and squinted for a light to turn on.

My eyes caught a floor lamp. I moved to it and pulled the cord, lighting up a tidy living room. There was a tidy bargain basement sofa with matching chairs, an imitation fireplace, cheesecake glossies of Rita Hayworth, Betty Grable and Ann Sheridan Scotch taped to the walls, what looked like a genuine captured Jap flag draped over the coffee table. The phone was on the floor by the sofa, with an address book next to it; I allotted half my time right there.

I checked every page. There was no Betty Short or Charles Issler, and none of the names listed were repeats from the master file or the names in Betty's "little black book." Five minutes down, five to go.

A kitchen, dinette and bedroom adjoined the living room. I turned off the lamp, moved in darkness to the half-open bedroom doorway and patted the inside wall for a light switch. Finding one, I flipped it on.

An unmade bed, four walls festooned with Jap flags and a big, scuffed chest of drawers were revealed. I opened the top drawer, saw three German Lugers, spare clips and a scattering of loose shells—and laughed at the taste of Axis Johnny. Then I opened the middle one, and a tingling was all over me.

Black leather harnesses, chains, whips, studded dog collars, Tijuana condoms that gave you a bludgeon-headed extra six inches. Smut books with pictures of naked women getting whipped by other women while they sucked harness-clad guys with big dicks. Close-up photos that captured fat, needle marks, chipped nail polish and dope-glazed eyes. No Betty Short, no Lorna Martilkova, no *Slave Girls from Hell* Egyptian backdrop or tie-in to Duke Wellington, but a parlay—whips to the coroner's "light lash marks"—that was enough to nail Johnny Vogel as Dahlia suspect number one.

I shut the drawers, flicked off the light, tingle walked into the living room and turned on the lamp, then reached for the address book. "Daddy & Mom's" number was GRanite-9401; if I got a no answer, B & E number two was a ten-minute drive away.

I dialed; Fritz Vogel's phone rang twenty-five times. I turned off the light and hauled ass.

Vogel Senior's small wood frame house was totally dark when I pulled up across from it. I sat behind the wheel remembering the layout from my previous visit, recalling two bedrooms off a long hallway, the kitchen, a rear service porch and a closed door across the hall from the bathroom. If Fritzie had a private den, that had to be it.

I took the driveway to the back of the house. The screen door to the service porch was open; I tiptoed past a washing machine to the barrier to the house proper. That door was solid wood, but feeling at the jamb I found it connected to the wall with a simple hook and eyelet. I shook the knob and felt plenty of give; if I could pop the little piece of metal, I was in.

I got down on my knees and patted the floor, stopping when my hand hit a skinny piece of metal. Pawing at it like a blind man, I realized I'd found an oil gauge dipstick. I smiled at my luck, stood up and popped the door open.

Thinking fifteen minutes tops, I moved through the kitchen, over to the hallway and down it, my hands in front of me to deflect unseen obstacles. A nightlight glowed inside the bathroom doorway—pointing me straight across to what I hoped was Fritzie's hideaway. I tried the knob—and the door opened.

The little room was pitch dark. I banged along the walls, hitting picture frames, feeling iceberg spooky until my leg grazed a tall wobbly object. It was about to topple when I snapped that it was a gooseneck lamp, reached for the top part and flipped the switch.

Light.

The pictures were photographs of Fritzie in uniform, in plainclothes, standing at attention with the rest of his 1925 Academy class. There was a desk positioned against the back wall, facing a window covered with a velvet curtain, a swivel chair and a filing cabinet.

I slid the top compartment open and fingered through manila folders stamped "Intelligence Rpt—Bunco Division," "Intelligence Rpt—Burglary Division," "Intelligence Rpt—Robbery Division"—all with the names of individuals typed on side tabs. Wanting some kind of common denominator, I checked the first sheets of the next three folders I came to—finding only one carbon page in each of them.

But those single pieces of paper were enough.

They were financial accountings, lists of bank balances and other assets, tallies made on known criminals that the Department couldn't legally touch. The routing designations at the top of each sheet spelled it out plain—it was the LAPD shooting the feds hot dope so that they could initiate tax evasion investigations. Handwritten notes—phone numbers, names and addresses—filled the margins, and I recognized Fritzie's Parker penmanship hand.

My breath came in short cold bursts as I thought: shakedown. He's either putting the screws to the hoods based on info in the rest of the files or selling them tip-offs on impending fed rousts.

Extortion, first degree.

Theft and harboring of official LAPD documents.

Impeding the progress of federal investigations.

But no Johnny Vogel, Charlie Issler or Betty Short.

I tore through another fourteen folders, finding the same scrawled-over financial reports in all of them. I memorized the side tab names, then moved to the bottom compartment. I saw "Known Offender Rpt—Administrative Vice Division" on the first file inside it—and knew I'd gotten the whole ball of wax.

Page one detailed the arrests, MO and confessing career of Charles Michael Issler, white male, born in Joplin, Missouri, in 1911; page two listed his "Known Associates." A June 1946 "whore book" check by his probation officer yielded six girls' names, followed by phone numbers and the arrest dates and dispositions of their hooking convictions. There were an additional four female names below the heading "?—No Prostitution Record." The third name was "Liz Short—Transient?"

I turned to page three and read down the column headed "KAs, cont"; one name harpooned me. "Sally Stinson" was in Betty Short's little black book, and none of the four questioning teams had been able to locate her. In brackets beside her name, some Ad Vice dick had penciled in, "Works out of Biltmore bar—conventioneer johns." Doodles in Fritzie's ink color surrounded the entry.

I forced myself to think like a detective, not a revenge-happy kid. The extortion stuff aside, it was certain that Charlie Issler knew Betty Short. Betty knew Sally Stinson, who hooked out of the Biltmore. Fritz Vogel didn't want anybody to know it. He probably arranged the warehouse stunt to find out how much

Sally and/or his other girls had told Issler about Betty and the men she was recently with.

"I proved I'm not no nancy boy. Homos couldn't do what I did. *I'm not cherry no more*, so don't say nancy boy."

I put the folders back in order, closed the cabinet, hit the light and relatched the backdoor before walking out the front like I owned the place, wondering briefly if there was any connection between Sally Stinson and the missing "S's" in the master file. Treading air to my car, I knew it couldn't be— Fritzie didn't know that the El Nido work room existed. Then another thought took over: if Issler had blabbed about "Liz" and her tricks I would have overheard. Fritzie was confident he could keep me quiet. It was an underestimation that I was going to bleed him for.

·   ·   ·

Russ Millard was waiting for me with two words: "Report, Officer."

I told him the whole story in detail. When I finished, he saluted Elizabeth Short on the wall, said, "We're making progress, dear," and formally stuck out his hand.

We shook, sort of like father and son after the big game. "What next, padre?"

"Next you go back to duty like none of this happened. Harry and I will brace Issler at the nut farm, and I'll assign some men to look for Sally Stinson on the QT."

I swallowed. "And Fritzie?"

"I'll have to think about it."

"I want him nailed."

"I know you do. But you keep one thing in mind. The men that he extorted are criminals who would never testify against him in court, and if he gets wind of this and destroys the carbons, we wouldn't even be able to get him for an inter-departmental offense. *All* of this is going to require corroboration, so for now it's just us. And *you* had better settle down and control your temper until it's over."

I said, "I want in on the collar.'

Russ nodded. "I wouldn't have it any other way." He tipped his hat to Elizabeth on the way out the door.

·   ·   ·

I went back to swingwatch and played sob sister; Russ put men out to look for Sally Stinson. A day later, he called me at home with one dose of bad news, one of good:

Charles Issler had found a lawyer to file him a writ of

habeaus corpus; he had been released from the Mira Loma ding farm three weeks before. His LA apartment had been cleaned out; he couldn't be found. That was a kick in the balls, but the confirmation on the Vogel extortion front made up for it.

Harry Sears checked Fritzie's felony arrest records—from Bunco in 1934 up through his current position in Central Detectives. At one time or another Vogel had arrested every single man on the LAPD-FBI financial carbons. And the feds did not indict a single one of them.

I rotated off-duty the next day, and spent it with the master file, thinking *corroboration*. Russ called to say that he hadn't got any leads on Issler, that it looked like he'd blown town. Harry was keeping Johnny Vogel under a loose surveillance on and off duty; a buddy working West Hollywood Sheriff's Vice had kicked loose with some KA addresses—friends of Sally Stinson. Russ told me a half dozen times to take it easy and not jump the gun. He knew damn well I already had Fritzie in Folsom and Johnny in the Little Green Room.

I was scheduled to go back on duty Thursday, and got up early in order to spend a long morning with the master file. I was making coffee when the phone rang.

I picked it up. "Yes?"

"It's Russ. We've got Sally Stinson. Meet me at 1546 North Havenhurst in half an hour."

"Rolling."

*   *   *

The address was a Spanish castle apartment house: white-washed cement shaped into ornamental turrets, balconies topped by sun-weathered awnings. Walkways led up to the individual doors; Russ was standing by the one on the far right.

I left the car in a red zone and trotted over. A man in a disheveled suit and paper party hat strutted down the walkway, a slap-happy grin on his face. He slurred, "Next shift, huh? Twosies on onesies, ooh la la!"

Russ led me up the steps. I rapped on the door; a not-young blonde with mussed hair and smeared makeup threw it open, spat, "What did you forget this time?," then, "Oh, shit."

Russ held out his badge. "LAPD. Are you Sally Stinson?"

"No, I'm Eleanor Roosevelt. Listen, I put out for the sheriff's more ways than one lately, so I'm tapped in the cash department. You want the other?"

I started to elbow my way inside; Russ grabbed my arm.

"Miss Stinson, it's about Liz Short and Charlie Issler, and it's here or the women's jail."

Sally Stinson clutched the front of her robe and pressed it to her bodice. She said, "Listen, I told the other guy," then stopped and hugged herself. She looked like the floozy victim confronting the monster in old horror movies; I knew exactly who *her* monster was. "We're not with him. We just want to talk to you about Betty Short."

Sally appraised us. "And he ain't gonna know?"

Russ flashed his father-confessor smile and lied. "No, this is strictly confidential."

Sally stood aside. Russ and I entered an archetypal trick pad front room—cheap furniture, bare walls, suitcases lined up in one corner for a quick getaway. Sally bolted the door. I said, "Who's this guy we're talking about, Miss Stinson?"

Russ straightened the knot in his necktie; I clammed up. Sally jabbed a finger at the couch. "Let's do this quicksville. Rehashing old grief is against my religion."

I sat down; stuffing and the point of a spring popped out a few inches from my knee. Russ settled into a chair and got out his notebook; Sally took a perch on top of the suitcases, back to the wall and eyes on the door like a seasoned getaway artist. She started with the most often heard Short case intro line: "I don't know who killed her."

Russ said, "Fair enough, but let's take it from the beginning. When did you meet Liz Short?"

Sally scratched a hickey on her cleavage. "Last summer. June, maybe."

"Where?"

"At the bar at the Yorkshire House Grill downtown. I was half in the bag, waiting for my . . . waiting for Charlie I. Liz was putting the moves on this rich-looking old hairbag, coming on too strong. She scared him off. Then we started talking and Charlie showed up."

I said, "Then what?"

"Then we all discovered we had a lot in common. Liz said she was broke, Charlie says 'you wanta make a quick double-saw,' Liz says 'yeah,' Charlie sends us over for a twosie at the textile salesman's convention at the Mayflower."

"And?"

"And Liz was gooood. You want details, wait till I publish my memoirs. But I'll tell you this. I'm pretty good at faking like I'm loving it, but Liz was great. She had this bee in her bonnet about keeping her stockings on, but she was like a virtuoso. Academy Award stuff."

I thought of the stag film—and the strange gash on Betty's left thigh. "Do you know if Liz ever appeared in any pornographic movies?"

Sally shook her head. "No, but if she did she'd be gooood."

"You know a man named Walter "Duke" Wellington?"

"No."

"Linda Martin?"

"Ixnay."

Russ took over. "Did you turn any other tricks with Liz?"

Sally said, "Four or five, last summer. Hotel jobs. All conventioneers."

"Remember any names? Organizations? Descriptions?"

Sally laughed and scratched her cleavage. "Mr. Policeman, my first commandment is keep your eyes shut and try to forget. I'm good at it."

"Were any of the hotel jobs at the Biltmore?"

"No. The Mayflower, the Hacienda House. Maybe the Rexford."

"Did any of the men react strangely to Liz? Get rough with her?"

Sally hooted. "Mostly they were just happy 'cause she faked it so good."

Itchy to get at Vogel, I changed the subject. "Tell me about you and Charlie Issler. Did you know he confessed to the Dahlia killing?"

Sally said, "Not at first I didn't. Then . . . well, anyway, I wasn't surprised when I did hear. Charlie's got this what you might wanta call compulsion to confess. Like if a prostie gets killed and it makes the papers, bye-bye Charlie and get out the iodine when he comes back, 'cause he always makes sure the rubber hose boys work him over."

Russ said, "Why do you think he does it?"

"How's a guilty conscience sound?"

I said, "How's this sound? You tell us where you were January tenth through fifteenth, and you tell us about this guy we all don't like."

"Sounds like I've really got a choice."

"You do. Talk to us here or to a butch matron downtown."

Russ tugged at his tie—hard. "Do you remember where you were on those dates, Miss Stinson?"

Sally fished cigarettes and matches from her pockets and lit up. "Everybody who knew Liz remembers where they were then. You know, like when FDR died. You keep wishing you could go back, you know, and change it."

I started to apologize for my tactics; Russ beat me to it. "My partner didn't mean to get nasty, Miss Stinson. This is a grudge thing for him."

It was the perfect come-on. Sally Stinson tossed her cigarette on the floor, ground it out with her bare feet, then patted the suitcases. "I'm adios as soon as you walk out the door. I'll tell you, but I won't tell no DAs, no Grand Juries, no other cops. I mean it. You walk out that door and it's bye-bye Sally."

Russ said, "It's a deal." Sally's color rose; that and the anger in her eyes knocked a good ten years off her. "On Friday the tenth I got a call at this hotel where I was staying. A guy said he's a friend of Charlie and he wants to buy me for this young guy he knows who's cherry. Two-day session at the Biltmore, a C-note and a half. I say I ain't seen Charlie in a while, how'd you get my number? The guy says 'Never mind, meet me and the kid outside the Biltmore tomorrow at noon.'

"I'm broke, so I say okay, and I meet the two guys. Big fat peas in a pod packing hardware, I know it's a father and son cop act. Money changes hands, sonny's got halitosis but I've seen worse. He tells me daddy's name and I get a little scared, but daddy amscrays and the kid's so lame I know I can take care of him."

Sally lit another cigarette. Russ passed me Personnel photos of the Vogel boys; I handed them to her. She said, "On the button," burned their faces off with the tip of her Chesterfield, then got on with it.

"Vogel had a suite set up. Sonny and I tricked, and he tried to get me to play with these creepy sex gadgets he brought. I said, 'Ixnay, ixnay, ixnay.' He said he'll give me an extra twenty if he can whip me soft for fun. I said, 'When hell freezes.' Then he—"

I broke off the story. "Did he talk about stag films? Lezzie stuff?"

Sally snorted. "He talked about baseball and his peter. He called it the Big Schnitzel, and you know what? It wasn't."

Russ said, "Go on, Miss Stinson."

"Well, we screw all afternoon, and I listen to the kid prattle about the Brooklyn Dodgers and the Big Schnitzel until I am blue in the face. Then I say, 'Let's get dinner and some fresh air,' and we go down to the lobby.

"And there's Liz, sitting all by herself. She tells me she needs money, and since I can tell sonny likes her, I set up a trick within a trick. We go back up to the suite, and I take a breather while they go at it in the bedroom. Liz skips out about twelve-thirty, whispers 'Little Schnitzel' to me, and I never saw her again until I saw her picture all over the papers."

I looked at Russ. He mouthed the word, "Dulange"; I nodded,

picturing Betty Short on the loose until she met Frenchman Joe on the morning of the twelfth. The missing Dahlia days were coming together.

Russ said, "And you and John Vogel went back to your assignation then?"

Sally tossed the Personnel photos on the floor. "Yes."

"Did he talk to you about Liz Short?"

"He said she loved the Big Schnitzel."

"Did he say that they'd made plans to meet again?"

"No."

"Did he mention his father and Liz in any context at all?"

"No."

"What did he say about Liz?"

Sally hugged herself. "He said she liked to play his kind of games. I said, 'What kind of games?' Sonny said, 'Master and Slave' and 'Cop and Whore.'"

I said, "Finish it up. Please."

Sally eyed the door. "Two days after Liz got in all the papers, Fritz Vogel came by my hotel and told me sonny said he'd tricked with her. He told me he'd got my name from some police file, and he questioned me about my . . . procurors. I mentioned Charlie I, and Vogel remembered him from when he worked this hotshot Vice detail. Then he got spooked, 'cause he remembered Charlie had this confessing problem. He called some partner of his on my phone and told him to yank some Vice file of Charlie's, then he made another call and went crazy, 'cause whoever he talked to told him Charlie was already in custody, that he'd already confessed to Liz.

"He beat me up then. He asked me all these questions, like whether Liz would mention tricking with a cop's son to Charlie. I told him Charlie and Liz were just acquaintances, that he'd just sent her out a few times, months and months ago, but he kept hitting me anyway, and he told me he'd kill me if I told the police about his son and the Dahlia."

I got up to go; Russ sat still. "Miss Stinson, you said that when John Vogel told you his father's name you got scared. Why?"

Sally whispered, "A story I heard." Suddenly she looked beyond used-up—ancient.

"What sort of story?"

Sally's whisper cracked. "How he got kicked off that hotshot Vice job."

I remembered Bill Koenig's rendition—that Fritzie caught syphilis from hookers when he worked Ad Vice, and was canned to take the mercury cure. "He caught a bad dose. Right?"

Sally dredged up a clear voice: "I heard he got the syph and went crazy. He thought a colored girl gave it to him, so he shook down this house in Watts and made all the girls do him before he took the cure. He made them rub his thing in their eyes, and two of the girls went blind."

My legs were weaker than they were the night at the warehouse. Russ said, "Thank you, Sally."

I said, "Let's go get Johnny."

•　•　•

We took my car downtown. Johnny had been working a daywatch foot beat with overtime on swing, so at 11:00 A.M. I knew there was a good chance of snagging him alone.

I drove slowly, looking for his familiar blue serge figure. Russ had a syringe and Pentothal ampule he'd kept from the Red Manley interrogations out on the dashboard; even he knew this was a muscle job. We were cruising the alley in back of the Jesus Saves Mission when I spotted him—solo rousting a pair of piss bums scrounging in a trash can.

I got out of the car and yelled, "Hey, Johnny!" Vogel Junior shook a finger at the winos and sidled over, thumbs in his Sam Browne belt.

He said, "What you doin' in civvies, Bleichert?" and I hooked him to the gut. He bent over double, and I grabbed his head and banged it into the roof of the car. Johnny slumped, his lights dimming. I held him; Russ rolled up his left sleeve and jacked the silly syrup into the vein at the crook of his elbow.

Now he was out cold. I took the .38 from his holster, tossed it on the front seat and stuffed Johnny into the back. I got in with him; Russ took the wheel. We peeled rubber down the alley, the piss bums waving their short dogs at us.

The ride to the El Nido took half an hour. Johnny giggled in his dope slumber, almost coming awake a couple of times; Russ drove silently. When we got to the hotel, Russ checked the lobby, found it empty and gave me the high sign from the door. I slung Johnny over my shoulder and hauled him up to room 204—the hardest minute's work of my life.

The trip upstairs half roused him; his eyes fluttered as I dumped him into a chair and cuffed his left wrist to a heating pipe. Russ said, "The Pentothal's good for another few hours. No way he can lie." I soaked a bath towel in the sink and swathed Johnny's face with it. He coughed, and I pulled the towel away.

Johnny giggled. I said, "Elizabeth Short," and pointed to the glossies on the wall. Johnny, rubber-faced, slurred, "What about her?" I gave him another dose of the towel, a cobweb-clearing bracer. Johnny sputtered; I let the wad of cold terrycloth drop into his lap. "How about *Liz* Short? You remember her?"

Johnny laughed; Russ motioned for me to sit beside him on the bed rail. "There's a method to this. Let me ask the questions. You just hold on to your temper."

I nodded. Johnny had the two of us in focus now, but his eyes were pinned and his features were slack and goofy. Russ said, "What's your name, son?"

Johnny said, "You know me, loot," the slur on its way out.

"Tell me anyway."

"Vogel, John Charles."

"When were you born?"

"May 6, 1922."

"What's sixteen plus fifty-six?"

Johnny thought for a moment, said, "Seventy-two," then fixed on me. "Why'd you hit me, Bleichert? I never did you no dirt."

Fat Boy seemed genuinely befuddled. I kept it zipped; Russ said, "What's your father's name, son?"

"You know him, loot. Oh . . . Friedrich Vogel. Fritzie for short.

"Short like in Liz Short?"

"Uh sure . . . like Liz, Betty, Beth, Dahlia . . . lots of monickers."

"Think about this January, Johnny. Your dad wanted you to lose your cherry, right?"

"Uh . . . yeah."

"He bought you a woman for two days, right?"

"Not a woman. Not a *real* one. A hooer. A hoooooer." The long syllable turned into a laugh; Johnny tried to clap his hands. One hand hit his chest; the other jerked at the end of its cuffed tether. He said, "This ain't right. I'll tell Daddy."

Russ answered him calmly: "It's only for a little while. You had the prostitute at the Biltmore, right?"

"Right. Daddy got a rate because he knew the house dick."

"And you met Liz Short at the Biltmore, too. Right?"

Spastic movements hit Johnny's face—eye tics, lip twitches, veins popping on his forehead. He reminded me of a knocked-down fighter trying to haul himself up off the canvas. "Uh . . . that's right."

"Who introduced you?"

"What's her name . . . The hooer."

"And what did you and Liz do then, Johnny? Tell me about it."

"We . . . divvied on ten scoots for three hours and played games. I gave her the Big Schnitz. We played 'Horse and Rider,' and I liked Liz, so I just whipped her soft. She was nicer than the blondie hooer. She kept her stockings on, 'cause she said she had this birthmark nobody could look at. She liked the Schnitz, and she let me kiss her without the Listerine like the blondie made me gargle."

I thought about Betty's thigh gouge and held my breath. Russ said, "Johnny, did you kill Liz?"

Fat Boy jerked in his chair. "No! No no no no no no! No!"

"Ssssh. Easy, son, easy. When did Liz leave you?"

"I didn't slice her!"

"We believe you, son. Now when did Liz leave you?"

"Late. Late Saturday. Maybe twelve, maybe one."

"You mean early Sunday morning?"

"Yeah."

"Did she say where she was going?"

"No."

"Did she mention any men's names? Boyfriends? Men she was going to see?"

"Uh . . . some flyboy she was married to."

"That's all?"

"Yeah."

"Did you see her again?"

"No."

"Did your father know Liz at all?"

"No."

"Did he force the house detective to change the name on the registration book after Liz's body was found?"

"Uh . . . yes."

"Do you know who killed Liz Short?"

"No! No!"

Johnny was starting to sweat. I was too—anxious for facts to nail him with now that it looked like he and the Dahlia were just a one-night stand. I said, "You told your father about Liz when she made the papers, is that right?"

"Uh . . . yes."

"And *he* told *you* about a guy named Charlie Issler? A guy who used to pimp Liz Short?"

"Yes."

"And he told you Issler was in custody as a confessor?"

"Uh . . . yes."

"Now you tell me what he said he was going to do about that, shitbird. You tell me damn good and slow."

Fat Boy's cut-rate heart rose to the challenge. "Daddy tried to get Ellis Jewboy to cut Issler loose, but he wouldn't. Daddy knew this morgue attendant who owed him, and he got this DOA cooze and talked Jewboy into this idea. Daddy wanted Uncle Bill for it, but Jewboy said no, take you. Daddy said you'd do it 'cause without Blanchard to tell you what to do you were jelly. Daddy said you were a sob sister, weak sister, buck tooth . . ."

Johnny started laughing hysterically, shaking his head, spraying sweat, rattling his cuffed wrist like a zoo animal with a new plaything. Russ stepped in front of me. "I'll make him sign a statement. You take a half hour or so to calm down. I'll feed him coffee, then when you get back we'll figure out what's next."

I walked out to the fire escape, sat down and dangled my legs over the edge. I watched cars head up Wilcox to Hollywood and got it all down, the cost to myself, the whole enchilada. Then I played license plate blackjack, southbound versus northbound, out-of-state cars as wild cards. Southbound was me, the house; northbound was Lee and Kay. Southbound stood on a chicken-shit seventeen; northbound got an ace and a queen for pure blackjack. Dedicating the enchilada to the three of us, I went back to the room.

Johnny Vogel was signing Russ's statement, flushed and sweaty, with a bad case of the shakes. I read the confession over his shoulder: it laid out the Biltmore, Betty, and Fritzie's beating of Sally Stinson succinctly, to the tune of four misde-meanors and two felonies.

Russ said, "I want to sit on this for now, and I want to talk to a legal officer."

I said, "No, padre," and turned to Johnny.

"You're under arrest for suborning prostitution, withholding evidence, obstruction of justice and accesory to first-degree assault and battery."

Johnny blurted, "Daddy" and looked at Russ. Russ looked at me—and held out the statement. I put it in my pocket and cuffed Junior's wrists behind his back while he sobbed quietly.

The padre sighed. "It's the shithouse until you retire."

"I know."

"You'll never get back to the Bureau."

"I've already got a taste for shit, padre. I don't think it'll be so bad."

* * *

I led Johnny down to my car and drove him the four blocks to Hollywood Station. Reporters and camera jockeys were lounging on the front steps; they went nuts when they saw the plainclothesman with the uniformed cop in bracelets. Flashbulbs popped, newshounds recognized me and shouted my name, I yelled back, "No comment." Inside, bluesuits goggle-eyed the sight. I shoved Johnny to the front desk and whispered in his ear: "Tell your daddy I know about his extortion deal with the fed reports, and about the syph and the whorehouse in Watts. Tell him I'm going to the papers with it tomorrow."

Johnny went back to his quiet sobbing. A uniformed lieutenant came over and blurted, "What on God's earth is this here?"

A flashbulb went off in my eyes; there was Bevo Means with his notepad at the ready. I said, "I'm Officer Dwight Bleichert and this is Officer John Charles Vogel." Handing the statement to the lieutenant, I winked. "Book him."

* * *

I dawdled over a big steak lunch, then drove downtown to Central Station and my regular tour of duty. Heading into the locker room, I heard the intercom bark: "Officer Bleichert, go to the watch commander's office immediately."

I reversed directions and knocked on Lieutenant Jastrow's door. He called out, "It's open." I walked in and saluted like an idealistic rookie. Jastrow stood up, ignored the salute and adjusted his horn-rims like he was seeing me for the first time.

"You're on two weeks vacation leave as of now, Bleichert. When you return to duty, report to Chief Green. He'll assign you to another division."

Wanting to milk the moment, I asked, "Why?"

"Fritz Vogel just blew his brains out. That's why."

My farewell salute was twice as crisp as my first one; Jastrow ignored it again. I walked across the hall thinking of the two blind whores, wondering if they'd find out or care. The muster room was crammed with blues waiting for roll call—a last obstacle before the parking lot and home. I took it slow, standing GI straight, meeting the eyes that sought mine, making them look down. The hisses of "Traitor" and "Bolshevik" all came when my back was turned. I was almost out the door when I heard applause and turned to see Russ Millard and Thad Green clapping good-bye.

213

CHAPTER TWENTY-FOUR

Exiled to the shithouse and proud of it; two weeks to kill before I began serving my sentence at some putrid LAPD outpost. The Vogel arrest-suicide whitewashed as interdepartmental offenses and a father's shame over the ignominy. I closed out my glory days the only way that seemed decent—I chased the gone man.

I started at the LA end of his vanishing act.

I got nothing from repeated readings of Lee's arrest scrapbook; I questioned the lezzies at La Verne's Hideaway, asking whether Mr. Fire showed up to abuse them a second time—and got no's and jeers. The padre sneaked me a carbon of the complete Blanchard felony arrest file—it told me nothing. Kay, content in our monogamy, told me I was worse than a fool for what I was doing—and I knew it scared her.

Dredging up the Issler/Stinson/Vogel connection had convinced me of one thing—that I was a detective. Thinking like one as far as Lee was concerned was another matter, but I forced myself to do it. The ruthlessness I had always seen—and secretly admired—in him came across even deeper, making me care for him even more unequivocally. As did the facts I always came back to:

Lee disappeared when the Dahlia, Benzedrine and Bobby De Witt's imminent parole converged on him;

He was last seen in Tijuana at a time when De Witt was heading there and the Short case was centered on the U.S.-Mexico border;

De Witt and his dope partner Felix Chasco were murdered then, and even though two Mexican nationals were nailed for the job, it could have been a railroad—the Rurales wiping an unwanted homicide off their books;

Conclusion: Lee Blanchard could have murdered De Witt and Chasco, his motive a desire to protect himself from revenge attempts and Kay from lounge lizard Bobby's possible abuse. Conclusion within that conclusion: I didn't care.

My next step was to study the transcript of De Witt's trial. At the Hall of Records, more facts sunk in:

Lee named the informants who gave him the dope on De Witt as the Boulevard-Citizens "brains," then said that they left town to avoid reprisals from Lizard's friends. My follow-up call to R&I was unsettling—the snitches had no records at all. De Witt asserted a police frame because of his prior dope arrests, and the prosecution based its case on the marked money from the robbery found at De Witt's house and the fact that he had no alibi for the time of the heist. Of the four-man gang, two were killed at the scene of the crime, De Witt was captured and the fourth man remained at large. De Witt claimed not to know who he was—even though stooling might have gotten him a sentence reduction.

Conclusion: maybe it *was* an LAPD frame, maybe Lee *was* in on it, maybe he initiated it to curry favor with Benny Siegel, whose money was clouted by the real heisters, and who Lee was terrified of for good reason—he had stiffed the Bug Man on his fight contract. Lee then met Kay at De Witt's trial, fell in love with her in his chaste-guilty way and learned to hate Bobby for real. Conclusion within that conclusion: Kay couldn't have known. De Witt was scum who got what he deserved.

And the final conclusion: I had to hear the man confirm or deny himself.

Four days into my "vacation," I took off for Mexico. In Tijuana, I passed out pesos and American dimes and showed snapshots of Lee, holding quarters back to barter for "información importante." I acquired an entourage, no leads and the certainty that I would be trampled if I kept showing coin. From then on, I stuck to the traditional gringo cop–Mex cop one-dollar handout confidential exchange.

215

The TJ cops were black-shirted vultures who spoke only broken English—but they understood the international language very well. I stopped a score of individual "patrolmen" on the street, flashed my shield and pictures, pressed dollar bills into their hands and asked questions in the best English-Spanish I could muster. The singles quickly snapped up, I got headshakes, bilingual bullshit broadsides and a strange series of tales that rang true.

One had "el blanco explosivo" weeping at a stag film smoker held at the Chicago Club in late January; another featured a big blond guy beating the shit out of three jack rollers, then buying off the cops with double-saws peeled from a large roll. The capper was Lee donating 200 scoots to a leper ministry priest he met in a bar, buying drinks for the house, then driving to Ensenada. That bit of dope earned a five spot and a demand for an explanation. The cop said, "The priest my brother. He ordain himself. Vaya con Dios. Keep your money in your pocket."

I took the coast road eighty miles south to Ensenada, wondering where Lee got that kind of money to throw around. The drive was pleasant—scrub-lined bluffs giving way to the ocean on my right, hills and valleys covered with dense foliage to the left of me. Car traffic was scarce, with a steady trickle of pedestrians walking north: whole families lugging suitcases, looking scared and happy at the same time, like they didn't know what their dash across the border would bring them, but it had to be better than sucking Mexican dirt and tourist chump change.

Approaching Ensenada at twilight, the trickle became a migration march. A single line of people hugged the northbound roadside, belongings wrapped in blankets and slung over their shoulders. Every fifth or sixth marcher carried a torch or a lantern, and all the small children were strapped papoose-style onto their mothers' backs. Coming over the last hill outside the city limits, I saw Ensenada, a smear of neon below me, torchlights punctuating the darkness until the overall fluorescence swallowed them.

I drove down into it, quickly sizing up the burg as a sea breeze version of TJ catering to a higher class of turista. The gringos were well behaved, there were no child beggars on the streets and no barkers in front of the profusion of juice joints. The wetback line originated out in the scrubland, and only cut through Ensenada to reach the coast road—and to pay tribute to the Rurales for letting them through.

It was the most blatant shakedown I had ever seen. Rurales

216

in brownshirts, jodhpurs and jackboots were walking from peasant to peasant, taking money and attaching tags to their shoulders with staple guns; plainsclothes cops sold parcels of beef jerky and dried fruit, putting the coins they received into changemakers strapped next to their sidearms. Other Rurales were stationed one man to a block to check the tags; when I turned off the main drag onto an obvious red light street, I glimpsed two brownshirts rendering a man senseless with the butts of their weapons: sawed-off pump shotguns.

I decided that it would be wise to check in with the law before going out to question the Ensenada citizenry. Also, Lee had been spotted talking to a group of Rurales up near the border shortly after leaving LA, and it might be possible to shake the locals for a line on him.

I followed a caravan of '30s-vintage prowl cars down the red light block and across to the street paralleling the beach—and there was the station. It was a converted church: barred windows, the word POLICÍA painted in black over religious scenes carved into the white adobe facade. A searchlight was stationed on the lawn; when I got out of the car, badge out, American grin on, it was shined right at me.

I walked into it, eyes shielded, face smarting from the heat blast. A man cackled, "Yanqui copper, J. Edgar, Texas Rangers." His hand was out as I passed him. I pressed a dollar bill into it and entered the station.

The interior was even more churchlike: velvet wall hangings depicting Jesus and his adventures decorated the entrance hall; the benches filled with lounging brownshirts looked like pews. The front desk was a big block of dark wood, Jesus on the cross carved into it—most likely a retired altar. The fat Rurale standing sentry there licked his lips when he saw me coming—he reminded me of a child molester who would never retire.

I had my obligatory onesky out, but held back. "Los Angeles Police to see the chief."

The brownshirt rubbed his thumbs and forefingers together, then pointed to my badge holder. I handed it over along with the dollar; he led me down a Jesus-frescoed hallway to a door marked CAPITÁN. I stood there while he went in and talked in rapid-fire Spanish; when he exited, I got a heel click and a belated salute.

"Officer Bleichert, come in please."

The non-accented words surprised me; I walked in to answer them. A tall Mexican man in a gray suit was standing there with his hand out—for a shake, not a dollar bill.

We shook. The man sat down behind a big desk and tapped a plate reading CAPITÁN VASQUEZ. "How can I help you, Officer?"

I grabbed my badge holder off the desk and put a picture of Lee down in its place. "That man is a Los Angeles police officer. He's been missing since late January, and when he was last seen he was heading here."

Vasquez examined the snapshot. The corners of his mouth twitched; he immediately tried to cover up the response by turning it into a negative head shake. "No, I haven't seen this man. I will put out a bulletin to my officers and have them inquire in the American community here."

I answered the lie. "He's a hard man to miss, Captain. Blond, six feet, built like a brick shithouse."

"Ensenada attracts rough trade, Officer. That is why the police contingent here is so well armed and vigilant. Will you be staying awhile?"

"At least overnight. Maybe your men missed him, and I can get some leads."

Vasquez smiled. "I doubt that. Are you alone?"

"I have two partners waiting for me in Tijuana."

"And what division are you assigned to?"

I lied big. "Metropolitan."

"You are very young for such prestigious duty."

I picked up the photo. "Nepotism, Captain. My dad's a deputy chief and my brother's with the consulate in Mexico City. Good night."

"And good luck, Bleichert."

* * *

I rented a room at a hotel within walking distance of the nightclub/red light strip. For two dollars I got a ground-floor flop with an ocean view, a bed with a pancake-thin mattress, a sink and a key to the community john outside. I dumped my grip on the dresser, and as a precaution on the way out, yanked two hairs from my head and spit-glued them across the door-doorjamb juncture. If the fascisti prowled the pad, I would know.

I walked to the heart of the neon smear.

The streets were filled with men in uniform: brownshirts, U.S. marines and sailors. There were no Mex nationals to be seen, and everyone was quite orderly—even the knots of jarheads weaving drunk. I decided that it was the walking Rurale arsenal that kept things pacified. Most of the brownshirts were scrawny bantamweights, but they were packing

218

firepower grande: sawed-offs, tommmys, .45 automatics, brass knucks dangling from their cartridge belts.

Fluorescent beacons pulsated at me: Flame Klub, Arturo's Oven, Club Boxeo, Falcon's Lair, Chico's Klub Imperial. "Boxeo" meant "boxing" in Spanish—so I made that dump my first stop.

Expecting darkness, I walked into a garishly lit room crowded with sailors. Mexican girls danced half naked on top of a long bar, dollar bills tucked into their G-strings. Canned marimba music and catcalls made the joint a deafening pocket of noise; I stood on my tiptoes looking for someone with the air of proprietor. At the back I saw an alcove papered with fight publicity stills. It drew me like a magnet, and I threaded my way past a new shift of nudies slinking to the bar to get to it.

And there *I* was, in great light heavyweight company, sandwiched between Gus Lesnevich and Billy Conn;

And there was Lee, right next to Joe Louis, who he could have fought if he'd dived for Benny Siegel.

Bleichert and Blanchard. Two white hopes gone wrong.

I stared at the pictures for a long time, until the raucousness around me dissipated and I wasn't in some upholstered sewer, I was back in '40 and '41, winning fights and rutting with giveaway girls who looked like Betty Short. And Lee was scoring knockouts and living with Kay—and, strangely, we were a family again.

"First Blanchard, now you. Who's next? Willie Pep?"

I was back in the sewer immediately, blurting, "When? When did you see him?"

Whirling around, I saw a hulking old man. His face was cracked leather and broken bones—a punching bag—but his voice was nothing like a stumblebum's: "A couple of months ago. The heavy rains in February. We musta talked fights for ten hours straight."

"Where is he now?"

"I ain't seen him since that one time, and maybe he don't want to see you. I tried to talk about that fight you guys had, but Big Lee won't have any. Says 'We ain't partners no more' and starts tellin' me the featherweights are the best division pound for pound. I tell him, nix—it's the middles. Zale, Graziano, La Motta, Cerdan, who you kiddin'?"

"Is he still in town?"

"I don't think so. I own this place, and he ain't been back here. You lookin' to settle a grudge? A rematch maybe?"

"I'm looking to get him out of a shitload of trouble he's in."

The old pug measured my words, then said, "I'm a sucker for

dancemasters like you, so I'll give you the only piece of skinny I've got. I heard Blanchard caused a ruckus over at the Club Satan, had to bribe his way out big with Captain Vasquez. You walk over five blocks to the beach, there's the Satan. You talk to Ernie the cook. He saw it. You tell him I said to be kosher with you, and take a deep breath when you walk in, 'cause there ain't nothin' like that place where you're comin' from."

• • •

The Club Satan was a slate-roofed adobe hut sporting an ingenious neon sign: a little red devil poking the air with a trident-headed hard-on. It had its very own brownshirt door-man, a little Mex who scrutinized incoming patrons while fondling the trigger housing of a tripod BAR. His epaulet flaps were stuffed with yankee singles; I added one to the collection as I walked in, bracing myself.

From the sewer to the shitstorm.

The bar was a urinal trough. Marines and sailors mastur-bated into it while they gash dived the nudie girls squatting on top. Blow jobs were being dispensed underneath tables facing the front of the room and a large bandstand. A guy in a Satan costume was dicking a fat woman on a mattress. A burro with red velvet devil horns pinned to his ears stood by, eating hay out of a bowl on the floor. To the right of the stage, a tuxedo-clad gringo was crooning into a microphone: "I've got a rich girl, her name's Roseanne, she uses a tortilla for a diaphragm! Hey! Hey! I've got a girl, her name is Sue, she's a one-way ticket to the big fungoo! Hey! Hey! I've got a girl her name's Corrine, she knows how to make my banana cream! Hey! Hey! . . ."

The "music" was drowned out by chants from the tables—"Donkey! Donkey!" I stood there getting sideswiped by revel-ers, then garlicky breath smothered me. "Joo want the bar, handsome? Breakfast of champions, one dollar. Joo want *me*? Roun' the world, two dollar."

I got up the guts to look at her. She was old, fat, her lips crusted with chancre sores. I pulled bills from my pocket and shoved them at her, not caring what denomination they were. The whore genuflected before her nightclub Jesus; I shouted, "Ernie. I have to see him now. The guy at Club Boxeo sent me over."

Mamacita exclaimed, "Vamanos!" and ran interference for me, pushing through a line of jarheads waiting for dinner seats at the bar. She led me to a curtained passageway beside the stage and down it to the kitchen. A spicy aroma perked my tastebuds—until I saw the rear end of a dog carcass hanging out of a stewpot. The woman spoke in Spanish to the chef—a strange-looking guy who came off as a Mex-Chink halfbreed. He nodded along, then walked over.

I had the snapshot of Lee out. "I heard this man gave you some trouble a while back."

The guy gave the photo a cursory eyeball. "Who wants to know?"

I flashed my badge, giving the breed a glimpse of hardware. He said, "He your friend?"

"My best friend."

The breed tucked his hands under his apron; I knew one of them was holding a knife. "Your friend drink fourteen shots of my best Mescal, house record. That I like. He make lots of toasts to dead women. That I don't mind. But he try to fuck with my donkey show, and that I don't take."

"What happened?"

"Four of my guys he take, fifth he don't. Rurales take him home to sleep it off."

"That's it?"

The breed pulled out a stiletto, popped the button and scratched his neck with the dull side of the blade. "Finito."

I walked out the backdoor into an alley, scared for Lee. Two men in shiny suits were lounging by a streetlight; when they saw me they picked up the tempo of their foot shuffling and studied the ground like dirt was suddenly fascinating. I took off running; gravel scraping behind me said the two were in hot pursuit.

The alley ended at a connecting road to the red light block, with another, barely navigable dirt fork angling off in the direction of the beach. I took it at a full sprint, my shoulders brushing chicken wire fencing, penned-up dogs trying to get at me from the opposite sides. Their barks destroyed the rest of the street noise; I had no idea if the two were still on my tail. I saw the ocean-front boulevard looming in front of me, got my bearings, figured the hotel to be a block to the right and slowed to a walk.

I was half a block off—in my favor.

The dump was about a hundred yards away. Catching my breath, I strolled there, Mr. Square American slumming. The courtyard was empty; I reached for my room key. Then light from the second floor fluttered across the door—now minus my spit hair warning trap.

I drew my .38 and kicked the door in. A white man sitting in the chair by the bed already had his hands up and a peace offering on his lips: "Whoa, boy. I'm a friend. I'm not heeled, and if you don't believe me then I'll stand a frisk right now."

I pointed my gun at the wall. The man got up and placed his palms on it, hands over head, legs spread. I patted him down, .38 at his spine, finding a billfold, keys and a greasy comb. Digging the muzzle in, I examined the billfold. It was stuffed with American cash; there was a California private investigator's license in a laminated holder. It gave the man's name as Milton Dolphine, his business address as 986 Copa De Oro in San Diego.

I tossed the billfold on the bed and eased the pressure on my gun; Dolphine squirmed. "That money's jackshit compared to what Blanchard was holding. You go partners with me and it's easy street."

I kicked his legs out from under him. Dolphine hit the floor and sucked dust off the carpet. "You tell me all of it, and you watch what you say about my partner, or it's a B&E roust and the Ensenada jail."

Dolphine pushed himself up onto his knees. He gasped, "Bleichert, how the fuck did you figure I knew to come here? It occur to you that maybe I was nearby when you did your gringo cop routine with Vasquez?"

I sized the man up. He was past forty, fat and balding, but probably tough—like an ex-athlete whose hardness reverted to smarts when his body went. I said, "Somebody else is tailing me. Who is it?"

Dolphine spat cobwebs. "The Rurales. Vasquez has got a vested interest in you not finding out about Blanchard."

"Do they know I'm staying here?"

"No. I told Cap I'd start the tail. His other boys must have picked you up. You lose them?"

I nodded and flicked Dolphine's necktie with my gun. "How come you're so cooperative?"

Dolphine put a light hand on the muzzle and eased it away from him. "I got my own vested interest, and I am damn good at playing both ends against the middle. I also talk a sight better sitting down. You think that's possible?"

I grabbed the chair and placed it in front of him. Dolphine got to his feet, brushed off his suit and plopped himself into it. I reholstered my piece. "Slow and from the beginning."

Dolphine breathed on his nails and buffed them on his shirt. I took the only other chair in the flop and sat down facing the slats so that I'd have something to grab. "Talk, goddamnit."

Dolphine obliged. "About a month ago, this Mexican woman walked into my office in Dago. Chubby, wearing ten tons of makeup, but dressed to the nines. She offered me five hundred to locate Blanchard, and she told me she thought he was somewhere down around TJ or Ensenada. She said he was an LA cop, some kind of lamster. Knowing the LA cops love that green stuff, I started thinking money pronto.

"I asked my TJ snitches about him, showed around this newspaper picture the woman gave me. I heard that Blanchard was in TJ around late January, getting in fights, boozing, spending lots of dough. Then a pal on the Border Patrol tells me he's hiding out in Ensenada, paying protection to the Rurales—who are actually letting him booze and brawl in their town—something Vasquez just about never tolerates.

"Okay, so I came down here and started tailing Blanchard, who's playing the rich gringo to the hilt. I see him beat up these two spics who insult this señorita, with Rurale troopers standing by doing nothing. That means the protection tip is straight dope, and I start thinking money, money, money."

Dolphine traced a dollar sign in the air; I grabbed the chair slats so hard that I could feel the wood start to give. "Here's where it gets interesting. This one pissed-off Rurale who's not on the Blanchard payroll tells me that he heard Blanchard hired a couple of Rurale plainclothesmen to kill two enemies of his in Tijuana in late January. I drive back to TJ, pay out some bribe money to the TJ cops and learn that two guys named Robert De Witt and Felix Chasco were bumped off in TJ on January twenty-third. De Witt's name sounded familiar, so I called a friend working San Diego PD. He checked around and called me back. Now get this, if you didn't already know. Blanchard sent De Witt up to Big Q in '39, and De Witt vowed to get even. I figure that De Witt got early parole, and Blanchard had him snuffed to protect his own ass. I called my partner in Dago, and left a message with him for the Mexican woman. Blanchard is in Ensenada, protected by the Rurales, who probably snuffed De Witt and Chasco for him."

I let go of the slats, my hands numb. "What was the woman's name?"

Dolphine shrugged. "She called herself Delores Garcia, but it was obviously a phony. After I heard about the De Witt-Chasco angle, I pegged her as one of Chasco's bimbos. He was supposed to be a gigolo with plenty of rich Mex gash on the line, and I figured the dame wanted revenge for the snuff. I figured she already knew somehow that Blanchard was responsible for the killings, and she just needed me to finger him."

I said, "You know the Black Dahlia thing up in LA?"

"The Pope a guinea?"

"Lee was working on the case right before he came down here, and in late January there was a Tijuana angle on it. Did you hear of him asking questions about the Dahlia?"

Dolphine said, "Nada. You want the rest of it?"

"Rapidamente."

"Okay. I went back to Dago, and my partner told me that the Mex dame got the message I left. I took off for Reno and a little vacation, and I blew the money she paid me at the crap table. I started thinking of Blanchard and all that money he had, wondering what the Mex dame had in mind for him. It really got to be a bug up my ass, and I went back to Dago, worked some missing persons jobs and came back to Ensenada about two weeks later. And you know whatt? There was no fucking Blanchard.

"Only a fool would've asked Vasquez or the troopers about him, so I hung around town picking up skinny. I saw this punk wearing Blanchard's old letterman's jacket, and this other punk with that Legion Stadium sweatshirt of his. I get word that two guys got hanged in Juarez for the De Witt-Chasco job, and I think, Rurale railroad all the way. I stay in town sucking up to Vasquez, snitching hopheads to him to stay on his good side. Finally I piece the Blanchard thing together. So if he was your buddy, get ready."

At "was," my hands broke off the chair slat I was grabbing. Dolphine said, "Whoa, boy."

I gasped, "Finish it."

The PI spoke slowly and calmly, like he was addressing a hand grenade. "He's dead. Chopped up with an axe. Some punks found him. They broke into the house he was staying in, and one of them blabbed to the troopers, so they wouldn't get tagged for it. Vasquez bought them off with pesos and some of Blanchard's belongings, and the Rurales buried the body outside town. I heard rumors that none of the money was found, and I stuck around because I figured Blanchard was rogue and sooner or later some American cop would come looking for him. When you showed up at the station with that horseshit about working Metropolitan, I knew it was you."

I tried to say no, but my lips wouldn't move; Dolphine speed-balled the rest of his pitch: "Maybe the Rurales did it, maybe it was the woman or friends of hers. Maybe one of them got the money and maybe they didn't, and *we* can. You *knew* Blanchard, you could get a grip on who—"

I leaped up and roundhoused Dolphine with the chair slat; he caught the blow on the neck, hit the floor and sucked carpet again. I aimed my gun at the back of his head; the shitbird private eye whimpered, then double-speeded a mercy plea: "Look, I didn't know it was so personal with you. I didn't kill him, and I'll back off if you want to get whoever did it. Please, Bleichert, goddamn it."

I whimpered myself. "How do I know it's true?"

"There's a sand pit by the beach. The Rurales dump stiffs there. A kid told me he saw a bunch of troopers burying a big white man right around the time that Blanchard got it. Goddamn you, it's true!"

I eased down the .38's hammer. "Then show me."

•   •   •

The burial ground was ten miles south of Ensenada, just off the coast road on a bluff overlooking the ocean. A big, burning cross marked the spot. Dolphine pulled up next to it and killed the engine. "It's not what you think. The locals keep the damn thing lit up because they don't know who's buried there, and lots of them have got missing loved ones. It's a ritual with them. They burn the crosses, and the Rurales tolerate it, like it's some kind of panacea to keep the great unwashed gun-shy. Speaking of which, you want to put that thing away?"

My service revolver was pointed at Dolphine's midsection; I wondered how long I'd been holding the bead. "No. Have you got tools?"

Dolphine swallowed. "Gardening stuff. Listen—"

"No. You take me to the spot the kid told you about, and we dig."

Dolphine got out of the car, walked around and popped open the trunk. I followed, watching him remove a large earth spade. Flame glow illuminated the PI's old Dodge coupe; I noticed a pile of fence pickets and rags next to the spare tire. Tucking the .38 into my waistband, I fashioned two torches out of them, wrapping the rags around the ends of the posts, then igniting them in the cross. Handing one to Dolphine, I said, "Walk ahead of me."

We strode into the sand pit, outlaws holding fireballs on a stick. The softness made the going slow; torchlight let me pick out grave offerings—little bouquets and religious statues placed atop dunes here and there. Dolphine kept muttering how gringos got dumped on the far side; I felt bones cracking beneath my feet. We reached an especially high drift, and Dolphine waved his torch at a tattered American flag spread out on the sand. "Here. The punk said by el bannero."

I kicked the flag away; a swarm of insects buzzed up.

Dolphine screeched, "Cocksuckers," and swatted them with his torch.

A putrid smell rose from a big crater at our feet. "Dig," I said.

Dolphine went at it; I thought of ghosts—Betty Short and Laurie Blanchard—waiting for the shovel to hit bones. The first time it did I recited a psalm the old man had force-fed me; the second time, it was the "Our Fathers" that Danny Boylan used to chant before our sparring sessions. When Dolphine said, "Sailor. I can see his jumper," I didn't know if I wanted Lee alive and in grief or dead and nowhere—so I pushed Dolphine aside and shoveled myself.

My first blow sheared off the sailor's skull, my second tore into the front of his tunic, pulling the torso free from the rest of the skeleton. The legs were in crumbled pieces; I shoveled past them into plain sand glinting with mica. Then it was maggot nests and entrails and a blood-mattted crinoline dress and sand and odd bones and nothing—and then it was sunburned pink skin and blond eyebrows covered with stitch scars that looked familiar. Then Lee was smiling like the Dahlia, with worms creeping out of his mouth and the holes where his eyes used to be.

I dropped the shovel and ran. Dolphine shouted, "The money!" behind me; I tore for the burning cross thinking that I put those scars on Lee, I did it to him. Reaching the car, I got in, gunned it in reverse, plowed the crucifix into the sand, then gnashed through the gears one-two-three going forward. I heard, "My car! The money!" as I fishtailed onto the coast road northbound, reaching for the siren switch, slamming the dashboard when it hit me that civilian vehicles didn't have them.

I made it to Ensenada, highballing at double the speed limit. I ditched the Dodge on the street by the hotel, then ran for *my* car—slowing when I saw three men approaching me in a flanking movement, their hands inside their jackets.

My Chevy ten yards away; the middle man coming into focus as Captain Vasquez, the other two fanning out to close me in from the sides. The only shelter a phone booth near the first door on the left U of the courtyard. Bucky Bleichert about to be DOA in a Mexican sand pit, his best friend along for the ride. I decided to let Vasquez get right up next to me and blow his brains out point-blank. Then a white woman walked out the left-hand door, and I saw my ticket home.

I ran over and grabbed her by the throat. She started to scream. I stifled the sound by moving my left hand to her mouth. The woman flailed with her arms, then clenched herself rigid. I pulled my .38 and pointed it at her head.

The Rurales advanced cautiously, hand cannons pressed to their sides. I shoved the woman into the phone booth, whispering, *"Scream and you're dead. Scream and you're dead."* Inside, I pinned her to the wall with my knees and removed my hand; the screams she put out were silent. I aimed my gun at her mouth to keep them that way, grabbed the receiver, fed the slot a nickel and dialed "O." Vasquez was standing in front of the booth now, livid, reeking of cheap American cologne. The operator came on the line with "Que?" I blurted, "Habla inglés?"

"Yes, sir."

I held the receiver chin to shoulder and fumbled all the coins in my pocket into the slot; I kept my .38 glued to the woman's face. When a shitload of pesos were swallowed up, I said, "Ferderal Bureau of Investigation, San Diego field office. It's an emergency."

The operator muttered, "Yes, sir." I heard the call going through. The woman's teeth chattered against my gun barrel. Vasquez tried bribery: "Blanchard was very rich, my friend. We could find his money. You could live very well here. You—"

"FBI, Special Agent Rice."

I stared daggers at Vasquez. "This is Officer Dwight Bleichert, Los Angeles Police Department. I'm in Ensenada, and I screwed up with some Rurales. They're getting ready to kill me for nothing, and I thought you could talk Captain Vasquez here out of it."

"What the—"

"Sir, I'm a legit LA policemen and you had better do this fast."

"You jerking my chain, son?"

"Goddamn it, you want proof? I worked Central Homicide with Russ Millard and Harry Sears. I worked DA's Warrants, I worked—"

"Put the spic fellow on, son."

I handed the receiver to Vasquez. He took it and leveled his automatic at me; I kept my .38 on the woman. Seconds ticked; the standoff held as the Rurale boss listened to the fed, getting paler and paler. Finally he dropped the phone and lowered his piece. "Go home, puta. Get out of my city and get out of my country."

I holstered my gun and squeezed out of the booth; the woman shrieked. Vasquez stood back and waved his men away. I got in my car and peeled out of Ensenada on fear overdrive. It was only when I was back in America that I started obeying speed laws—and that was when it got bad with Lee.

• • •

Dawn was pushing up over the Hollywood Hills when I knocked on Kay's door. I stood on the porch shivering, storm clouds and streaks of sunlight looming as strange things I didn't want to see. I heard "Dwight?" inside, followed by the sound of bolts being unlatched. Then the other remaining partner in the Blanchard/Bleichert/Lake triad was there, saying, "And all that."

It was an epitaph I didn't want to hear.

I walked inside, stunned at how strange and pretty the living room was. Kay said, "Lee's dead?"

I sat down in his favorite chair for the first time. "The Rurales or some Mexican woman or her friends killed him. Oh, babe, I—"

Using Lee's endearment jarred me. I looked at Kay, standing by the door, backlighted by the weird sunstreaks. "He hired the Rurales to kill De Witt, but that doesn't mean shit. We've got to get Russ Millard and some decent Mexican cops on it . . ."

I stopped, noticing the phone on the coffee table. I started dialing the padre's home number. Kay's hand halted me. "No. I want to talk to you first."

I moved from the chair to the couch; Kay sat beside me. She said, "You'll hurt Lee if you go crazy with this."

That was when I knew she'd been expecting it; that was when I knew she knew more than I did. "You can't hurt something dead."

"Oh, yes you can, babe."

"Don't call me that! That's his!"

Kay moved closer and touched my cheek. "You can hurt him and you can hurt us."

I pulled away from the caress. "You tell me why, *babe*."

Kay cinched the belt on her robe and fixed me with a cold look. "I didn't meet Lee at Bobby's trial," she said. "I met him before. We became friends, and I lied about where I was staying so Lee wouldn't know about Bobby. Then he found out on his own, and I told him how bad it was, and he told me about a business opportunity he had coming up. He wouldn't tell me the details, and then Bobby was arrested for bank robbery and everything was chaos.

"Lee planned the robbery and got three men to help him. He'd bought his way out of his contract with Ben Siegel, and it cost him every cent he'd made as a boxer. Two of the men were killed during the robbery, one escaped to Canada, and Lee was the fourth. Lee framed Bobby because he hated him for what he did to me. Bobby didn't know we were seeing each other, and we made it look like we met at the trial. Bobby knew it was a frame, but he didn't suspect Lee, just the LAPD in general.

"Lee wanted to give me a home, and he did. He was very cautious with his part of the robbery money, and he always talked up his boxing savings and his gambling so the brass wouldn't think he was living above his means. He hurt his career by living with a woman, even though we weren't together that way. It was like a happy fairy tale until last fall, right after you and Lee became partners."

I moved toward Kay, awed by Lee as the most audacious rogue cop in history. "I knew he had it in him."

Kay drew away from me. "Let me finish before you get sentimental. When Lee heard about Bobby getting an early parole date, he went to Ben Siegel to try to get him killed. He was afraid of Bobby talking about *me*, upsetting our fairy tale with all the ugly things he knew about yours truly. Siegel wouldn't do it, and I told Lee it didn't matter, that there were three of us now and the truth couldn't hurt us. Then, right before New Year's, the third man from the robbery showed up. He knew that Bobby De Witt was getting out on parole, and he made a blackmail demand: Lee was to pay him ten thousand dollars, or he would tell Bobby that Lee masterminded the robbery and framed him.

"The man said Lee's deadline was Bobby's release date. Lee put him off, then went to Ben Siegel to try to borrow the money. Siegel wouldn't do it, and Lee begged him to have the man killed. He wouldn't do that either. Lee learned that the man hung out with some Negroes who sold marijuana, and he—"

I saw it coming, huge and black like the headlines it got me, Kay's words the new fine print: "That man's name was Baxter Fitch. Siegel wouldn't help Lee, so he got you. The men were armed, so I guess you were legally justified, and I guess you were damn lucky that no one looked into it. It's the one thing I can't forgive him for, the one thing I hate myself for tolerating. Still feeling sentimental, triggerman?"

I couldn't answer; Kay did it for me. "I didn't think so. I'll finish up, and you tell me if you still want revenge.

"The Short thing happened then, and Lee latched on to it for his little sister and who knows what else. He was terrified that Fitch had already talked to Bobby, that Bobby knew about the frame. He wanted to kill him or have him killed, and I begged and pleaded with him to just let it be, no one would believe Bobby, so just don't hurt anybody else. If it wasn't for that fucking dead girl I might have convinced him. But the case went down to Mexico, and so did Bobby and Lee and you. I knew that the fairy tale was over. And it is."

FIRE AND ICE COPS KO NEGRO THUGS

SOUTHSIDE SHOOTOUT—COPS: 4, HOODLUMS: 0

FOUR HOPHEADS SLAIN BY BOXER—POLICEMEN IN BLOODY LA GUN BATTLE

Limp all over, I started to stand up; Kay grabbed my belt with both hands and brought me back down. "No! You don't pull the patented Bucky Bleichert retreat this time! Bobby took pictures of me with animals, and Lee stopped it. He pimped me to his friends and hit me with a razor strap, and Lee stopped it. He wanted to love me, not fuck me, and he wanted us to be together, and if you weren't so intimidated by him you would have known it. We can't drag his name down. We have to give it all up and forgive him and get on with just us and—"

I retreated then, before Kay destroyed the rest of the triad.

• • •

Triggerman.

Stooge.

Bumfuck detective too blind to clear the case he was a homicide accessory to.

The weak point in a fairy tale triangle.

Best friend to a cop—bank robber, now the keeper of his secrets.

"Give it all up."

I stuck to my apartment for the next week, killing off the remainder of my "vacation." I hit the heavy bag and skipped rope and listened to music; I sat on the back steps and took finger sights at blue jays perching on my landlady's clothesline. I convicted Lee of four homicides connected to the Boulevard-Citizens bank job and granted him a pardon based on homicide number five—himself. I thought of Betty Short and Kay until they blurred together; I reconstructed the partnership as a mutual seduction and figured out that I lusted for the Dahlia because I had her number, that I loved Kay because she had mine.

And I examined the past six months. It was all there:

The money Lee had been spending in Mexico was probably a separate stash of robbery swag.

On New Year's Eve I heard him weeping; Baxter Fitch had made his blackmail demand a few days before.

That fall, Lee had sought out Benny Siegel—in private— every time we went to the fights at the Olympic; he was trying to talk him into killing Bobby De Witt.

Right before the shoot-out, Lee had spoken on the phone to a snitch—allegedly about Junior Nash. The "snitch" had fingered Fitch and the Negros, and Lee came back to the car looking spooked. Ten minutes later four men were dead.

On the night I met Madeleine Sprague, Kay shouted at Lee: *"After all that might happen"*—a portentous line, probably her predicting disaster with Bobby De Witt. During our time working the Dahlia case, she had been jittery, morose, concerned for Lee's well-being, yet weirdly accepting of his lunatic behavior. I thought she was upset over Lee's obsession with Betty Short's murder; she was really running toward and from the fairy tale's finale.

It was all there.

"Give it all up."

When my refrigerator was empty, I took the patented Bucky Bleichert retreat down to the market to stock up. Walking in, I saw a box boy reading the local section of the morning *Herald*. Johnny Vogel's picture was at the bottom of the page; I looked over the kid's shoulder and saw that he'd been dismissed from the LAPD on a graft whitewash. A column over, Ellis Loew's name caught my eye—Bevo Means was quoting him that "The Elizabeth Short investigation is no longer my raison d'etre—I have more pertinent fish to fry." I forgot all about food, and drove to West Hollywood.

It was recess. Kay was in the middle of the schoolyard, supervising kids flopping around in a sandbox. I watched her awhile from the car, then walked over.

The kids noticed me first. I flashed my teeth at them until they started laughing. Kay turned around then. I said, "It's the patented Bucky Bleichert advance."

Kay said, "Dwight"; the kids looked at us like they knew it was a big moment. Kay caught on a second later. "Did you come here to tell me something?"

I laughed; the kids chortled at another shot of my choppers. "Yeah. I decided to give it all up. Will you marry me?"

Kay, expressionless, said, "And we'll bury the rest of it? The f-ing dead girl too?"

"Yes. Her too."

Kay stepped into my arms. "Then yes."

We embraced. The children called out, "Miss Lake's got a boyfriend, Miss Lake's got a boyfriend!"

• • •

We were married three days later, May 2, 1947. It was a rush job, the vows given by the LAPD Protestant chaplain, the service held in the backyard of Lee Blanchard's house. Kay wore a pink dress to satirize her lack of virginity; I wore my blue dress uniform. Russ Millard was best man, and Harry Sears came along as a guest. He started out with a stutter, and for the first time I saw that it was precisely his fourth drink that quashed it. I got the old man out of the rest home on a pass, and he didn't know who the hell I was, but seemed to have a good time anyway—swigging from Harry's flask, goosing Kay, hopping around to the music from the radio. There was a table laid out with sandwiches and punch, hard and soft. The six of us ate and drank, and total strangers walking down to the Strip heard the music and laughter and crashed the party. By dusk the yard was filled with people I didn't know, and Harry made a run to the Hollywood Ranch Market for more food and booze. I unloaded my service revolver and let the unknown civilians play with it, and Kay danced polkas with the chaplain. When darkness hit, I didn't want it to end, so I borrowed strings of Christmas lights from the neighbors and strung them over the backdoor and the clothesline and Lee's favorite Yucca tree. We danced and drank and ate under a fake constellation, the stars red and blue and yellow. Around 2:00 A.M., the clubs on the Strip let out, revelers from the Trocadero and Mocambo made the scene, and Errol Flynn hung around for a while, his tux coat doffed for my jacket, replete with badge and pistol medals. If it weren't for the thunderstorm that struck, it might have gone on forever—and I wanted it to. But the crowd broke up amidst frantic kisses and hugs, and Russ drove the old man back to the rest bin. Kay Lake Bleichert and I retired to the bedroom to make love, and I left the radio on to help distract me from Betty Short. It wasn't necessary—she never crossed my mind.

III

Kay and Madeleine

CHAPTER TWENTY-FIVE

Time passed. Kay and I worked and played at being a young married couple.

After our quickie San Francisco honeymoon, I returned to what remained of my police career. Thad Green talked turkey to me: he admired what I did with the Vogels, but considered me useless as a patrol cop—I had earned the enmity of rank and file blues, and my presence in a uniformed division would only create grief. Since my year of junior college showed straight A's in chemistry and math, he assigned me to the Scientific Investigation Detail as an evidence technician.

The job was quasi-plainclothes—smocks in the lab and gray suits in the field. I typed blood, dusted for latent prints and wrote ballistics reports; scraped ooze off the walls at crime scenes and examined it under a microscope, letting the Homicide dicks take it from there. It was test tubes and beakers and clinical gore—an intimacy with death that I never became inured to; a constant reminder that I wasn't a detective, that I couldn't be trusted to follow up on my own findings.

From various distances I followed the friends and enemies the Dahlia case had given me.

Russ and Harry kept the El Nido file room intact, continuing to work overtime hours on the Short investigation. I had a key to the door, but didn't use it—per my promise to Kay to bury "that ————— dead girl." Sometimes I met the padre for lunch and asked him how it was going; he always said, "Slowly," and I knew that he would never find the killer and never quit trying.

In June of '47, Ben Siegel was shot to death in his girlfriend's Beverly Hills living room. Bill Koenig, assigned to 77th Street dicks after Fritz Vogel's suicide, caught a shotgun blast in the face on a Watts street corner early in '48. Both killings went unsolved. Ellis Loew was soundly trounced in the June '48 Republican primary, and I celebrated by cooking up beakers of moonshine on my Bunsen burner, getting everyone in the crime lab fried.

The '48 general election brought me news of the Spragues. A slate of reform Democrats were running for seats on the LA City Council and Board of Supervisors, "City Planning" their basic campaign theme. They asserted that there were faultily designed, unsafe dwellings all over Los Angeles, and were calling for a grand jury probe on the contractors who built the structures back during the '20s real estate boom. The scandal tabloids took up the hue and cry, running articles on the "boom barons"—Mack Sennett and Emmett Sprague among them— and their "gangster ties." *Confidential* magazine ran a series on Sennett's Hollywoodland tract and how the Hollywood Chamber of Commerce wanted to lop the L-A-N-D off the giant Hollywoodland sign on Mount Lee, and there were photographs of the Keystone Kops director standing beside a stocky man with a cute little girl in tow. I couldn't quite tell if it was Emmett and Madeleine, but I clipped the pictures anyway.

My enemies;

My friends;

My wife.

I processed evidence and Kay taught school, and for a while we reveled in the novelty of living a squarejohn life. With the house paid off in full and two salaries, there was plenty of money to spend, and we used it to pamper ourselves away from Lee Blanchard and the winter of '47. We took weekend trips to the desert and the mountains; we ate in restaurants three and four nights a week. We checked into hotels pretending to be illicit lovers, and it took me well over a year to realize that we did those things because it got us out of the pad the Boulevard-Citizens bank job paid for. And I was so heedless in my pursuit of pampering that it required a live-wire shock to spell it out.

A floorboard in the hallway came loose, and I pulled it all the way off so I could reglue it. Looking in the hole, I found a cash roll, two thousand dollars in C-notes secured by a rubber band. I didn't feel joyous or shocked; my brain went tick, tick, tick, and came up with the questions my rush into normal life had quashed:

If Lee had this money, plus the dough he was spending in Mexico, why didn't he pay off Baxter Fitch?

If he had the money, why did he go to Ben Siegel to try to borrow ten grand to meet Fitch's blackmail demand?

How could Lee have bought and furnished this house, put Kay through college and still have had a substantial sum left when his cut from the aborted heist couldn't have amounted to more than fifty grand or so?

Of course I told Kay; of course she couldn't answer the questions; of course she loathed me for dredging up the past. I told her we could sell the house and get an apartment like other normal squarejohns—and of course she wouldn't have it. It was comfort, style—a link to her old life that she would not give up.

I burned the money in Lee Blanchard's Deco-streamline fireplace. Kay never asked me what I did with it. The simple act gave me back some smothered part of myself, cost me most of what I had with my wife—and returned me to my ghosts.

Kay and I made love less and less. When we did it was perfunctory reassurance for her and a dull explosion for me. I came to see Kay Lake Bleichert as wasted by the obscenity in her old life, just short of thirty and already going chaste. I brought the gutter to our bed then, the faces of hookers I saw downtown attached to Kay's body in the darkness. It worked the first few times, until I saw where I really wanted to go. When I finally made the move and came gasping, Kay stroked me with mothering hands, and I sensed that she knew I'd broken my marriage vow—with her right there.

1948 became 1949. I turned the garage into a boxing gym, complete with speed bag and heavy bag, jump ropes and barbells. I got back into fighting trim, and decorated the garage walls with fight stills of young Bucky Bleichert, circa '40–'41. My own image glimpsed through sweat-streaked eyes brought me closer to her, and I scoured used book stores for Sunday supplements and news magazines. I found sepia candids in *Colliers*; some family snapshots reproduced in old issues of the Boston *Globe*. I kept them out of sight in the garage, and the stack grew, then vanished one afternoon. I heard Kay sobbing inside the house that evening, and when I went to talk to her the bedroom door was locked.

CHAPTER TWENTY-SIX

The phone rang. I reached for the bedside extension, then snapped that I'd been a couch sleeper for the past month and flailed at the coffee table. "Yeah?"

"You still sleeping?"

It was the voice of Ray Pinker, my supervisor at SID. "I was sleeping."

"Past tense is right. Are you listening?"

"Keep going."

"We've got a gunshot suicide from yesterday. 514 South June Street, Hancock Park. Body removed, looks open and shut. Do a complete work-up and drop the report off with Lieutenant Reddin at Wilshire dicks. Got it?"

I yawned. "Yeah. Premises sealed?"

"The stiff's wife will show you around. Be courteous, this is filthy rich we're dealing with."

I hung up and groaned. Then it hit me that the Sprague mansion was a block from the June Street address. Suddenly the assignment was fascinating.

●   ●   ●

I rang the bell of the pillared colonial manse an hour later. A handsome gray-haired woman of about fifty opened the door, dressed in dusty work togs. I said, "I'm Officer Bleichert, LAPD. May I express my condolences, Mrs.—"

Ray Pinker hadn't given me a name. The woman said, "Condolences accepted, and I'm Jane Chambers. Are you the lab man?"

The woman was trembling underneath her brusqueness; I liked her immediately. "Yes. If you'll point me to the place I'll take care of it and leave you alone."

Jane Chambers ushered me into a sedate, all-wood foyer. "The study in back of the dining room. You'll see the rope. Now, if you'll excuse me I want to do some gardening."

She took off dabbing at her eyes. I found the room, stepped over the crime scene rope and wondered why the bastard did himself in where his loved ones would see the gore.

It looked like a classic self-inflicted shotgun job: overturned leather chair, the outline of the stiff chalked on the floor beside it. The weapon, a double-barreled .12 gauge, was right where it should have been—three feet in front of the body, the muzzle coated with blood and shredded tissue. The light plaster walls and ceiling showed off blood and caked-on brains to full advantage, the teeth fragments and buckshot a dead giveaway that the victim had stuck both barrels in his mouth.

I spent an hour measuring trajectories and spatter marks, scraping matter into test tubes and dusting the suicide weapon for latents. When I finished, I took a bag from my evidence kit and wrapped up the shotgun, knowing full well it would end up the property of some LAPD sportsman. Then I walked out to the entrance hall, stopping when I saw a framed painting hung at eye level.

It was a portrait of a clown, a young boy done up in court jester's garb from long, long ago. His body was gnarled and hunched; he wore a stuporous ear-to-ear smile that looked like one continuous deep scar.

I stared, transfixed, thinking of Elizabeth Short, DOA at 39th and Norton. The more I stared the more the two blended; finally I pulled my eyes away and settled them on a photo of two arm-linked young women who looked just like Jane Chambers.

"The other survivors. Pretty, aren't they?"

I turned around. The widow was twice as dusty as before, smelling of insect spray and soil. "Like their mother. How old are they?"

"Linda's twenty-three and Carol's twenty. Are you finished in the study?"

I thought of the daughters as contemporaries of the Sprague girls. "Yes. Tell whoever cleans it up to use pure ammonia. Mrs. Chambers—"

"Jane."

"Jane, do you know Madeleine and Martha Sprague?"

Jane Chambers snorted, "Those girls and that family. How do you know them?"

"I did some work for them once."

"Count yourself lucky it was a brief encounter."

"What do you mean?"

The hallway phone rang. Jane Chambers said, "Back to condolences. Thank you for being so nice, Mr.—"

"It's Bucky. Good-bye, Jane."

"Good-bye."

• • •

I wrote out my report at Wilshire Station, then checked the routine suicide file on Chambers, Eldridge Thomas, DOD 4/2/49. It didn't tell me much: Jane Chambers heard the shotgun explosion, found the body and called the police immediately. When detectives arrived, she told them her husband was depressed over his failing health and their eldest daughter's failing marriage. Suicide: case closed pending forensic crime scene work-up.

My work-up confirmed the verdict, plain and simple. But it didn't feel like enough. I liked the widow, the Spragues lived a block away, I was still curious. I got on a squadroom phone and put in calls to Russ Millard's newspaper contacts, giving them two names: Eldridge Chambers and Emmett Sprague. They did their own digging and calling, and got back to me on the station extension I was hogging. Four hours later I knew the following:

That Eldridge Chambers died enormously wealthy;

That from 1930 to 1934 he was president of the Southern California Real Estate Board;

That he nominated Sprague for membership in Wilshire Country Club in 1929, but the Scotsman was rejected because of his "Jewish business associates"—i.e. East Coast hoodlums;

And the kicker: Chambers, through intermediaries, got Sprague kicked off the real estate board when several of his houses collapsed during the '33 earthquake.

It was enough for a juicy newspaper obit, but not enough for a test-tube cop with a foundering marriage and time on his hands. I waited four days; then, when the papers told me Eldridge Chambers was in the ground, I went back to talk to his widow.

She answered the door in gardening clothes, holding a pair of shears. "Did you forget something or are you as curious as I thought you were?"

"The latter."

Jane laughed and wiped dirt from her face. "After you left I put your name together. Weren't you some sort of athlete?"

I laughed. "I was a boxer. Are your daughters around? Have you got someone staying with you?"

Jane shook her head. "No, and I prefer it that way. Will you join me for tea in the backyard?"

I nodded. Jane led me through the house and out to a shaded veranda overlooking a large bent grass yard more than half dug up into furrows. I sat down in a lounge chair; she poured iced tea. "I've done all that garden work since Sunday. I think it's helped more than all the sympathy calls I've gotten."

"You're taking it well."

Jane sat down beside me. "Eldridge had cancer, so I half expected it. I didn't expect a shotgun in our own home, though."

"Were you close?"

"No, not anymore. With the girls grown up, we would have divorced sooner or later. Are you married?"

"Yes. Almost two years."

Jane sipped tea. "God, a newlywed. There's nothing better, is there?"

My face must have betrayed me. Jane said, "Sorry," then changed the subject. "How do you know the Spragues?"

"I was involved with Madeleine before I met my wife. How well do you know them?"

Jane considered my question, staring out at the uprooted yard. "Eldridge and Emmett went way back," she said finally. "They both made a lot of money in real estate and served on the Southern California board together. Maybe I shouldn't be saying this, since you're a policeman, but Emmett was a bit of a crook. A lot of his houses went down during the big quake in '33, and Eldridge said that he has lots of other property that has to go bad sooner or later—houses made out of *the* worst possible material. Eldridge got Emmett booted off the board when he found out that phony corporations controlled the rentals and sales—he was enraged that Emmett would never be held responsible if more lives were lost."

I remembered talking with Madeleine about the same thing. "Your husband sounded like a good man."

Jane's lips curled into a smile—it looked like against her will. "He had his moments."

"He never went to the police about Emmett?"

"No. He was afraid of his gangster friends. He just did what he could, a little nuisance to Emmett. Being removed from the board probably cost him some business."

"'He did what he could' isn't a bad epitaph."

Now Jane's lips curled into a sneer. "It was out of guilt. Eldridge owned slum blocks in San Pedro. When he learned he had cancer, he really started feeling guilty. He voted Democratic last year, and when they got in he had meetings with some of the new City Council members. I'm sure he gave them his dirt on Emmett."

I thought of the Grand Jury probe the scandal sheets were predicting. "Maybe Emmett's heading for a fall. Your husband could have been—"

Jane rapped her ring finger on the tabletop. "My husband was rich and handsome and did a mean Charleston. I loved him until I found out he was cheating on me, and now I'm starting to love him again. It is so strange."

"It's not so strange," I said.

Jane smiled very softly. "How old are you, Bucky?"

"Thirty-two."

"Well, I'm fifty-one, and I think it's strange, so it is strange. You shouldn't be so all-accepting of the human heart at your age. You should have illusions."

"You're teasing me, Jane. I'm a cop. Cops don't have illusions."

Jane laughed—heartily. "Touché. Now *I'm* curious. How did an ex-boxer cop get involved with Madeleine Sprague?"

Now I lied. "I stopped her for a red light and one thing led to another." My gut clenching, I asked casually, "What do you know about her?"

Jane stomped her foot at a crow eyeing the rose bushes just off the veranda. "What I know about the distaff Spragues is at least ten years old and quite strange. Baroque, almost."

"I'm all ears."

Jane said, "Some might say all teeth." When I didn't laugh, she looked across the dug-up yard to Muirfield Road and the boom baron's estate. "When my girls and Maddy and Martha were little, Ramona directed pageants and ceremonies on that huge front lawn of theirs. Little enactments with the girls

dressed up in pinafores and animal costumes. I let Linda and
Carol participate, even though I knew Ramona was a disturbed
woman. When the girls all got a bit older—in their teens—the
pageants got stranger. Ramona and Maddy were very good at
makeup, and Ramona staged these . . . epics, reenacting the
things that happened to Emmett and his friend Georgie Tilden
during World War I.

"So, she had children wearing soldier kilts and pancake
faces, carrying toy muskets. Sometimes she smeared fake
blood on them, and sometimes Georgie actually filmed it. It got
so bizarre, so out of proportion, that I made Linda and Carol
quit playing with the Sprague girls. Then one day Carol came
home with some pictures Georgie took of her. She was playing
dead, all smeared with red dye. That was the last straw. I
stormed over to the Sprague house and berated Georgie,
knowing Ramona wasn't really responsible for her actions. The
poor man just took my abuse, and I felt terrible about it later—
he was disfigured in a car wreck, and it turned him into a bum.
He used to manage property for Emmett, now he just does yard
work and weeds lots for the city."

"And what happened to Madeleine and Martha then?"

Jane shrugged. "Martha turned into some sort of art prodigy
and Madeleine turned into a roundheels, which I guess you
already know."

I said, "Don't be catty, Jane."

Tapping the table with her ring, Jane said, "I apologize.
Maybe I'm wishing *I* could pull it off. I certainly can't spend
the rest of my life gardening, and I'm too proud for gigolos.
What do you think?"

"You'll find yourself another millionaire."

"Unlikely, and one was enough to last me a lifetime. You
know what I keep thinking? That it's almost 1950 and I was
born in 1898. That floors me."

I said what I'd been thinking for the past half hour. "You
make me wish things were different. That time was different."

Jane smiled and sighed. "Bucky, is that the best I can expect
from you?"

I sighed back. "I think it's the best anyone can."

"You're a bit of a voyeur, you know."

"And you're a bit of a gossip."

"Touché. Come on, I'll walk you out."

We held hands on the way to the door. In the entrance hall,
the scar mouth clown painting grabbed me again. Pointing to
it, I said, "God, that is spooky."

"Valuable, too. Eldridge bought it for my forty-ninth birthday, but I hate it. Would you like to take it with you?"

"Thanks, but no thanks."

"Thank you, then. You were my best condoler."

"And you were mine."

We embraced for a moment, then I took off.

CHAPTER TWENTY-SEVEN

Bunsen burner jockey.

Couch sleeper.

Detective without a case.

I worked at all three throughout the spring of '49. Kay left for school early each morning; I pretended to sleep until she was gone. Alone in the fairy tale house, I touched my wife's things—the cashmere sweaters Lee bought her, her essays to be graded, the books she had stacked up waiting to be read. I kept looking for a diary, but never found one. At the lab I pictured Kay prowling *my* belongings. I toyed with the idea of writing a journal and leaving it out for her to find—detailed accounts of my coupling with Madeleine Sprague—rubbing her nose in it to either gain forgiveness for my fix on the Dahlia or blow our marriage out of its stasis. I got as far as five pages scrawled in my cubicle—stopping when I smelled Madeleine's perfume melding with the Lysol stench of the Red Arrow Motel. And wadding the pages up and throwing them away only fanned the brush fire into a blaze.

I kept the Muirfield Road mansion under surveillance for four nights running. Parked across the street, I watched lights go on and off, saw shadows flicker across leaded glass windows. I played with notions of crashing the Spragues' family

245

life, cashing in on being a hard boy to Emmett, coupling with Madeleine all over hot sheet row. None of the family left the manse during those nights—all four of their cars remained on the circular driveway. I kept wondering what they were doing, what shared history they were rehashing, what the odds were on someone mentioning the cop who came to dinner two years before.

On the fifth night, Madeleine, dressed in slacks and a pink sweater, walked to the corner to mail a letter. When she returned, I saw her notice my car, passing headlights illuminating the surprise on her face. I waited until she hurried back inside the Tudor fortress, then drove home, Jane Chambers' voice taunting, "Voyeur, voyeur."

Walking in, I heard the shower running; the bedroom door was open. Kay's favorite Brahms quintet was on the phonograph. Remembering the first time I saw my wife naked, I undressed and lay down on the bed.

The shower went off; Brahms came on that much stronger. Kay appeared in the doorway wrapped in a towel. I said, "Babe," she said, "Oh, Dwight," and let the towel drop. We both began talking at once, apologies from both sides. I couldn't quite make out her words, and I knew that she couldn't unscramble mine. I started to get up to turn off the phonograph, but Kay moved to the bed first.

We fumbled at kisses. I went open-mouthed too fast, forgetting how Kay liked to be coaxed. Feeling her tongue, I pulled away, knowing she hated it. Closing my eyes, I trailed my lips down her neck; she moaned, and I knew it was a fake. The love sounds got worse—like something you'd expect from a stag film actress. Kay's breasts were flaccid in my hands, her legs closed, but braced up against me. A knee nudge parted them—the response was jerky, spasmodic. Hard now, I made Kay wet with my mouth and went inside her.

I kept my eyes open and on hers so she would know it was just us; Kay turned away, and I knew she saw through it. I wanted to ease off and go slowly, softly, but the sight of a vein throbbing in Kay's neck made me go as hard as I could. I came grunting, "I'm sorry goddamn you I'm sorry," and whatever Kay said back was muffled by the pillow she was burying her head in.

CHAPTER TWENTY-EIGHT

The following night I was parked across the street from the Sprague mansion, this time in the unmarked Ford I drove to SID field jobs. Time was lost on me, but I knew that every second was bringing me closer to knocking on the door or bolting outright.

My mind played with Madeleine nude; I wowed the other Spragues with killer repartee. Then light cut across the driveway, the door slammed and the Packard's headbeams went on. It pulled out onto Muirfield, hung a quick left turn on Sixth Street and headed east. I waited a discreet three seconds and followed.

The Packard stayed in the middle lane; I dogged it from the right one, a good four car lengths behind. We traveled out of Hancock Park into the Wilshire District, south on Normandie and east on 8th Street. I saw glittery bar beacons stretching for a solid mile—and knew Madeleine was close to something.

The Packard stopped in front of the Zimba Room, a dive with crossed neon spears above the entrance. The only other parking space was right behind it, so I glided up, my headlights catching the driver locking the door, my brain wires unraveling when I saw who it wasn't and *was*.

Elizabeth Short.

Betty Short.
Liz Short.
The Black Dahlia.
My knees jerked into the steering wheel; my trembling hands hit the horn. The apparition shielded her eyes and squinted into my beams, then shrugged. I saw familiar dimples twitch, and returned from wherever it was I was going.

It was Madeleine Sprague, completely made over as the Dahlia. She was dressed in an all-black clinging gown, with makeup and hairdo identical to Betty Short at her portrait photo best. I watched her sashay into the bar, saw a dot of yellow in her upswept black curls and knew that she'd taken her transformation all the way to the barrette Betty wore. The detail hit me like a Lee Blanchard one-two. On punch-drunk legs, I pursued the ghost.

The Zimba Room interior was wall-to-wall smoke, GI's and juke box jazz; Madeleine was at the bar sipping a drink. Looking around, I saw that she was the only woman in the place and already creating a hubbub—soldiers and sailors were elbowing the good news to one another, pointing to the black-clad figure and exchanging whispers.

I found a zebra-striped booth at the back; it was filled with sailors sharing a bottle. One glance at their peach fuzz faces told me they were underage. I held out my badge and said, "Scram or I'll have the SP's here inside of a minute." The three youths took off in a blue swirl, leaving their jug behind. I sat down to watch Madeleine portray Betty.

Guzzling half a tumbler of bourbon calmed my nerves. I had a diagonal view of Madeleine at the bar, surrounded by would-be lovers hanging on her every word. I was too far away to hear anything—but every gesture I saw her make was *not* hers, but that of some other woman. And every time she touched a member of her entourage my hand twitched toward my .38.

Time stretched, in a haze of navy blue and khaki with a jet back center.

Madeleine drank, chatted and brushed off passes, her attention narrowing down to a stocky sailor. Her coterie dwindled out as the man shot them mean looks; I killed off the bottle. Staring at the bar kept me from thinking, the loud jazz kept my ears perked for the sound of voices above it, the booze kept me from rousting the stocky man on a half dozen trumped-up charges. Then the woman in black and the sailor in blue were out the door, arms linked, Madeleine inches taller in her high heels.

I gave them a bourbon-calmed five seconds, then hauled. The

Packard was turning right at the corner when I got behind the wheel; gunning it and hanging a hard right myself, I saw taillights at the end of the block. I zoomed up behind them, almost tapping the rear bumper; Madeleine's signal arm shot out the window, and she veered into the parking lot of a brightly lit auto court.

I skidded to a stop, then backed up and killed my headlights. From the street I could see sailor boy standing by the Packard smoking a cigarette, while Madeleine hit the motel office for the room key. She came outside with it a moment later, just like our old routine; she made the sailor walk ahead of her, just like she did with me. The lights went on and off inside the room, and when I listened outside it the blinds were drawn and our old station was on the radio.

* * *

Rolling stakeouts.

Field interrogations.

The Bunsen burner jockey now a detective *with* a case.

I kept Madeleine's Dahlia act under surveillance for four more nights; she pulled the same MO every time: 8th Street gin mill, hard boy with lots of confetti on his chest, the fuck pad at 9th and Irolo. When the two were ensconsed, I went back and questioned bartenders and GIs she gave the ixnay to.

What name did the black-clad woman give?

None.

What did she talk about?

The war and breaking into the movies.

Did you notice her resemblance to the Black Dahlia, that murdered girl from a couple of years ago, and if so, what do you think she was trying to prove?

Negative answers and theories: She's a loony who thinks she's the Black Dahlia; she's a hooker cashing in on the Dahlia's look; she's a policewoman decoy out to get the Dahlia killer; she's a crazy woman dying of cancer, trying to attract the Dahlia slasher and cheat the Big C.

I knew the next step was to roust Madeleine's lovers—but I didn't trust myself to do it rationally. If they said the wrong thing or the right thing, or pointed me in the wrong/right direction, I knew I couldn't be held accountable for what I would do.

The four nights of booze, catnaps in the car and couch naps at home with Kay sequestered in the bedroom took their toll on me. At work I dropped slides and mislabeled blood samples, wrote evidence reports in my own exhaustion shorthand and twice fell asleep hunched over a ballistics miscroscope, awakening to jagged shots of Madeleine in black. Knowing I couldn't hack night five by myself or give it a pass, I stole some Benzedrine tablets awaiting processing for Narcotics Division. They juiced me out of my fatigue and into a clammy feeling of disgust for what I'd been doing to myself—and they gave me a brainstorm to save me from Madeleine/Dahlia and make me a real cop again.

Thad Green nodded along as I plea-bargained him: I had seven years on the Department, my run-in with the Vogels was over two years before and mostly forgotten, I hated working SID and wanted to return to a uniformed division—preferably nightwatch. I was studying for the Sergeant's Exam, SID had served me well as a training ground for my ultimate goal—the Detective Bureau. I started to launch a tirade on my shitty marriage and how nightwatch would keep me away from my wife, faltering when images of the lady in black hit me and I realized I was close to begging. The Chief of Detectives finally silenced me with a long stare, and I wondered if the dope was betraying me. Then he said, "Okay, Bucky," and pointed to the door. I waited in the outer office for a Benzedrine eternity; when Green walked out smiling, I almost jumped loose of my skin. "Newton Street nightwatch as of tomorrow," he said. "And try to be civil with our colored brethren down there. You've got a bad case of the yips, and I wouldn't want you passing it on to them."

• • •

Newton Street Division was southeast of downtown LA, 95 percent slums, 95 percent Negroes, all trouble. There were bottle gangs and crap games on every corner; liquor stores, hair-straightening parlors and poolrooms on every block, code three calls to the station twenty-four hours a day. Footbeat hacks carried metal-studded saps; squadroom dicks packed .45 automatics loaded with un-regulation dum-dums. The local winos drank "Green Lizard"—cologne cut with Old Monterey white port, and the standard pop for a whore was one dollar, a buck and a quarter if you used "her place"—the abandoned cars in the auto graveyard at 56th and Central. The kids on the street were scrawny and bloated, stray dogs sported mange and perpetual snarls, merchants kept shotguns under the counter. Newton Street Division was a war zone.

I reported for duty after twenty-two hours of sack time, booze-weaned off the Benzies. The station commander, an ancient lieutenant named Getchell, supplied a warm welcome, telling me that Thad Green said I was kosher, and he'd accept me as such until I fucked up and proved otherwise. Personally, he hated boxers and stoolies, but he was willing to let bygones be bygones. My fellow officers would probably take some persuading, however; they *really* hated glory cops, boxers and Bolsheviks, and Fritzie Vogel was warmly remembered from his Newton Street tour years before. The cordial CO assigned me to a single-o foot beat, and I left that initial briefing determined to out-kosher God himself.

My first roll call was worse.

Introduced to the watch by the muster sergeant, I got no applause and a wide assortment of fisheyes, evil eyes and averted eyes. After the reading of the crime sheet, seven men out of the fifty-five or so stopped to shake my hand and wish me good luck. The sergeant gave me a silent tour of the division and dropped me off with a street map at the east edge of my beat; his farewell was, "Don't let the niggers give you no shit." When I thanked him, he said, "Fritz Vogel was a good pal of mine," and sped off.

I decided to kosherize myself fast.

My first week at Newton was muscle rousts and gathering information on who the *real* bad guys were. I broke up Green Lizard parties with my billy club, promising not to roust the winos if they fed me names. If they didn't kick loose, I arrested them; if they did, I arrested them anyway. I smelled reefer smoke on the sidewalk outside the gassed hair joint on 68th and Beach, kicked the door in and drew down on three grasshoppers holding felony quantities of maryjane. They snitched off their supplier and fingered an upcoming rumble between The Slausons and Choppers in return for my promise of leniency; I called in the info to the squardroom and flagged down a black-and-white to haul the hopheads to the station. Prowling the hooker auto dump got me prostitution collars, and threatening the girls' johns with calls to their wives got me more names. At week's end I had twenty-two arrests to my credit—nine of them felonies. And I had names. Names to test my courage on. Names to make up for the main events I'd dodged. Names to make the cops who hated me afraid of me.

I caught Downtown Willy Brown coming out of the Lucky Time Wine Bar. I said, "Your mother sucks a mean dick, Sambo"; Willy charged me. I took three to give six; when it was over Brown was blowing teeth out his nose. And two cops shooting the breeze across the street saw the whole thing.

Roosevelt Williams, paroled rape-o, pimp and policy runner, was tougher. His response to "Hello, shitbird" was "You a whitey motherfuck"—and he hit first. We traded shots for close to a minute, in full view of a cadre of Choppers lounging on front stoops. He was getting the better of me, and I almost went for my baton—not the stuff of which legends are made. Finally I pulled a Lee Blanchard move, rolling upstairs-downstairs sets, wham-wham-wham-wham, the last blow sending Williams to dreamland and me to the station nurse for two finger splints.

Bare knuckles were now out of the question. My last two names, Crawford Johnson and his brother Willis, operated a rigged card game out of the rec room of the Mighty Reedeemer Baptist Church on 61st and Enterprise, catty corner from the greasy spoon where Newton cops ate for half price. When I came in the window, Willis was dealing. He looked up and said, "Huh?" my billy club took out his hands and the card table. Crawford went for his waistband; my second baton blow knocked a silencer-fitted .45 from his grip. The brothers crashed out the door howling in pain; I picked up my new off-duty piece and told the other gamblers to grab their money and go home. When I walked outside, I had an audience: bluesuits chomping sandwiches on the sidewalk, watching the Johnson brothers hotfoot it, holding their broken paws. "Some people don't respond to civility!" I yelled. An old sergeant rumored to hate my guts yelled back, "Bleichert, you're an honorary white man!" and I knew I was kosherized.

• • •

The Johnson Brothers roust made me a minor legend. My fellow cops gradually warmed to me—the way you do to guys too crazy-bold for their own good, guys that you're grateful not to be yourself. It was like being a local celebrity again.

I got straight 100's on my first month's fitness report, and Lieutenant Getchell rewarded me with a radio car beat. It was a promotion of sorts, as was the territory that came with it.

Rumor had it that both the Slausons and the Choppers were out to do me in, and if they failed, Crawford and Willis Johnson were next in line to try. Getchell wanted me out of harm's way until they cooled off, so he assigned me to a sector on the western border of the division.

The new beat was an invitation to boredom. Mixed white and Negro, small factories and tidy houses, the best action you could hope for was drunk drivers and hitchhiking hookers soliciting motorists, trying to pick up a few bucks on their way down to the niggertown dope pads. I busted DDs and thwarted assignations by flashing my cherry lights, wrote traffic tickets by the shitload and generally prowled for anything out of the ordinary. Drive-in restaurants were popping up on Hoover and Vermont, spangly modern jobs where you could eat in your car and listen to music on speakers attached to the window posts. I spent hours parked in them, KGFJ blasting be-bop, my two-way on low in case anything hot came over the air. I eyeballed the street while I sat and listened, trawling for white hookers, telling myself that if I saw any who looked like Betty Short, I'd warn them that 39th and Norton was only a few miles away and urge them to be careful.

But most of the whores were jigs and bleached blondes, not worth warning and only worth busting when my arrest quota was running low. They were women, though, safe places to let my mind dawdle, safe substitutes for my wife at home alone and Madeleine crawling 8th Street gutters. I toyed with the idea of picking up a Dahlia/Madeleine lookalike for sex, but always quashed it—it was too much like Johnny Vogel and Betty at the Biltmore.

Going off-duty at midnight, I was always itchy, restless, in no mood to go home and sleep. Sometimes I hit the all-night movies downtown, sometimes the jazz clubs on South Central. Bop was moving into its heyday, and all-night sessions with a pint of bonded were generally enough to ease me home and into a dreamless sleep shortly after Kay left for work in the morning.

But when it didn't work, it was sweats and Jane Chambers' smiling clown and Frenchman Joe Dulange smashing cockroaches and Johnny Vogel and his whip and Betty begging me to fuck her or kill her killer, she didn't care which. And the worst of it was waking up alone in the fairy tale house.

Summer came on. Hot days sleeping it off on the couch; hot nights patrolling west niggertown, bonded sourmash, the Royal Flush and Bido Lito's, Hampton Hawes, Dizzy Gillespie, Wardell Gray and Dexter Gordon. Restless attempts to study for the Sergeant's Exam and the urge to blow off Kay and the fairy tale house and get a cheap pad somewhere on my beat. If it weren't for the spectral wino it might have gone on forever.

I was parked in Duke's Drive-in, eyeing a gaggle of trampy-looking girls standing by the bus stop about ten yards in front of me. My two-way was off, wild Kenton riffs were coming out of the speaker hook-up. The breezeless humidity had my uniform plastered to my body; I hadn't made an arrest in a week. The girls were waving at passing cars, one peroxide blonde gyrating her hips at them. I started synchronizing the bumps and grinds to the music, playing with the idea of pulling a shakedown, running them through R&I for outstanding warrants. Then a scraggy old wino entered the scene, one hand holding a short dog, the other out begging for chump change.

The bottle blonde quit dancing to talk to him; the music went haywire—all screeches—without her accompaniment. I flashed my headlights; the wino shielded his eyes, then shot me the finger. I was out of the black-and-white and on top him, Stan Kenton's band my backup.

Roundhouse lefts and rights, rabbit punches. The girl's shrieks out-decibeling Big Stan. The wino cursing me, my mother, my father. Sirens in my head, the smell of rotting meat at the warehouse, even though I knew it couldn't be. The old geez blubbering, "Pleeese."

I staggered to the corner pay phone, gave it a nickel and dialed my own number. Ten rings, no Kay, WE-4391 without thinking. Her voice: "Hello, Sprague residence." My stammers; then, "Bucky? Bucky, is that you?" The wino weaving toward me, sucking his bottle with bloody lips. Hands inside my pockets, pulling out bills to throw him, cash on the pavement. "Come over, sweet. The others are down at Laguna. It could be like old—"

I left the receiver dangling and the wino scooping up the better part of my last paycheck. Driving to Hancock Park, I ran, just this one time, just to be inside the house again. Knocking on the door, I had myself convinced. Then Madeleine was there, black silk, upswept coiffure, yellow barrette. I reached for her; she stepped back, pulled her hair loose and let it fall to her shoulders. "No. Not yet. It's all I have to keep you with."

IV

Elizabeth

CHAPTER TWENTY-NINE

For a month she held me in a tight velvet fist.

Emmett, Ramona and Martha were spending June at the family's beach house in Orange County, leaving Madeleine to look after the Muirfield Road estate. We had twenty-two rooms to play in, a dream house built from immigrant ambition. It was a big improvement over the Red Arrow Motel and Lee Blanchard's monument to bank robbery and murder.

Madeleine and I made love in every bedroom, tearing loose every silk sheet and brocade coverlet, surrounded by Piscassos and Dutch masters and Ming Dynasty vases worth hundreds of grand. We slept in the late mornings and early afternoons before I headed for niggertown; the looks I got from her neighbors when I walked to my car in full uniform were priceless.

It was a reunion of avowed tramps, rutters who knew that they'd never have it as good with anyone else. Madeleine explained her Dahlia act as a strategy to get me back; she had seen me parked in my car that night, and knew that a Betty Short seduction would keep me returning. The desire behind it moved me even as the elaborateness of the ruse elicted revulsion.

She dropped the look the second the door shut that first time. A quick rinse brought her hair back to its normal dark brown, the pageboy cut returned, the tight black dress came off. I tried everything but threats of leaving and begging; Madeleine kept me mollified with "Maybe some day." Our implicit compromise was Betty talk.

I asked questions, she digressed. We exhausted actual facts quickly; from then on it was pure interpretation.

Madeleine spoke of her utter malleability, Betty the chameleon who would be anyone to please anybody. I had her down as the center of the most baffling piece of detective work the Department had ever seen, the disrupter of most of the lives close to me, the human riddle I had to know *everything* about. That was my final perspective, and it felt bone shallow.

After Betty, I turned the conversation to the Spragues themselves. I never told Madeleine that I knew Jane Chambers, broaching Jane's inside stuff in roundabout ways. Madeleine said that Emmett was mildly worried about the forthcoming demolitions up by the Hollywoodland sign; that her mother's pageantry and love of strange books and medieval lore were nothing but "Hophead stuff—Mama with time on her hands and a snootful of patent medicine." After a while, she came to resent my probes and demanded turnabout. I told lies and wondered where I would go if my own past was all I had left.

CHAPTER THIRTY

Pulling up in front of the house, I saw a moving van in the driveway and Kay's Plymouth, top down, packed with boxes. The run for clean uniforms was turning into something else.

I double-parked and bolted up the steps, smelling Madeleine's perfume on myself. The van started backing out; I yelled, "Hey! Goddamn it, come back here!"

The driver ignored me; words from the porch kept me from going after him. "I didn't touch your things. And you can have the furniture."

Kay was wearing her Eisenhower jacket and tweed skirt, just like when I'd first met her. I said, "Babe," and started to ask "Why?" My wife counterpunched: "Did you think I'd let my husband vanish for three weeks and do nothing about it? I've had detectives following you, Dwight. She looks like that fucking dead girl, so you can have *her*—not me."

Kay's dry eyes and calm voice were worse than what she was saying. I felt shakes coming on, bad heebie-jeebies. "Babe, goddamn it—"

Kay backed out of grabbing range. "Whoremonger. Coward. *Necrophile.*"

The shakes got worse; Kay turned and made for her car, a

deft little pirouette out of my life. I caught another scent of Madeleine and walked into the house.

The bentwood furniture looked the same, but there were no literary quarterlies on the coffee table and no cashmere sweaters folded in the dining room cabinet. The cushions on my couch-bed were neatly arrayed, like I'd never slept there. My phonograph was still by the fireplace, but all Kay's records were gone.

I picked up Lee's favorite chair and threw it at the wall; I hurled Kay's rocker at the cabinet, reducing it to glass rubble. I upended the coffee table and rammed it into the front window, then tossed it out on the porch. I kicked the rugs into sloppy piles, pulled out drawers, tipped over the refrigerator and took a hammer to the bathroom sink, smashing it loose from the pipes. It felt like going ten rounds full blast; when my arms were too limp to inflict more damage I grabbed my uniforms and my silencer .45 and got out, leaving the door open so scavengers could pick the place clean.

With the other Spragues due back in LA anyday, there was only one place to go. I drove to the El Nido, badged the desk clerk and told him he had a new tenant. He forked over an extra room key; seconds later I was smelling Russ Millard's stale cigarette smoke and Harry Sears' spilled rye. And I was eyeball to eyeball with Elizabeth Short on all four walls: alive and smiling, dumbstruck with cheap dreams, vivisected in a weedy vacant lot.

And without even saying it to myself, I knew what I was going to do.

I removed the file cases from the bed, stacked them in the closet and ripped off the sheets and blankets. The Dahlia photos were nailed to the wall; it was easy to drape the bedding over them so that they were completely covered. The pad perfect, I went prowling for props.

I found a jet-black upswept wig at Western Costume, a yellow barrette at a dime store on the Boulevard. The heebie-jeebies came back—worse than bad. I drove to the Firefly Lounge, hoping it still had Hollywood Vice's sanction.

One eyeball circuit inside told me it did. I sat down at the bar, ordered a double Old Forester and stared at the girls congregating on a matchbook-size bandstand. Footlights set in the floor shined up at them; they were only thing in the dump illuminated.

I downed my drink. They all looked typical—hophead whores in cheap slit kimonos. Counting five heads, I watched the girls smoke cigarettes and adjust their slits to show more leg. None was anywhere near close.

Then a skinny brunette in a flouncy cocktail dress stepped onto the bandstand. She blinked at the glare, scratched her pert button nose and toed figure eights on the floor.

I hooked a finger at the bartender. He came over with the bottle; I held a palm over my glass. "The girl in the pink. How much to take her to my place for an hour or so?"

The barman sighed. "Mister, we've got three rooms here. The girls don't like—"

I shut him up with a crisp new fifty. "You're making an exception for me. Be generous with yourself."

The fifty disappeared, then the man himself. I filled my glass and downed it, eyes on the bartop until I felt a hand on my shoulder.

"Hi, I'm Lorraine."

I turned around. Close up she could have been any pretty brunette—perfect molding clay. "Hi, Lorraine. I'm . . . B-B-Bill."

The girl snickered, "Hi, *Bill*. You wanna go now?"

I nodded; Lorraine walked outside ahead of me. Straight daylight showed off the runs in her nylons and old needle scars on her arms. When she got in the car I saw that her eyes were dull brown; when she drummed her fingers on the dashboard I saw that her closest link to Betty was chipped nail polish.

It was enough.

We drove to the El Nido and walked up to the room without saying a word. I opened the door and stood aside to let Lorraine enter; she rolled her eyes at the gesture, then gave a low whistle to let me know the place was a dive. I locked the door behind us, unwrapped the wig and handed it to her. "Here. Take off your clothes and put this on."

Lorraine did an inept strip. Her shoes clunked on the floor, she snagged her nylons pulling them off. I made a move to unzip her dress, but she saw it coming, turned away and did it herself. With her back to me, she unhooked her bra, stepped out of her panties and fumbled with the wig. Facing me, she said, "This your idea of a big thrill?"

The coiffure was askew, like a gag rug on a vaudeville comic; only her breasts were a good match. I took off my jacket and started to work at my belt. Something in Lorraine's eyes stopped me; I snapped that she was afraid of my gun and handcuffs. I got the urge to calm her down by telling her I was a cop—then the look made her seem more like Betty, and I stopped.

The girl said, "You won't hurt—"; I said, "Don't talk," and straightened the wig, bunching her lank brown hair up inside it. The fit was still all wrong, whorish and out of kilter. Lorraine was shaking now; head-to-toe shivers as I stuck the yellow barrette into the coif to make things right. All it did was rip loose strands of black as dry as straw and tilt everything off to one side, like the girl was the slash mouth clown, not my Betty.

I said, "Lie down on the bed." The girl complied, legs rigid and pressed together, hands underneath her, a skinny length of tics and twitches. Prone, the wig was half on her head, half on the pillow. Knowing the pictures on the wall would spark perfection, I pulled off the sheets covering them.

I stared at portrait-perfect Betty/Beth/Liz; the girl screamed, *"No! Killer! Police!"*

Wheeling around, I saw a naked fraud transfixed by 39th and Norton. I hurled myself onto the bed, pressed my hands over her mouth and held her down, talking it right and perfect: "It's just that she has all these different names to be, and this woman won't be her for me, and I can't be just anybody like her, and every time I try I fuck it up, and my friend went crazy because his little sister might have been her if somebody didn't kill her—"

"KILL—"

The wig in disarray on the bedspread.

My hands on the girl's neck.

I let go and stood up slowly, palms out, no harm meant. The girl's vocal cords stretched, but she couldn't come up with a sound. She rubbed her throat where my hands had been, the imprint still bright red. I backed off to the far wall, unable to talk.

Mexican standoff.

The girl massaged her throat; something like ice came into her eyes. She got off the bed and put on her clothes facing me, the ice getting colder and deeper. It was a look I knew I couldn't match, so I got out my ID buzzer and held up LAPD badge 1611 for her to see. She smiled; I tried to imitate her; she walked up to me and spat on the piece of tin. The door slammed, the pictures on the wall fluttered, my voice came back in racking fits, "I'll get him for you, he won't hurt you anymore, I'll make it up to you, oh Betty Jesus fuck I will."

CHAPTER THIRTY-ONE

The airplane flew east, slicing through cloud banks and bright blue sky. My pockets were stuffed with cash from my all but liquidated bank account, Lieutenant Getchell had bought my line about a grievously ill high school pal in Boston and had granted me a week's accumulated sick leave. A stack of notes from the Boston PD's background check was on my lap—laboriously copied from the El Nido file. I already had an interrogation itinerary printed out, aided by the metropolitan Boston street atlas I'd purchased at the LA airport. When the plane landed, it would be Medford/Cambridge/Stoneham and Elizabeth Short's past—the part that didn't get smeared across page one.

I'd hit the master file yesterday afternoon, as soon as I quit shaking and was able to put how close I'd gotten to havoc out my brain—at least the front part of it. One quick skimming told me that the LA end of the investigation was dead, a second and third told me it was deader, a fourth convinced me that if I stayed in town I'd go batshit over Madeleine and Kay. I had to run, and if my vow to Elizabeth Short was to mean anything, it had to be in her direction. And if it was a wild-goose chase, then at least it was a trip to clean territory—where my badge and live women wouldn't get me into trouble.

The revulsion on the hooker's face wouldn't leave me; I could still smell her cheap perfume and imagined her spitting indictments, the same words Kay had used earlier that day, only worse—because she knew what I was: a whore with a badge. Thinking about her was like scraping the bottom of my life on my knees—the only comfort in it the fact that I couldn't go any lower—that I'd chew the muzzle of my .38 first.

The plane landed at 7:35; I was the first in line to disembark, notebook and satchel in hand. There was a car rental place in the terminal; I rented a Chevy coupe and headed into the Boston metropolis, anxious to take advantage of the hour or so of daylight left.

My itinerary included the addresses of Elizabeth's mother, two of her sisters, her high school, a Harvard Square hash house where she slung plates in '42 and the movie theater where she worked as a candy girl in '39 and '40. I decided on a loop through Boston to Cambridge, then Medford—Betty's real stomping ground.

Boston, quaint and old, hit me like a blur. I followed street signs to the Charles River Bridge and crossed over into Cambridge: ritzy Georgian pads and streets packed with college kids. More signs led me to Harvard Square; there was stop one— Otto's Hofbrau, a gingerbread structure spilling the aroma of cabbage and beer.

I parked in a meter space and walked in. The Hansel and Gretel motif extended to the whole place—carved wood booths, beer steins lining the walls, waitresses in dirndl skirts. I looked around for the boss, my eyes settling on a smock-clad older man standing by the cash register.

I walked over, and something kept me from badging him. "Excuse me. I'm a reporter, and I'm writing a story on Elizabeth Short. I understand that she worked here back in '42, and I thought you could tell me a little about her then."

The man said, "Elizabeth who? She some sort of movie star?"

"She was killed in Los Angeles a few years ago. It's a famous case. Do you—"

"I bought this place in '46, and the only employee I got left from the war is Roz. Rozzie, come here! Man wants to talk to you!"

The battle-axe waitress of them all materialized—a baby elephant in a thigh-length skirt. The boss said, "This guy's a reporter. Wants to talk to you about Elizabeth Short. You remember her?"

Rozzie popped her gum at me. "I told the *Globe* and the *Sentinel* and the cops the first time around, and I ain't changing my story. Betsy Short was a dish dropper and a dreamer, and if she didn't bring in so much Harvard business, she wouldn't a lasted a day. I heard she put out for the war effort, but I didn't know none of her boyfriends. End of story. And you ain't no reporter, you're a cop."

I said, "Thank you for that perceptive comment," and left.

My atlas placed Medford twelve miles away, a straight run out Massachusetts Avenue. I got there just as night was falling, smelling it first, then seeing it.

Medford was a factory town, smoke-belching foundry stacks forming its perimeter. I rolled up my window to hold off the sulfur stink; the industrial area dwindled into blocks of narrow red-brick houses crammed together with less than a foot between them. Every block had at least two gin mills, and when I saw Swasey Boulevard—the street the movie theater was on—I opened my wind wing to see if the foundry stench was dissipating. It wasn't—and the windshield was already bearing a film of greasy soot.

I found the Majestic a few blocks down, a typical Medford red-brick building, the marquee heralding *Criss Cross* with Burt Lancaster and *Duel in the Sun*—"All Star Cast." The ticket booth was empty, so I walked straight into the theater and up to the snack stand. The man behind it said, "Anything wrong, officer?" I groaned that the locals had my number—three thousand miles from home.

"No, nothing's wrong. Are you the manager?"

"The owner. Ted Carmody. You BPD?"

I reluctantly displayed my shield. "Los Angeles Police Department. It's about Beth Short."

Ted Carmody crossed himself. "Poor Lizzie. You got some hot leads? That why you're here?"

I put a nickel on the counter, grabbed a Snickers bar and unwrapped it. "Let's just say I owe Betty one, and I've got a few questions."

"Ask on."

"First off, I've seen the Boston Police background check file, and your name wasn't listed on the interview sheet. Didn't they talk to you?"

Carmody handed me back my nickel. "On the house, and I didn't talk to the Boston cops because they talked Lizzie up like she was some sort of tramp. I don't cooperate with bad-mouthers."

"That's admirable, Mr. Carmody. But what would you have told them?"

"Nothing dirty, that's for damn sure. Lizzie was all aces to me. If the cops had been properly respectful of the dead, I'd have told 'em that."

The man was exhausting me. "I'm a respectful guy. Pretend that it's two years ago and tell me."

Carmody couldn't quite peg my style, so I chomped the candy bar to ease him into some slack. "I'd have told 'em Lizzie was a bad worker," he said finally. "And I'd have told 'em I didn't care. She brought the boys in like a magnet, and if she kept sneaking in to watch the picture, so what? For fifty cents an hour I didn't expect her to slave for me."

I said, "What about her boyfriends?"

Carmody slammed the counter; Jujubees and Milk Duds toppled over. "Lizzie wasn't no roundheels! The only boyfriend I knew she had was this blind guy, and I knew it was just palship. Listen, you want to know what kind of kid Lizzie was? I'll tell you. I used to let the blind guy in for free, so he could listen to the picture, and Lizzie kept sneaking into tell him what was on the screen. You know, describe it to him. That sound like tramp behavior to you?"

It felt like a punch to the heart. "No, it doesn't. Do you remember the guy's name?"

"Tommy something. He's got a room over the VFW Hall down the block, and if he's a killer I'll flap my arms and fly to Nantucket."

I stuck out my hand. "Thanks for the candy bar, Mr. Carmody."

We shook. Carmody said, "You get the guy who killed Lizzie, I'll buy you the factory that makes the goddamn things."

As I said the words, I knew it was one of the finest moments of my life:

"I will."

The VFW Hall was across the street and down from the Majestic, yet another red-brick structure streaked with soot. I walked there thinking of blind Tommy as a big washout, someone I had to talk to soften up Betty, make her live more easily in me.

Side steps took me upstairs, past a mailbox labeled T. GILFOYLE. Ringing the bell, I heard music; looking in the one window I saw pitch darkness. Then a soft male voice came from the other side of the door. "Yes? Who is it?"

"Los Angeles Police, Mr. Gilfoyle. It's about Elizabeth Short."

Light hit the window, the music died. The door opened, and a tall pudgy man wearing dark glasses pointed me inside. He was immaculate in striped sportshirt and slacks, but the room was a pigsty, dust and grime everywhere, an army of bugs scattering from the unaccustomed blast of brightness.

Tommy Gilfoyle said, "My Braille teacher read me the LA papers. Why did they say such nasty things about Beth?"

I tried diplomacy. "Because they didn't know her like you did."

Tommy smiled and plopped into a ratty chair. "Is the apartment really disreputable?"

The couch was littered with phonograph records; I scooped a handful aside and sat down. "It could use a lick and a promise."

"I get slothful sometimes. Is Beth's investigation active again? Priority stuff?"

"No, I'm here on my own. Where did you pick up the cop lingo?"

"I have a policeman friend."

I brushed a fat bug off my sleeve. "Tommy, tell me about you and Beth. Give me something that didn't make the papers. Something good."

"Is this personal with you? Like a vendetta?"

"It's more than that."

"My friend said policemen who take their work personally get in trouble."

I stomped a cockroach exploring my shoe. "I just want to get the bastard."

"You don't have to yell. I'm blind, not deaf, and I wasn't blind to Beth's little faults, either."

"How so?"

Tommy fingered the cane by his chair. "Well, I won't dwell on it, but Beth was promiscuous, just like the newspapers implied. I knew the reason, but I kept still because I didn't want to disgrace her memory, and I knew that it wouldn't help the police find her killer."

The man was wheedling now, caught between wanting to kick loose and keep secrets. I said, "You let *me* judge that. I'm an experienced detective."

"At your age? I can tell by your voice that you're young. My friend said that to make detective you have to serve at least ten years on the force."

"Goddamn it, don't dick me around. I came here on my own and I didn't come to—"

I stopped when I saw that the man was frightened, one hand going for the telephone. "Look, I'm sorry. It's been a long day, and I'm a long way from home."

Tommy surprised me by smiling. "I'm sorry, too. I was just being coy to prolong the company, and that's rude. So I'll tell you about Beth, her little foibles and all.

"You probably know she was star-struck, and that's true. You probably guessed that she didn't have much talent, and that's true, too. Beth read plays to me—acting all the parts, and she was a terrible ham—just awful. I understand the spoken word, so believe me, I know.

"What Beth was good at was writing. I used to sit in on movies at the Majestic, and Beth used to describe things so I'd have something to go with the dialogue. She was brilliant, and I encouraged her to write for the movies, but she just wanted to be an actress like every other silly girl who wanted to get out of Medford."

I would have committed mass murder to get out. "Tommy, you said you know the reason Beth was promiscuous."

Tommy sighed. "When Beth was sixteen or seventeen, these two thugs assaulted her, somewhere in Boston. One actually raped her, and the other was going to, but a sailor and a marine came by and chased them away.

"Beth thought the man might have made her pregnant, so she went to a doctor for an examination. He told her she had benign ovarian cysts, that she'd never be able to have children. Beth went crazy, because she'd always wanted lots of babies. She looked up the sailor and marine who'd saved her, and she begged them to father her child. The marine turned her down, and the sailor . . . he used Beth until he was shipped overseas."

I thought immediately of Frenchman Joe Dulange—his account of the Dahlia hipped on being pregnant, how he fixed her up with a "doctor buddy" and a bogus exam. That part of Dulange's story obviously wasn't as booze-addled as Russ Millard and I had originally thought—it was now a solid lead on Betty's missing days, the "doctor buddy" at least a major witness, maybe a major suspect. I said, "Tommy, do you know the names of the sailor and marine? The doctor?"

Tommy shook his head. "No. But that was when Beth became so loose with servicemen. She thought they were her saviors, that they could give her a child, a little girl to be a great actress in case she never made it. It's sad, but the only place I heard Beth was a great actress was in bed."

I stood up. "What happened with you and Beth then?"

"We lost touch. She left Medford."

"You've given me a good lead, Tommy. Thanks."

The blind man tapped his cane at the sound of my voice. "Then get who did it, but don't let Beth get hurt anymore."

"I won't."

CHAPTER THIRTY-TWO

The Short case was hot again—
if only with me.

Hours of Medford pub crawling gave me promiscuous Betty,
East Coast style—a big anticlimax after Tommy Gilfoyle's
revelations. I caught a midnight flight back to LA and called
Russ Millard from the airport. He agreed: Frenchman Joe's
"roach doctor" was probably legit, independent of Dulange's
DTs. He proposed a call to the Fort Dix CID to try to get more
details from the discharged loony, then a three-man canvassing
of downtown doctor's offices, concentrating on the area around
the Havana Hotel, where Dulange coupled with Betty. I sug-
gested that the "doctor" was most likely a barfly, an abortionist
or a quack; Russ concurred. He said he would talk to R&I and
his snitches, and he and Harry Sears would be knocking on
doors inside of an hour. We divvied up the territory: Figueroa
to Hill, 6th Street to 9th Street for me; Figueroa to Hill, 5th to
1st for them. I hung up and drove straight downtown.

I stole a Yellow Pages and made a list: legitimate MD's and
chiropractors, herb pushers and mystics—bloodsuckers who
sold religion and patent medicine under the "doctor" aegis.
The book had a few listings for obstetricians and gynocologists,

but instinct told me that Joe Dulange's doctor ploy was happenstance—not the result of his consciously seeking a specialist to calm Betty down. Running on adrenaline, I worked.

I caught most of the doctors early in their day, and got the widest assortment of sincere denials I'd ever encountered as a cop. Every solid citizen croaker I talked to convinced me a little bit more that Frenchy's pal had to be at least a little bit hinky. After a wolfed sandwich lunch, I hit the quasi types.

The herb loonies were all Chinese; the mystics were half women, half squarejohn lames. I believed all of their bewildered no's; I pictured all of them too terrified by the Frenchman to consider his offer. I was about to start hitting bars for scuttlebutt on barfly docs when exhaustion hit me. I drove "home" to the El Nido and slept—for all of twenty minutes.

Too itchy to try sleep again, I tried thinking logically. It was 6:00, doctors' offices were closing for the day, the bars wouldn't be *ripe* for canvassing for at least three hours. Russ and Harry would call me if they got something hot. I reached for the master file and started reading.

Time flew; names, dates and locations in police jargon kept me awake. Then I saw something that I'd perused a dozen times before, only this time it seemed off.

It was two memo slips:

1/18/47: Harry - Call Buzz Meeks at Hughes and have him call around on possible E. Short movie bus. associations. Bleichert says the girl was star struck. Do this independent of Loew - Russ.

1/22/47: Russ - Meeks says goose egg. Too bad. He was anxious to help - Harry.

With Betty's movie mania fresh in my mind, the memos looked different. I remembered Russ telling me that he was going to query Meeks, the Hughes security boss and the Department's "unofficial liaison" to the Hollywood community; I recalled that this was during the time when Ellis Loew was suppressing evidence on Betty's promiscuity in order to secure himself a better prosecuting attorney's showcase. Also: Betty's little black book listed a number of lower-echelon movie people—names that were checked out during the '47 black book interrogations.

The big question:

If Meeks really had checked around, why didn't he come up

271

with at least a few of the black book names and forward them to Russ and Harry?

I went out to the hall, got the Hughes Security number from the White Pages and dialed it. A singsong woman answered: "Security. May I help you?"

"Buzz Meeks, please."

"Mr. Meeks is out of his office right now. Whom shall I say is calling?"

"Detective Bleichert, LAPD. When will he be back?"

"When the budget meeting breaks up. May I ask what this is in reference to?"

"Police business. Tell him I'll be at his office in half an hour."

I hung up and leadfooted it to Santa Monica in twenty-five minutes. The gate guard admitted me to the plant parking lot, pointing to the security office—a Quonset hut at the end of a long string of aircraft hangars. I parked and knocked on the door; the woman with the singsong voice opened it. "Mr. Meeks said you should wait in his office. He won't be very long."

I walked in; the woman left, looking relieved that her day's work was over. The hut was wallpapered with paintings of Hughes aircraft, military art on a par with the drawings on cereal boxes. Meeks' office was better decorated: photos of a burly crewcut man with various Hollywood hotshots—actresses I couldn't place by name along with George Raft and Mickey Rooney.

I took a seat. The burly man showed up a few minutes later, hand out automatically, like someone whose job was ninety-five percent public relations. "Hello there. Detective Blyewell, is it?"

I stood up. We shook; I could tell that Meeks was put off by my two-day clothes and three-day beard. "It's Bleichert."

"Of course. What can I do for you?"

"I have a few questions about an old case you helped Homicide out with."

"I see. You're with the Bureau, then?"

"Newton Patrol."

Meeks sat down behind his desk. "A little out of your bailiwick, aren't you? And my secretary said you were a detective."

I closed the door and leaned against it. "This is personal with me."

"Then you'll top out your twenty rousting nigger piss bums. Or hasn't anyone told you that cops who take things personal end up from hunger?"

"They keep telling me, and I keep telling them that's my hometown. You fuck a lot of starlets, Meeks?"

"I fucked Carole Lombard. I'd give you her number, but she's dead."

"Did you fuck Elizabeth Short?"

Tilt, bingo, jackpot, lie detector perfect as Meeks flushed and fingered the papers on his blotter; a wheezing voice to back it up: "You catch a few too many in the Blanchard fight? The Short cooze is dead."

I pulled back my jacket to show Meeks the .45 I was carrying. "Don't call her that again."

"All right, tough guy. Now suppose you tell me what you want. Then we settle up and end this little charade before it gets out of hand. Comprende?"

"In '47, Harry Sears asked you to query your movie contacts on Betty Short. You reported back that it was a washout. You were lying. Why?"

Meeks picked up a letter opener. He ran a finger along the blade, saw what he was doing and put it down. "I didn't kill her and I don't know who did."

"Convince me, or I call up Hedda Hopper and give her tomorrow's column. How's this sound: 'Hollywood hanger-on suppressed Dahlia evidence because blank, blank, blank'? You fill in those blanks for me, or I fill them in for Hedda. Comprende?"

Meeks gave bravado another try. "Bleichert, you are fucking with the wrong man."

I pulled out the .45, made sure the silencer was on tight and slid a round into the chamber. "No, you are."

Meeks reached for a decanter on the sideboard by his desk; he poured himself a bracer and gulped it. "What I got was a dead-end lead, but you can have it if you want it so bad."

I dangled my gun by the trigger guard. "From hunger, shitbird. So give it to me."

Meeks opened up a safe built into his desk and pulled out a sheaf of papers. He studied them, then swiveled his chair and spoke to the wall. "I got a tip on Burt Lindscott, a producer at Universal. I got it from a guy who hated Lindscott's pal Scotty Bennett. Scotty was a pimp and a bookie, and he gave out Lindscott's home phone number in Malibu to all the good-looking young stuff who applied at the Universal casting office. The Short girl got one of Scotty's cards, and she called Lindscott.

"The rest, the dates and so forth, I got from Lindscott

himself. On the night of January tenth, the girl called from the Biltmore downtown. Burty had her describe herself, and he liked what he heard. He told the girl he'd give her a screen test in the morning, when he got back from a poker session at his club. The girl said she didn't have any place to go until then, so Lindscott told her to come over and spend the night at his place—his houseboy would feed her and keep her company. She took a bus out to Malibu, and the houseboy—he was queer—did keep her company. Then, the next day around noon, Lindscott and three buddies of his came home drunk.

"The guys thought they'd have some fun, so they gave the girl this screen test, reading from a screenplay Burt had lying around. She was bad, and they laughed her out, then Lindscott made her an offer: service the four of them and he'd give her a bit part in his next picture. The kid was still mad at them for laughing at her screen test, and she threw a tantrum. She called them draft dodgers and traitors and said they weren't fit to be soldiers. Burt kicked her out around two-thirty that afternoon, Saturday the eleventh. The houseboy said she was broke and that she said she was gonna walk back downtown."

So Betty walked, or hitched, twenty-five miles downtown, meeting Sally Stinson and Johnny Vogel in the Biltmore lobby six hours or so later. I said, "Meeks, why didn't you report this? And look at me."

Meeks swiveled around; his features were smeared with shame. "I tried to get ahold of Russ and Harry, but they were out in the field, so I called Ellis Loew. He told me not to report what I'd found out, and he threatened to revoke my security clearance. Later on I found out that Lindscott was a Republican bigwig, and he'd promised Loew a bundle for his run at DA. Loew didn't want him implicated with the Dahlia."

I shut my eyes so I wouldn't have to look at the man; Meeks copped pleas while I ran pictures of Betty hooted at, propositioned, kicked out to die. "Bleichert, I checked out Lindscott and his houseboy and his buddies. These are legit depositions I've got—the megillah. None of them could have killed her. They were all at home and at their jobs from the twelfth straight through Friday the seventeenth. None of them could have done it, and I wouldn't have sat on it if one of the bastards snuffed her. I've got the depositions right here, and I'll show you."

I opened my eyes; Meeks was twirling the dial of a wall safe. I said, "How much did Loew pay you to keep quiet?"

Meeks blurted, "A grand," and backed off as if fearing a blow. I loathed him too much to give him the satisfaction of punishment, and left with his price tag hanging in the air.

• • •

I now had Elizabeth Short's missing days halfway filled in:

Red Manley dropped her in front of the Biltmore at dusk on Friday, January tenth; she called Burt Lindscott from there, and her Malibu adventures lasted until 2:30 the following afternoon. She was back at the Biltmore that evening, Saturday the eleventh, met Sally Stinson and Johnny Vogel in the lobby, tricked with Johnny until shortly after midnight, then took off. She met Corporal Joseph Dulange then, or later in the morning, at the Night Owl Bar on 6th and Hill—two blocks from the Biltmore. She was with Dulange, there and at the Havana Hotel, until the afternoon or evening of Sunday, January twelfth, when he took her to see his "doctor buddy."

Driving back to the El Nido, some missing piece of legwork nagged at me through my exhaustion. Passing a phone booth it came to me: if Betty called Lindscott in Malibu—a toll call— there would be a record with Pacific Coast Bell. If she made other toll calls, at that time or on the eleventh, before or after her coupling with Johnny Vogel, P.C.B. would have the information in its records—the company saved tallies of pay phone transactions for cost and price studies.

My fatigue nosedived once more. I took side streets the rest of the way, running stop signs and red lights; arriving, I parked in front of a hydrant and ran up to the room for a notebook. I was heading for the hallway phone when it foiled me by ringing.

"Yes?"

"Bucky? Sweet, is that you?"

It was Madeleine. "Look, I can't talk to you now."

"We had a date yesterday, remember?"

"I had to leave town. It was for work."

"You could have called. If you hadn't told me about this little hideaway of yours I'd have thought you were dead."

"Madeleine, Jesus Christ—"

"Sweet, I need to see you. They're tearing those letters off the Hollywoodland sign tomorrow, *and* demolishing some bungalows Daddy owns up there. Bucky, the deeds lapsed to the city, but Daddy bought that property and built those places under his own name. He used *the* worst materials, and an investigator from the City Council has been nosing around Daddy's tax lawyers. One of them told him this old enemy of his who committed suicide left the Council a brief on Daddy's holdings and—"

It sounded like gibberish—tough guy Daddy in trouble, tough boy Bucky the second choice for consolation duty. I said, "Look, I can't talk to you now," and hung up.

Now it was real detective shitwork. I arrayed my notebook and pen on the ledge by the phone and emptied a four-day accumulation of coins from my pockets, counting close to two dollars—enough for forty calls. First I called the night supervisor at Pacific Coast Bell, requesting a list of all toll and collect calls made from Biltmore Hotel pay phones on the evenings of January 10, 11, and 12, 1947; the names and addresses of the called parties and the times of the calls.

I stood nervously holding the receiver while the woman did her work, shooting dirty looks to other El Nido residents who wanted to use the phone. Then, a half hour later, she came back on the line and started talking.

The Lindscott number and address was there among the 1/10 listings, but nothing else that night registered as hinky. I wrote all the information down anyway; then, when the woman got to the evening of 1/11—right around the time Betty met Sally Stinson and Johnny Vogel in the Biltmore lobby—I hit paydirt:

Four toll calls were made to obstetricians' offices in Beverly Hills. I took down the names and numbers, along with the numbers for the doctors' night answering services, and the immediately following toll call listings. They produced no sparks—but I copied them anyway. Then I attacked Beverly Hills with an arsenal of nickels.

It took all my change to get what I wanted.

I told the answering service operators it was a police emergency; they put me through to the doctors at home. They had their secretaries drive to the office to check their back records, then call me at the El Nido. The whole process took two hours. At the end of it I had this:

On the early evening of January 11, 1947, a "Mrs. Fickling" and a "Mrs. Gordon" called a total of four different obstetricians' offices in Beverly Hills, requesting appointments for pregnancy testing. The after-hours service operators made appointments for the mornings of January 14 and 15. Lieutenant Joseph Fickling and Major Matt Gordon were two of the war heros Betty dated and pretended to be married to; the appointments were never kept because on the fourteenth she was getting tortured to death; on the fifteenth she was a mutilated pile of flesh at 39th and Norton.

I called Russ Millard at the Bureau; a vaguely familiar voice answered: "Homicide."

"Lieutenant Millard, please."

"He's in Tucson extraditing a prisoner."

"Harry Sears, too?"

"Yeah. How are you, Bucky? It's Dick Cavanaugh."

"I'm surprised you could place my voice."

"Harry Sears told me you'd be calling. He left a list of doctors for you, but I can't find it. That what you want?"

"Yeah, and I need to talk to Russ. When's he coming back?"

"Late tomorrow, I think. Is there someplace I can call you if I find the list?"

"I'm rolling. I'll call you."

The other phone numbers had to be tried, but the obstetrician lead was too potent to sit on. I headed back downtown to look for Dulange's doctor buddy, my exhaustion dropped like a hot rock.

I kept at it until midnight, concentrating on the bars around 6th and Hill, talking up barflies, buying them drinks, racking up booze rebop and a couple of tips on abortion mills that almost sounded legit.

Another sleepless day ended; I took to driving from bar to bar, playing the radio to keep from dozing off. The news kept droning on about the "milestone refurbishing" of the Hollywoodland sign—playing up the lopping off of L-A-N-D as the biggest thing since Jesus. Mack Sennett and his Hollywoodland tract got a lot of air time, and a theater in Hollywood was reviving a bunch of his old Keystone Kops pictures.

Toward bar-closing time, I felt like a Keystone Kop and looked like a bum—scraggly beard, soiled clothes, fevered attention that kept wandering off. When drunks eager for more booze and camaraderie began giving me the brush, I took it as a strong hint, drove to a deserted parking lot, pulled in and slept.

* * *

Leg cramps woke me up at dawn. I stumbled out of the car looking for a phone; a black-and-white cruised by, the driver giving me a long fisheye. I found a booth at the corner and dialed the padre's number.

"Homicide Bureau. Sergeant Cavanaugh."

"Dick, it's Bucky Bleichert."

"Just the man I wanted to talk to. I've got the list. You got the pencil?"

I dug out a pocket notebook. "Shoot."

"Okay. These are licensed-revoked doctors. Harry said they were practicing downtown in '47. One, Gerald Constanzo, 1841½ Breakwater, Long Beach. Two, Melvin Praeger, 9661 North Verdugo, Glendale. Three, Willis Roach. That's Roach like in the bug, in custody at Wayside Honor Rancho, convicted of selling morph in . . ."

Dulange.

The DTs.

"So I take Dahlia down the street to see the *roach doctor*. I slip him a tensky, and he gives her a fake examination . . ."

Breathing shallowly, I said, "Dick, did Harry write down the address where Roach was practicing?"

"Yeah. 614 South Olive."

The Havana Hotel was two blocks away. "Dick, call Wayside and tell the warden that I'll be driving up immediately to question Roach on the Elizabeth Short homicide."

"Mother dog."

"Motherfucking dog."

* * *

A shower, shave and change of clothes at the El Nido had me looking like a homicide detective; Dick Cavanaugh's call to Wayside would give me the rest of the juice I needed. I took the Angeles Crest Highway north, laying 50–50 odds that Dr. Willis Roach was Elizabeth Short's murderer.

The trip took a little over an hour; Hollywoodland sign spiel accompanied me on the radio. The deputy sheriff in the gate hut examined my badge and ID card and called the main building to clear me; whatever he was told made him snap to attention and salute. The barbed-wire fence swung open; I drove past the inmate barracks and over to a large Spanish-style structure fronted by a tile portico. As I parked, an LASD captain in uniform walked over, hand out, nervous grin on. "Detective Bleichert, I'm Warden Patchett."

I got out and gave the man a Lee Blanchard bonecrusher. "A pleasure, Warden. Has Roach been told anything?"

"No. He's in an interrogation room waiting for you. Do you think he killed the Dahlia?"

I started walking; Patchett steered me in the right direction. "I'm not sure yet. What can you tell me about him?"

"He's forty-eight years old, he's an anesthesiologist, and he was arrested in October of '47 for selling hospital morphine to an LAPD narcotics officer. He got five to ten, did a year at Quentin. He's down here because we needed help in the infirmary and the Adult Authority thought he'd be a safe risk. He's got no prior arrests, and he's been a model prisoner."

We turned into a low, tan brick building, a typical county "utility" job—long corridors, recessed steel doors embossed with numbers and no names. Passing a string of one-way glass windows, Patchett grabbed my arm. "There. That's Roach."

I stared in. A bony middle-aged man in county denims was seated at a card table, reading a magazine. He was a smart-looking bird—high forehead covered by wisps of thinning gray hair, bright eyes, the kind of large, veiny hands you associate with doctors. I said, "Care to sit in, Warden?"

Patchett opened the door. "Wouldn't miss it."

Roach looked up. Patchett said, "Doc, this is Detective Bleichert. He's with the Los Angeles Police, and he's got a few questions for you."

Roach put down his magazine—*American Anesthesioligist*. Patchett and I took seats across from him; the doctor/dope peddler said, "However I can be of service," his voice eastern and educated.

I went right for the throat. "Dr. Roach, why did you kill Elizabeth Short?"

Roach smiled slowly; gradually his grin spread ear to ear. "I expected you back in '47. After Corporal Dulange made that sad little confession of his, I expected you to break down my office door any second. Two and a half years after the fact surprises me, however."

My skin was buzzing; it felt like bugs were getting ready to eat me for breakfast. "There's no statute of limitations on murder."

Roach's grin disappeared, replaced by a serious look, the movie doctor getting ready to deliver some bad news. "Gentlemen, on Monday, January 13, 1947, I flew to San Francisco and checked in at the Saint Francis Hotel, preparatory to delivering my Tuesday night keynote speech at the annual convention of the Academy of American Anesthesiologists. I gave the speech Tuesday night, and was featured speaker at the farewell breakfast, Wednesday morning, January fifteenth. I was in the constant company of colleagues through the afternoon of the fifteenth, and I slept with my ex-wife at the Saint Francis both Monday and Tuesday nights. If you would like corroboration, call the Academy at their Los Angeles number, and my ex-wife, Alice Carstairs Roach, at San Francisco CR-1786."

I said, "Check that out for me, would you please, Warden?,"
my eyes on Roach.

Patchett left; the doctor said, "You look disappointed."

"Bravo, Willis. Now tell me about you and Dulange and
Elizabeth Short."

"Will you inform the Parole Board that I cooperated with
you?"

"No, but if you don't tell me I'll have the LA District Attorney
file charges on you for obstruction of justice."

Roach acknowledged match point with a grin. "Bravo,
Detective Bleichert. You know, of course, that the reason the
dates are so well fixed in my mind is due to all the publicity
Miss Short's death garnered. So please trust my memory."

I got out a pen and notepad. "Go, Willis."

Roach said, "In '47 I had a lucrative little sideline selling
pharmaceuticals. I sold them primarily in cocktail lounges,
primarily to servicemen who had discovered their pleasures
overseas during the war. That was how I met Corporal
Dulange. I approached him, but he informed me that he
appreciated the pleasures of Johnnie Walker Red Label scotch
whisky exclusively."

"Where was this?"

"At the Yorkshire House Bar, 6th and Olive Streets, near my
office."

"Go on."

"Well, that was the Thursday or Friday before Miss Short's
demise. I gave Corporal Dulange my card—injudiciously, as it
turned out—and I assumed that I would never see the man
again. Sadly, I was wrong.

"I was in poor shape financially at that time, owing to the
ponies, and I was living in my office. On the early evening of
Sunday, January twelfth, Corporal Dulange showed up at my
door with a lovely young woman named Beth in tow. He was
quite drunk, and he took me aside, pressed ten dollars into my
hand and told me lovely Beth was hipped on being pregnant.
Would I please give her a quick examination and tell her it was
so?

"Well, I obliged. Corporal Dulange waited in my outer office,
and I took lovely Beth's pulse and blood pressure and informed
her that yes indeed, she was pregnant. Her response was quite
strange: she seemed sad and relieved at the same time. My
interpretation was that she needed a reason to justify her
obvious promiscuity, and child bearing seemed like the ticket."

I sighed. "And when her death became news, you didn't go to the police because you didn't want them nosing around your dope racket?"

"Yes, that's correct. But there's more. Beth asked to use my phone. I acceded, and she dialed a number with a Webster prefix and asked to speak to Marcy. She said, 'It's Betty,' and listened for a while, then said, 'Really? A man with a medical background?' I didn't hear the rest of the conversation, and Beth hung up and said, 'I've got a date.' She joined Corporal Dulange in my waiting room, and they left. I looked out the window, and she was giving him the brush-off. Corporal Dulange stormed away, and Beth walked across 6th Street and sat down at the westbound Wilshire Boulevard bus stop. That was about seven-thirty, Sunday the twelfth. There. You didn't know that last part, did you?"

I finished up my shorthand version of it. "No, I didn't."

"Will you tell the Parole Board that I gave you a valuable clue?"

Patchett opened the door. "He's clean, Bleichert."

"No shit," I said.

* * *

Another piece of Betty's missing days revealed; another trip back to the El Nido, this time to check the master file for Webster prefix phone numbers. Going through the paperwork, I kept thinking that the Spragues had a Webster number, the Wilshire bus passed within a couple of blocks of their place and Roach's "Marcy" could be a mistaken "Maddy" or "Martha." It didn't follow logically—the whole family was down at their Laguna beach house the week of Betty's disappearance, Roach was certain about the "Marcy" and I had squeezed every ounce of Dahlia knowledge out of Madeleine.

Still, the thought simmered, like some buried part of me wanted to hurt the family for the way I'd rolled in the gutter with their daughter and sucked up to their wealth. I threw out another hook to keep it going; it fell flat when confronted with logic:

When Lee Blanchard disappeared in '47, his "R," "S" and "T" files were missing; maybe the Sprague file was among them.

But there was no Sprague file, Lee did not know that the Spragues existed, I kept everything pertaining to them away from him out of a desire to keep Madeleine's lesbian bar doings under wraps.

I continued skimming the file, sweating in the hot, airless room. No Webster prefixes appeared, and I started getting nightmare flashes: Betty sitting on the westbound Wilshire bus stop, 7:30 P.M., 1/12/47, waving bye-bye Bucky, about to jump into eternity. I thought about querying the bus company, a general rousting of drivers on that route—then realized it was too cold, that any driver who remembered picking up Betty would have come forward during all the '47 publicity. I thought of calling the other numbers I'd gotten from Pacific Coast Bell—then jacked that chronologically they were off— they didn't jibe with my new knowledge of where Betty was at what time. I called Russ at the Bureau and learned that he was still in Tucson, while Harry was working crowd control up by the Hollywoodland sign. I finished my paper prowl, with a total of zero Webster prefixes. I thought of yanking Roach's P.C.B file, nixing the notion immediately. Downtown LA, Madison prefix to Webster, was *not* a toll call—there would be no record, ditto on the Biltmore listings.

It came on then, big and ugly: bye-bye Bleichert at the bus stop, adios shitbird, has-been, never-was, stool pigeon niggertown harness bull. You traded a good woman for skunk pussy, you've turned everything that's been handed you to pure undiluted shit, your "I will's" amount to the eighth round at the Academy gym when you stepped into a Blanchard right hand—pratfalling into another pile of shit, clover that you turned to horse dung. Bye-bye Betty, Beth, Betsy, Liz, we were a couple of tramps, too bad we didn't meet before 39th and Norton, it just might have worked, maybe *us* would've been the one thing we wouldn't have fucked up past redemption—

I bolted downstairs, grabbed the car and rolled code three civilian, peeling rubber and grinding gears, wishing I had red lights and siren to sanction me faster. Passing Sunset and Vine, traffic got bottlenecked: shitloads of cars turning north on Gower and Beachwood. Even from miles away I could see the Hollywoodland sign dripping with scaffolding, scores of antlike people climbing up the face of Mount Lee. The lull in movement calmed me down, gave me a destination.

I told myself it wasn't over, that I'd drive to the Bureau and wait for Russ, that with two of us we'd put the rest of it together, that all *I* had to do was get downtown.

The traffic jam got worse—film trucks were shooting straight north while motorcycle bulls held back east- and westbound vehicles. Kids walked the lanes hawking plastic Hollywoodland sign souvenirs and passing out handbills. I heard, "Keystone Kops at the Admiral! Air-cooled! See the great new revival!" A piece of paper was shoved in my face, the printed "Keystone Kops," "Mack Sennett" and "Deluxe Air-Cooled Admiral Theatre" barely registering, the photo on the bottom registering hugely loud and wrong, like your own scream.

Three Keystone Kops were standing between pillars shaped like snakes swallowing each other's tails; a wall inset with Egyptian hieroglyphics was behind them. A flapper girl was lying on a tufted divan in the right-hand corner of the picture. It was unmistakably the background that appeared in the Linda Martin/Betty Short stag film.

I made myself sit still; I told myself that just because Emmett Sprague knew Mack Sennett in the '20s and had helped him build sets in Edendale, *this* didn't mean that he had anything to do with a 1946 smut film. Linda Martin had said the movie was shot in Tijuana; the still unfound Duke Wellington admitted making it. When traffic started moving, I hung a quick left up to the Boulevard and ditched the car; when I bought my ticket at the Admiral box office the girl recoiled from me—and I saw that I was hyperventilating and rank with sweat.

Inside, the air-conditioning froze that sweat, so that my clothes felt like an ice dressing. Final credits were rolling on the screen, replaced immediately by new opening ones, superimposed on papier mâché pyramids. I balled my fists when "Emmett Sprague, Assistant Director," flashed; I held my breath for a title that said where the thing was shot. Then a printed prologue came on, and I settled into an aisle seat to watch.

The story was something about the Keystone Kops transplanted to biblical days; the action was chases and pie throwing and kicks in the ass. The stag film set recurred several times, confirmed by more details each showing. The exterior shots looked like the Hollywood Hills, but there were no outside-inside scenes to pin down whether the set was in a studio or a private dwelling. I knew what I was going to do, but I wanted another hard fact to buttress all the logical "What if's" that were stacking up inside me.

The movie dragged on interminably; I shivered from icy sweats. Then the end titles rolled, "Filmed in Hollywood, U.S.A.," and the "What if's" fell like tenpins.

I left the theater, shaking from the blast-oven heat outside. I saw that I'd left the El Nido without either my service revolver or off-duty .45, took side streets back and grabbed the handcannon. Then I heard, "Hey, fella. Are you Officer Bleichert?"

It was the next-door tenant, standing in the hallway holding the phone at the end of its cord. I made a running grab for it, blurting, "Russ?"

"It's Harry. I'm up at the end of B-B-Beachwood Drive. They're tearing down a b-bunch of b-bungalows, and t-t-this patrolman f-f-found t-this shack all b-b-b-bloodstained. T-T-There was an FI card filed up here on the twelfth and th-th-thirtenth and I-I-I—"

And Emmett Sprague owned property up there; and it was the first time I'd heard Harry stutter in the afternoon. "I'll bring my evidence kit. Twenty minutes."

I hung up, took the Betty Short print abstract from the file and ran down to the car. Traffic had slackened; in the distance I could see the Hollywoodland sign missing it's last two letters. I hauled east to Beachwood Drive, then north. As I approached the park area that bordered Mount Lee, I saw that all the excitement was contained behind ropes guarded by a cordon of bluesuits; double-parking, I glimpsed Harry Sears walking over, badge pinned to his coat front.

His breath was now rife with liquor, the stutter gone. "Jesus Christ, what a piece of luck. This foot hack was assigned to clear out the vagrants before they started the demolitions. He stumbled onto the shack and came down and got me. It looks like tramps have been in and out since '47, but maybe you could still forensic it."

I grabbed my evidence kit; Harry and I walked uphill. Wrecking crews were tearing down bungalows on the street paralleling Beachwood, the workers shouting about gas leaking from pipes. Fire trucks stood by, hoses manned and pointed at huge rubble heaps. Bulldozers and earthmovers were lined up on the sidewalks, with patrolmen shepherding the locals out of potential harm's way. And up ahead of us, vaudeville reigned.

A system of pulleys was attached to the face of Mount Lee, supported by high scaffolding sunk into the ground at its base. The "A" of Hollywoodland, some fifty feet high, was sliding down a thick wire while cameras rolled, photographs snapped, rubberneckers gawked and political types drank champagne. Dust from uprooted scrub bushes was everywhere; the Hollywood High School band sat in folding chairs on a jerry-built bandstand a few feet from the pulley wire's terminus. When the letter "A" crashed to the dirt, they struck up "Hooray for Hollywood."

Harry said, "This way." We veered off on a dirt hiking trail circling the foot of the mountain. Dense foliage pressed in from both sides; Harry took the lead, walking sideways on a footpath pointing straight up the slope. I followed, scrub bushes snagging my clothes and brushing my face. After fifty uphill yards, the path leveled off into a small clearing fronted by a shallow stream of running water. And there was a tiny, pillbox-style cinderblock hut, the door standing wide open.

I walked in.

The side walls were papered with pornographic photographs of crippled and disfigured women. Mongoloid faces sucking dildoes, nudie girls with withered and brace-clad legs spread wide, limbless atrocities leering at the camera. There was a mattress on the floor; it was caked with layers and layers of blood. Bugs and flies were laced throughout the crust, stuck there as they feasted themselves to death. The back wall held tacked-on color photos that looked like they were torn from anatomy texts: close-up shots of diseased organs oozing blood and pus. There were spray and spatter marks on the floor; a small spotlight attached to a tripod was stationed beside the mattress, the light fixture aimed at the center of it. I wondered about electricity, then examined the gizmo's base and saw a battery hook-up. A blood-sprayed stack of books rested in one corner—mostly science fiction novels, with *Gray's Advanced Anatomy* and Victor Hugo's *The Man Who Laughs* standing out among them.

"Bucky?"

I turned around. "Go get ahold of Russ. Tell him what we've got. I'll do a forensic here."

"Russ won't get back from Tucson till tomorrow. And kid, you don't look too healthy to me right—"

"Goddamn it, get out of here and let me do this!"

Harry stormed out, spitting crushed pride; I thought of the proximity to Sprague property and dreamer Georgie Tilden, bum shack dweller, son of a famous Scottish anatomist. "Really? A man with a medical background?" Then I opened up my kit and raped the nightmare crib for evidence.

First I examined it top to bottom. Aside from obviously recent mud tracks—Harry's tramps probably—I found narrow strands of rope under the mattress. I scraped what looked like abraded flesh particles off them; I filled up another test tube with blood-matted dark hair taken from the mattress. I checked the blood crust for different color shadings, saw that it was a uniform maroon and took a dozen samples. I tagged and packed the rope away, along with the anatomy pages and smut pictures. I saw a man's bootprint, blood-outlined, on the floor, measured it and traced the sole treads onto a sheet of transparent paper.

Next it was fingerprints.

I dusted every touch, grab and press surface in the room; I dusted the few smooth spines and glossy pages in the books on the floor. The books yielded only streaks; the other surfaces brought up smudges, glove marks and two separate and distinct sets of latents. Finishing, I took a pen and circled the smaller digits on the door, doorjamb and wall molding by the mattress headboard. Then I got out my magnifying glass and Betty Short's print blow-up and made comparisons.

One identical point;

Two;

Three—enough for a courtroom.

Four, five, six, my hands shaking because this was unimpeachably where the Black Dahlia was butchered, shaking so hard I couldn't transfer the other set of latents to plates. I hacked a four-digit spread off the door with my knife and wrapped it in tissue—forensic amateur night. I packed up my kit, tremble-walked outside, saw the running water and knew that was where the killer drained the body. Then a strange flash of color by some rocks next to the stream caught my eye.

A baseball bat—the business end stained dark maroon.

I walked to the car thinking of Betty alive, happy, in love with some guy who'd never cheat on her. Passing through the park, I looked up at Mount Lee. The sign now read just *Hollywood*; the band was playing, "There's No Business Like Show Business."

• • •

I drove downtown. The LA city personnel office and the office of the Immigration and Naturalization Service were closed for the day. I called R&I and got goose egg on Scotland-born George Tildens—and I knew I'd go crazy if I waited overnight to make the print confirmation. It came down to calling in a superior officer, breaking and entering or bribery.

Remembering a janitor cleaning up outside the personnel

office, I tried number three. The old man heard my phony story out, accepted my double-sawbuck, unlocked the door and led me to a bank of filing cabinets. I opened a drawer marked CITY PROPERTY CUSTODIAL—PART-TIME, got out my magnifying glass and powder-dusted piece of wood—and held my breath.

Tilden, George Redmond, born Aberdeen, Scotland, 3/4/1896. 5 foot 11, 185 pounds, brown hair, green eyes. No address, listed as "Transient—contact for work thru E. Sprague, WE-4391." California Driver's license # LA 68224, vehicle: 1939 Ford pickup, license 6B119A, rubbish-hauling territory Manchester to Jefferson, La Brea to Hoover—39th and Norton right in the middle of it. Left- and right-hand fingerprints at the bottom of the page; one, two, three, four, five, six, seven, eight, nine matching comparison points—three for a conviction, six more for a one-way to the gas chamber. Hello, Elizabeth.

I closed the drawer, gave the janitor an extra ten-spot to keep him quiet, packed up the evidence kit and walked outside. I pinpointed the moment: 8:10 P.M., Wednesday, June 29, 1949, the night a flunky harness bull cracked the most famous unsolved homicide in California history. I touched the grass to see if it felt different, waved at office workers passing by, pictured myself breaking the news to the padre and Thad Green and Chief Horrall. I saw myself back at the Bureau, a lieutenant inside of a year, Mr. Ice exceeding the wildest Fire and Ice expectations. I saw my name in the headlines, Kay coming back to me. I saw the Spragues squeezed dry, disgraced by their complicity in the killing, all their money useless. And *that* was what kiboshed my reverie: there was no way for me to make the arrest without admitting I suppressed evidence on Madeleine and Linda Martin back in '47. It was either anonymous glory or public disaster.

Or back-door justice.

I drove to Hancock Park. Ramona's Cadillac and Martha's Lincoln were gone from the circular driveway; Emmett's Chrysler and Madeleine's Packard remained. I parked my lackluster Chevy crossways next to them, the rear tires sunk into the gardener's rose bush border. The front door looked impregnable, but a side window was open. I hoisted myself up and into the living room.

Balto the stuffed dog was there by the fireplace, guarding a score of packing crates lined up on the floor. I checked them out; they were filled to the top with clothes, silverware and ritzy bone china. A cardbox box at the end of the row was overflowing with cheap cocktail dresses—a weird anomaly. A sketch pad, the top sheet covered with drawings of women's faces, was wedged into one corner. I thought of commerical artist Martha, then heard voices upstairs.

I went to them, my .45 out, the silencer screwed on tight. They were coming from the master bedroom: Emmett's burr, Madeleine's pout. I pressed myself to the hallway wall, eased down to the doorway and listened.

". . . besides, one of my foremen said the goddamn pipes are spewing gas. There'll be hell to pay, lassie. Health and safety code violations at the very least. It's time for me to show the three of you Scotland, and let our Jew friend Mickey C. utilize his talent for public relations. He'll put the onus on old Mack or the pinkos or some convenient stiff, trust me he will. And when things are kosher again, we'll come home."

"But I don't *want* to go to Europe, Daddy. Oh God, *Scotland*. You've never been able to talk about it without saying how dreadful and provincial it is."

"Is it your toothy chum you think you'll be missing? Ahh, I suspect it is. Well, let me put your heart to rest. Aberdeen's got strapping plowboys who'll put that piss-poor excuse for a man to shame. Less inquisitive, lads who know their place. You'll not lack for sturdy cocksmen, let me assure you. Bleichert served his purpose to us a long time ago, and it's just the danger-loving part of you that took him back in. An injudicious part, I might add."

"Oh Daddy, I don't—"

I wheeled and stepped into the bedroom. Emmett and Madeleine were lying on the big canopied bed, clothed, her head on his lap, his rough carpenter's hands massaging her shoulders. The father-lover noticed me first; Madeleine pouted when Daddy's caresses stopped. My shadow hit the bed; she screamed.

Emmett silenced her, a whip-fast hand glinting with gem-stones over her mouth. He said, "This isn't a cuckold, lad. It's just affection, and we've a dispensation for it."

The man's reflexes and dinner table tone were pure style. I aped his calm: "Georgie Tilden killed Elizabeth Short. She called here on January twelfth, and one of you fixed her up with Georgie. She took the Wilshire bus out here to meet him. Now you fill the rest of it in."

Madeleine, eyes wide, trembled under her father's hand. Emmett looked at the none too steady gun aimed at him. "I

don't dispute that statement and I don't dispute your some-
what belated desire to see justice done. Shall I tell you where
George can be found?"

"No. First you tell me about you two, then you tell me about
your dispensation."

"It's not germane, lad. I'll congratulate you on your detective
work and tell you where Georgie can be found, and we'll leave
it at that. Neither of us wants to see Maddy hurt, and
discussing dour old family matters would affect her adversely."

As if to underline paternal concern, Emmett released his
hand. Madeleine wiped smeared lipstick off her cheeks and
murmured, "Daddy, make him stop."

I said, "Did Daddy tell you to fuck me? Did Daddy tell you to
invite me to dinner so I wouldn't check your alibi? Did you all
figure that a little hospitality and some cunt would brazen
things out for you? Did you—"

"*Daddy make him stop!*"

Emmett's whip hand flashed again; Madeleine buried her
face in it. The Scotchman made the next logical move. "Let's
get down to brass tacks, lad. Put the Sprague family history out
of your mind. What do you want?"

I looked around the bedroom, picking out objects—and the
price tags that Madeleine had bragged to me. There was the
Picasso oil on the back wall—a hundred and twenty grand.
Two Ming vases resting on the dresser—seventeen big ones.
The Dutch Master above the headboard cost two hundred odd
thou; the ugly Pre-Columbian gargoyle on the nightstand a
cool twelve and a half. Emmett, smiling now, said, "You
appreciate nice things. I appreciate that, and nice things like
those can be yours. Just tell me what you want."

I shot the Picasso first. The silencer went "Pffft" and the .45
hollow point blew the canvas in half. The two Mings were next,
crockery fragments exploding all over the room. I missed the
gargoyle with my first shot—a gold-bordered mirror the
consolation prize. Daddy and darling daughter huddled on the
bed; I took sight on Rembrandt or Titian or whoever the fuck it
was. My bull's-eye blew a dandy hole out of it, along with a
chunk of the wall. The frame toppled and hit Emmett's
shoulder; the heat of the weapon singed my hand. I held on to it
anyway, one round still in the chamber to get me my story.

Cordite, muzzle smoke and plaster haze making the air
almost unbreathable. Four hundred grand in bits and pieces.
The two Spragues a tangle of limbs on the bed, Emmett

coming out of it first, stroking Madeleine, rubbing his eyes and squinting.

I placed the silencer to the back of his head. "You, Georgie, Betty. Make me believe it or I'll take your whole fucking house down."

Emmett coughed and patted Madeleine's stray curls; I said, "You and your own daughter."

My old brass girl looked up then, tears drying, dust and lipstick mottling her face. "Daddy's not my real daddy and we've never really . . . so it's not wrong."

I said, "Then who is?"

Emmett turned, gently pushing my gun hand out of the way. He didn't look broken or angry. He looked like a businessman warming to the task of negotiating a tough new contract. "Dreamer Georgie is Maddy's father, Ramona is her mother. Do you want the details, or will that fact suffice?"

I sat down in a silk brocade chair a few feet from the bed. "All of it. And don't lie, because I'll know."

Emmett stood up and tidied his person, giving the room damage a weather eye. Madeleine went into the bathroom; a few seconds later I heard water running. Emmett sat on the edge of the bed, hands firm on his knees, like it was man-to-man confessional time. I knew he thought he could get away with telling me only what he wanted to; I knew I was going to make him spill it all, whatever it took.

"Back in the mid-20's Ramona wanted a child," he said. "I didn't, and I got damn sick and tired of being nagged about fatherhood. One night I got drunk and thought, 'Mother, you want a child I'll give you a lad just like me.' I did her without wearing a skin, sobered up and put it out of my mind. I didn't know it, but she took up with Georgie then, just to get that foal she craved so dearly. Madeleine was born, and I thought she was from that one mean time. I took to her—my little girl. Two years later I decided to go for a matched set, and we made Martha.

"Lad, I know you've killed two men, which is more than I can brag. So I know you know what it is to hurt. Maddy was eleven when I realized she was the stark spitting image of Georgie. I found him and played tic-tac-toe on his face with a nigger shiv. When I thought he'd die I took him to the hospital and bribed the administrators into putting 'car crash victim' on their records. When Georgie got out of the hospital he was a pitiful disfigured wreck. I begged him to forgive me, and I gave him money and I got him work tending my property and hauling rubbish for the city."

I recalled thinking that Madeleine resembled neither of her parents; I remembered Jane Chambers mentioning Georgie's car crash and descent to stumblebum. So far, I believed Emmett's story. "What about Georgie himself? Did you ever think he was crazy? Dangerous?"

Emmett tapped my knee, man-to-man empathy. "Georgie's father was Redmond Tilden, quite a celebrated doctor in Scotland. He was an anatomist. The Kirk was still strong in Aberdeen back then, and Doc Redmond could only legally dissect the corpses of executed criminals and the child molesters the villagers caught and stoned. Georgie liked to touch the organs his dad threw out. I heard a tale when we were boys, and I credit it. It seems that Doc Redmond bought a stiff from some body snatchers. He cut into the heart, and it was still beating. Georgie saw it, and it thrilled him. I credit the tale because in the Argonne Georgie used to take his bayonet to the dead Jerries. I'm not sure, but I think he's burgled graves here in America. Scalps and inside organs. Ghastly, all of it."

I saw an opening, a stab in the dark that might hit home. Jane Chambers had mentioned Georgie and Ramona filming pageants that centered on Emmett's World War I adventures, and two years ago at dinner, Ramona had said something about "Reenacting episodes out of Mr. Sprague's past he would rather forget." I swung out with my hunch: "How could you put up with someone so crazy?"

Emmett said, "You've been idolized in your time, lad. You know how it is when a weak man needs you to look after him. It's a special bond, like having a daft little brother."

I said, "I had a daft big brother once. I looked up to him."

Emmett laughed—fraudulently. "That's a side of the fence I've never been on."

"Oh yeah? Eldridge Chambers says otherwise. He left a brief with the City Council before he died. It seems that he witnessed some of Ramona and Georgie's pageants back in the thirties. Little girls with soldier kilts and toy muskets, Georgie holding off the Germans, you turning tail and running like a goddamn chickenshit coward."

Emmett flushed and tried to dredge up a smirk; his mouth twitched spastically with the effort. I shouted, "Coward!" and slapped him full force—and the hardcase Scotchman son of a bitch sobbed like a child. Madeleine came out of the bathroom,

291

fresh makeup, clean clothes. She moved to the bed and embraced her "Daddy," holding him the way he'd held her just a few minutes before.

I said, "Tell me, Emmett."

The man wept on the shoulder of his ersatz daughter; she stroked him with ten times more tenderness than she'd ever given me. Finally he got out a shell-shocked whisper: "I couldn't let Georgie go because he saved my life. We got separated from our company, all alone in a big field of stiffs. A German patrol was reconnoitering, sticking bayonets in everything British, dead or alive. Georgie piled Germans on top of us. They were all in pieces from a mortar attack. Georgie made me crawl under all these arms and legs and guts and stay there, and when it was over he cleaned me up and talked about America to cheer me up. So you see I couldn't . . ."

Emmett's whisper died out. Madeleine caressed his shoulders, ruffled his hair. I said, "I know that the stag film with Betty and Linda Martin wasn't shot in TJ. Did Georgie have anything to do with it?"

Madeleine's voice had the timbre Emmet's had earlier, when he was the one holding up the front. "No. Linda and I were talking at La Verne's Hideaway. She told me she needed a place to make a little movie. I knew what she meant, and I wanted to be with Betty again, so I let them use one of my daddy's vacant houses, one that had an old set in the living room. Betty and Linda and Duke Wellington shot the movie, and Georgie saw them doing it. He was always sneaking around Daddy's empty houses, and he got crazy over Betty. Probably because she looked like me . . . his daughter."

I turned away to make it easier for her to spill the rest. "Then?"

"Then, around Thanksgiving, Georgie came to Daddy and said, 'Give me that girl.' He said he'd tell the whole world that Daddy wasn't my daddy, and he'd lie about what we did together, like it was incest. I looked around for Betty, but I couldn't find her. Later I found out she was in San Diego then. Daddy was letting Georgie stay in the garage, because he was making more and more demands. He gave him money to keep him quiet, but he was still acting nasty and awful.

"Then, that Sunday night, Betty called, out of the blue. She'd been drinking, and she called me Mary or something like that. She said she'd been calling all the friends in her little black book trying to get a loan. I put Daddy on, and he offered Betty money to date a nice man he knew. You see, we thought Georgie just wanted Betty for . . . sex."

I said, "After all you knew about him, you believed that?"

Emmett shouted, "He liked to touch dead things! He was passive! I didn't think he was a goddamned killer!"

I eased them into the rest. "And you told them Georgie had a medical background?"

"Because Betty respected doctors," Madeleine said. "Because we didn't want her to feel like a whore."

I almost laughed. "Then?"

"Then I think you know the rest."

"Tell me anyway."

Madeleine delivered, hate oozing out of her. "Betty took the bus out here. She and Georgie left. We thought they'd go someplace decent to be together."

"Like the Red Arrow Motel?"

"No! Like one of Daddy's old houses that Georgie took care of! Betty forgot her purse, so we thought she'd be back for it, but she never came back and neither did Georgie, and then the papers came out and we knew what must have happened."

If Madeleine thought her confession was over, she was wrong. "Tell me what you did then. How you covered things up."

Madeleine caressed Emmett while she spoke. "I went looking for Linda Martin, and I found her at a motel in the Valley. I gave her money and told her that if the police picked her up and asked her about the movie she was to say it was filmed in Tijuana with a Mexican crew. She kept her part of the bargain when you captured her, and she only mentioned the movie because she had the print in her purse. I tried to find Duke Wellington, but I couldn't. That worried me, then he sent in his alibi to the *Herald-Express*, and it didn't mention where the movie was shot. So we were safe. Then—"

"Then I came along. And you pumped me for dope on the case, and you threw me little tidbits about Georgie to see if I bit."

Madeleine quit stroking Daddy and studied her manicure. "Yes."

"What about the alibi you gave me? Laguna Beach, check with the servants?"

"We gave them money in case you actually did check. They don't speak English too well, and of course you believed me."

Madeleine was smiling now. I said, "Who mailed Betty's

pictures and little black book in? There were envelopes sent, and you said Betty left her purse here."

Madeleine laughed. "That was genius sister Martha. She knew I knew Betty, but she wasn't home that night Betty and Georgie were here. She didn't know Georgie was blackmailing Daddy or that he killed Betty. She ripped the page with our number on it out of the book, and she scratched the faces off the men in the pictures as her way of saying, 'Look for a lesbian,' namely me. She just wanted me smeared, implicated. She also called the police and gave them a tip on La Verne's. The scratched faces were très genius Martha—she always scratches like a cat when she's mad."

Something in her statement hit me as wrong, but I couldn't pin it down. "Martha told you this?"

Madeleine buffed her red claws. "When the little black book stuff made the papers, I knew it had to be Martha. I scratched a confession out of her."

I turned to Emmett "Where's Georgie?"

The old man stirred. "He's probably staying at one of my vacant houses. I'll bring you a list."

"Bring me all four of your passports, too."

Emmett walked out of the battlefield bedroom. Madeleine said, "I really did like you, Bucky. I really did."

"Save it for Daddy. You're wearing the pants now, so save the sugar for him."

"What are you going to do?"

"First I'm going home and putting all of this on paper, attached to material witness warrants for you and Daddy. Then I'm leaving them with another officer in case Daddy goes to his friend Mickey Choen with an offer for my head. Then I'm going after Georgie."

Emmett came back and handed me four U.S. passport holders and a sheet of paper. Madeleine said, "If you turn in those warrants, we'll ruin you in court. Everything about us will come out."

I stood up and kissed the brass girl hard on the lips. "Then we'll all go down together."

• • •

I didn't drive home to write it all out. I parked a few blocks from the Sprague manse and studied the list of addresses, spooked by the juice Madeleine had shown, by her sense of how deep our stalemate went.

The houses were situated in two locales: Echo Park and Silverlake, and across town in Watts—bad territory for a fifty-three-year-old white man. Silverlake-Echo was several miles due east of Mount Lee, a hilly area with lots of twisting streets, greenery and seclusion, the kind of terrain a necrophiliac might find soothing. I drove there, five addresses circled on Emmett's sheet.

The first three were plain deserted shacks: no electricity, broken windows, Mexican gang slogans painted on the walls. No '39 Ford pickup 6B119A nearby—only desolation accompanied by Santa Ana winds blowing down from the Hollywood Hills. Heading toward the fourth pad just after midnight was when I got the idea—or the idea got me.

Kill him.

No public glory, no public disgrace—private justice. Let the Spragues go or coerce a detailed confession out of Georgie before you pull the trigger. Get it on paper, then figure out a way to hurt them with it at your leisure.

Kill him.

And try to live with it.

And try to lead a normal life with Mickey Cohen's good pal running the same type of schemes on you.

I put it all out of mind when I saw that the fourth house was intact at the dead end of a cul-de-sac—chaste exterior, the lawn neatly tended. I parked two doors down, then prowled the street on foot. There were no Ford trucks—and plenty of curbside spaces for them.

I studied the house from the sidewalk. It was a '20s stucco job, small, cube-shaped, off-white with a wood-beam roof. I circled it, driveway to tiny backyard and around a flagstone path to the front. No lights—the windows were all covered with what looked like thick blackout curtains. The place was utterly silent.

Gun out, I rang the buzzer. Twenty seconds, no answer. I ran my fingers down the door-doorjamb meeting point, felt cracked wood, got out my handcuffs and wedged in the narrow part of one ratchet. The teeth held; I whittled at the wood near the lock until I felt the door play slacken. Then I gave it a gentle kick—and it opened.

Light from outside guided me to a wall switch; I flipped it on, saw a cobweb-streaked empty room, walked to the porch and shut the door. The blackout curtains held in every bit of illumination. I moved back into the house, closed the door and stuck wood slivers into the bolt fixture to jam the lock.

With front access blocked off, I walked to the rear of the house. A medicinal stench was issuing from a room adjoining the kitchen. I toed the door open and tapped the inside wall for a switch. I hit one; harsh light blinded me. Then my vision cleared and I placed the smell: formaldehyde.

The walls were lined with shelves holding jars of preserved organs; there was a mattress on the floor, half covered by an army blanket. A red-headed scalp and two notebooks lay on top of it. I took a wheezing breath and forced myself to see it *all*.

Brains, eyes, hearts and intestines floating in fluid. A woman's hand, wedding ring still attached to her finger. Ovaries, glots of shapeless viscera, a jar filled with penises. Gum sections replete with gold teeth.

I felt dry heaves coming on, and squatted by the mattress so I wouldn't have to see any more gore. I picked up one of the notebooks and leafed through it; the pages were filled with neatly typed descriptions of grave robberies—cemeteries, plot names and dates in separate columns. When I saw "East Los Angeles Lutheran," where my mother was buried, I dropped the book and reached for the blanket for something to hold; crusted semen top to bottom made me throw it at the doorway. I opened the other binder to the middle then, neat masculine printing taking me back to January 14, 1947:

> When she woke up Tuesday morning I knew she couldn't take much more and I knew I couldn't risk staying in the hills much longer. Derelicts and lovebirds were sure to be out and about sooner or later. I could tell she was so damn proud of her little titties even while I took Chesterfields to them yesterday. I decided to cut them off slowly.
>
> She was still in a stupor, maybe even shock. I showed her the Joe DiMaggio Louisville Slugger which had given me so much pleasure since Sunday night. I teased her with it. That took her out of her shock. I poked it at her little hole and she almost swallowed her gag. I wished there were nails to put in it, like the iron maiden or a chastity belt she would not soon forget. I held the bat in front of her, then I opened up a cigarette burn on her left tittie with my knife. She bit on her gag and blood from where I took the Joe DiMaggio to her teeth came out due to her biting so hard. I stuck the knife down to a little bone I felt, then I twisted it. She tried to scream and the

gag slipped deeper into her throat. I pulled it out for one second and she yelled for her mother. I put it back in hard and cut her again on the right tittie.

She's getting infected where's she's tied up now. The ropes are cutting her ankles and they're squishy with pus . . ."

I put the notebook down, knowing I could do it, knowing if I faltered, a few more pages would turn me around. I stood up; the organ jars caught my attention, dead things all in a row, so neat, so perfect. I was wondering whether Georgie had ever killed before when I noticed a jar all by itself on the window ledge above the head of the mattress.

A triangular piece of flesh, tattooed. A heart with the Army Air Corps insignia inside it, the words "Betty & Major Matt" below.

I closed my eyes and shook head to toe; I wrapped my arms around myself and tried to tell Betty I was sorry I'd seen that special part of her, that I didn't mean to pry so far, that I was just trying to help. I tried to say it and say it and say it. Then something touched me softly, and I was grateful for the gentleness.

I turned around and saw a man, his face all scars, his hands holding little hooked instruments, tools for cutting and probing. He touched the scalpels to his cheeks; I gasped at where I'd been and reached for my gun. Twin streaks of steel lashed at me; the .45 slipped out of my waistband and hit the floor.

I sidestepped; the blades snagged my jacket and ripped a piece of my collarbone. I sent a kick at Tilden's groin; the grave raper caught the blow off balance, buckled and leaped forward, crashing into me, knocking me back into the wall shelving.

Jars broke, formaldehyde sprayed, awful pieces of flesh were loosed. Tilden was right on top of me, trying to bring his scalpels down. I held his wrists up, then shot a knee between his legs. He grunted but didn't retreat, this face getting closer and closer to mine. Inches away, he bared his teeth and snapped; I felt my cheek tearing. I kneed him again, his arm pressure slackened, I caught another bite on the chin, then dropped my hands. The scalpels hit the shelf in back of me; I flailed for a weapon and touched a big piece of glass. I dug it into Georgie's face just as he yanked the blades free; he screamed; steel dug into my shoulder.

The shelving collapsed. Georgie fell on top of me, blood

pouring from an empty eye socket. I saw my .45 on the floor a few feet away, dragged the two of us there and grabbed it. Georgie raised his head, making animal screeches. He went for my throat, his mouth huge in front of me. I jammed the silencer into his eye hole and blew his brains out.

CHAPTER THIRTY-THREE

Russ Millard supplied the Short case epitaph.

Adrenaline-fried, I left the death house and drove straight to City Hall. The padre had just gotten in from Tucson with his prisoner; when the man was ensconced in a holding cell, I took Russ aside and told him the entire story of my involvement with the Spragues—from Marjorie Graham's lez tip to the shooting of Georgie Tilden. Russ, dumbstruck at first, drove me to Central Receiving Hospital. The emergency room doc gave me a tetanus shot, said, "God, those bites look almost human," and sutured them up. The scalpel wounds were superficial—and required only cleansing and bandaging.

Outside, Russ said, "The case has to stay open. You'll be canned from the Department if you tell anyone else what happened. Now let's go take care of Georgie."

It was 3:00 A.M. when we got to Silverlake. The padre was shaken by what he saw, but held his composure ramrod stiff. Then the best man I ever knew astonished me.

First he said, "Go over and stand by the car"; then he fiddled with some pipes on the side of the house, paced off twenty yards and emptied his service revolver at the spot. Gas ignited; the house went up in flames. We highballed out of there without headlights. Russ shot me his line: "That obscenity did not deserve to stand."

Then it was incredible exhaustion—and sleep. Russ dropped me at the El Nido, I dived onto the bed and into twenty-odd hours of pitch-black unconsciousness. Waking up, the first thing I saw was the four Sprague passports on the dresser: the first thing I thought was: *they have to pay.*

If health and safety code violations or worse came down, I wanted the family in the country where they would suffer. I called the U.S. passport office, impersonated a detective captain and put a police hold on passport reissues for all four Spragues. It felt like an impotent gesture—a slap on the wrist. I shaved and showered then, extra careful not to wet my bandages or sutures. I thought about the end of the case so I wouldn't think about the shambles my life was in. I recalled that something Madeleine said the other day was off, wrong, out of sync. I played with the question while I dressed; going out the door to get something to eat, it hit home:

Madeleine said that Martha called the police with a tip on La Verne's Hideaway. But: I knew the Short case paperwork better then any cop alive, and there were no notations anywhere pertaining to the place. Two incidents sparked me then. Lee getting a long call during our phone-answering stint the morning after I met Madeleine; Lee going directly to La Verne's after he cracked up at the stag film showing. Only "Genius" Martha could give me answers. I drove to Ad Agency Row to brace her.

* * *

I found Emmett Sprague's real daughter alone, eating lunch on a bench in the shade of the Young & Rubicam Building. She didn't look up when I sat down across from her; I remembered that Betty Short's little black book and pictures were taken out of a mailbox a block away.

I watched the pudgy girl-woman nibble a salad and read the newspaper. In the two and a half years since I'd seen her she'd held her own against fat and bad skin—but she still looked like a tough distaff version of Emmett.

Martha put the paper down and noticed me. I expected rage to light up her eyes; she surprised me by saying, "Hello, Mr. Bleichert," with just a touch of a smile.

I walked over and sat down beside her. The *Times* was folded over to a Metro section piece: "Bizarre Fire in Silverlake Foothills—Body Found Charred Beyond Recognition."

Martha said, "I'm sorry for that picture I drew of you that night you came to dinner."

I pointed to the newspaper. "You don't seem surprised to see me."

"Poor Georgie. No, I'm not surprised to see you. Father told me you knew. I've been underestimated all my life, and I always had a feeling Maddy and Father were underestimating you."

I pushed the compliment aside. "Do you know what 'Poor Georgie' did?"

"Yes. From the beginning. I saw Georgie and the Short girl leave the house that night in Georgie's truck. Maddy and Father didn't know I knew, but I did. Only Mother never figured it out. Did you kill him?"

I didn't answer.

"Are you going to hurt my family?"

The pride in the "my" knifed me. "I don't know what I'm going to do."

"I don't blame you for wanting to hurt them. Father and Maddy are dreadful people, and I went way out on a limb to hurt them myself."

"When you sent in Betty's things?"

Now Martha's eyes fired up. "Yes. I tore out the page in the book that had our number, but I thought there might be other numbers to lead the police to Father and Maddy. I didn't have the courage to send *our* number in. I should have. I—"

I held up a hand. "Why, Martha? Do you know what would have happened if the police got the whole story about Georgie? Accessory charges, court, jail."

"I didn't care. Maddy had you and Father, Mother and I had nothing. I just wanted the whole ship to sink. Mother has lupus now, she's only got a few years left. She's going to die, and that is so unfair."

"The pictures and scratch marks. What did you mean by them?"

Martha laced her fingers together and twisted them until the knuckles were white. "I was nineteen, and all I could do was draw. I wanted Maddy smeared as a dyke, and the last picture was Father himself—his face scratched out. I thought he might have left fingerprints on the back. I was desperate to hurt him."

"Because he touches you like he touches Madeleine?"

"Because he doesn't!"

I braced myself for the spooky stuff. "Martha, did you call the police with a tip on La Verne's Hideaway?"

Martha lowered her eyes. "Yes."

"Did you talk to—"

"I told the man about my dyke sister, how she met a cop named Bucky Bleichert at La Verne's last night and had a date with him tonight. Maddy was gloating to the whole family about you, and I was jealous. But I only wanted to hurt her—not you."

Lee taking the call while I sat across a desk from him in University squadroom; Lee going directly to La Verne's when *Slave Girls From Hell* drove him around the twist. I said, "Martha, you come clean on the rest of it."

Martha looked around and clenched herself—legs together, arms to her sides, fists balled. "Lee Blanchard came to the house and told Father he'd talked to women at La Verne's—lesbians who could tie Maddy in to the Black Dahlia. He said he had to leave town, and for a price he wouldn't report his information on Maddy. Father agreed, and gave him all the money he had in his safe."

Lee, Benzie-crazed, absent from City Hall and University Station; Bobby De Witt's imminent parole his reason for blowing town. Emmett's money the cash he was flaunting in Mexico. My own voice numb: "Is there more?"

Martha's body was coiled spring-tight. "Blanchard came back the next day. He demanded more money. Father turned him down, and he beat Father up and asked him all these questions about Elizabeth Short. Maddy and I heard it from the next room. I loved it and Maddy was wicked mad. She left when she couldn't take any more of her beloved daddy-poo groveling, but I kept listening. Father was afraid that Blanchard would frame one of us for the killing, so he agreed to give him a hundred thousand dollars and told him what happened with Georgie and Elizabeth Short."

Lee's bruised knuckles; his lie: "Penance for Junior Nash." Madeleine on the phone that day: "Don't come over. Daddy's having a business soiree." Our desperate rutting at the Red Arrow an hour later. *Lee filthy rich in Mexico. Lee letting Georgie Tilden go scot fucking free.*

Martha dabbed at her eyes, saw that they were dry and put a hand on my arm. "The next day a woman came by and picked up the money. And that's all of it."

I took out my wallet snapshot of Kay and showed it to her. Martha said, "Yes. That's the woman."

I stood up, alone for the first time since the triad was formed. Martha said, "Don't hurt my family anymore. Please."

I said, "Get out, Martha. Don't let them ruin you."

•   •   •

I drove to West Hollywood Elementary School, sat in the car and kept an eyeball fix on Kay's Plymouth in the faculty parking lot. Lee's ghost buzzed in my head as I waited—bad company for close to two hours. The 3:00 bell rang right on time; Kay exited the building in a swarm of children and teachers a few minutes later. When she was alone by her car, I walked over.

She was arranging a load of books and papers in the trunk, her back to me. I said, "How much of the hundred grand did Lee let you keep?"

Kay froze, her hands on a stack of fingerpaintings. "Did Lee tell you about Madeleine Sprague and me back then? Is that why you've hated Betty Short all this time?"

Kay ran her fingers over the kiddie artwork, then turned and faced me. "You are so, so good at some things."

It was another compliment I didn't want to hear. "Answer my questions."

Kay slammed the trunk, her eyes dead on mine. "I did not accept a cent of that money, and I didn't know about you and Madeleine Sprague until those detectives I hired gave me her name. Lee was going to run away no matter what. I didn't know if I'd ever see him again, and I wanted him to be comfortable, if such a thing was possible. He didn't trust himself to deal with Emmett Sprague again, so I picked up the money. Dwight, he knew I was in love with you, and he wanted us to be together. That was one of the reasons he left."

I felt like I was sinking in a quicksand of all our old lies. "He didn't leave, he *ran* from the Boulevard-Citizens job, from the frame on De Witt, from the trouble he was in with the Depart—"

"He loved us! Don't take that away from him!"

I looked around the parking lot. Teachers were standing by their cars, eyeing the husband and wife spat. They were too far away to hear; I imagined them chalking up the fight to kids or mortgages or cheating. I said, "Kay, Lee knew who killed Elizabeth Short. Did you know that?"

Kay stared at the ground. "Yes."

"He just let it go."

"Things got crazy then. Lee went down to Mexico after Bobby, and he said he'd go after the killer when he got back. But he didn't come back, and I didn't want you going down there too."

I grabbed my wife's shoulders and squeezed them until she looked at me.

"And you didn't tell me later? You didn't tell *anyone*?"

Kay lowered her head again; I jerked it back up with both my hands. "And you didn't tell anyone?"

In her calmest schoolteacher voice, Kay Lake Bleichert said, "I almost told you. But you started whoring again, collecting her pictures. I just wanted revenge on the woman who ruined the two men I loved."

I raised a hand to hit her—but a flash of Georgie Tilden stopped me.

CHAPTER THIRTY-FOUR

I called in the last of my accumulated sick leave and spent a week killing time at the El Nido. I read and played the jazz stations, trying not to think about my future. I pored over the master file repeatedly, even though I knew the case was closed. Child versions of Martha Sprague and Lee racked my dreams; sometimes Jane Chambers' slash-mouth clown joined them, hurling taunts, speaking through gaping holes in his face.

I bought all four LA papers every day, and read them cover to cover. The Hollywood sign hubbub had passed, there was no mention of Emmett Sprague, Grand Jury probes into faulty buildings or the torched house and stiff. I began to get a feeling that something was wrong.

It took a while—long hours spent staring at the four walls thinking of nothing—but finally I nailed it.

"It" was a tenuous hunch that Emmett Sprague set Lee and I up to kill Georgie Tilden. With me he was blatant: "Shall I tell you where Georgie can be found?"—perfectly in character for the man—I would have been more suspicious if he had tried a roundabout approach. He sent Lee after Georgie immediately after Lee beat him up. Was he hoping Lee's anger would peak when he saw the Dahlia killer? Did he know of Georgie's grave

robbery treasure trove—and count on it making us killing
mad? Did he count on Georgie to initiate a confrontation—one
that would either eliminate him or the greedy/nosy cops who
were creating such a nuisance? And why? For what motive? *To
protect himself?*

The theory had one huge hole: namely, the incredible, almost
suicidal audacity of Emmett, not the suicidal type.

And with Georgie Tilden—the Black Dahlia killer pure and
clean—nailed—there was no logical reason to pursue it. But
"It" was backstopped by a tenuous loose end:

When I first coupled with Madeleine in '47, she mentioned
leaving notes for Betty Short at various bars: "Your lookalike
would like to meet you." I told her the act might come back to
haunt her; she said, "I'll take care of it."

The most likely one to have "taken care of it" was a
policeman—and I refused to. *And*, chronologically, Madeleine
spoke those words right around the time Lee Blanchard made
his initial blackmail demand.

It was tenuous, circumstantial and theoretical, probably just
another lie or half truth or thread of useless information. A
loose end unraveled by a coming-from-hunger cop whose life
was built on a foundation of lies. Which was the only good
reason I could think of to pursue the ghost of a chance. Without
the case, I had nothing.

• • •

I borrowed Harry Sears' civilian car and ran rolling skate-
outs on the Spragues for three days and nights. Martha drove
to work and back home; Ramona stayed in; Emmett and
Madeleine shopped and did other daytime errands. All four
stuck to the manse on evenings one and two; on the third night
Madeleine prowled as the Dahlia.

I tailed her to the 8th Street bar strip, to the Zimba Room, to
a cadre of sailors and flyboys and ultimately the 9th and Irolo
fuck pad with a navy ensign. I felt no jealously, no sex pull this
time. I listened outside room twelve and heard KMPC; the
venetian blinds were down, no visual access. The only depar-
ture from Madeleine's previous MO was when she ditched her
paramour at 2:00 A.M. and drove home—the light going on in
Emmett's bedroom a few moments after she walked in the
door.

I gave day four a pass, and returned to my surveillance spot
on Muirfield Road shortly after dark that night. I was getting
out of the car to give my cramped legs a breather when I heard,
"Bucky? Is that you?"

It was Jane Chambers, walking a brown and white spaniel. I felt like a kid with his hand caught in the cookie jar. "Hello, Jane."

"Hello, yourself. What are you doing? Spying? Torching for Madeleine?"

I remembered our conversation on the Spragues, "Enjoying the crisp night air. How's that sound?"

"Like a lie. Want to enjoy a crisp drink at my place?"

I looked over at the Tudor fortress; Jane said, "Boy, have you got a bee in your bonnet with that family."

I laughed—and felt little aches in my bite wounds. "Boy, have you got my number. Let's go get that drink."

We walked around the corner to June Street. Jane unhooked the dog's leash; he trotted ahead of us, down the sidewalk and up the steps to the front door of the Chambers' colonial. We caught up with him a moment later; Jane opened the door. And there was my nightmare buddy—the scar mouth clown.

I shuddered. "That goddamn thing."

Jane smiled. "Shall I wrap it up for you?"

"Please don't."

"You know, after that first time we talked about it, I looked into its history. I've been getting rid of a lot of Eldridge's things, and I was thinking about giving it to charity. It's too valuable to give away, though. It's a Frederick Yannantuono original, and it's inspired by an old classic novel—*The Man Who Laughs* by Victor Hugo. The book is about—"

There was a copy of *The Man Who Laughs* in the shack where Betty Short was killed. I was buzzing so hard I could hardly hear what Jane was saying.

"—a group of Spaniards back in the fifteenth and sixteenth centuries. They were called the Comprachicos, and they kidnapped and tortured children, then mutilated them and sold them to the aristocracy so that they could be used as court jesters. Isn't that hideous? The clown in the painting is the book's main character, Gwynplain. When he was a child he had his mouth slashed ear to ear. Bucky, are you all right?"

MOUTH SLASHED EAR TO EAR.

I shuddered, then forced a smile. "I'm fine. The book just reminded me of something. Old stuff, just a coincidence."

Jane scrutinized me. "You don't look fine, and you want to hear another coincidence? I thought Eldridge wasn't on speaking terms with any of the family, but I found the receipt. It was Ramona Sprague who sold him the painting."

For a split second I thought Gwynplain was spitting blood at me. Jane grabbed my arms. "Bucky, what is it?"

I found my voice. "You told me your husband bought that picture for your birthday two years ago. Right?"

"Yes. What—"

"In '47?"

"Yes. Buck—"

"What *is* your birthday?"

"January fifteenth."

"Let me see the receipt."

Jane, spooky eyed, fumbled at some papers on the end table across the hall. I stared at Gwynplain, transposing 39th and Norton glossies against his face. Then: "Here. Now will you tell me what's going on?"

I took the piece of paper. It was purple stationery, covered with incongruously masculine block printing: "Received from Eldridge Chambers, $3500.00 for the sale of the Frederick Yannantuono painting 'The Man Who Laughs.' This receipt constitutes Mr. Chambers' proof of ownership. Ramona Cathcart Sprague, January 15, 1947."

The printing was identical to the script in the torture diary I read just before I killed Georgie Tilden.

Ramona Sprague murdered Elizabeth Short.

I grabbed Jane in a hard bear hug, then took off while she stood there looking stunned. I went back to the car, decided it was a single-o play, watched lights go on and off in the big house and sweated through a long night of reconstructions: Ramona and Georgie torturing together, separately, bisecting, divvying up the spare parts, running a two-car caravan to Leimert Park. I played every kind of variation imaginable; I ran riffs on how the thing ignited. I thought of everything but what I was going to do when I got Ramona Sprague alone.

At 8:19 Martha walked out the front door carrying an art portfolio, and drove east in her Chrysler.

At 10:37, Madeleine, valise in hand, got into her Packard and headed north on Muirfield. Emmett waved from the doorway; I decided to give him an hour or so to leave—or take him down along with his wife. Shortly after noon, he played into my hand—tooling off, his car radio humming light opera.

My month of playing house with Madeleine had taught me the servants' routine: today, Thursday, the housekeeper and gardener were off; the cook showed up at 4:30 to prepare dinner. Madeleine's valise implied some time away; Martha wouldn't return from work until 6:00. Emmett was the only wild card.

I walked across the street and reconnoitered. The front door was locked, the side windows were bolted. It was either ring the bell or B&E.

Then I heard tapping on the other side of the glass and saw a blurry white shape moving back into the living room. A few seconds later the sound of the front door opening echoed down the driveway. I walked around to meet the woman head on.

Ramona was standing in the doorway, spectral in a shapeless silk dressing gown. Her hair was a frizzy mess, her face was blotchy red and puffed up—probably from tears and sleep. Her dark brown eyes—identical in color to mine—were scary alert. She pulled a ladylike automatic from the folds of her gown and pointed it at me. She said, "You told Martha to leave me."

I slapped the gun out of her hand; it hit a straw welcome mat emblazoned with THE SPRAGUE FAMILY. Ramona gnawed at her lips; her eyes lost their focus. I said, "Martha deserves better than a murderer."

Ramona smoothed her gown and patted at her hair. I pegged the reaction as the class of a well-bred hophead. Her voice was pure cold Sprague: "You didn't tell, did you?"

I picked up the gun and put it in my pocket, then looked at the woman. She had to be jacked on a twenty-year residue of drugstore hop, but her eyes were so dark that I couldn't tell if they were pinned or not. "Are you telling me Martha doesn't know what you did?"

Ramona stood aside and bid me to enter. She said, "Emmett told me it was safe now. He said that you'd taken care of Georgie and you had too much to lose by coming back. Martha told Emmett you wouldn't hurt us, and he said you wouldn't. I believed him. He was always so accurate about business matters."

I walked inside. Except for the packing crates on the floor, the living room looked like business as usual. "Emmett sent me after Georgie, and Martha doesn't know you killed Betty Short?"

Ramona shut the door. "Yes. Emmett counted on you to take care of Georgie. He was confident that he wouldn't implicate me—the man was quite insane. Emmett is a physical coward, you see. He didn't have the courage to do it, so he sent an underling. And my God, do you honestly think I'd let Martha know what I'm capable of?"

The torture murderess was genuinely aghast that I'd impugned her as a mother. "She'll find out sooner or later. And I know she was here that night. She saw Georgie and Betty leave together."

"Martha left to visit a chum in Palm Springs an hour or so

later. She was gone for the next week. Emmett and Maddy know. Martha doesn't. And my dear God, she mustn't."

"Mrs. Sprague, do you know what you've—"

"I'm not Mrs. Sprague, I'm Ramona Upshaw Cathcart! You can't tell Martha what I did or she'll leave me! She said she wants to get her own apartment, and I haven't that much more time left!"

I turned my back on the spectacle and walked around the living room, wondering what to do. I looked at the pictures on the walls: generations of kilt-clad Spragues, Cathcarts cutting the ribbons in front of orange groves and vacant lots ripe for development. There was a fat little girl Ramona wearing a corset that must have strictured her bloody. Emmett holding a dark-haired child, beaming. Glassy-eyed Ramona poising Martha's brush hand over a toy easel. Mack Sennett and Emmett giving each other the cuckold's horns. At the back of an Edendale group shot I thought I could see a young Georgie Tilden—handsome, no scars on his face.

I felt Ramona behind me, trembling. I said, "Tell me all of it. Tell me why."

•   •   •

Ramona sat down on a divan and spoke for three hours, her tone sometimes angry, sometimes sad, sometimes brutally detached from what she was saying. There was a table covered with tiny ceramic figurines beside her; her hands played with them constantly. I circled the walls, looking at the family pictures, feeling them meld into her story.

She met Emmett and Georgie in 1921, when they were Scottish immigrant boys on the make in Hollywood. She hated Emmett for treating Georgie like a lackey—and she hated herself for not speaking up about it. She didn't speak up because Emmett wanted to marry her—for her father's money, she knew—and she was a homely woman with slender husband prospects.

Emmett proposed. She accepted and settled into married life with the ruthless young contractor and budding real estate tycoon. Who she gradually grew to hate. Who she passively fought by gathering information.

Georgie lived in the apartment above the garage the first years they were married. She learned that he liked to touch dead things, and that Emmett reviled him for it. She took to poisoning the stray cats who trampled her garden, leaving them on Georgie's doorstep. When Emmett spurned her desire for him to give her a child, she went to Georgie and seduced him—exulting that she had the power to excite him with something alive—the fat body that Emmett derided and only plundered at odd times.

Their affair was brief, but resulted in a child—Madeleine. She lived in terror of a resemblance to Georgie asserting itself, and took to doctor-prescribed opiates. Two years later Martha was born of Emmett. This felt like a betrayal of Georgie—and she went back to poisoning stray animals for him. Emmett caught her in the act one day; he beat her for taking part in "Georgie's perversion."

When she told Georgie of the beating, he told her of saving the coward Emmett's life in the war—putting the lie to Emmett's version of the story: that *he* saved Georgie. She started planning her pageants then—how she would get back at Emmett symbolically in ways so subtle that he would never know he was being thrashed.

Madeleine cleaved to Emmett. She was the lovely child, and he doted on her. Martha became her mother's little girl—even though she was Emmett's spitting image. Emmett and Madeleine disdained Martha as a fatso and a crybaby; Ramona protected her, teaching her to draw, putting her to bed each night with admonishings not to hate her sister and father—even though she did. Protecting Martha and instructing her in the love of art became her reason for living, her strength in the intolerable marriage.

When Maddy was eleven, Emmett noted her resemblance to Georgie, and slashed her real father's face beyond recognition. Ramona fell in love with Georgie; he was now even more physically bereft than she—and she felt a parity had been achieved between them.

Georgie rebuffed her persistent advances. She came across Hugo's *The Man Who Laughs* then, and was moved by both the Comprachicos and their disfigured victims. She bought the Yannantuono painting and kept it hidden, staring at it as a memento of Georgie in her private hours.

When Maddy hit her teens she became promiscuous, sharing the details with Emmett, cuddling on the bed with him. Martha drew obscene pictures of the sister she hated; Ramona forced her to draw pastoral landscapes to keep her anger from going haywire. To get back at Emmett she staged her long-planned pageants; they spoke obliquely of his greed and cowardice. Toy houses falling down signified Emmett's jerry-built shacks crashing in the '33 earthquake; children hiding under store mannequins dressed in ersatz German uniforms portrayed Emmett the yellow. A number of parents found the pageants disturbing, and forbade their children to play with the Sprague girls. Around that time Georgie drifted out of their lives, doing his yard work and rubbish hauling, living in Emmett's abandoned houses.

Time passed. She concentrated on looking after Martha, pressing her to finish high school early, establishing funds at Otis Art Institute so that she would get special treatment. Martha thrived and excelled at Otis; Ramona lived through her accomplishments, on and off sedatives, often thinking of Georgie—missing him, wanting him.

Then, in the fall of '46, Georgie returned. She overheard him make his blackmail demand of Emmett: "Give him" the girl in the dirty movie, or risk exposure of a good deal of the family's sordid past and present.

She became frighteningly jealous and hateful of "that girl," and when Elizabeth Short showed up at the Sprague house on January 12, 1947, her rage exploded. "That girl" looked so much like Madeleine that it felt like the cruelest of jokes was being played on her. When Elizabeth and Georgie left in his truck, she saw that Martha had gone to her room to pack for her Palm Springs trip. She left a note on her door saying good-bye, that she was sleeping now. Then she casually asked Emmett where "that girl" and Georgie were going.

He told her he heard Georgie mention one of his abandoneds up on North Beachwood. She went out the backdoor, grabbed their spare Packard, sped to Hollywoodland and waited. Georgie and the girl arrived at the base of the Mount Lee park area a few minutes later. She followed them on foot to the shack in the woods. They went inside; she saw a light go on. It cast shadows over a shiny wood object leaning against a tree trunk—a baseball bat. When she heard the girl giggle, "Did you get those scars in the war?" she went in the door, bat first.

Elizabeth Short tried to run. She knocked her unconscious and made Georgie strip her and gag her and tie her to the mattress. She promised him parts of the girl to keep forever. She took a copy of *The Man Who Laughs* from her purse and read aloud from it, casting occasional glances at the girl spread-eagled. Then she cut her and burned her and batted her and wrote in the notebook she always carried while the girl was passed out from the pain. Georgie watched, and together they shouted the chants of the Comprachicos. And after two full days of it, she slashed Elizabeth Short ear to ear like Gwynplain, so she wouldn't hate her after she was dead. Georgie cut the body in two, washed the halves in the stream outside the shack and carried them to her car. Late at night,

312

they drove to 39th and Norton—a lot that Georgie used to tend for the city. They left Elizabeth Short there to become the Black Dahlia, then she drove Georgie back to his truck and returned to Emmett and Madeleine, telling them that soon enough they would find out where she had been and finally respect her will. As an act of purging, she sold her Gwynplain painting to the bargain-loving art worshipper Eldridge Chambers down the street—making a profit on the deal. Then it was days and weeks of the horror that Martha would find out and hate her—and more and more laudanum and codeine and sleep potion to make it go away.

●   ●   ●

I was looking at a row of framed magazine ads—award-winning Martha artwork—when Ramona stopped talking. The silence jarred me; her story rolled on in my head, back and forth in sequence. The room was cool—but I was sweating.

Martha's 1948 Advertising Council first prizer featured a handsome guy in a seersucker suit walking on the beach, ogling a blonde dish sunbathing. He was so oblivious to everything else around him that he was about to get creamed by a big wave. The caption at the top of the page read: "Not to worry! In his Hart, Shaffner & Marx Featherweight he'll be dried out and crisp—and ready to woo her at the club tonight!" The dish was sleek. Her features were Martha's—a soft, pretty version. The Sprague mansion was in the background, surrounded by palm trees.

Ramona broke the silence. "What are you going to do?"

I couldn't look at her. "I don't know."

"Martha mustn't know."

"You told me that already."

The guy in the ad was starting to look like an idealized Emmett—the Scotchman as a Hollywood pretty boy. I threw out the one cop question Ramona's story inspired: "In the fall of '46 someone was throwing dead cats into cemeteries in Hollywood. Was that you?"

"Yes. I was so jealous of her then, and I just wanted Georgie to know I still cared. *What are you going to do?*"

"I don't know. Go upstairs, Ramona. Leave me alone."

I heard soft footfalls moving out of the room, then sobs, then nothing. I thought about the family's united front to save Ramona, how arresting her would blow my police career: charges of withholding evidence, obstruction of justice. Sprague money would keep her out of the gas chamber, she'd get eaten alive at Atascadero or a women's prison until the lupus got her, Martha would be ravaged, and Emmett and Madeleine would still have each other—withholding/obstruction beefs against them would be too second-hand to prosecute on. If I took Ramona in I was shot to shit as a policeman; if I let her go I was finished as a man, and in either case Emmett and Madeleine would survive—together.

So the patented Bucky Bleichert advance, stymied and stalemated, sat still in a big plush room full of ancestor icons. I looked through the packing crates on the floor—the Sprague getaway if the City Council got uppity—and saw the cheap cocktail dresses and the sketch pad covered with women's faces, no doubt Martha sketching alter egos to plaster over ads huckstering toothpaste and cosmetics and cornflakes. Maybe she could design an advertising campaign to spring Ramona from Tehachapi. Maybe without torturer Mommy she wouldn't have the guts to work anymore.

I left the manse and killed time making rounds of old haunts. I checked out the rest home—my father didn't recognize me, but looked full of malicious spunk. Lincoln Heights was rife with new houses—prefab pads waiting for tenants—"No Down Payment" for GIs. The Eagle Rock Legion Hall still had a sign ballyhooing Friday night boxing, and my Central Division beat was still winos, rag suckers and Jesus shriekers. At twilight, I gave in: one last shot at the brass girl before I took her mommy down; one last chance to ask her why she was still playing Dahlia when she knew I'd never touch her again.

I drove to the 8th Street bar strip, parked at the corner of Irolo and waited with an eye on the Zimba Room entrance. I was hoping that the valise I'd seen Madeleine carrying in the morning didn't mean a trip somewhere; I was hoping her Dahlia prowl of two nights ago wasn't a one-shot deal.

I sat there eyeballing foot traffic: servicemen, civilian boozehounds, neighborhood squares going in and out of the hash house next door. I thought of packing it in, then got frightened of the next stop—Ramona—and stuck. Just past midnight Madeleine's Packard pulled up. She got out—carrying her valise, looking like herself, not Elizabeth Short.

Startled, I watched her walk into the restaurant. Fifteen minutes passed slowly. Then she sashayed out, Black Dahlia to the nines. She tossed her valise in the Packard's backseat and hit the Zimba Room.

I gave her a minute's slack, then went over and peered in the doorway. The bar was serving a skeleton crew of army brass; the zebra-striped booths were empty. Madeleine was drinking by herself. Two soldiers were primping at stools down from her, getting ready to make the big move. They swooped a half second apart. The dump was too deserted for me to hold surveillance in; I retreated to the car.

Madeleine and a first lieutenant in summer dress khakis walked out an hour or so later. Per her old MO, they got in the Packard and headed around the corner to the 9th and Irolo auto court. I was right behind them.

Madeleine parked and walked to the manager's hut for the key; the soldier waited by the door of room twelve. I thought of frustration: KMPC on loud, venetian blinds down to the sill. Then Madeleine left the office, called to the lieutenant and pointed across the courtyard to a different unit. He shrugged and went over; Madeleine joined him and opened the door. The light went on and off inside.

I gave them ten minutes, then moved to the bungalow, resigned to big band standards and darkness. Moans were coming from inside, unaccompanied by music. I saw that the one window was open two feet or so, dried paint on the runner holding it stuck. I found shelter beside a trellis overgrown with vines, squatted down and listened.

Heavier moans, bed springs creaking, male grunts. Her love sounds reaching fever pitch—stagy, more soprano than when she was with me. The soldier groaning hard, all noise subsiding, then Madeleine, speaking with a feigned accent:

"I wish there was a radio. Back home all the motels had them. They were bolted down and you had to put dimes in, but at least there was music."

The soldier, trying to catch his breath: "I heard Boston's a nice town."

I placed Madeleine's fake voice then: New England blue collar, the way Betty Short was supposed to speak. "Medford's not nice, not nice at all. I had one lousy job after another. Waitress, candy girl at a theater, file clerk at a factory. That was why I came to California to seek my fortune. Because Medford was so awful."

Madeleine's "A's" were getting broader and broader; she sounded like a Boston guttersnipe. The man said, "You came out here during the war?"

"Uh-huh. I got a job at the Camp Cooke PX. This soldier beat me up, and this rich man, this award-winning contractor, he saved me. He's my stepdaddy now. He lets me be with whoever I want to be with so long as I come home to him. He bought me my nice white car and all my nice black dresses, and he gives me back rubs 'cause he's not my real daddy."

"That's the kind of dad to have. My dad bought me a bicycle

once, and he gave me a couple of bucks toward a soap box derby racer. But he never bought me any Packards, that's for damn sure. You've got yourself a real sugar daddy, Betty."

I knelt down lower and peered through the window crack; all I could see were dark shapes on a bed in the middle of the room. Madeleine/Betty said, "Sometimes my stepdaddy doesn't like my boyfriends. He never makes a fuss, because he's not my real daddy and I let him give me backrubs. There was this one boy, a policeman. My stepdaddy said he was wishy-washy with a mean streak. I didn't believe him, because the boy was big and strong, and he had these cute buck teeth. He tried to hurt me, but Daddy settled his hash. Daddy knows how to deal with weak men who suck around money and try to hurt nice girls. He was a big hero in the First World War and the policeman was a draft dodger."

Madeleine's accent was slipping, moving into another voice, low and guttural. I braced myself for more verbal lashing; the soldier said, "Draft dodgers should either be deported to Russia or shot. No, shooting's too merciful. Hanged by the you know what, that's more like it."

Madeleine, a vibrato rasp, a perfect Mexican accent: "An axe ees better, no? The policeman have a partner. He tie up some loose ends for me—some notes I should not 'ave lef' for a not so nice girl. The partner beat up my stepdaddy an' run away to May-hee-co. I draw pictures of a face to be and buy cheap dress. I hire a detective to find him, an' I make a pageant. I go down to Ensenada in dees-guise, I wear cheap dress, preten' to be beggar and knock on hees door. 'Gringo, gringo, I need money.' He turn hees back, I grab axe an' chop him down. I take money he steal from stepdaddy. Seventy-one thousan' dollar I bring back home."

The soldier jabbered, "Look, is this some kind of joke?" I pulled out my .38 and cocked the hammer. Madeleine as Milt Dolphine's "rich Mex woman" slipped into Spanish, a streak of raspy obscenities. I aimed through the window crack; the light went on inside; lover boy thrashing himself into his uniform spoiled my shot at the killer. I saw Lee in a sand pit, worms crawling out of his eyes.

The soldier bolted out the door, half dressed. Madeleine, slipping into her tight black gown, was an easy target. I drew a bead; a last flash of her nakedness made me empty the gun into the air. I kicked the window in.

Madeleine watched me climb over the sill. Undaunted by gunshots and flying glass, she spoke with soft savoir faire: "She was the only thing real to me, and I had to tell people about her. I felt so contrived next to her. She was a natural and I was just an imposter. And she was ours, sweet. You brought her back to me. She was what made it so good with us. She was ours."

I mussed up Madeleine's Dahlia hairdo, so that she looked like just another raven-clad floozy; I cuffed her wrists behind her back and saw myself in the sand pit, worm bait along with my partner. Sirens bared down from all directions; flashlights shined in the broken window. Out in the Big Nowhere, Lee Blanchard reprised his line from the Zoot Suit riot:

"Cherchez la femme, Bucky. Remember that."

CHAPTER THIRTY-FIVE

We took the fall together.

Four black-and-whites responded to my shots. I explained to the officers that it was a lights and siren roll to Wilshire Station—I was booking the woman for Murder One. At the Wilshire squadroom, Madeleine confessed to the killing of Lee Blanchard, concocting a brilliant fantasy—a lovers' triangle of Lee/Madeleine/Bucky, how she was intimately involved with both of us in the winter of 1947. I sat in on the interrogation, and Madeleine was flawless. Seasoned Homicide dicks bought her tale hook, line and sinker: Lee and I rivals for her hand, Madeleine preferring me as a potential husband. Lee going to Emmett, demanding that he "give him" his daughter, beating the man half to death when he refused. Madeleine revenge-stalking Lee in Mexico, axing him to death in Ensenada. No mention of the Black Dahlia murder case at all.

I corroborated Madeleine's story, saying that I only recently figured out that Lee had been murdered. I then confronted Madeleine with a circumstantial run-though on the snuff and coerced a partial confession out of her. Madeleine was transported to the LA women's jail, and I went back to the El Nido—still wondering what I was going to do about Ramona.

The next day I returned to duty. At the end of my tour a team

318

of Metro goons was waiting for me in the Newton locker room. They grilled me for three hours; I ran with the fantasy ball Madeleine started rolling. The grit of her story and my wild departmental rep carried me through the interrogation—and nobody mentioned the Dahlia.

Over the next week the legal machinery took over.

The Mexican government refused to indict Madeleine for the murder of Lee Blanchard—without a corpse and backup evidence extradition proceedings could not be initiated. A Grand Jury was called up to decide her fate; Ellis Loew was slated to present the case for the City of Los Angeles. I told him I would testify only by deposition. Knowing my unpredictability only too well, he agreed. I filled up ten pages with lies on the "lovers' triangle," fantasy embellishments worthy of romantic Betty Short at her best. I kept wondering if she would appreciate the irony.

Emmett Sprague was indicted by a separate Grand Jury— for health and safety code violations stemming from his mob-fronted ownership of dangerously faulty property. He was given fines in excess of $50,000—but no criminal charges were filed. Counting the $71,000 that Madeleine stole from Lee, he was still close to twenty grand in the black on the deal.

The lovers' triangle hit the papers the day after Madeleine's case went to the Grand Jury. The Blanchard-Bleichert fight and the Southside shootout were resurrected, and for a week I was big-time local stuff. Then I got a call from Bevo Means of the *Herald*: "Watch out, Bucky. Emmett Sprague's about to hit back, and the shit's about to hit the fan. 'Nuff said."

It was *Confidential* magazine that nailed me.

The July 12 issue ran an article on the triangle. It featured quotes from Madeleine, leaked to the scandal rag by Emmett. The brass girl had me ditching out on duty to couple with her at the Red Arrow Motel; stealing fifths of her father's whiskey to see me through nightwatch; giving her the inside lowdown on the LAPD's traffic ticket quota system and how I "beat up niggers." Innuendos pointed to worse offenses—but everything Madeleine said was true.

I was fired from the Los Angeles Police Department on grounds of moral turpitude and conduct unbecoming an officer. It was the unanimous decision of a specially convened board of inspectors and deputy chiefs, and I did not protest it. I thought of turning over Ramona in hopes of pulling a grand-stander's turnabout, but kiboshed the idea. Russ Millard might be compelled to admit what he knew and get hurt; Lee's name would get coated with more slime; Martha would *know*. The firing was about two and a half years overdue; the *Confidential* exposé my final embarrassment to the Department. No one knew that better than I did.

I turned in my service revolver, my outlaw .45 and badge 1611. I moved back to the house that Lee bought, borrowed $500 from the padre and waited for my notoriety to die down before I started looking for work. Betty Short and Kay weighed on me, and I went by Kay's school to look for her. The principal, eyeing me like a bug who just crawled out of the woodwork, said that Kay left a resignation letter the day after I hit the newsstands. It stated that she was going on a long cross-country automobile trip and would not be returning to Los Angeles.

The Grand Jury bound Madeleine over for trial on Manslaughter Three—"premeditated homicide under psychological duress and with mitigating circumstances." Her lawyer, the great Jerry Giesler, had her plead guilty and request a judge's chambers sentencing. Taking into account the recommendations of psychiatrists who found Madeleine to be a "severely delusional violent schizophrenic adept at acting out many different personalities," the judge sentenced her to Atascadero State Hospital for an "indeterminate period of treatment not to subscribe below the minimum time allotted by the state penalties code: ten years of imprisonment."

So the brass girl took the heat for her family and I took it for myself. My farewell to the Spragues was a front-page photo in the LA *Daily News*. Matrons were leading Madeleine out of the courtroom while Emmett wept at the defense table. Ramona, hollow-cheeked with disease, was being shepherded by Martha, all good strong business in a tailored suit. The picture was a lock on my silence forever.

CHAPTER THIRTY-SIX

A month later I got a letter from Kay.

Sioux Falls, S.D.
8/17/49

Dear Dwight,

I didn't know if you'd moved back to the house, so I don't know if this letter will reach you. I've been checking the library for L.A. papers, and I know you're not with the Department anymore, so that's another place where I can't write to you. I'll just have to send this out and see what happens.

I'm in Sioux Falls, living at the Plainsman Hotel. It's the best one in town, and I've wanted to stay here since I was a little girl. It's not the way I imagined it, of course. I just wanted to wash the taste of L.A. out of my mouth, and Sioux Falls is as antithetical to L.A. as you can get without flying to the moon.

My grade school girlfriends are all married and have children, and two of them are widows from the war. Everyone talks about the war like it's still going on, and the high prairies outside of town are being plowed for housing developments. The ones that have been constructed so far are so ugly, such bright, jarring colors. They make me miss our old house. I know you hate it, but it was a sanctuary for nine years of my life.

Dwight, I've read all the papers and that trashy magazine piece. I must have counted a dozen lies. Lies by omission and the blatant kind. I keep wondering what happened, even though I don't really want to know. I keep wondering why Elizabeth Short was never mentioned. I would have felt self-righteous, but I spent last night in my room just counting lies. All the lies I told you and things I never told you, even when it was good with us. I'm too embarrassed to tell you how many I came up with.

I'm sorry for them. And I admire what you did with Madeleine Sprague. I never knew what she was to you, but I know what arresting her cost you. Did she really kill Lee? Is that just another lie? Why can't I believe it?

I have some money that Lee left me (a lie by omission, I know) and I'm going to head east in a day or so. I want to be far away from Los Angeles, someplace cool and pretty and old. Maybe New England, maybe the Great Lakes. All I know is that when I see the place, I'll know it.

Hoping this finds you,

Kay.

P.S. Do you still think about Elizabeth Short? I think about her constantly. I don't hate her, I just *think* about her. Strange after all this time.

K.L.B.

I kept the letter and re-read it at least a couple of hundred times. I didn't think about what it meant, or implied about my future, or Kay's, or ours together. I just re-read it and thought about Betty.

I dumped the El Nido master file in the garbage and thought about her. H.J. Caruso gave me a job selling cars, and I thought about her while I was hawking the 1950 line. I drove by 39th and Norton, saw that houses were going up on the vacant lot and thought about her. I didn't question the morality of letting Ramona walk or wonder whether Betty would approve. I just thought about her. And it took Kay, always the smarter of the two of us, to put it together for me.

Her second letter was postmarked Cambridge, Massachusetts, and was written on stationery for the Harvard Motor Lodge.

9/11/49

Dear Dwight—

I'm still such a liar, proscrastinator and chicken heart. I've known for two months, and I just got up the courage to tell you. If this letter doesn't reach you I'll actually have to call the house or Russ Millard. Better to try this way first.

Dwight, I'm pregnant. It had to have happened that one awful time about a month before you moved out. I'm due around Christmas and I want to keep it.

This is the patented Kay Lake retreat advancing. Will you please call or write? Soon? Now?

That's the big news. Per the P.S. on my last letter, something strange? Elegiac? Plain funny happened.

I kept thinking about Elizabeth Short. How she disrupted all our lives, and we never even knew her. When I got to Cambridge (God, how I love academic communities!) I remembered that she was raised nearby. I drove to Medford, stopped for dinner and got into a conversation with a blind man sitting at the next table. I was feeling gabby and mentioned Elizabeth Short. The man was sad at first, then he perked up. He told me about an L.A. policeman who came to Medford three months ago to find "Beth's" killer. He described your voice and verbal style to a "T." I felt very proud, but I didn't tell him that cop was my husband, because I don't know if you still are.

Wondering,

Kay

I didn't call or write. I put Lee Blanchard's house on the market and caught a flight to Boston.

CHAPTER THIRTY-SEVEN

On the plane I thought of all the things I'd have to explain to Kay, evidence to keep a new foundation of lies from destroying the two—or three—of us.

She would have to know that I was a detective without a badge, that for one month in the year 1949 I possessed brilliance and courage and the will to make sacrifices. She would have to know that the heat of that time would always make me vulnerable, prey to dark curiosities. She would have to believe that my strongest resolve was not to let any of it hurt her.

And she had to know that it was Elizabeth Short who was giving us our second chance.

Nearing Boston, the plane got swallowed up by clouds. I felt heavy with fear, like the reunion and fatherhood had turned me into a stone plummeting. I reached for Betty then; a wish, almost a prayer. The clouds broke up and the plane descended, a big bright city at twilight below. I asked Betty to grant me safe passage in return for my love.